Chapters in a Lucky Life

Chapters in a Lucky Life

by
Clara Thomas

August 18 2000

To Ross, with love and many many happy memories

Clara

*Borealis Press
Ottawa, Canada
1999*

Copyright © by Clara Thomas, 1999

All rights reserved. No part of this book may be used or reproduced in any manner whatsoever without written permission of the publisher, except in the case of brief quotations embodied in critical articles and reviews.

The Publishers gratefully acknowledge the financial assistance of the multiculturalism program of the Department of Canadian Heritage and of the Canada Council for the Arts.

Canadian Cataloguing in Publication Program

Thomas, Clara, 1919-
  Chapters in a lucky life

ISBN 0-88887-866-4

1. Thomas, Clara, 1919-   2. Critics—Canada—Biography.
I. Title.

PS8025.T56A3 1999   C810.9'00092   C99-900311-9
PR9183.T56A3 1999

Illustration front cover by J. Kolstein; photo of author by John Dawson, York University; all Retirement photos by Dr. Paul Craven.

"Prayer for Passion and Easter," by Margaret Laurence, pp. 323-24, courtesy Jocelyn Laurence per the Estate of Margaret Laurence.

Cover design by Bull's Eye Design, Ottawa, Canada

Printed and bound in Canada on acid free paper

Borealis Press
110 Bloomingdale Street
Ottawa, Ontario K2C 4A4
Canada

Illustrations

1. 1924 — Grandma McCandless and Clara, Grand Bend, Lake Huron, 1924.
2. 1926 — Samuel Mccandless
3. 1937 — Morley Thomas
4. 1943 — Martha Mccandless
5. 1944 — Agatha Cavers
6. 1944 — Basil McCandless, Flight Sergeant Vernon McCandless
7. 1944 — Mabel McCandless, Flight Sergeant Vernon McCandless
8. 1949 — Caroline and Brandon Conron, wedding photograph
9. 1951 — Alice Thomas and John
10. 1952 — Clara, Steve, John
11. 1952 — Steve
12. 1952 — John
13. 1952 — Morley
14. 1956 — The Sullivan Sisters, from left, Annie Fidler, Mabel McCandless, Dorothy Davis, Margery Durocher
15. 1960 — A.S.P. Woodhouse in his office, University College, Toronto
16. 1961 — Clara, first year at Glendon College, York University
17. 1967 — Oxford England, Blackwell's Bookstore, English publication of *Love and Work Enough*
18. 1977 — Margaret Laurence's Honorary Degree from York University: Clara Thomas, Margaret Laurence, President Ian Macdonald, Chancellor John Robarts

19. John Lennox, Clara, Publication of *William Arthur Deacon: A Canadian Literary Life*
20. 1984 — Retirement Party at Glendon College, York University, Clara presiding over birthday cake
21. 1984 — Chinua Achebe, Eugene Hallman, Margaret Laurence
22. 1984 — Northrop Frye, Carl Klinck
23. 1984 — Margaret Laurence
24. 1984 — Clara Thomas, Northrop Frye
25. 1984 — From left Adele Wiseman, Murdo McKinnon, Chinua Achebe, Ian Macdonald, Margaret Laurence, Jim Nelson, Elizabeth McKinnon
26. 1984 — Clara Thomas, John Lennox
27. 1984 — Michèle Lacombe
28. 1984 — Morley Thomas
29. 1984 — Edith Fowke
30. 1985 — Margaret Laurence with Jane Lennox, Mary Matheson
31. 1985 — Left Jack David, Right Robert Lecker of ECW Press, publishers of Clara's Festshrift #29 of *Essays in Canadian Writing*
32. 1985 — Mary Louise Craven, who with John Lennox and Michèle Lacombe organized the retirement party, Northrop Frye in foreground
33. 1985 — Rideau Hall, Ottawa, Morley Thomas awarded the Massey medal by Gov. Gen. Jeanne Sauvé. From left, John Thomas, Morley Thomas, Steve Thomas
34. 1983 — Our grandson Tyler's christening. Margaret Laurence, his Godmother.

Abbreviations

A.C.U.T.E. (recently A.C.C.U.T.E.) — Association of College and University Teachers of English

A.T.C.M. — Associate of the Toronto Conservatory of Music

B.Y.P.U. — Baptist Young People's Union

C.A.A. — Canadian Authors Association

C.A.R.A.L. — Canadian Abortion and Reproductive Rights Action League

C.B.C. — Canadian Broadcasting Corporation

C.C.F. — Canadian Commonwealth Federation, later N.D.P., (New Democratic Party)

C.G.I.T. — Canadian Girls in Training

C.N.R. — Canadian National Railway

C.O.T.C. — Canadian Officer Training Corps

C.U.S.O. — Canadian University Services Overseas

C.W.A.C. — Canadian Women's Army Corps

D Day — Day one of the W.W. II Allied invasion of Europe, 6 June 1944

I.O.D.E. — Imperial Order of Daughters of the Empire

M.A. — Master of Arts

M.P. — Member of Parliament of Canada

N.C.L. — New Canadian Library (McClelland & Stewart serial)

O.A.C. — Ontario Arts Council

O.A.C. — Ontario Agricultural College

O.C.E. — Ontario College of Education

Ph.D. — Doctorate of Philosophy

R.C.A.F. — Royal Canadian Air Force

R.M.C. — Royal Military College

S.S.H.R.C.C. — Social Science and Humanities Research Council of Canada

U.B.C. — University of British Columbia

U.N.B. — University of New Brunswick

U. of T. — University of Toronto

U.S.S.R. — Union of Soviet Socialist Republics

V.I.P.s — Very Important Persons

W.W.I. — World War One

W.W.II — World War Two

Y.M.C.A. — Young Men's Christian Association

Contents

List of Illustrations v

Abbreviations vii

I Before Memory 1

II Awakenings 6

III The Wider World 30

IV Church 50

V Reading 59

VI Western 1937-1941 65

VII Bright's Grove and the Three Poos 88

VIII 1941-1945 Wartime 94

IX Family Matters 114

X The Apprenticeship Years 126

XI Glendon in the Early Years 148

XII The Golden Years 1968-1980 160

XIII Canadian Literature Abroad 193

XIV Biography 213

XV	Grandma's Story of Her Life, written at age 90	232
XVI	Telling Dot's Life Like a Story	244
XVII	Vi and Evan 1925-1993	263
XVIII	My Friend, Agatha	272
XIX	Jim and Trudi Rowe	279
XX	Malcolm and Eve Elwin	287
XXI	Friends and Sisters	299
Index		325
Illustrations		333

Chapter I

Before Memory

Strathroy, the town where I was born and grew up, was in every way a perfect fit for our various archetypal Canadian small towns. Like Leacock's Mariposa, it could be seen as a hotbed of inflated self-esteem and unlikely get-rich-quick schemes. Like Sara Jeannette Duncan's Elgin it was the commercial centre for the farming land around it, its citizens possessed of a strong sense of their special importance in the life of the entire country. Like Margaret Laurence's Manawaka it could be seen as stifling and repressive, but still a homeland from which it was impossible to ever really separate. Like Robertson Davies' Deptford, it could also be seen as "more varied in what it offered to the observer than people from more sophisticated places generally think, and if it had sins and follies and roughnesses, it also had much to show of virtue, dignity and even nobility (*Fifth Business*)." In the early twenties when I came to consciousness it was a town of 2,500, and because of the political clout of some of its 19th century inhabitants, fortunately situated on the main line of the C.N.R. between Sarnia and London. George Ross, who built the grandest house in town about 1890, was a Minister of Education, then Premier of Ontario, then Senator (Liberal), and two other Senators, businessmen Calvert and O'Connor, had also added to Strathroy's Liberal lustre. So close-knit with politics were the townspeople that my Grandfather, seeking a teaching position for his Normal

School daughter, took her on the train to Ross's office at Queen's Park, reminded the Minister of his Liberal loyalties—and got the school he wanted.

Founded around a mill in the 1830s, the town had struggled along until the railway boom made it a specially thriving community with its full share, and perhaps a few more, of civically-minded men who saw to it that schools and churches mirrored their expectations and their confidence. The High School, an imposing building of yellow brick, was a matter of special pride, because quite soon it became one of Ontario's first "Collegiate Institutes" boasting teachers who were specialists in their fields, especially Classics, and one man in particular, James Wetherell, who was unusually gifted and industrious by any standards. He was a writer and an enthusiastic early Canadianist, producing many anthologies for the Department of Education from the 90s to after W.W.I. His anthology of 1893, *Later Canadian Poets*, and *The Great War In Prose And Verse* (1919), are especially memorable, the former for its admittedly afterthought inclusion of a few women poets, the latter for a truly distinguished collection, including a number of speeches by war leaders, both soldiers and statesmen. James Carson, an indefatigable inspector of schools, certainly the most taxing educational job of the time, was the father of two of the earliest of Canada's women doctors, Susanna and Jenny, both graduates of the Collegiate Institute. Probably the most famous of its graduates was James Shotwell, who became a renowned historian, Professor at Columbia, Editor-in-Chief of the *Encyclopaedia Britannica* and then Head of the huge Carnegie Foundation historical project on Canadian-American relations funded by the Carnegie Endowment and eventually responsible for instigating and publishing some thirty-five volumes. Shotwell had the crowning distinction of being one of the architects of the League of Nations, chosen by Woodrow Wilson as one of the group of founding advisors who accompanied him to the Peace Conference. He is commemorated in Geneva's Palais des Nations by photographs and citations. In sum, Strathroy had had a proud tradition by the time of my birth, particularly in education; in the early twenties, when W.W.I. was fresh in every adult mind and many families had lost a son, the United Nations and Shotwell's part in it had a special cachet, signified by the enthusiastic prominence it was given by some of our elementary school teachers.

The enormous importance of education was instilled in me from my earliest days, both from my mother's family, the Sullivans, and my father's, the McCandlesses. Like most of the townspeople, they were only a generation away from back-breaking work on the farm; both my grandparents and my mother and father had lived on farms in their youth. For their children and grandchildren they knew that schooling was the blessedly available way up and out and they promoted it with all their might. So from babyhood I grew up with Sullivan stories of the cleverness of my Uncle Vernon, killed in the war, who before he came home to join up had been teaching and homesteading in the Peace River District of the West. My grandfather McCandless, who, before he married and began to support a family, had been a schoolteacher, loved to hold up the Baptist university, McMaster, to me as my goal and as his goal and pledge for me.

I think now that there were three additional lucky strikes with me from the start: I was the first child of young and healthy parents, born red-headed, and too soon. The advantages of a health heritage are obvious; to be red-headed in our family was to be special, "taking after" a much revered great-grandmother on my mother's side, and having an immediately established bond with my aunt Dot, the only one of my mother's family who had happened to inherit her colour. That aunt, younger than my mother by several years, looked after me often when I was young, and she certainly did her best to make me confident that red hair was special. She liked to tell about meeting an acquaintance when I was with her who called me his "little red-haired darling" and my all-too-cute reply: "I know my hair is red, but my mother likes me to call it golden." A friend and academic colleague and I have talked for years about doing a poll of redheads, certain that we would find, contrary to the dislike of *Anne Of Green Gables* for her red head, that they all developed an early awareness of difference that was positive in its effects on self-image. My earliest photograph, taken at about nine months for my grandparents and grandly set off in convex, ornately-framed gilt, shows me with a bright orange tuft of hair, wearing a modest little shirt which, I was always told, was painted on at my grandparents' request. They didn't approve of the naked original.

By "too soon," I mean that my parents were married in March of 1919; I was born in May. In the small town that Strathroy was then, such an event was almost a "Scarlet Letter" disgrace to some. In fact, my parents had been courting for a couple of years and their eventual marriage was a foregone conclusion. They were both young, Mother just over 20, Father 22, and Mother in particular was determined from the start that I would confound all comment by being front and centre—by being an achiever from the very beginning. My first memories have to do with learning "recitations" by heart, for that was the day of children being expected to perform for

Sunday School concerts, family gatherings and the many popular entertainments of the day. I'm told that "Betty and Her Cow" was my specialty piece, very long, and contained in one of the many compendiums of such recitations, then a popular item among family volumes. It was certainly not long before I was quite happy to perform, and that early drilling, I am convinced, set up the basis for a very good memory which, in my schooldays, was far more essential for success than brain power. It wasn't exactly easy, mind you, to be my mother's daughter, but her determination did a very great deal for me. I can see that now and admit it, though then I was afraid of her for much of the time—and with reason.

My debt to her extends far beyond early childhood training, however: Mother was an advanced woman in her day, a feminist long before the word was current, and in her way an adventuress in a man's world. For almost all of my childhood she worked in a dress shop, loving clothes and colour as I do, and intensely possessive of her position as a saleswoman, finally becoming, to her intense pleasure, manager. The coincidence of the Depression and my grandfather's death, making "S. McCandless and Sons, Grocers and Butchers," responsible for the upkeep of three households, their own and my grandmother's, certainly made it easier for her to break out of the accepted housewifely mould. However, she would have managed the breakaway somehow, of that I am sure, because in my brother's and my early years she was an intensely frustrated woman. Circumstances aided and abetted her aggressive need for independence and gave her a career that was vastly satisfying until her early sixties. With a working mother, one moreover who throve on work, it was entirely natural for me to look forward to a similar future.

Chapter II

Awakenings

On the beach at Grand Bend on Lake Huron, when I was five years old, I saw my first airplane. I was paddling around in the water, wearing my navy blue cotton jersey bathing suit with the orange stripe around the modest skirt. My Grandmother McCandless, done up in the navy blue serge bathing suit that she had had since well before World War I, excitedly told me to "look up, look up, there's an airplane!" An old snapshot reminds me and jolts my memory into turning black-and-white film into colour—white sand, blue water, green fringe of trees bordering the beach, and Grandma luxuriating in the holiday she loved. She still had that bathing suit when she died at ninety-five in the late fifties, a heavy serge top with a round neck and a full short skirt, trimmed with white braid, over full bloomers to below the knee, black stockings and little rubber sand shoes. She wore it with a matching gathered mob cap like the cotton ones she wore for housework, and in the picture she looks charming, much younger than her age, then mid-sixties.

Grandma had been coming to Grand Bend for a two-week holiday every summer since early in the century when her four sons, my father the youngest, were children. She loved to tell me how she would pack up a large wooden box with her baking, and meat and groceries from Grandpa's store, and take off on the train from Strathroy to Forest, and then on to the Bend by wagon, and the big, ramshackle frame cottage rented every year.

Now, as the century closes there are still some of those cottages at the Bend, but then they lined the streets back of the lake, two-storey structures, built up high over the sand, with unfinished partitions and bare beams inside on the second floor, everything smelling of wood and coal oil from the lamps and the little three burner oil stove where all the cooking was done. Everything was wonderful to me, though not to my mother who disliked the lake intensely and wouldn't come near the water. The year my memories begin my mother did the current daring and newly fashionable thing and had her hair cut while we were at the Bend. I remember a small commotion, but she was pregnant at the time, which of course I didn't know, and that was her excuse. Eccentricities were excused when a woman was "in the family way."

In small-town southwestern Ontario, it was still early in the car era, but Grandpa was a successful merchant who prided himself on his modernity and his Grey Dort was an elegant car of its time. One of my memories, even earlier, was of being in the Grey Dort's back seat and someone pulling down the isinglass window shades when it began to rain. When we were at the Bend, early Sunday morning, for the "shop" as it was always called was open to midnight on Saturdays, my father, Uncle Evan and Grandpa would arrive at the cottage. It must have been at least two o'clock in the morning, but they'd sit down to the traditional Saturday night 'lunch,' really a hearty meal of cold meat, bread, biscuits, pickles, preserves, and, always, pie. On Sunday my Uncle Roy would arrive from Sarnia where he had a drug store, and often other company as well, for with cars the visiting that Grandma loved so well was easier than it had ever been, and everyone made the most of it. The more people Grandma had for Sunday dinner, the happier she was, and being at the lake gave a special relish to everything, always.

My birth year, 1919, and my birth month, May, seem lucky to me now, for when I began to take notice and remember, we were at the very cross-over of an old world to a new. At Grandma's house, where I spent a lot of time, there were copies of the *London Illustrated News* and war-time newspapers piled on the shelves of the "little room" where books, old school books and some cast-off furniture found a home. There was also a huge, garishly coloured picture of four generations of royalty, Victoria, Edward, George and young David, staring complacently out of an ornate gilt frame. It was my favourite room in the whole house. I spent hours poring over drawings in the *Illustrated News* of ships upending for the final plunge, and pages on pages of small sepia photographs of officers killed in battle. By the time I was five I could read, spurred on by Grandpa's promise of the handsome illustrated copy of Hurlbut's *Story Of The Bible* as soon as I could read it. Grandma had been particularly caught up in the tragic story of the Russian Royal family, and I drank in all the many pictures of them and to the extent I could understand, the accounts of their murder from black-bordered pages of the *London Advertiser*.

My own Uncle Vernon, my mother's brother, had been reported missing in August of 1918, and very early I was awed by that tragedy and by its circumstances which quickly became family myth. Vernon had been the oldest child of Will Sullivan and Rachel Clark, born on a farm in Adelaide and followed by Frieda, Mabel, Harold, Marge and Dorothy. In 1904 Rachel had died with the next baby and in 1910 Will had remarried and moved to Strathroy, where his wife, Margaret McColl, had given birth to Annie in 1911 and twins, Hugh and Lloyd, in

1914. In 1913 Vern had gone west to Saskatoon to Model School, and then to the Peace River district to teach and homestead. He hated both teaching and homesteading and was only too anxious to give it up and come home to join up when young Harold lied about his age and at fifteen joined A Company of the 135th Battalion, recruited in Strathroy. Pious family myth always had it that Vern had come home to be with him, official policy for brothers in that war; his letters home from the west tell a different story. But the sad result was the same: for years, all through the twenties, my grandfather would hear of some poor veteran who had lost his mind and his memory and would make yet another trip to Westminster Hospital in London, hoping to identify him as the lost Vern. My brother, born in 1925, was named for him, and ever after, Will Sullivan treated him as a surrogate Vernon, with a fatherly affection that seemed stronger than he showed to his own son, Hugh, the only surviving twin.

Harold had come home from the trenches with lasting damage to his back, a condition that caused him lifelong pain and the wearing of a shoulder to thigh cast. His pain he controlled by liberal uses of painkillers, 222s with codeine, and multiple coffees and cokes. He lived hard, popular, active and always adventurous, a particular lover of good cars, until his death at 50, in 1951. In the twenties he had a good trucking business, carting supplies of all kinds between Strathroy and London. Later on he had a gas station, and then, finally, a small haberdashery store where he was in his element, for like my mother, he loved fashion. He married Beatrice Burdon about 1925, and the two of them brought constant movement and vitality to the whole family circle. The first and only "rumble seat" I ever rode in was in Harold's snappy Buick; and one of the peaks of my pre-teen existence was a trip to London to see *King Kong*, the apex of movie thrillerdom in its day. Mother and Father got their first car, a Chev, in 1925, the summer after Vernon was born. Fred Morningstar, a fat, middle-aged man who sold Chevs and also had a restaurant, taught Mother to drive, and great was the teasing about that among the Sullivans.

Many of the good early memories depend on transportation. Largely at Harold's instigation, the Sullivans were given to picnics, with fried chicken and potato salad, or, on some memorable occasions, fried potatoes too; for if we went to Kettle Point on Lake Huron, close to the nearby Indian reserve, Will Sullivan, "Dad," thought nothing of asking an Indian woman (squaws, they were always called then) to use her stove for heating a pan full of potatoes. Rock Glen was another favourite spot, with its picturesque little Falls and its famous fossil rock formations, though I always thought it far behind Lake Huron for picknicking—no swimming. The crowning expedition of all, talked about for decades in the family, was a great outing to Boblo, Detroit's Coney Island, a twenties and thirties embryonic Disneyland in the Detroit River, only accessible by steamer from the Jefferson docks in Detroit. I have an indelible mind's-eye picture of Dad Sullivan and brother Vernon, arriving with a suitcase bulging with food, including, unbelievably, muskmelons, much later than the rest of us, at the picnic grounds. A hot day, I was horribly seasick throughout the boat part of this outing and I've detested boats ever since.

Although both families were Baptists, the McCandlesses were far stricter than the Sullivans. There were no Sunday picnics for them, though they "visited" a lot on Sundays, and sometimes took me with them as far as Woodstock where Grandpa's sister, Polly Smiley lived, the matriarch of a large family of cousins. A widow, she lived with her daughter, Violet, who had a husband and also a boarder. There were a good many remarks made about Violet and her doubly male household, but about that and many another family mystery I learned young not to ask questions. From a very young age I was known as a book-worm and heard a great deal when I was sitting with a book in front of me, looking like an engrossed reader, but listening to family chat on Sunday evenings after supper at Grandma's.

Dad Sullivan was the caretaker of the Strathroy Cemetery and had, as he was fond of saying, two thousand people under him. Mother used to give Vernon and me a good supply of sandwiches and send us out, on sunny summer days, to picnic in the cemetery with him. Except that the treat involved riding out in his rig, high behind Bob, his skittish horse, I loved going there, and it had absolutely no creepy fears for me. Close by was a swampy woods, with beautiful wild iris (flags) and marsh marigolds, and always a lover of wild flowers, I revelled in them. Bob had been a race-horse, but had gone blind, and Dad had got him for a song, but he was a one-man animal and had no use for me, nor I for him, especially as Dad was as impatient as Bob and they both seemed to delight in my nervousness. The Sullivans never had a car, and until the end of his life in the '50s Bob ferried him back and forth to the cemetery, finally finding his way home one day with Dad in the driver's seat as usual, but unconscious from a stroke suffered en route.

My very first experiences with horses I don't remember but feel as if I should. Before memory begins I'm told that I took great pleasure in riding in Grandpa McCandless's delivery wagon, driven by young Doney Marshall. It went around town every morning to the regular customers to take orders for the day's meat, which was then cut at the store and delivered back to them in time to be cooked for the noon meal. I certainly remember thinking that the young driver was wonderful, and anyone who says that a five-year-old can't have a crush on a young man is, simply, wrong! The carriage trade service was exchanged when I was about six for a town delivery, the Crandon brothers, who drove in horse and covered cab all day long servicing all the merchants. From time to time I was behind a horse with my Uncle Ed Sullivan who lived about seven miles northwest of Strathroy in Adelaide. He would come into town on errands and take me back with him to the farm. He was really my great-uncle, Dad's brother, and the one who, with Aunt Clara, for whom I am named, had taken my mother in after her mother died and kept her for some half-dozen years. He had an Essex car, but he was teased incessantly by the whole family about his driving, and I think he always preferred a horse and wagon, though it seemed to me to take forever to get out to the farm that way. Every summer and some Easter holidays I spent out there, especially enchanted by the attic, stretching across the full width of the house, and stocked with discarded chests of drawers, old trunks filled with cast-off clothing and high-button shoes, books, and stacks of magazines, including years of *Saturday Evening Posts* and, one summer, when I was in my teens, a priceless cache of *Ladies Home Journals*, carrying a serial story about American teenagers, Maudie and David, who immediately became my role models.

My two cousins, Helen (Hon) and Stewart, both considerably older than I, cheerfully put up with me, and their home was a wonderful treat. Uncle Ed was a successful farmer who had begun on the Sullivan "Home Farm," established in the 1830s. He married Clara

Carruthers, a neighbor's daughter, whose brother, Lou, was city architect for London. Right after W.W.I., flush with the prosperity that had come with the high price of wartime wheat, Ed and Clara had demolished the old house and built a new one, designed by Lou, the pride of the whole family and, for that matter, of the whole Second Line where they lived. Hardwood floors, a black and white tiled bathroom with a flush toilet, spacious rooms, an electric light system, battery operated, called Delco, a wall telephone where Hon and I delighted in "listening in" to some of the neighbors' conversations, everything was up-to-date and completely out of the ordinary then for a town house, let alone a country one. Aunt Clara was a wonderful gardener; her flowers were a lavish treat that had to be paid for, however, by pail after pail of water carried to the hard-baked clay in which they flourished. I was usually out there at haying time, and when I wasn't in the attic, happily sweltering as I made play-houses, dressed up, or read old books, I was in the barn playing with the kittens who inhabited the hay lofts. Day after day the hay would be put in, higher and higher, until I finally had to give up and move out, leaving the kittens behind, to my sorrow. Sometimes I hung around to help Hon drive the horses as the men forked off the hay, and sometimes in the late afternoon I was sent back to the field in front of the woods to get the cows for milking. I thoroughly disliked cows because they scared me, a town child, but they knew far better than I what was required and dutifully they came home to the barn. The roadside ditch on the way was lush and perfumed with fat red clover and that I loved.

Uncle Ed's family went to Bethesda church down the road about two miles from their home and sometimes there would be special gatherings for which Aunt Clara would bake. One summer I was at the farm for threshing, the climax of the harvest season, an occasion that put every farm wife on her mettle as a cook. The presence of the telephone meant that due notice was given of the arrival of the threshing machine, usually a full day ahead, and great was the bustle: pies, cakes, canned fruit brought up from the cellar; chickens killed and readied for frying, for Uncle Ed had an incubator and all the young males were for eating—in fact everyone in the family was heartily sick of fried chicken long before summer ended. There was a big wood range in the kitchen and a coal oil stove with attached oven in the summer kitchen; both of these worked full-time in preparation, and the temperature in the kitchen must have been well up into the 90s Fahrenheit. The threshers were always there for both dinner and supper. They came in starving hungry at noon and again at 6 o'clock, having rinsed off some of the dust in a tub of water outside the door. The amount of food they ate was as amazing as the speed with which they ate it—shovelled it in, would be a closer description—roasts, fried chicken and sausages, fried potatoes, fresh-picked yellow beans in rich butter and cream (real cream) sauce, pies, cakes, fruit, and gallons of strong tea. After they went back to their work the women ate, usually two or three neighbors helping out and having a good gossip as well.

 Sometimes I would go visiting with Hon, down the road a quarter of a mile and across to another farm, Uncle John's and Aunt Mandana's home with their children, Fred, Laura, Hazel and Jack. Except for Jack, the others were considerably older than Hon and Stewart. In family lore, Uncle John was the least favourite Sullivan; but he gave me my first McIntosh apple and I couldn't believe the shock of the big red apple, the most delicious I ever tasted,

I thought, and its little new tree that he was proud of getting from O.A.C. in Guelph. Apples had been a big crop on the Second Line in the generations before mine, but now the orchards were let go to ruin, though their Snow-apples, Spies and Astrakhans, Jonathans, Wealthies, Duchesses, Russets and Pippins were, to my mind, without equal. They lay on the ground in their hundreds, windfalls for the taking, and aside from home cooking, applesauce, pies, and for some farmers but not the abstemious Sullivans, cider, they were only food for the pigs. Grain was the thing to grow and prosper on, and the proper maintenance of an orchard was too labour-intensive to bother with. Besides, everyone had apples—and most people had a barrel in their cellar for eating all winter long. Mother's favourite was Jonathan, and long before spring I got heartily sick of Jonathan apples.

What was holiday bliss for me was isolation for my cousins and their friends who had gone to the one-room school up the road a mile from Uncle Ed's. My mother had gone there too, before Dad Sullivan remarried and she came into town unwillingly, to be reunited with her family and the new family in the big McColl house on Victoria Street in Strathroy. The house was on "Quality Hill," so called only half-jokingly, because Premier George Ross and Senators O'Connor and Calvert had built impressive 19th century mansions in the neighborhood. My Grandmother McCandless, too, born in 1863, had gone to school on the Second Line, though conditions in her young days were those of pioneer times. One fine winter day when she was seven or eight, her father, Samuel Martin, had walked some six miles into town for provisions. There he was stranded by a blizzard while his wife, Beulah, found that her twin baby boys had diphtheria, a much-dreaded, often fatal disease rampant at the time. Late in her life Grandma told me of having to help her mother make a coffin out of rough boards for one little boy, leaving him out in the cold, for the ground for a grave could not be dug in the winter. It was a searing memory, and for all of her long life Grandma retained a terror of anything connected with a sore throat striking "the young ones." That had always been the beginning of diphtheria. Choking was the end.

It was on the Second Line too that my cousin Stewart was the victim of what was considered the thirties' most thrilling adventure—travelling barnstorming pilots who charged a few dollars for an airplane ride. With a crowd of onlookers he was watching a Labour Day performance too close to a makeshift runway and was struck on the side of the head by a wing. He died two days later. Quite soon, Uncle Ed sold the farm and moved to Strathroy.

When I was a child, the piano in the "front room," not "parlour" (old-fashioned), and not yet "living-room" (new-fangled), was a status symbol, a sign of prosperity and modernity and a highly important instrument of family pleasure to all my relatives. In the early 1920s, just before the arrival of radio, gatherings always included singing, for pleasure (both sentimental old tunes of the Stephen Foster ilk and current Tin Pan Alley hits), patriotism (songs of World War I), uplift (hymns and "sacred songs" like "Beautiful Isle of Somewhere"), or all three. I'm sure I heard the piano and the singing before I recognized individual people, for my father loved to play for others to sing and, therefore, he was the pianist for an extended group of family and friends. Until the Royal Bank insisted that he put a stop to it (unseemly for one of their young tellers), he had even played piano at the Lyceum, the town concert hall and movie theatre, when the cowboys galloped over the sagebrush to the tempo of the "William Tell Overture," and the heroine was delivered safely from the dastardly villain to the strains of "Home Sweet Home." Almost the only pastime in Strathroy that men and women customarily shared was involved with music, from church "socials" and choirs to ambitious Gilbert and Sullivan operettas and the ever popular Minstrel Shows. My most unforgettable memory of my mother is of her 'rendering' of the heart-tugging "Take my Back to Dear Old Childhood" in black-face, with a bright red turban, looking, she hoped, like Aunt Jemima. I wasn't at all averse to performance either, quite fancying myself at age ten, all draped in cheesecloth with tinsel trim, warbling "Star of the East, O Bethlehem's Star," at the Sunday School Christmas Concert. In our teens Dorrie, my best friend and I, learned many a duet , "The March of the Tin Soldiers" being our best number, to play at church socials. The Baptist 'Irish Tea' on St. Patrick's Day and the Anglican 'Shrove Tea', at the beginning of Lent, were our most prestigious engagements.

Such joys were some, but not total, compensation for the dreary drudgery involved in passing the Toronto Conservatory Music Exams each spring. Tens of thousands of Canadian children were hounded into practising the required programme for a series of exams culminating in the A.T.C.M.(Associate of the Toronto Conservatory of Music), which only a miniscule percentage of them ever finished. Small town music teachers by the score put pupils through their paces (Bach, Chopin, Czerny exercises, scales, sight readings and one boring party piece), and parents relentlessly played their drill-sergeant roles as well as paying for lessons. In our town the top price was 75 cents a week. To take the exam under the eye of a bored and beady-eyed examiner we had to go by train to

London. But the ordeal had great compensations: dinner at Wong's Cafe, and a big-time, first-run movie at Loew's or the Capitol theatre. I still remember the thrill of seeing *The Divine Lady* with Corinne Griffith, the story of Nelson and Emma Hamilton, after a music exam.

When Grandma McCandless was ninety years old, she wrote an account of her life for me in which she said that all her life music had been of next importance to her family. Very young she had begun to sing in a country church choir where, shortly, she was playing the organ. Before that, when there was no accompanying instrument, the leader had used a tuning-fork to get them all started, and then they sang by the 'tonic-sol-fa scale' (Do ra me so la te do), a method that was still in use in my years of public school, brought back to prominence by Julie Andrews in *The Sound Of Music*. Grandma continued to sing in the Strathroy Baptist choir until she was eighty years old. She was her own and her family's harshest critic: Woe Betide either one of the two daughters-in-law who sang there also and didn't achieve her standard of anthem singing. As for the year that the choir practised a much watered-down version of the Hallelujah Chorus as an Easter specialty, our cousin who sang tenor through his nose proved himself once and for all beyond the pale. One of Grandma's sisters who had 'gone over' to the Anglicans was a leader in the Gilbert and Sullivan productions that were for a time the pride of the town, but weren't quite permissible for a Baptist. The most famous sister of all had moved with her husband to Toronto, and actually sang in the Mendelssohn choir whose leader, Sir Ernest MacMillan, was one of Grandma's heroes; her other hero was Edward Johnson, the boy from Guelph who had become a famous tenor at the Metropolitan Opera. In the thirties he had become General Manager of the Met. That was why I began, in my early teens, to listen with Grandma to the first Texaco broadcasts of the opera from New York on Saturday afternoons. The "Great Golden Horseshoe," so often mentioned in the broadcasts, seemed to me then the most glamorous place on earth. I remember one of Madame Ernestine Schummann-Heink's innumerable farewell broadcasts, and I also remember, much more clearly, the day that the great Wagerian soprano, Kirsten Flagstadt, made her debut at the Met in *Lohengrin*.

Because my father and mother were young, and because they were the first to marry in both families, our house was a prime site for family gatherings and company meals. Also, mother loved to cook, and the ready availability of both meat and vegetables from the store where my father had become the grocer and Grandpa and my Uncle Evan the butchers, meant that the open-house policy was never questioned. The Sullivans, split up among relatives when their mother died and only reunited when they were in their teens, couldn't get enough of one another. They were noisy, funny, quarrelsome, articulate (gabby), Irish in the most stereotypical sense of the word, and they were never happier than when they were all together, eating, singing, laughing, teasing, at our house, "Base and Mabe's."

On Frank Street in Strathroy, above stores and next to the Post Office, the town's pride, was the Lyceum, home of the movies in my early days and of stage plays until the war. It was an elegant structure for a town of 2,000, dating back to about 1880, with a proper stage with curtain, fire curtain, boxes on either side and plenty of room for dressing rooms behind. It also had some kind of a lift for raising scenery and furniture to the stage. There was an auditorium that would seat, I suppose, about 200, with a shallow balcony on three sides. In my early youth, before I was five, I'd be taken to movies there with Mother and Father, and on one special occasion I went with them to *Birth Of A Nation*, the D.W. Griffiths classic. I have two distinct memories of that—real horses on stage, and mother making us leave, self-censoring the greatest of the old silents. My horse-memory was shouted down in many an argument until fairly recently when I read a biography of Griffiths telling of the astounding success of *Birth*, including an account of the railway cars packed with stage props and *Live Horses* that accompanied the show until well into the twenties. I also saw several stage plays there, for a winter or early spring local production every year was the rule. A travelling impresario called Sarah Gibney would arrive in town with the rights to a show, boxes and crates of costumes and props, and the promise of sponsorship by one of Strathroy's organizations, often the I.O.D.E.(Imperial Order of the Daughters of the Empire). Great was the excitement as Miss Gibney took up residence in the Alexandra Hotel and the jockeying for parts began. Our family was usually involved for Father was invaluable as an accompanist, and either the shows themselves were musicals or they featured musical numbers between acts. I remember my brother at four years old, drilled endlessly beforehand, warbling "When the Organ Plays at Twilight" at one such entertainment (this was an era when "cute" little child performers were the rage). I also remember an even earlier production of *Peg O' My Heart*, a very successful Broadway production. Our little terrier, Teddy, was co-opted as a performer and my aunt Dorothy was the female lead, opposite Ned Lewis, a glamorous bachelor shoe-store owner. There was a memorable *Uncle Tom's Cabin* in my time, in which mother played Miss Ophelia with Civil War crinolines and fake ringlets and I envied the fragile blonde child who played little Eva and was hauled up to Heaven most convincingly.

In that production three of my aunts was featured in a between-act chorus of "Ramona," a ragingly popular pseudo-Spanish ballad of the late twenties. Miss Gibney's son stalked around the stage in a Spanish matador's costume, singing "Ramona, at break of day I hear you call / Ramona, I'll wait beside the waterfall, etc." while the girls, dressed in black skirts and magenta shawls with black fringe, with fake roses in their hair, swooped about in a kind of dance. Thrillingly romantic, and for years I dressed up in one of the shawls, discarded at our house.

I made my own Lyceum debut in High School, in a large production of George M. Cohen's *The Beauty Parlour*. It had been a great Broadway success with the usual romantic plot, great songs and dances and great choruses. To my delight I was chosen for the ingénue part, and had a song of my own and a dance, "The Hesitation Waltz" with a young man whose identity I've completely forgotten. I vividly remember my first evening dress, though, bought for that occasion at the Artistic where mother worked, a pale yellow organdy with matching short cape. The leading man, Clarke Wright, a lawyer and the most eligible bachelor in town and his leading lady, the truly beautiful Jean Thompson, a still-young spinster who worked in Stepler's drug store, left trails of envious sighs behind them. In his tails and a red satin-lined evening cape, he was an unforgettable sight, one never before seen by most of us, certainly not by me. Mother was in that show too, for there was, for Strathroy, a huge cast and two choruses, one of matrons like her, one of young women like myself. The whole thing was a rousing community success, wiping out the sour Depression taste of life for its duration. In the course of the show I was cut out of the budding affections of the shy young man, later to become an undertaker, who had been taking me to the odd movie and once, never-to-be-forgotten, to a magician show in Sarnia. He and his best boyfriend were madly into magic tricks and juggling—the number of billiard balls they could keep in the air was a matter of great importance to them, and crashing boredom to me. However, I got my comeuppance when a newcomer to town, Mary Ellen, whose last name I've forgotten, was given the part of the Spanish vamp in *The Beauty Parlour* with her own song and solo dance and a black mantilla on her hair. My erstwhile escort fell for her like a ton of bricks and I saw him no more. I was not downcast—he did not dance.

In the late twenties the King Theatre opened at the west end of Front Street's business strip. It showed two movies a week, plus a Saturday matinee, and it speedily became my dearest wish to see both of them, every week. This was Hollywood's hey-day, and the King's proprietor, who also owned a couple of theatres in neighboring small towns, got a surprising number of first-run features. From the twenties I remember numbers of Westerns, always accompanied by two short comedy features and a newsreel, and on Saturday afternoon by a continued thriller. When I was about ten our mother began to work on Saturdays for the Artistic Ladies Wear, and I was charged with taking my small brother to the "show." He was terrified by one serial, *The Wolf Woman*, and began to have nightmares that no one could account for, certainly not I, who loved every moment of it. Cartoons were then in the embryonic stage, but soon they appeared in all their glorious mayhem, along with the jerky, blurry Pathé newsreels. Once in a while a film showing only in

London would become a 'must' for the whole family, *Sonny Boy*, with the wildly popular Al Jolson, for instance. In the two main London theatres, the tail-ends of the vaudeville age were still a part of the entertainment. An excruciating "Roses of Picardy," rendered by a large blonde sitting on a swing decorated with paper roses stays stubbornly in my memory, as do various whistlers, jokesters and accordion players. On one great occasion in the twenties the Dumbells, the famous World War I entertainers, came to the Grand Theatre in London and we went. I remember much laughing and grand male voices.

By the time I was in High School, 1932, we were getting all the up-to-the-minute films in Strathroy and I missed few of the entire now-famous roster—Myrna Loy, Claudette Colbert, Katherine Hepburn, the Bennett sisters, Constance and Joan, Olivia de Havilland and Joan Fontaine, who were also sisters, Joan Crawford, Bette Davis and their leading men, Gable, Cooper, Tracy, Powell, Flynn, Fairbanks Jr., Grant—and of course the greatest stars of all, Garbo and Dietrich. Because the mother of my friend, Agatha, actually bought movie magazines, I was at least as familiar with the official romance-versions of their lives as I was with the people around me. Even in the depths of the Depression there always seemed to be fifteen cents available from my father for one movie at least. Father had been a local baseball star, a catcher, long before I was born; before memory begins I was the mascot of the team and, I'm told, enjoyed a great deal of attention. Throughout his life Father was a devoted sports enthusiast with baseball always at the head of his lineup. In later life he watched football games on television and, at the same time, listened to baseball games on a radio by his ear, always intensely involved in the fortunes of the Detroit Tigers.

Strathroy was on the C.N.R. line that went from Chicago through Sarnia and on to join the Windsor line at London. Consequently all the Sunday papers came in on Saturday night from east and west. Every Sunday morning our house was littered with the papers that had come in to town the night before, the *Detroit News* and *Free Press* and the Chicago papers especially. Out of bed long before the adults, my brother and I fell upon the comics. In those days weekly coloured "funny papers" were extensive—the Gumps, Maggie and Jiggs, Tillie the Toiler, Happy Hooligan, Popeye and Olive Oyl, the Katzenjammer Kids and, a little later, Flash Gordon with his prototypical space ship—they all were meat to us. Children and adults alike followed "the funnies"; the death of Uncle Bim Gump's young wife, Marigold, was a cross-country headline. For years, because of sports reporting we took *The Border Cities Star*, spurning London's *Free Press* and *Advertiser*.

Many, maybe most young girls of my time, were stage-struck, but I was more so than most. I embarked on a dramatization of *Little Women* in Entrance Class (Grade 8), and once in High School, where we were allowed to present skits instead of giving individual speeches in "Oral Composition" classes, I was well away, dramatizing Kenilworth and a serial story by Alice Duer Miller running in *The Ladies Home Journal* called "Just the Maid," as well as bossing around all my friends in short chorus productions, such as "Pop-Eye the Sailor man," and "The Man on the Flying Trapeze." All three of the High School literature teachers encouraged, or at least put up with, such excursions, Miss Goulding, Miss McCormick and Miss Waugh. As well, Miss Goulding directed a full-length play every year. I was thrilled with the idea of a real, three-act play, and was made understudy in my first year, because, of course, a first-year student couldn't expect a major part. I compensated by memorizing all the parts, and developing a mighty "crush" on the senior boy who took a leading role. Though no one of the actors fell sick or in any way gave me a chance to perform, I was quite happy to be even such a marginal part of it all.

Later on when I was in fourth form we presented an operetta, *The Riddle Of Isis*, and there I realized my leading-lady dream. I was Isis herself, a centuries-dead mummy, who woke beside her mate, Rameses, in the midst of being visited by a group of travelling students who were being harassed by an unruly group of Bedouins. This production gave great scope to many of my friends as well; it was a clever little operetta with some catchy choruses. I was garbed in yards of green-dyed cheesecloth (Nile green, of course), enhanced by all the rhinestone clips and pins I could beg or borrow. I thought my solo, "My Star," was gorgeous, but I'm sure that Rameses' song, "Just call me Rameses with the accent on the Ram," was deservedly the show-stopper. As the school-mistress in charge of a group of touring students, my friend, Ruth Sands, was memorably funny, undoubtedly the best thing in the production, but no one made comparisons, not to our faces at least, and so for all of us the effort was a great success.

By this time, 1936, radio had made its enormous impact on our family life. We had a crystal set by the mid-twenties, again largely because of father's preoccupation with the ball scores. I remember him listening with earphones to Lindbergh's huge welcome home in New York in 1927, relaying the talk of Wall Street tickertape and roaring crowds to the rest of us. In World Series time he would always come home for Jimmy Stevenson's ball scores at 6.30 on WJR Detroit, even on Saturdays when the store was open in the evening and he'd have to go right back again. By the time I was in High School, almost everyone I knew had a free-standing De Forest Crossley in the living room, and no one, child or adult, would have dreamed of missing the evening programmes, Myrt and Marge and Amos 'n Andy weeknights and on Sundays, Jack Benny (Jello), Fibber McGee and Molly, Fred Waring (Pond's Cold Cream), or the Lux Radio Theatre. By our mid-teens we were all listening to the Hit Parade, and it was a matter of pride to know the 'top ten.' Boys at school liked to twiddle the dial and brag about bringing in WLW Cincinnati or stations from even more far-flung places, but we girls were satisfied with programmes, and quickly became fans of the "soaps."

From the day we began High School, dancing was the prime entertainment, and to be known as a good dancer was an absolute necessity for popularity. We began dancing at noon hour in our first year of High School, upstairs in the Assembly Hall, not girls and boys mixed, but the girls together, with one of us playing the piano for the rest, and the experienced girls dragging around the starters. Soon we were, or thought we were, accomplished enough to venture forth to the Saturday night dances at the Town Hall, with Strathroy's own Casa Loma orchestra, led by Lionel Thornton, playing the music. Most of us weren't allowed to go regularly until Third Form when we were approaching sixteen and by that time the boys seemed miraculously to have learned to dance—and dance well—for we bragged about the footwork of Strathroy teenagers, always. There weren't many adults at the Saturday night dances, but the New Year's Dance was different. Then members of the I.O.D.E. were sponsors, women wore evening dresses and men wore dark suits or tuxes, if they had such glamorous apparel. Until we were "sophisticated" grown-ups that dance was not for the High School crowd. At the High School itself we had just one regular formal, as we called it, the yearly At Home, held at the beginning of the Christmas holidays in the gym, well-decorated, and again with the town orchestra. It was the occasion for intense rivalry for partners and concern for clothes. I first went in Third Form, and then my Uncle (half uncle) Hugh kindly asked me, a thoughtful attention that I will always remember and be grateful for. Because I had been in *The Beauty Parlour*, I had the beautiful yellow organdy, and I went with Hugh with the greatest pleasure.

The admission to Town Hall dances was a quarter, and it always seemed to be forthcoming, just as 15 cents for the movie was. There was no disgrace attached to going by oneself, or spending the time dancing with girl friends, though as we got older we separated into boy-girl pairs, in our group always at the instigation of the boys. Though we kept on arriving at the dance by ourselves, it became the thing to go home with one of the boys, stopping at Prangley's for a coke on the way if he had any money. Prangleys was a big, old-fashioned ice-cream parlour on Front Street, with an upstairs where the first juke-box in town was installed. We were all so crazy about dancing that we'd go there after four, or on Friday nights, or just any time anyone had a dime or two. There my most vivid memories are of my friend, Agatha Cavers, jitterbugging with Donnie Leitch. They were wonderfully matched and a joy to watch. Donnie became a pilot in the R.C.A.F. and was killed.

Courting was cheap in those days. On Saturday nights through the summer and early fall, one or other of the boys would get his father's car, either Cecil Wright or Jack Fowlie, and we would pile in, to drive out to Bright's Grove on Lake Huron to dance to Jack Kennedy's orchestra. This was in the hey-day of the big bands, and sometimes we were even taken as far afield as Port Stanley on Lake Erie, where Benny Goodman, Artie Show, the Dorseys and Glen Miller played every once in a while in the years leading up to the war. When we really got in the presence of one of the "Greats," we did far more pushing to the front of the floor and listening and looking than dancing. I don't remember dancing at all to Artie Show, just being entranced with watching and seeing him play the fabulous clarinet.

Twice in the early years of High School we went to C.G.I.T. camp at Hillsboro on Lake Huron, sleeping in tents, my friend Dorrie and I in a pup-tent that would barely hold us, having a wonderful free time, swimming, having beach fires and sing-songs, and eating—always eating! We were isolated from big resorts with dancing, and so there was nothing to distract us from enjoying the beach all day every day. Our leaders had their own tent and paid little attention to us, the first lesbian couple I had ever met, though I certainly had no idea of that until twenty or thirty years later. To me, and I think to the rest of us, they were just especially dear friends. In the summer after Fourth form and again after Fifth, however, we had our very peak experience as teenagers, for Williston Downham was allowed to take a group of us to the family cottage just down the road about half a mile from the dance hall at Bright's. Willie, Agatha Cavers, Libby Lambert, Dorrie Fowlie, Joyce Houston, Grace Crawforth and I were there, spending each day on the beach and each evening at the open air dance hall, where Jack Kennedy and his orchestra played their own arrangements of the hits of the day, and did very creditable imitations of Sammy Kay and his orchestra. The dance hall, at five cents a dance, was well patronized with young people from the cottages around, as well as from Sarnia and

Petrolia, and the dancing was superb. We all developed "crushes" on one boy or another, mine on Ross Drummond from Petrolia, Willie's on Bill Kirk from Sarnia. Libby "loved" Willie's brother, George, and Joyce, Jack Fowlie, who with Cecil Wright and Walter Bowley camped out in a big tent pitched next to the Downham's cottage, so that we all did a lot of eating and beaching together. We had glorious times and glorious dances—and never, I'm sure, was there a more innocent group of teenagers. It was terribly exciting if anyone even talked of kissing, let alone did such a thing, and anyone who showed signs of wanting to wander off with a boy was taken speedily to task.

The summers of '36 and '37 were the last before the war, and the last before the real world began to move into our growing up. Certainly they were the last summer when parents could feel as secure and without anxiety as ours obviously did. We did everything in a gang, and though the boys from time to time showed signs of wanting to establish "girl friends," we simply didn't buy into the idea of "going steady." Night after night I'd come in long after midnight, for the drive from Bright's Grove took at least an hour, and our house would be peacefully dark and sleeping. We were a lucky gang, and ours were also lucky parents! In some respects, I was doubly lucky, for my parents were young, and with my father's love of sports and the piano, and mother's love of fashion, all the popular sheet music and many current periodicals, *McCall*'s and *The Ladies' Home Journal* especially, found their way to our house in spite of the Depression. Until the radio gave almost everyone a taste of the times, I lived in a much more stimulating atmosphere than did most of my friends.

Chapter III

The Wider World

Public School, 1925-32

The schools in Strathroy were always called the Public School (actually there were two, Colborne and Maitland), and High School (really Collegiate Institute and a source of great town pride). For a town of about 2,500 in the twenties, it seems strange to have two elementary schools, but even so, many of us walked a good distance. Both were south of Front Street, the business street, Colborne just north of the C.N.R. tracks and Maitland, some blocks to the west and just south of them. Children knew each other according to the school they went to, and to me the Maitland crowd might as well have been living in another town entirely. We all met each other in Junior Fourth, when everyone went to Maitland school (Grade 7), as in Senior Fourth (Entrance Class), they all went to Colborne. Traditionally the Principal of Colborne Street School was the senior town teacher, and male; Junior Fourth's teacher, also male, was second in command. All the other teachers in my time were women.

I was five years old on May 22, 1924, and I began school in September. From the time of my earliest memories school had been held up to me as a great goal, and I was correspondingly anxious to get at it. When I was very young Grandpa McCandless had told me that he was going to make sure I went to university. I remember sitting on his knee and being told that. I was aware that something momentous was being said, and that it had to do with school, and from then on I didn't for a moment doubt that school was the most important event in my life and that the grand-sounding university (for Grandpa the Baptist McMaster), was to be my future. From the Sullivan side of the family I was infected with awe and respect for education as well. In fat, I believe that for all of "old Strathroy" education was considered the cornerstone of civilization, advancement in life and in general, bringing credit to one's family. I have never deviated from the goals set down for me so early.

There were probably between thirty and forty children who began school together that day, starting in First Card Class with "The Little Red Hen" in the primer and Miss Sadleir as our teacher. She was a spinster, then in her late thirties, with short bobbed hair plastered down with a "spit curl" on each side of her face, and absolutely no memorable dress or mannerism. We learned to read that year, but I could already read, and so found our primer insufferably boring. We also learned to write numbers from one to one hundred, beginning with slates and screechy slate-pencils but quickly progressing to scribblers, pencils and erasers. I have a clear memory of a smudgy column of figures, my first scholastic achievement. I longed to get on to the "First Book" and its unknown delights, for by the age of five I was away beyond the Primer in expectation. I'd been brought up on stories, both oral and printed, and at four had been given Hurlbut's *Story Of The Bible*, long promised to me when I could read. I had haunted the small, book-filled room at my Grandfather's house since I could walk, poring over the bibles, books and old newspapers on its shelves, fascinated by impenetrable prose and poetry and in my element, shut away from everyone "playing school."

At the real school we sat in single desks in rows in a large downstairs classroom, its one side all windows overlooking the girls' playground, its other three sides all blackboards rimmed with elegantly-drawn letters and numbers and dusty with the chalky remains of hundreds of lessons. Its floor was oiled and smelled of pine, and its front was dominated by the teacher's desk and, above the blackboard, by a colour picture of King George and Queen Mary, imposing in their crowns and regalia. They were obligatory icons in thousands of classrooms throughout the Empire where the sun was still comfortably far from setting. They were balanced by one blackboard displaying the words of "The Maple Leaf Forever," though I'm perfectly certain that, for every time we sang about the dauntless Wolfe, we sang "God Save the King" a dozen times. Mary Dampier soon became my friend—by good luck she still is. We call each other "Oldest," talk and see each other often. The boys in the room stand out in my memory far more than the other girls, particularly Cecil Wright, Norman Dickson, and Billy Bowie who teased us and talked to us from the beginning. Our teachers soon learned to part us, putting four of us at the four corners of classrooms where we couldn't break the paramount rule of law "No talking."

Strathroy was proud of its schools and by the standards of the twenties they were, no doubt, good. Today they seem almost as punitive as Oliver's orphanage. Colborne School was a bare, forbidding, dirty-cream brick building, set in the middle of a large, sandy lot. The girls' playground, with a single, large maple tree, was on the north side, the boys' on the south. In each playground was an outhouse, a four-holer, and credit must certainly be given to a long-ago janitor, for in them it was the smell of pine floor cleaner that was pervasive, though I hated the whole set-up and, as my grandfather's house was just up the street, seldom had to venture inside. The sand in our playground was excellent for hop-scotch, played obsessively by all the girls in the Spring and Fall. Competition was keen for attractive pieces of broken crockery for hop-scotch counters, especially for pieces of the iridescent glass now known as "Carnival Glass" which we traded enthusiastically. School began at nine and ended at four, with two fifteen minute periods of recess at 10.30 and three, signalled by the Principal's ringing of a large, brass handbell. At noon, at the sound of the furniture-factory whistle, we were out until one-thirty, time enough for some of us to make a good fifteen minute walk home and back again. Everybody had hot dinner at noon then; only in the direst of winter storms were we allowed to take our lunches.

We had a ten days' holiday at Easter, July and August in the summer and another ten days at Christmas. The 24th of May, Queen Victoria's birthday, was the traditional late spring holiday and the 23rd was Empire Day, not a holiday, but a day when we took part in various patriotic exercises drilled by our teachers. In the Fall, we had a half-holiday for the town Fair, when we all swarmed out to the Fairgrounds and, if money permitted, spent nickels and dimes on the Merry-Go-Round and Ferris Wheel. The most exciting school day of each year was the day of the Inspector's visit, when the younger and more nervous teachers were wrecks and the show-offs among the students (I was one such), were delighted to perform for his benefit.

In those days schools operated largely through fear, but I can remember no fear in Miss Sadlier's room though there was plenty of it in Florence Newton's First Book the next year. Her job may well have been a harder one, for in that year we had to learn a lot of arithmetic and certainly two-column adding was, for awhile, a nemesis for me. But mostly, I believe, she was a repressed and cruel woman who relished ruling through fear, as she certainly relished strapping the entire class from time to time and, often, individual children, particularly the big boys and the two Indian girls who sat slightly apart from the rest of us at the back of the room. In every grade there were certain marginalised children, often boys who hadn't been sent to school regularly or who, probably unfairly, were considered below par mentally. Certainly the two Indian girls were far bigger and older than the rest of us, and they were isolated and shunned, first by the teacher and then, following her lead, by us. I have a vivid memory of one boy in our room that year who had only one scribbler for the entire year. When it was used he had to rub it all out and start again on the scarred pages. Florence Newton made fun of him, and we skirted around his desk as if he were contagious. I also remember her creating a first-class crisis because of the loss of someone's silver pencil. Mr. Cuddy was called in, every desk searched, and hanging over the culprit the terrible certainty of a strapping in front of the whole class by the Principal. I can't remember the outcome of it all, just the atmosphere of excited terror. My mother always insisted on canonizing Florence Newton, as indeed did many others, for the local branch of the I.O.D.E. still bears her name. Those of us who sat in her class think differently.

Most of the time we were drilled in the three R's, but once a week we had "Art," and were told to copy something that the teacher provided, a pumpkin, perhaps, or always a favourite, a maple leaf in its fall glory. Certainly there were absolutely no free-hand paintings allowed us—the very thought would have been shocking in those days. I loved my paintbox, though, and also doodled a lot in the margins of my scribblers, hurriedly rubbing out if the teacher came down the aisle. Once a week, too, we had a singing lesson, for Strathroy was proud to consider itself a progressive town. Then a portly elderly gentleman (later not considered a gentleman at all and advised to leave town!), called by courtesy only Professor Gordon, came along and taught us pieces according to the 'tonic sol fa' method. Once in a very long while, we were given squares of brightly coloured paper which we then folded and cut, according to instructions, to make amazing patterns. And always, the teachers read us a few pages from a book once or twice a week, a very harmless book with, usually, a minimum of excitement and adventure and a maximum of moral lesson—something like Nellie McClung's *Sowing Seeds In Danny*. We always began school with the Lord's Prayer, and singing The King, and there was a short spell when the town ministers (Protestant only) took turns coming around to read us passages of scripture. There was always a Christmas Concert, but the most memorable festival was Valentine's Day, when we had a "candy feast" and deposited our valentines to one another in a decorated box. Great was the orgy of paste, scissors and red paper hearts, and great was the competition and teasing. Once Ted, Mary's brother, put all his valentines in the box for me—as I recall, 17, my greatest claim to popularity then or since. I think fondly of him still.

When we were in Third book we suddenly had a 'School Nurse,' Mrs. Wilson, who examined our heads once in a while for nits and, in my brother's time, found some. Great was the consternation, the washing of all heads in coal oil and the painful fine-tooth-combing of the hair. I was lucky to escape that plague, though my brother didn't. Mrs. Wilson supervised a great smallpox vaccination project. She also began a school milk project which I had no part of. I would have had to bring money from home to pay for the milk and my mother thought, rightly, that I drank plenty of it at home. I certainly did take part in the Penny Bank project begun in the twenties by the Bank of Commerce and that seemed very exciting, actually bringing pennies from home and having individual bankbooks. Boys were expected to hate school then, and many, no doubt, did, but most girls, and especially born show-off girls like myself and my friends, thoroughly enjoyed school, especially when safely away from Florence Newton. We idolized Miss Denning, our Second-Book teacher, and she lives forever in our memory for the pageant she put on one Empire Day. Mary Dampier, Myrtle Haight and I together made up the flag, Mary red, Myrtle white, and I, blue. We marched to the cenotaph with all the town's public school children, with the Maitland School crowd complete strangers to us. We sang and recited our pieces, a great and memorable public triumph. As a reward, Mother drove Mary and me out to pick violets, growing lushly by a roadside near Mt. Brydges. Miss Denning had us come over to her house on the south side of town, across the railroad tracks, to be fitted for our crepe paper dresses, and gave us lemonade, an unforgettable treat.

 We were ten when we went to Miss Cameron in Junior Third. I believe that children, certainly girls, really begin to wake up at that age and for the first time are ready, eager, and hungry to learn, and besides that, are avid observers of everything around them. Certainly I doubt now that Miss Alison Cameron was as remarkable as Mary and I thought she was—so much so that years and years later, grown up, we called on her to reminisce about our two years in her room. She did have initiative, though, beyond what the teachers' manual told her to do. She entered at least two of the boys in a singing contest for area schools and drilled them endlessly in "All Through the Night". She introduced Junior Red Cross into our lives, and engaged us in a money-making scheme on its behalf, distributing flyers for Grieve's Drugstore. We had real meetings of the Red Cross, and real elections for its officers (I was eager to be President, and was duly elected). We began to learn something of the running of meetings and committees and of Parliamentary Procedure. We also got the *Junior Red Cross Magazine*, which opened our eyes on the wider world, as did the burgeoning League of Nations, very much featured in it. Miss Cameron was an enthusiast for the League and for all of my life Geneva and the League's headquarters have had a special importance for me that dates back to that year and probably before that, to the mythical James Shotwell of Strathroy who had been an advisor at its founding. A combination of Miss Cameron's enthusiasm and tales of Shotwell and the League imprinted internationalism on me deeply and early, and so it has remained.

By this time in our lives Mary Dampier and I were in a healthy competition for everything going. First in importance was, of course, the Honour Roll, printed in the Age Dispatch three times a year for all the grades in Public and High School as well—a barbarous ritual which was carried on in the school system at least until the war. Mary and I vied with might and main over being first, and when I lost out to her my Grandfather McCandless persuaded me that I should congratulate her—a hypocritical exercise on my part if ever there was one, and one that was mightily watered down by my grudging delivery, as

Mary still reminds me: "my Grandfather told me I should say 'congratulations.'" Socially Mary and I made our debuts in Third Book too. We were suddenly very popular with the boys and went to Cecil Wright's, Alan Campbell's and Billy Bowie's birthday parties. Once there, all dressed up, we ate, mostly, especially the obligatory cake and ice cream, though once, at Brian Engel's party, we had pumpkin pie. Brian was a New Zealander who had been sent to live with relatives, the Boyds, on Metcalfe Street, almost in the country. In the Fall we used to have grand games of Cowboy and Indians among the corn shooks in someone's adjacent field near his place. The Thomas boys, Randy and Stewart, notoriously tough redheads, lived near the Boyds too. We girls didn't have birthday parties, though once Myrtle Haight told us she was having one and we arrived at her house with great expectations, only to be met by a wickedly angry mother. Very sad to remember that!

Besides making our days adventurous, Miss Cameron charmed us by the books she read to us. No wishy washy pap for her. It was with her that I first heard *The Secret Garden*, a book I still read every few years. And then, thrill upon thrill, she read us *Tarzan of the Apes*—this was a few years before Johnny Weismuller and Maureen O'Hara made the film. Never had we been exposed to anything so exciting—I spent hours trying to figure out how Tarzan taught himself to read, and as for the denouement, his being Lord Greystoke, it was beyond measure a dream-come-true. We waited for each Friday afternoon's chapter practically holding our breath. Then, finally, with Jane tied to a stake by savages and Tarzan winging through the jungle to her rescue, Miss Cameron did the unthinkable. She refused to finish the book. We had talked too much, she said, and this was our punishment. No final chapter, no appeal. The teacher's word was law. It was years before we forgave her and we never forgot. Somehow, though, the warm memories of her Third Book overcame that final blow, though at the time it was crushing.

The next year, Junior Fourth, was almost as thrilling as the thought of High School in the not-too-far-off future. Colborne pupils had to move to Maitland across the tracks and on the other side of town to join the Fourth book pupils there in the class of Mr. MacVicar, our first male teacher. He had just come to Strathroy. He was young, attractive and newly married, all conditions guaranteed to thrill to the core romantic eleven-year-olds. He became our hero immediately, and we used to try to think of excuses to knock on his door and see what his wife was like. He had a good deal of initiative in introducing us to thrilling projects: Health Books, involving the rifling of magazines for delectable illustrations of food; Garden Books, encouraging the collection of vivid seed catalogue pictures of gorgeous fruit and blossoms. One of my friends remembers the year because she was good at Mental Arithmetic, and always finished and was allowed out of school fifteen minutes early on Friday afternoons when we had those exercises. I doubt that I ever did! For me it was the year of the *Anne Of Green Gables* influence, the self-conscious making of "best friends," the forming of Clubs, and the hiving together of various little groups and cliques. Strathroy was a town of about 2,500 then, but for all we had previously known the students at Maitland school, it might as well have been 25,000. Once we were thrown together, we mixed and melded, and friendships were formed, some of them to last a lifetime.

My route to school changed too. Instead of walking down Caradoc street, past Grandma's house to Colborne,

I had to walk down Victoria, over the tracks to Maitland. That meant following a one-lane dirt road, through the 'Back Flats,' land that was still wild then, with all the country delights of wild flowers and, best of all, an intriguing roadside dump well filled with pieces of broken china and wonderful hop-scotch glass. I usually walked with Agatha Cavers and Jean Swift, younger girls whose regular school was Maitland. One day we found what seemed to us to be a fabulous hoard of broken coloured china, obviously originally a vase. It demanded some special symbolic use and meaning and because somewhere I had heard fabulous things about flamingoes and because the sound of the word intrigued me, I founded the Flamingo Club with the broken crockery its talismans. I can't remember that we ever did much, if anything, though we had a Club House in an empty hen-run at the Swifts' house.

Dorrie Fowlie, whose father had recently come to town to be Manager of the Royal Bank, became a 'best friend' of that and many future years. She and I, Mary Dampier, Evelyn Brown and Jean Bowley, became a clique, paper dolls our passion and our club, a big secret, the PD Club. Our great gambit was to cadge old pattern books from Butler's and Evoy's Dry Goods stores and then cut out our dolls and trade, trade, trade. At one time I was the proud possessor of triplets with numbers of identical dresses. I also had a spell of designing and painting dresses for a 'Blondie' doll, cut out from the comics. I lived quite easily in several worlds by then, and kept them quite separate—my home, Grandpa and Grandma McCandless's, Aunt Rate's, where my Aunt Dot lived, Dad Sullivan's, my mother's father, up Victoria Street from us, where Annie, my youngest aunt, only eight years older than I, and Hugh, her younger brother, lived. None of these overlapped, nor do I remember any strangeness in moving from one to another. There was also Agatha from up the street, who, like me, loved reading. We had both imbibed Anne and her making of her own secret places, and we spent hours and hours down in the wild gully that ran behind Victoria street, a wonderful, natural playground, with its swimming hole, wild flowers, trailing wild grapes which we tried to use as Tarzan's tree ropes, and all kinds of natural playhouses. We even had a deserted cottage to explore, the house where the famous Shotwell had grown up, its grounds overgrown with huge old lilac bushes.

Senior Fourth, when I was twelve, going on thirteen, was the year of the big challenge. We were back at Colborne Street School and in Mr. Cuddy's room, with the notorious Entrance Examinations looming ahead of us and giving status and importance to everything we did and learned. Mary Dampier's father had died suddenly, leaving her and her brother Ted under the guardianship of Mrs. Pugsley, the widow of a former Anglican clergyman and mother herself of two teen-age daughters. She had moved her enlarged family to a large semi-detached house on Front Street and Mary and Dorrie Fowlie became pals. Suddenly, I was sometimes on the outside of their twosome, a place I wasn't used to being and that I didn't like at all. This was the year I discovered the thrill of writing 'plays,' the first one being, predictably, "Little Women," at least as much a favourite as Anne, if not more so. Teachers were always easy about letting us "put on" these affairs, probably because they had to give some time to what was called Oral Composition—public speaking. It was certainly easier for them to let us act, than to hear us drone away on dreary subjects like "My Summer Holidays," and it was certainly more fun for us.

We had the required five players for "Little Women" in our group—Jean Bowley as Amy, Eveyln Brown as Beth, Mary Dampier, Jo, Me Meg, and Dorrie, Marmee. I recall a whole lot of running around which I thoroughly enjoyed bossing, and minimal costumes, except for Dorrie who had a bona fide 19th-century dress. It was all stimulating, certainly, and lots of fun. Later we did more of them, but that was when we were in High School. At this late date I wonder why absolutely no one suggested to me that I should keep on trying to write— because I, then and later, always wrote the plays. Of course I know the answer to that one: such nonsense was just a waste of time according to the pedagogic wisdom of the day.

Arithmetic and Grammar were the main subjects of 'the Entrance,' as we all called it. We were endlessly drilled in both, and spent much time working over old papers, for the exam we would take in the spring was a province-wide one, and the papers were actually printed ones, looking fearsomely official. To have its students do well on The Entrance was crucially important to our teacher, and to Strathroy's pride in its school records. The fourth reader seemed totally adult compared to what had gone before. It was imperialist to a degree, a full-colour Union Jack its frontispiece, and poems like "The Private of the Buffs" (which I can still recite and also sing, to the tune of "Oh God our help in ages past"), and "Invictus"— ("the sand of the desert is sodden red / red with the wreck of a square that broke / The gatling's jammed and the Colonel's dead / And the men are all blind from dust and smoke ... But the voice of a schoolboy rallies the ranks ... Play up, Play up, and Play the game!") As much as, if not more than anything else, we had been drilled in memory work throughout Public School, again according to the pedagogic wisdom of the day, but based, I believe, on a sound theory—memory that is used, will expand, memory that is not used will atrophy.

At least once in that year Mr. Cuddy was not well, visibly confused, to our combined fear and curiosity. However, he did finish the year, and we duly presented ourselves at the High School, up the cinder path from Caradoc Street, clustering around the steps until the doors were opened, suffering fearsome pre-examination suspense, and anxious post-mortems morning and afternoon for three days. The spring had been a hard one for our family, because Grandpa McCandless had died, painfully, of cancer in May, after a long illness. Even though this was the first year when students with high averages were excused from writing Entrance Exams, I knew that the family wanted me to write the exams and qualify for the J.C. Elliott medal for highest marks in the district. So I did. In any case, after a year's drilling it would have been a disappointment not to write the exams. I was the winner, Father told me that Grandpa would have been proud, and I was satisfied. I dearly loved my Grandfather, always.

High School, 1932-37
Strathroy Collegiate Institute

In June, 1932, sixty-four of us had written the Entrance Examinations in Strathroy. In September we started up the hill to High School, a relatively new building opened in 1922. Both my parents had gone to the old High School over the tracks on Caradoc Street south. It was a landmark initiation each year for the First Form class—out of childhood and into a whole new world of multiple teachers, thrilling—and frightening—new subjects, Latin and

French, for instance, and all kinds of extra-curricular involvements, not only within the school, but in competition with other schools from as far away as Petrolia and Sarnia. We felt grown up, at least compared to the Public School kids, though certainly not to our experienced elders from Second Form on to the Fifth. There were 233 pupils in High School then, 130 girls, 103 boys, 113 from Strathroy and 120 from the country around.

There were eight teachers: Mr. Summerhayes, Principal, Math and Science, Mr. French, Latin and History, Greek and German by request, Mr. Manning, Agriculture and P.T., Mrs. Thompson, Mathematics, Miss Goulding, English and assorted subjects, Miss Waugh, English, Mrs. Hall, French, and Miss McCormick, also French and P.T. We referred to them behind their backs as Vic, Pa French, Corp Manning, Madam Hall, Hannah Goulding, Marian Waugh and Anne McCormick. In the spring of 1933 Mrs. Thompson resigned, to be followed by Mr. Armstrong, who was sadly inadequate and left after a turbulent year, and then in 1934 by Earl Marcy who had obviously been hired to bring discipline to a rowdy situation, and who forthwith scared most of us out our wits, some of the girls, literally! Mrs. Hall resigned in 1933 and she was not replaced, having been sadly inadequate in any case. Henceforth, until 1937, there were only seven teachers, undoubtedly a Depression cutback.

Strathroy had a long tradition of pride in its 'Collegiate', its colours blue and gold, and its motto "Live to Learn and Learn to Live": long-time residents were quick to correct anyone who called it a High School. It had been one of the first Collegiates in Ontario, a designation that meant a certain number of specialists on its teaching staff. Both my parents had gone to the 'Old High School' over the tracks on south Caradoc Street, and not demolished until 1933. At the time its history was commemorated by a celebratory write-up in *The Age Dispatch*, celebrating its history and the renown of certain of its graduates, The town had some reason for academic pride: on the 1931 department examinations for Middle School (Junior Matriculation), 274 papers had been written, of which 206 got over 75%.

Times were bad, of course, the pit of the Depression in fact. In the Fall of 1932 the Secondary School Federation suspended the minimum for teachers' salaries, which meant that each School Board would pay as little as it possibly could. Government Grants were cut by 10% in 1933. In the same year Dr. McCabe, Chairman of the Trustees, gave a report to the town Council: the Principal, he said, was being paid $3,325, the provincial average was $3900; female teachers were being paid $1,957, the provincial average $2,175. Male teachers were being paid $2,375, the average $2,763; the provincial average for all teachers was $2,638, the average for Strathroy teachers $2,232,50. Dr. McCabe's report reassured the Council somewhat—there had been complaints of unnecessary extravagance in paying teachers. As we who were there will remember, we were well taught according to the ideas of the day—the town was getting a large bargain, and had nothing to be proud of in paying below the provincial average.

The ads in *The Age Dispatch* tell their own story of hard times: "Mother thinks there is no medecine like Dr. Williams' Pink Pills for nervous High-strung girls," or, under the heading "Fat Girls Out of Fashion," "All over the world Kruschen Salts is appealing to girls and women who are striving for an attractive, free-from-fat figure.... Every morning they take a teaspoon of Kruschen Salts in a glass of water before breakfast." In June of 1932 the

Artistic Lady's Outfitters was having a dress sale for $1.89, with 15% off on Wednesday mornings. In the Fall they had a coat sale—$9.95 to $22.50. All stores were pushing specials: at Stepler's Drug Store you got 3/15 cent cakes of Piccadilly soap plus 1 washcloth for 29 cents; at Grieve's the offer was 2 golf balls plus 1 tube of Lifebuoy shaving cream for 99 cents. The Hydro Shop advertised ranges for $100 and electric washers for $99. McIntosh's Jewellry offered the Mikado pattern in Royal Crown Derby for $1.45 a cup and saucer and $1.65 a dinner plate. The Regent Theatre advertised Marlene Dietrich, Clive Brook and Anna May Wong in *Shanghai Express*, adults 25 cents, children 15, and, as a coming attraction, *Lives Of A Bengal Lancer*, with Gary Cooper and Franchot Tone. The Statham Orchestra was playing in the Town hall on Saturday nights and the C.N.R. was advertising its cent-a-mile specials. In the Fall the West Adelaide Presbyterian Church Ladies Aid Fowl Supper charged 25 cents for adults and 20 cents for children—the feasts of their time, with tables laden with roast chicken, mashed potatoes and gravy, cabbage salads and pies—and what pies! Multitudinous and delectable. Strathroy business men were caught up in numbers of schemes to stimulate trade, from "Popularity Contests" to a gala day in which airplane rides over the town were featured for 98 cents a time.

On the most ominous Depression note, in every issue of the paper there was a large ad listing the properties to be sold at auction for taxes. The taxes owing ranged from as high as $202 to as low as $11. Sometimes there were boxed inserts containing the appeal of Mrs. Wilson, Public Health Nurse, for clothes for needy families, and sometimes reports of Strathroy's Relief Committee: "There are presently 24 families receiving Relief food and fuel." For every family accepting 'Relief,' however, there were a dozen who were living on credit, and grocery and butcher businesses like my family's had to carry them or lose their goodwill. There were thousand of dollars of debts chalked up in those years that were never reclaimed, and only once or twice can I remember my father most unwillingly going after a bad debt. When he died in 1972, the house contained a trunkload of grocery bills still unpaid.

As far as necessities were concerned, our family was not touched by the Depression. Food was lavish, always, because my mother was an enthusiastic cook, and it was taken for granted that we would have the very best, especially of meat. Most young people then were not used to having money in hand, and as long as 25 cents was forthcoming for a movie, I saw nothing to complain of. I wore a lot of hand-me-downs to High School, mostly from my Aunt Marge, who lived in Windsor. When mother began working for the Artistic on Saturday and later in the decade full-time, I was among the very few favoured ones, for she loved buying me clothes, and always I had lots of them.

All of our High School teaching was directed toward the passing of exams, Lower School after Second Form, Middle School (Junior Matriculation) after Third Form, and Upper School, split between Fourth and Fifth Form. It was customary to write off Upper School English Literature and Composition after Fourth Form. Young men were then taken into the banks as "Juniors" after Fourth Form, and numbers of others left school at that time, so Fifth Form was a much smaller group than we had been used to. Those of us who hoped for university or Normal School had to have Senior Matriculation subjects, and those most likely to get good scholarships needed the three maths, Geometry, Algebra and Trigonometry. Foolishly, and because of the widespread prejudice against Mr. Marcy, I refused to take Upper School Trig, and therefore cut myself out of a number of good scholarships, a source of continuing, lifelong, embarrassment and regret. When I think back on High School in search of the learning challenges that came to mean so much to me at Western, I can think of only Mr. French's classes in History, Ancient and Modern, Latin, which I loved, and German, as difficult for him, I suspect, as for me. He was, though, a scholar, trained in classics in the old style, and sometimes that came through. The other teachers were certainly competent, but examination-obsessed, and the courses they had to teach contained the bare minimum of challenging material, and the maximum of dull, "learn by rote' material. I think now that the Upper School course was a scandal: having taken *Macbeth* in Fourth Form, we had to take it again in Fifth. The two collections, *Shorter Poems* And *Short Stories And Essays* were, in content as well as appearance, utterly dull. I recall nothing about the context of their contents being given to us, but plenty about the teacher's anxiety that we should know every word, particularly of Macbeth.

Miss Waugh would get emotionally distraught if the class seemed to be dimmer than usual, and never since have I been able to face a performance of *Macbeth* with tolerance, let alone anticipation. One novel a year we read, at a creeping pace, The ones I remember are Conrad's *Typhoon*, probably the least likely to intrigue a group of teenagers of any novel I can think of, and Hudson's *Green Mansions*, which had a sad effect on one of my friends who tended toward hysteria; she fancied herself as the airy-fairy Rima the Bird-Woman! As for French, its teaching was totally from the book: we translated with agonizing slowness, and then we wrote out sentences in

French. There was no French conversation, and the French of Quebec, or in fact Quebec itself, was non-existent in the classroom. "Lisez" and "traduisez" were the extent of the French we heard, aside from the endless "vocabularies" the main feature of every lesson. Everything was geared to memorization and having a first-class memory from early days, I did extremely well. Until, that is, it came to the maths which did, from time to time, require the use of the brain. I still did well, but I hated them, or thought I did, and I regret that. My first shock at Western was finding that most subjects required an effort beyond easy memorization.

Intellectually, High School was a wasteland. Why then are our memories of it kinder than they should be? I think it is because we were so busy growing up, finding out who we were, and how we could fit in with our peers that we were really not fit or ready for anything meatier than we got. For most of us it was the world around us that dominated our thoughts and minds: for girls the world of dances and boys, movies and marriage, careers—well perhaps—of clothes and makeup, and for some, but not for me, of sports; for boys of sports, cars, jobs-to-come and, of course, of girls as well. Although we had a Cadet Corps and a yearly parade with Bugle Band, there were few thoughts of the future war that was to dominate all our young adulthood. We were cocooned, really, largely because of the intense self-absorption of the teenager. Certainly the outside world was available to us through radio and the movies' omnipresent newsreels, but compared to our own concerns, its voices were a distant clamour only. Public school has a very different clientele: there, before the distractions of adolescence, children are opening their eyes and exploring the avenues of their own curiosities.

Chapter IV

Church

In Strathroy in the twenties, as in most other small towns at that time, family church affiliation was an important part of a child's identity. The McCandlesses were Baptists and my grandfather was Superintendent of the Sunday School, an office he held proudly for sixteen years. From infancy on I went to Sunday School at 2.30 on Sunday afternoons throughout the year except for July and August, when it was held at 10 in the morning, before church, instead. My mother was a faithful attendant too as, later, was my brother. Everyone gathered according to their classes in the big basement with the two furnaces that heated the church and there we had prayers and sang rousing "Sunday School hymns" like "Dare to be a Daniel" and "Onward Christian Soldiers," hymns that everyone enjoyed belting out and that were considered a little too robust for more formal church services. Next came our classes, and then a final gathering, more hymns and the all-important report on collection, often a short homily from the Superintendent, and then dismissal.

When we separated into our classes we were led through a lesson prescribed in the official Sunday School paper, *The Northern Messenger*. The teacher usually had us read the appropriate *Bible* passage taking turns, verse by verse. Sometimes she expounded a bit, or added a bit of moral message, but seldom. When she did, it could be terrible; I well remember the teacher who solemnly assured us that Catholics wouldn't go to Heaven, and I also remember my mother's anger when I asked her about that. Mother was notably tolerant of religion and race. In Sunday School I remember learning by memory scripture passages, but little else. Certainly the exciting *Bible* stories that I read in my Hurlbut's collection, about Moses, David, Saul, Sampson and all the rest of the *Old Testament*'s larger-than-life characters, officially took a distant second place to the *New Testament*'s Gospel message, usually watered down to a thin and anaemic consistency. Our teachers were pious women, no doubt, and except for one of them, totally uninspiring. Frieda Oakes, though, was an attractive young woman who worked in an office in London, was engaged to be married to a stalwart of the Presbyterian church and wore a handsome diamond. She was just the right teacher for us when we were in our early teens, and she regaled us beyond the lessons with stories of her marriage plans, and even instituted class-meetings, held in the church kitchen and featuring enthusiastic pot luck supper meetings.

She also brought Vesta Gast, a friend of hers, also a Presbyterian, who had been teaching on the Indian Reservation at Muncey, to talk to us and, a thing absolutely new to all of us, to share with us her real affection for the Indian children she had known. Vesta was a walking demonstration of the golden rule, "Do unto others as you would be done by." She had resolved to live by it when she was very young, and until she died, well into her eighties, she was a personification of Love to me. From that first early encounter in Sunday School she was one of the prime friends and influences of my life. Later I was fortunate to live in her home for more than two years, and until her death we remained dear friends. The phrase "role model" was unknown then, but Vesta was exactly that to me: she had an irresistible combination of human kindness, humour and intellectual curiosity that drew all kinds of people to her all her life. She never stopped growing and learning, and she was an inadvertent, but very important gift of Sunday School to me.

Church I usually attended with my grandfather. Grandma was, of course, in the choir, as were my mother and my Aunt Vi. Church services as I remember them were neither interesting nor excruciatingly boring, but rather predictably the same—same faces in the choir, same organist and, in general, same congregation. Summer Sundays, though, were often excruciatingly hot, and older women used freely the paper fans that were provided along with hymnals and Bibles in the pews. Once a month the members took communion after the regular service, at which time my mother left with a flourish, for she was not a member and only members were welcome at communion. She resented exclusion, but she wasn't about to capitulate and be a 'baptized Christian.' Children, of course, left as well, and a few others, but only mother made her exit with such consciousness of difference. In fact there were very mixed messages about the Baptist church emanating from our family, for my father had not been baptized either, nor did he ever go to church. He had disgraced the family early in his teens by playing baseball rather than attending certain important 'revival meetings,' and had even gone so far as to go to Detroit for a Sunday game. Grandpa and Grandma both considered him beyond the pale as far as church was concerned; whether they themselves really believed the prevalent Baptist nonsense about damnation, I never found out. I can't imagine that they did—rather I can imagine it very well, but I'd rather not believe it. Father had a lifelong anxiety and regret about his alienation, but he could not and would not pretend what he did not believe.

A series of revival meetings happened once in my youth, too. These times, when travelling preachers of fire and brimstone would be invited by the church to come to town and hold special services, were dear to the heart of Baptists. They were permissible orgies of emotionalism, descended from the notorious 'camp meetings' of earlier times. This revivalist, called Mr. Torrey, had the entire Sunday School up in the church for a blood and gore performance of Christ's journey to the Cross and Crucifixion, after which we were all sobbingly invited to come to the front and be saved. I was totally revolted, and at about age eight, probably frightened as well, though I've always linked the stubborn resolve to stay in my seat with disgust, not fright. And I've also remembered equally, and with pride, that I was the only one in the whole Sunday School to do so. Later, back at my grandparents' my grandfather began to lead me gently in the same direction when suddenly my mother erupted into the room, the only time I ever saw her defy Grandpa whom she loved: "Leave that child alone!" and home we went.

Clara the unsaved remained so until after my grandfather's death, when I consented to baptism to please my grandmother. I had a brief pious period when I was reading the Elsie Dinsmore books. Elsie was a dreadful child who was too holy to practice her music on Sunday and would sit on the piano bench until she fainted rather than risk offending the Lord. One of my cousins, of Father's vintage, owned all thirty-four of the Elsie books, and because I would read anything within my reach, I ate them up, and tried to make my friend, Mary Dampier, play Elsie sometimes. She had far too much sense, and still holds it against me! Equally sickening were the Pansy books, some of which were in our Sunday School "Library," a sad collection of a dozen or so books, none of them enjoyable. I didn't even persevere with them, I am now relieved to remember.

Every Baptist church has a baptismal tank, usually built in above the pulpit and choir loft, so that viewing it is like looking at a movie screen for the congregation. It has always struck me as absolutely ridiculous, but then many religious rituals are ridiculous. Total immersion, the basis of the Baptist faith is, however, especially ridiculous, and for anyone self-conscious, demeaning to boot. After a good evangelical campaign, hordes of people affected by the crowd hysteria that ensues, are baptized, and in warm climates, this happens in a handy river. Reminiscent of the Jordan, which is *the* traditional baptismal river. In cold climates and more conventional churches, however, times of baptism are announced by the minister well in advance, and happen only at intervals, quarterly perhaps. In our Strathroy church baptisms were done during the evening service with the choir in attendance, singing the doleful hymn "Take me, Oh Lord," at a snail's pace, to accompany the procedure.

The candidate for the church's blessing, and presumably the Lord's as well, traditionally wears white. The minister is covered head to foot with a rubberized boiler suit. He prays a while, and then quickly dunks the candidate, being careful to avoid dropping, ducking, or otherwise damaging her/him. I was a good sized teenager of 13 and neither he nor I had trouble; what a minister must encounter with hefty males or obese females does not bear imagining. I expect that a course, called something like "The techniques of Baptism" must be the subject of many a ribald joke in theological colleges. The water is lukewarm—I remember the whole thing being an embarrassing but quickly-over experience, one that left me completely unchanged, but my grandmother satisfied.

Neither of my parents, needless to say, being unbaptized themselves, were present. After baptism one is a full-fledged member of the church, and welcome to take the bread and weak, unsugared grape-juice of communion.

Throughout my teens I continued Sunday School and, usually, church as well, but I never joined the young people's association, the BYPU. For that kind of affiliation I went to C.G.I.T. at the United Church, and speedily became convinced that the United was the "joyful" church. I once said that to Northrop Frye, who laughed heartily, having had a rigorous, obviously not joyful, early experience of the old Methodist church, from which the United evolved. But in Strathroy, where there was always a flourishing continuing Presbyterian Church, and still is, the United seemed to me to be a melange of cheery people. My Aunt Dot, to whom I was always close, was a Sunday School teacher there, and a choir member. I was impressed by their policy of accepting young people into the choir, a practice unheard of in our church, where matrons and grandmothers ruled the roost, and it would have been considered frivolous for a young person to dream of joining them. Best of all, though, was the United Church's sponsoring of the C.G.I.T. group in the early thirties, with keen, attractive young women in charge who brought new ideas, enthusiasms, and activities to all the girls who joined from all the town's churches.

We had weekly meetings in the church basement, when we pledged our allegiance to high ideals and sang the official song, "Follow the Gleam," its pleasant tune and service-directed words entirely satisfying to a group of romantically minded girls:

> To the knights in the days of old,
> Keeping watch on the mountain height
> Came a vision of Holy Grail
> And a voice through the waiting night
> Follow follow follow the gleam
> Banners unfurl'd o'er all the world
> Follow follow follow the gleam
> Of the chalice that is the grail.
>
> And we who would serve the King
> And loyally him obey
> In the consecrate silence know
> That the challenge still holds today
> Follow follow follow the gleam,
> Standards of worth, O'er all the earth
> Follow follow follow the gleam
> Of the light that shall bring the dawn.

That song, I have since learned, was the official song of Bryn Mawr College, and it was, and is, an attractive call to service, especially appealing to young girls newly dazzled by the high idealism of the Grail legends. Certainly it was so to us—and, a bonus, completely without denominational reference.

On a more everyday basis, we wove baskets of coloured crepe paper, made doll beds out of empty cigar boxes, and exulted in our prowess with easily available crafts. We also put on skits, my particular love, involving much happy dressing up and noisy rushing about. One in particular, "The Landlord's Daughter," was especially rowdy and joyous fun. And best of all, in the summers we went to the camp at Hillsboro in tents, with two young women as our leaders. I am grateful to both my parents for their willingness for me to stretch my horizons, for I was not only encouraged, I was urged to join, while the stricter Baptists, of course, would have none of it. I was certainly the only girl from our church who attended, and I remember it fondly, a truly liberating teenage experience. The leaders, two of them over the course of three years or so, were both, I now understand, exceptional young women who became exceptional adults as well.

My divorce from the Baptist church was certainly hastened in my later teens by the arrival of a new, young minister, who had the temerity to preach a sermon against the film *One Night of Love*, starring Grace Moore and Franchot Tone. After the victory of sound, movies in the thirties were quick to experiment with music. The day of Josi Iturbi, Deanna Durbin, Gladys Swarthout and Lily Pons and even the great Stokowski dawned to my utter enchantment. Grace Moore was my first brush with an opera star; I was totally bedazzled, especially, of course, by her signature song, "Ciri Biri Bin" and her rendition of Kreisler's "The Old Refrain." I used to sit in church and imagine her sudden arrival in a blue velvet gown, amongst the choir in front of me, a fantasy that whiled away many a dull moment. The puritanical young minister also contrived to visit my grandmother one day when I was with her, and seriously advised me against dancing—and this when I, like my chums, danced at least once a week, and prided ourselves on our prowess! He wasn't a bad-looking young man, and I believe that he and his wife could be good company, but to my mind he personified every ridiculous restriction that I resented and intended to shake off as soon as I left town for university. And of course, I did just that. I cannot remember ever going into a church for all the Western years.

Much later on, when our sons were young and we lived in West Toronto, church attendance resumed out of a feeling of responsibility for properly bringing up a family. We were faithful attendants at the High Park United Church, and for several years I was a happy teacher of a large Sunday School class of teenage girls. I instituted the class supper meetings that I had enjoyed, though they were at our house, not in the church. The food was lavish and much more abundant than in the Baptist basement in the thirties. They were a very good group, outgoing and intelligent, though one year a good many of them who took part in Bloor Collegiate's performance of *South Pacific* were notable failures in their Grade XIII examinations. Their performance sticks in my mind, though, as the most enjoyable musical I ever attended. The stage simply lit up with their youth and energy. I gave up the class, regretfully, when I began in earnest to qualify for the Ph.D. at the University of Toronto.

After we moved to Lawrence Park in 1963 I attended the Lawrence Park Community church faithfully for many years, enjoying and benefiting from the sermons of Douglas Bradford, a gifted speaker. I was too busy at Glendon and then at the main York campus to belong to a women's group, and both boys promptly gave up church as soon as they were confirmed at age 13. My husband, Morley, was never interested though he still supports the church with yearly givings. I dropped away after one historic Sunday, Palm Sunday in fact, when a money-raising drive was begun with "Kick-Off" Sunday. I couldn't bear that kind of hucksterism and I still can't. I have been always, however, and I still am, extremely interested in religion, particularly in the history of various religions. Teaching Medieval and Renaissance History for Western fuelled my interest, a lasting and a fruitful one. I am, I believe, a religious person, but emphatically not an institutional one. I do recognize, however, a throwback to the radical individualism of the Baptist sect in my attitudes to church as to many other facets of my life.

Chapter V

Reading

At least as important as school to me was reading. Along with their respect for education, from the earliest age, my family on all sides was definitely for the encouragement of reading. Before my brother was born I think my mother herself read a fair amount, and certainly she took me to the town Library, at that time in a store on Front Street East, before I went to school. My first library book was *The Bobbsey Twins On A Houseboat*, and I also remember Uncle Wiggly and Nurse Jane, especially their adventure in a hot-air balloon. I read before I went to school, spurred on by my grandfather's promise of the coveted Hurlbut's story of the *Bible*. But the most thrilling memories come from a bout of chickenpox at age nine, when my young half-uncle and aunt, Hugh and Annie, brought me their old copies of *Robinson Crusoe*, The *Wonderful Wizard of Oz* and a thick collection of tales from the *Arabian Nights*. I've never been happier than I was then, itchy, blotchy, in bed, and reading. All of those books, even their appearance, *Robinson Crusoe* smelly and spotty, are vivid memories. Nothing I had ever heard had prepared me for the exoticism of Aladdin or Sinbad the Sailor—they were landmarks.

At about the same time I found in Grandma's "little room," effectively a small study with two walls filled with books, the 1912 issue of *Chums*. That was another great joy, especially a pirate story continued through many weekly (or monthly?) issues, and providing endless thrills, buried treasure, sword-fighting, and all the proper attributes of the pirate genre for young people. I was struck then, and I am still surprised, at the demonizing of Germany and Germans as early as 1912. Perhaps it began earlier than that. I've read very little about pre-war popular taste and propaganda. But certainly these stories were lavishly illustrated with uniformed and helmeted 'Hun' sharing the villains' roles with shifty Arabs in white robes, plotting their insurrections against the stalwart British soldiers of Victoria's far-flung empire.

At about the same time, again demonstrating my conviction that children really begin to wake up and eagerly grasp whatever is available to them, I began to read L.M. Montgomery's Anne books. They were not as exciting to me as the boys' adventure stories I adored, nor did they become so until on in my teens the three Emily books provided me with a vista on adolescence that I loved and could relate to my own longings. But from *Anne Of Green Gables* on, the importance of friendship as written into Anne's life by Montgomery did affect me; from that time on, and throughout my life, tried and true friendship was and is of primary importance, bringing me then as it does now, its warm and constant blessings. Because of my father's baseball enthusiasm and the presence every weekend of the American papers, I lapped up scandalous stories as well as the comics, the Lindbergh kidnapping tragedy, certain horrendous murders which even now I remember too well, and a bewildering hodgepodge of news and views, trash and legitimate news, anything at all in fact, for I read everything that my eyes lighted on.

Mother loved the women's magazines which just then were in their heyday and after she began to work at the Artistic Ladies' Wear on Saturdays and had a little bit of money to spend, we had *McCalls* and *The Ladies Home Journal* in the house almost every month. From time to time Grandma had a subscription given to her, and I remember *Delineator* and *The Canadian Home Journal* at her house. Of course I read all the fiction in all of them and in my play-writing days adapted at least one of the stories, Alice Duer Miller's *Just The Maid* to a High School production. Occasionally Mother would get concerned about what all of this was doing to my eyes, and I would be forbidden the town library and the splendid romances of such as Berta Ruck and Mary Roberts Rinehart, but her concern never lasted long enough to really deprive me.

The movies did a great deal to stimulate reading among reading addicts—my friend Agatha was an addicted reader as I was. The thirties were the days of frenetic activity in Hollywood, which translated itself into two shows a week in Strathroy, ranging from the huge historical productions such as *David Copperfield* and *Anna Karenina* to contemporary social commentary in productions of *The Grapes Of Wrath* and *Tobacco Road* to elegantly entertaining fluff like Ginger Rogers' and Fred Astaire's *Top Hat* and *Flying Down To Rio*. Every movie we saw, and we saw them all, suggested more reading to us, and while the town library didn't stretch to *Tobacco Road* or *Grapes Of Wrath,* it did provide us with *David Copperfield* and the more standard classics. A friendly, free-thinking cousin even sent me *Anna Karenina* from Galt where she taught—to my father's slight dismay, in case I became smirched by its contents.

To a born book-worm, anything in print was fodder, and perhaps the most enjoyable adventures of all were the random discoveries here and there. For one year my cousin Stewart boarded with us when he was in High

School, and I found Hawthorne's *Tanglewood Tales*, obviously one of his school books, left behind in a clothes closet—my introduction to the great Greek myths, an eye-widening, unforgettable experience sometime before I was eight, for then we moved from the house where I found the discard. Various volumes by Horatio Alger, *Mark The Match Boy*, *From Rags To Riches* and such, were the finds of one summer's holiday, all piled helter skelter in the attic out on Uncle Ed's farm. I read straight through everything in Grandma's 'little room': Nellie McClung, Ralph Connor, Philip Gibbs, E. Philip Oppenheim, Edgar Wallace, and, most thrilling of all, the book version of *The Birth Of A Nation*, with photographs from the film of Lilian Gish and various heroic military men. I can remember reading it sitting in a corner of the living room after a Sunday supper, with all the family present, and no one paying the slightest attention to Clara, who "always had her head in a book." Little did they know that I was reading of the famous rape scene, after which the image of the killer was forever imprinted on the eyes of the victim. I puzzled about that for a long time, but I was much too canny to ask anyone about it.

In general I grazed freely. When Aggie and I became friends, I saw many movie magazines, which somehow her mother afforded. We spent hours poring over them, speculating about the love-lives of the stars, totally deodorized versions of which were the only topic of those magazines. They did also have gorgeous still pictures, though, and my collection of Garbo stills is a pleasure to browse through, even now.

In school, anything that broke the monotony of the set "Readers" was a great treat, and the appearance of a handsome supplementary reading text, *Explorers, Soldiers And Statesmen*, when we were in Entrance Class, was a very special event. I am quite sure that the seed of my biography of Egerton Ryerson is to be found in his chapter there. I have already written about our adventure with Miss Alison Cameron and her reading of *Tarzan Of The Apes*. After the film, in our entrance year, which Mr. Fowlie took us to London to see, the Library, amazingly, purchased the whole Edgar Rice Burroughs series. What excitement amongst the devoted readers!

In High School, the boys I knew were more satisfactory reading adventurers than girls. Jack Fowlie, Cecil Wright and I used to talk endlessly about Rafael Sabatini's *Captain Blood*, the exploits of "The Saint" and all the rest of the currently popular tales of dare-devil soldiers of fortune, whose Hollywood impersonator was Errol Flynn. Of course we idolized Flynn with absolutely no suspicion of his lecherous reality, and also Basil Rathbone, the prime villain of the day. Richard Haliburton's *Royal Road To Romance*, followed by his other travel adventures, made devoted armchair travellers of us all, and in those Depression years, gave us tastes of the wide world that were impossibly far from our own experience. The thirties was a decade of popular biography—I remember *Poor Splendid Wings*, for instance, and the best-selling *Oil For The Lamps Of China* was much discussed, as were the various novels of Pearl Buck, especially the famous *The Good Earth*. Because we were all radio fans, we were aware of best-sellers of the day, and because of movies, I certainly read books that otherwise I would not have seen for years. Between movies and the books that they generated, we were really quite well and widely informed.

Mind you, some censorship was practised, but not, thankfully, by my family. Our town Librarian, Margaret McIntyre, would not let any of us read *Gone With The*

Wind, though the publicity surrounding it and the film were driving us mad with longing to experience the book. I doubt that her motives were as much concern for the morals of the young as for the convenience of her older readers who were, undoubtedly, avid for it as well. It was the first book I bought after we were married, though by then I'd long since read it!

Chapter VI

Western
1937-1941

From my earliest days university had been a large part of my expectation of the future, dating from very early days when my grandfather declared that he would "see me through McMaster." Also, from earliest days school was held up to me as *the* arena in which to make good.

My mother was enormously anxious to make me outstanding and I took to her ambition with gusto, becoming both highly motivated and highly competitive in any academic situation. Strangely enough, I was and am totally uncompetitive in any other context, games for instance, saving all my enthusiasm and drive for school, about which I quickly became obsessive. I ought to have been a royal pain, but oddly enough I don't think I was, for my friends were always almost agonizingly important to me. Besides, like many another female, I took great pains to downplay my academic prowess, pretending to be much more stupid than I was, especially in things to do with the male world, sports and cars for instance. In spite of Depression-bound Strathroy in the thirties, we all had a wonderful teenage as those of us who are still around never cease to testify. As I approached Fifth Form and the final Departmental examinations I became absolutely focused on a scholarship-to-come, and I didn't give a thought to other university expenses. I had never been used to having money, and witlessly I thought, if I thought at all, that once tuition was paid by scholarship, all would be well. In spite of the Depression, we had led a very sheltered life in Strathroy, my parents, I now see, as well as myself.

Therefore, it was not at all surprising that my first days at Western in the Fall of '37 were the unhappiest of my four years there, and my first year was certainly so. I had won only the two-year tuition scholarship, though I had passed the departmentals with ten first-class grades and one second (German composition). I had foolishly resisted taking Trigonometry, because of the current fear and loathing of Mr. Marcy among my schoolmates and therefore I was not eligible for any of the better scholarships. I really had not known that at the time: guidance counselling was non-existent, and though Principal Summerhayes had suggested that I take another year in Fifth Form, as many scholarship students did, I was totally determined to get away from home. Mother and I were at the apex of one of our periodic incompatibility periods and she had also made it quite clear that I should look for a place to work for my board. Father was depressed about the whole thing. He told me he'd do his best, but he didn't know how long that would last; he was thinking of Vernon coming along behind, he said, little knowing that what was coming along behind was the war—and that would change everything.

There was a "Big Sister" plan in operation at Western to look after the "freshettes" as we were called, and I had been contacted early in August by mine, a good-natured girl called Betty Lang, of a large and wealthy Kitchener family. Betty was a Pi Phi, which in the Western hierarchy meant that she was a part of the North-London-based social set—hardly a part of my milieu, but she cheerfully did her duty, taking me out to Boomers, *the* leading

London ice-cream parlour, for a sandwich and a sundae. Through the Camerons, the Strathroy Presbyterian minister's daughters, undergrads at the time, it was suggested that I board at Ranahans, where Noreen, a recent graduate, ran her big family home as a Boarding House. Annie took me in to London one day to buy some clothes (two sweaters and a skirt), and later, took Mother and me to the Ranahans, where I was left, with my luggage, to deal with orientation week.

I was utterly unprepared for any of rituals that followed, and was thoroughly miserable, quickly developing a nervous stomach flu that made me even more so. I had never before had a full physical exam, and though the doctor who examined me was Jean Campbell, capable and kind, I felt mauled and mussed. I knew nothing about registering, and when I found myself in front of Miss Allison, the Associate Registrar, after what seemed an age spent standing in line, she informed me that the English and History course, which I had looked forward to, had been discontinued, and that I should go into French and German: "Language teachers are needed." So I did, and that was my first big mistake.

I asked her, miserably, if she knew of any place where I could work for my board. "Won't your father stand behind you?" she said, making me both furious and more miserable. When I mumbled something about my brother, she said she'd see what she could do, and that was the end of my initial meeting with her. The shortness and impatience with which she treated me were quite out of character for the Helen Allison who was Dean Neville's right-hand woman and universally loved. She was having a bad day. However, only a few days later I had a summons to go to an apartment on Waterloo Street just south of the tracks to meet Mrs. Dean, who wanted a likely girl to help with her baby, David, and the housework as well. I went and was judged acceptable: Mrs. Pugsley, our Strathroy Anglican minister's widow, lived downstairs and was my friend, Mary Dampier's guardian. I was mightily cheered by the thought of my old friend, Mary, so close by, and moved out of the Ranahans' room and into the Deans' apartment immediately.

I was to come home every afternoon right after three o'clock, take David for a ride in his stroller, and then help get the dinner and wash the dishes. On Wednesday night I was free, and every third weekend I could go home. On top of beginning Western with all the novelty of strange surroundings and professors, it was a heavy schedule, but it never occurred to me to turn it down or to complain at home. After all, what choice did I have? Annie's friend, Marge Waters, had 'worked for her board' with the city librarian, Mr. Crouch, and had loved it, or so the story went. Mind you, she had also failed her year, but that wasn't mentioned. And Mary Dampier, who was starting Western too, in Nursing, was indeed downstairs. What a comfort!

After registration, Freshman initiation was the next ordeal to get through. That happened in the first week, before I moved to the Deans'. It turned out to be boring, humiliating and embarrassing. I was the girl in the notorious Western 'Kiss Picture' which resulted in orientation horseplay being cut out entirely for some years. Two sophomores collared a girl and a boy and ordered them to chew on opposite ends of a piece of string. Some smart photographer took a picture of the two of us as we reached the middle, Canadian Press picked it up and it was reproduced all over Canada—ministers and the inevitable guardians of public morals viewed it with alarm and a tempest in a teapot ensued. It was a bad Fall for

Western's Freshman orientation: a court case followed the forcible shaving of the head of one young man. I don't remember any further initiations during my years there. I certainly would never have taken part in them.

Throughout all the bewildering first weeks, Grace Crawforth, another Strathroy undergraduate, then in her third year, befriended me, advising me on books, courses, professors and, uppermost to her, the sorority, Gamma Phi Beta. The year before Mary Wright had taken me to London to a tea at the Gamma Phi house, and I was considered a good prospect from the start. In those days Western's administration, without women's residences, had an agreement with the three sororities, Gamma Phi Beta, Kappa Alpha Theta, and Pi Beta Phi. Organization details were looked after in the Registrar's Office; the chapter members themselves did the picking and choosing among first-year women every year after a spring 'Rushing Week', and the resulting crop of pledges were eligible to board at the sorority houses, large old North London establishments. Each house had a House Mother, in Gamma Phi's case, Miss Fox, an elderly, well-off spinster. A sizeable percentage of first year women became sorority members, and for those who 'lived in,' the experience was a memorable part of their university years.

In the spring of '38 I was 'rushed' by all three sororities, as were most others, and was dizzy with the complications of getting time off from the Deans, dreading the looming examinations, and general depression and exhaustion. It never occurred to me not to join when asked, and likewise it never occurred to me to question the social elitism of sororities and their out-and-out racism. Jewish and Chinese girls were not eligible and Blacks, of course, were unthinkable. The sororities were all based in the States and their American High Councils were all-powerful. It took the war to make me realize how deplorable their exclusionary policies were, and it was not until the sixties that I made some sort of recompense. In the very early days of York one of my young male colleagues and myself successfully barred sororities and fraternities from York, a ban that lasted at least twenty years. However, in that first year, the sorority was a hospitable refuge for me on my nights off, and I heard lots of gossip and general Western doings that I would not have known without the connection. Also, Ruth Sands, a Strathroy girl and in her second year at Western, became a close friend that first year, and remained so until she died in 1986.

    I rapidly discovered a lively dancing life at Western, the first occasion being the Frosh Hop, for which one's Big Sister traditionally found an escort. Betty Lang had roped in John Murray, a very young and shy Londoner, and Mother had taken me out to Aunt Clara's where my cousin Helen was staying home that Fall and had given me the evening dress that I still remember the most fondly of any formal wear I ever had. It was deep turquoise lace over green satin, with little satin-covered buttons all down the front, long sleeves, a flared skirt and a deep collar. It was gorgeous and I loved it. That night, possibly because they were in the same course, Math and Physics, John Murray and Morley Thomas exchanged dances— and that began a lifetime commitment! Morley was a marked freshman. Besides being the recipient of two scholarships, a Leonard, for his mother was a widow, and the prestigious Currie football scholarship, he was strikingly good-looking. I was *very* interested from the start, and though we didn't go out together that year, I made a point of bumping into him as streams of us walked back and forth from the Arts to the Science Building. Once, with Ruth Sands, we saw him coming and I well remember saying, "There's the man I'm going to marry," and her astonished double-take as she turned around for another look. Even if I did not remember the occasion, as I do, from then on Ruth would never let me forget it.

My courses were all bewildering, and, mostly, terrifying, partly because I really didn't have money for books, and had to scrounge or borrow, and partly because I was simply at sea. I remember Biological Science with Helen Battle as being fascinating, and totally new to me, but strangely, English 20, the survey, with Mrs. Albright, was a nightmare. We used the McCutcheon and Vann anthology and I borrowed one from somebody, but Chaucer and Old English, her favourites, were alien lands to me. Our German classes were small and totally in the hands of three clever hard-workers, Chris Jensen, Kay Liddy, and Mary Sinclair. I don't remember any German or French literature taught that year, just the boring drudgery of Grammar and endless translations. Mr. Bassett of the French Department did single me out in front of the whole class as one who could develop a passable French accent, but that meant going to Western's Quebec Summer School at Trois Pistoles and the $100 fee was quite out of the question for me. But the worst course of all was English History, taught by Hartley Thomas, a fine scholar, but probably bored to death by a large, first-year class, and almost completely unintelligible, to me at least. About November 1 he gave a test which most of the class failed, and then dropped the course, I among them, for I had got the disgraceful mark of 27—and in History too. In those days a first set of exams was written right after Christmas and I didn't do badly, and so blundered along through second term, finally passing the year with half B grades and Half A's, the latter in areas I somewhat enjoyed, Public Speaking with Jean Walker, Composition with Doris Lidicott, and the one it was almost impossible to fail, Library Science with Catherine Campbell.

At Christmas-time Annie and Art, married just over a year, had a dinner-party for me and my friends, before the all-important Strathroy High School "At Home" dance. They were enormously good to me always, and this was very special, for I asked Ross Drummond, my hero from Petrolia, who was at Dental College in Toronto. Ross was to be paired with Willie Downham, Libby Lambert with George Downham, Norman Dickson with Agatha Cavers, Grace Crawforth with Hugh Sullivan, Jack Fowlie with Joyce Houston, and Cecil Wright with me. Datewise, it was all a comedy of errors, for no one was paired with the man of her choice, or if she was, the man would have preferred someone else. We were wearing long dresses, and Willie had her first, in which she was so sure she was too skinny that she wore a thick wool skirt underneath and nearly cooked, Norman Dickson, a Catholic, had to leave early to go to midnight mass. Besides he didn't dance—and Aggie was the best dancer there. I, of course, wanted to be with Ross. Joyce was unhappy in a short dress, for her mother had been insulted when Annie had offered to let her wear her lovely pink organdy wedding dress.

At Western I was fortunate socially, for the Strathroy High School 'Old Boys Network' was strong, and such kindly men as Colin McKeen in 3rd year Science, and Ralph Parker, formerly of Strathroy, asked me to important dances, giving me a chance to wear a new formal, a full-skirted white net with a glittery trimmed bolero jacket. I got very very tired in second term though, and turned down several invitations because I was too down and depressed to bother with them. In the spring, Ruth Sands sprang into action, talking me into asking Father if I could board with her at Mrs. Gregory's for three weeks, studying and writing exams. Those were hilarious weeks, talking, laughing and studying until all hours, and I'm sure they saved my grades from being far worse than they were. I ended up on good terms with the Deans, too, and Mrs. Dean even had me to dinner after I had gone to live with Ruth. But I had absolutely had enough of the 'work for board' bit, and was determined that, rather than go through that for another year I would give up Western and go to Normal School.

I don't know now how serious I was about that, but I was certainly afraid of not doing well on the exams, and I desperately wanted the freedom that I had always looked forward to at University. To counteract that, though, I was certainly proud of my status as the only one of my Fifth Form year who had gone on to university. Dorrie Fowlie was at Business School in Toronto, and Jean Bowley and Evelyn Brown were at Westervelt's Business School in London. Cecil Wright had long since gone into the bank, and the other boys in our gang, and the other girls, were still in High School. I think I had the roots of intellectual snobbery well-developed in me even then—and of course, for years I had been massively affected by American college stories, especially by *The Girl Of The Limberlost*, and a lively series in *The Ladies Home Journal* featuring Maudie and David, college-age sweethearts. I had also idealized the great American women's colleges, the "Seven Sisters" which were familiar to me through journals and the Sunday papers that came into our house every weekend.

When I told Annie how discouraged I was, she

utterly rejected the thought of my quitting and drove me into London to find a place where I could room, paying only a token amount and bringing my food in from Strathroy. That was an enormously lucky trip. I had taken note of a house at 805 Richmond, where, it was said, two girls had roomed before my time. We went to call on the people there and found Mrs. Bertrand, her daughter, Ivy, and her brother, Mr. James, an elderly, former military man who was a bank messenger. They agreed to rent me a room for $3.00 a week, with the use of their kitchen, bathroom and a living room opening out of the bedroom. The house was an old, one-storey cottage on Richmond Street, near the corner of Sydenham, a centre-hall plan with spacious rooms. Better still, Joyce Houston, a year behind me in Strathroy Collegiate, was certainly going to win a scholarship and was planning on one year at Western and then Normal School. She was anxious to share with me, which meant that we only paid $1.50 each. We were both happy at the thought, and I went out to work at Bright's Grove with Dorothy Stevenson from Petrolia, a Gamma Phi with whom I'd become friendly, secure in next year's plans. Then, finally, I would have the freedom I had always associated with going to university.

I had learned much that first year and had made the most important friend of my university years, and one of the especially important friends of my lifetime. I think Brandy Conron and I met briefly on registration day—at least he always said so—but certainly as soon as I began to live at the Deans' he turned up daily in his father's car to drive me up the hill to school. His father was a United church minister and the family lived almost across from us on Waterloo Street. Amazingly, and as it turned out constantly, Brandy drove the car, for his father didn't like to drive and in return for being chauffeured around when he needed it, Brandy had the car. From then on, for four years, Brandy drove me and whoever happened to be my room-mate, to Western. Furthermore, we had many of the same classes. He was going into English with Latin and Greek his minors, and already was startlingly knowledgeable and confident about what he wanted from university. We swiftly became friends, talking endlessly about the academic world, and the possibilities before us. At the end of year one, it was easy for him to persuade me that I should get out of French and German and into English and French, and at the end of year two, his master plan was to move himself from English Language and Literature to Classics, leaving me to move to his vacated programme. That way, he figured (and he was right), we would each get the $100 prize for highest standing in our respective fields and each of us needed that money. Before London, Brandy's father had been stationed in Burford, near Brantford, and Brandy had become an expert car-repairman at a garage there, so in fact, he always had a well-paid summer job, and his need for the prize was more a matter of prestige than anything else.

Brandy was one of five children, the second youngest, I believe, born in 1919, after his father, a Methodist, then United Church minister, had returned from being a chaplain overseas in W.W.I. He was his father's academic pride and hope and had grown up reading on quite a different level from anyone I had known before. He had read all of *Paradise Lost*, for instance. He and his father had talked for years about literature and the Classics as familiar and accessible branches of knowledge. I could not have imagined making such a friend and the making was all on his side. I am forever grateful. There was not a trace of romance about our association—looking back it had a definite Pygmalion flavour, for Brandy was interested in 'improving me,' my mind, attitudes and ambitions—but there was a totally uninhibited sharing of current concerns and future hopes and dreams that would have been quite impossible with any other person, male or female, whom I had ever known and that lasted through the war, through our marriages and until his death in 1994.

1938-1939

When Joyce Houston and I moved into 805 Richmond St., shortly after Labour Day in 1938, the whole world bloomed for me. For one thing, Dot Stevenson, Ruth Sands and I (the three Poohs as we happily called ourselves), had had a wonderful summer working for the Nicholson brothers at Bright's Grove on Lake Huron, about ten miles north of Sarnia. I still had, I thought, a huge crush on Ross Drummond, but I was by no means as fixated about that as I had been the year before. We settled into our quarters with great enthusiasm, Joyce even buying some china brightly decorated with orange and yellow nasturtiums that we both loved, and proceeded to taste our freedom as well as our cooking with the greatest pleasure. We had a double bed, a curtained off portion of one side of our room for a closet, a table for a desk, a pretty little vanity dresser and a washstand where we kept our dishes, cutlery, cooking pots and food. I brought food in from home and the store, Joyce brought food from home, and all in all we were very well supplied. Whenever we cooked we were free to use Mrs. Bertrand's stove in the kitchen. We could use the telephone, and also the big bathroom adjoining our room. Most important of all to me, we were free—to come and go as we pleased, to sleep in, or work late, and when the mood struck us, to use the sitting room that opened off our bedroom, and even to play the piano there. After the restrictions of year one, it was heaven. I firmly believe that every university student should live away from home, and should, as we did, live freely. Even if I could have afforded the Sorority House I would not have wanted to live there once I had tasted our quite untrammeled and totally unsupervised existence.

There was one quick and important result for me of such an unlocking of doors and possibilities: I began to wake up, and quickly, to the interest of my classes. Having moved to English and French made a great difference, for I found that I loved the English courses, and especially loved the Medieval history course taught by Dr. Maine. Maine's history covered both the Renaissance and Reformation and he did a first-class job of awakening a fascination for the period that has never left me. Twenty years later, picking on a extra-departmental course for my Ph.D. qualifications at the U. of T., I chose Professor Powicke's Renaissance and Reformation History, and by that time, I had taught Dr. Maine's course several times myself in Extension for Western.

Throughout Western I kept on with German Literature, and was filled with enthusiasm for the Romantic Movement in Germany by the bubbling enthusiasm of Dr. Kalbfleisch, for Goethe by Dr. Allen, in French, for the great early woman novelists by Dr. Dorothy Turville, the Dean of Women, and in History, by any of the courses taught by Drs. Maine or Dorland. This second year we began to have the senior men in the department for various English classes, Drs. Tamblyn and Spenceley, and memorably, again for the Romantics, the latest addition to the Department, Frank Stiling. Brandy's and my friendship flourished and we did a lot of studying together that year, most unforgettably for the spring exams, when he would drive out to the Wishing Well near Komoka and we would sit, in a memory that must be much heightened by time, among blooming wild flowers, going over our texts and our notes and fantasizing about some day starting our own university. In our later lives we both came closer to that far-off wish than anyone would have thought possible, for he superintended the building of Western's Middlesex College, becoming its first principal, and I was one of the first York faculty.

The second great event of that year, and fairly early that year too, was Morley's and my getting together. I had not given up my practice of being noticed by hook or by crook whenever he was around, and on one weekend during the summer he had come into the store at Bright's Grove much to the excitement of Ruth and Dot, for my mates too were much aware of my interest. It was the custom at Western for numbers of the boys to stand about between classes underneath the clock in the lower hall, and there, one Fall day, he separated himself from the group to ask me if I'd like to go to the dance in Convocation Hall after the football game on Saturday. From that night on, I at least considered our pairing off to be a done thing. Dot Stevenson and I went together to Toronto for Football Weekend, staying in the Royal York with all the rest of the Western gang, and going to the dance with our dates, for her Bill Ewener, for me, Morley, both of them members of the Mustangs, the winning team. During Sadie Hawkins' Week, when women were the instigators of dating, our dating had a temporary set-back, for Morley was asked to Western's Sadie Hawkins' dance by Jean Phillips, and I, my nose somewhat out of joint, asked Jack Cluny, a Sarnia boy. But when I asked Morley to come over to our house on Richmond Street one night that week, he was glad to do so, and that night, for me at least, was the deciding factor in what became the rest of my life. We were comfortable together—I couldn't think of any male presence but my grandfather who made me feel so peaceful and with whom talking was so effortless. With Brandy there was always challenge, friendly, mind you, but challenge and some rivalry—much later in life I realized that Brandy and I were always a good deal like siblings. But with Morley it was different, and somehow just right. I don't think Morley was by any means as swiftly committed as I was, but the customs of our youth dictated that the women would be the hunters, the men the prizes. As far as I was concerned I had found my prize.

The year passed on an upward swing. I had been initiated into Gamma Phi, a ritualized performance that I found ridiculous and that did a great deal toward turning me off sororities forever. I did steadily better in my courses, and in the final exams especially well in History, so that I got the coveted $100 prize. Dot had graduated in 1938 and was working in Petrolia, so couldn't plan on waitressing with me at Bright's, and Ruth was in training at Wellesley Hospital in Toronto, but I was going back to Bright's and looked forward to it, as well as to their visits. This, remember, was the summer of '39, when every day brought the war nearer, and finally, Labour Day brought the war itself. Morley came to pick me up on Labour Day, took me to dinner in Sarnia, and from then on we considered ourselves engaged.

The Bertrands had told us that Mr. James was too unwell to tolerate roomers in the house the next year, and before I left London, Brandy took me around to find another place to room, and moved all my things into it. However, during the summer, the landlady had a change of mind, wrote to Mother, and she in turn wrote to Vesta

Stocks, formerly Vesta Gast, recently married to Harry, a barber, and living on Epworth Avenue in London. I had known Vesta since she came as a guest to our Sunday School class when I was in my early teens, and in my last year in High School we had been in a play at the Lyceum together. I truly loved Vesta, then and now, and fortunately for me, it was not difficult for mother to arrange for us to have a room with her, again at $3.00 a week between two of us. Joyce was not going at Western, but was going to Normal school, and again we would be living together.

1939-1940

Living with Vesta was a wonderful experience. The house on Epworth had three very small bedrooms, ours opening into the kitchen. No closet, but a curtain hiding our clothes, somewhat, and no room for such conveniences as a chair or desk. I didn't care in the least, however, for Vesta made an atmosphere that was so warm and loving that we were quite oblivious to ordinary comforts. She gave us shelves in the kitchen for our things, room in the icebox for our food, and all the welcome we could possibly want, plus her own unique brand of love and friendship. The Fall day when I first arrived I'll always remember, for the smell of cooking chili sauce hung all over the house, a welcoming smell if ever there was one. Vesta was my true friend and mentor from that day forward, and when I went back to Western to work in the Library in 1943 I gladly returned to 212 Epworth and her warm and welcoming presence. In 1939 the middle bedroom was taken by a freshman, Norma Ready from St. Marys, a boarder, not a roomer as we were. She was a good sort and remained a good friend until well into the fifties, when she disappeared to Florida, later marrying and settling there.

Harry worked for long hours in his barbershop, downstairs from Graham's drugstore on Richmond street, just south of the Western gates. He didn't eat his evening meal at home, and didn't arrive home until about nine o'clock, and so the house for most of the time was a house of women—thoroughly enjoying themselves and one another. Vesta loved discussions about philosophy, the world situation, the war, just anything, because she had, always, a lively and enquiring mind. She thrived on hearing about my lectures and Norma's, and having been through Normal School herself, she knew just what Joyce's course was like. Often we all ate together, and certainly we talked together all the time. She loved me to have my books out on the kitchen table, and she equally loved calling off the studying and going into the front room, where the pride of her life was her grand piano, and where she could and would play anything at all by ear, and sing along with it. Many times we would also light the fireplace, and Brandy got into the habit of bringing us wood—often for Morley and I to court by. She was permissiveness itself, and described with great gusto hers and Harry's courtship out on the farm north of Strathroy, when her father insisted they leave a light on, and they put a lamp on the floor behind the piano.

Vesta admired both Morley and Brandy from day one. I think Brandy endeared himself to Harry by adopting him as his barber, and Morley earned his good opinion both by being a Mustang and, later, as they got to know each other, by being himself. In the Fall of 1939 the Mustangs won the Inter-Collegiate Championship, the celebration dances were especially joyous, and every Mustang's stock went sky-high. Joyce, who by this time was courting with Harry Whicher, was not so lucky. Harry took a dislike to him, and could hardly stand the sight of him. Harry Stocks was even then a strange guy, and later, much later, developed Huntington's Chorea which affected his mind, and ruined his last years and many years for Vesta as well. If he disliked, he loathed—Morley and I were fortunate in his tolerance.

As the winter of 1940 approached spring, the worst of the war days unrolled. The Germans overran Holland and Belgium, the Battle of Britain raged daily in the skies over England, France fell and the British Expeditionary Force was trapped on the beach of Dunkirk. For the first time the war was terrifyingly real to us, and for the first time, all the men we knew began to realize that for them the future held only war service. Vesta's was a wonderful place to be that year. Not only was her faith in the Allies totally steadfast, she was far more conversant with the news than we were, and she made very sure that, when we came home for dinner, we too knew all that had happened each day.

This year I was spreading my wings a little about summer work. I applied to Banff, Bigwin Inn, and Oakwood Inn at Grand Bend. I was accepted at all three, and, of course, because of seeing Morley, I chose Oakwood, the closest, a terrible choice as far as the working conditions went, but one where the pay, at $10 a week, was twice as much as at Bright's. I also worked hard at courses that year, and studied again with Brandy, for I was steadily more involved with and fascinated by literature. Sorority meetings were supposed to be compulsory, but I didn't spend much time at the sorority. It was really far more interesting at Vesta's.

We were disappointed in the spring when Harry decided that we couldn't return the next year. He thought, rightly, that it was foolish to let us have the room for $3, when a boarder would pay double that, and besides, his business landlord, the druggist, Dunc Graham, wanted to come and live there. However, things turned out wonderfully for me: when I went down to the Bertrands again at 805 Richmond I found, to my great delight, that I could return there. This year Joyce wouldn't be with me, Mr. James had died, and Ivy, now working at Western, and her mother were alone again. Once again, Brandy moved my things for me before I left for the summer, and I was secure for the Fall.

This was the year, too, when I had taken Brandy's advice and moved from English and French to straight English Language and Literature. He had moved to Classics. That meant, as he predicted, that I got the $100 scholarship for English, and he got it for Classics, satisfying to us both. For the second year, I also got the $100 prize for History, this time a course of Dr. Dorland's. Oakwood Inn was not a good experience—too regimented, with all the other waitresses local girls who did not particularly enjoy me in their midst. Morley's visits on Saturday nights were the redeeming feature, but a very large redeeming feature. Finally the summer was over and we were back for our final year.

1940-41

I had loved being with Vesta, but I also loved being on my own back at 805 Richmond. Morley visited often, on weekends and on Wednesday night after C.O.T.C., now compulsory for all male students. We still had a football season, and still a gala Toronto weekend in the Fall, and still the many formals that we were used to. Perhaps they had an urgency they hadn't had before, but in large measure we were still protected from the war, and still largely unconscious of it. At Vesta's, with her interest and the radio, we were aware of all the disasters of that fateful spring of 1940, but at 805 Richmond, without a radio, I was relatively cocooned against outside events. I was working hard, partly because Professor Spenceley had stopped me in the hall one day to tell me that I would get the Governor-General's Gold Medal for English if I tried. As always, Brandy and I were much involved with our courses, studying together and talking of them and everything else that seemed important to us, especially, for him, the war.

It was through Brandy that year that the war came close. From early Fall on, he talked of going into the army, specifically the First Hussars, a cavalry regiment centred in London, that was being converted, as they all were, to an armoured regiment. From his knowledge of cars, his interest in tanks was a natural step, and from mid-fall on he knew that he would be leaving shortly after Christmas for training at Camp Borden. The university would grant his degree, a war-time favour to men enlisting that was begun that year and continued throughout the war years. So far, there was no compulsory military training for women, though in the next years, after I graduated, that came about too, though it was rather a farce.

From being largely uninterested in the sorority in my second and third years, I had been named 'Rushing Chairman' for this fourth year. Unexpectedly, I was intrigued by my job. I entertained many of the incoming class of women, either at the sorority house or at 805, making them fudge, and generally big-sistering them. They were a good crew that year, among them Joan Brown from Meaford, and Edith Whicher from Wiarton, both of them destined to be much involved with our future lives. Edith was the sister of Harry Whicher who by this time was seriously courting with Joyce and was anxious for us to know his young sister. Joan was her room-mate in a boarding house, and the two of them speedily became regulars at 805 Richmond, so much so that Edith broached the idea of living with me after Christmas and I acquiesced. She had taken up with Jim Grandy, a Huron College contemporary of Harry's, and in the winter and spring there were many sessions at which Harry and Joyce, Morley and I, Edith and Jim courted together in our room. The Bertrands were endlessly patient with troops of us tracking in an out of their house, and we did have a good, and an innocent, time. Edith's father, Carl Whicher, had a general store in Colpoy's Bay outside of Wiarton, and he sent down groceries, though most of our meals kept on coming from Strathroy.

That year I made a little extra money by working in the university Library for 50 cents an hour, minding the main desk usually, though sometimes the Reserve Room desk. I loved doing that, and did a good deal of exploring the stacks when things weren't busy. We also had many courses. This was the year of the dreaded Anglo-Saxon, both language and literature. However, Professor Spenceley was notorious for setting exactly the same examinations year after year, and by dint of studying former ones, both Brandy and I ended with ridiculously high marks, 95, I think. Anglo-Saxon grammar was all memory work, and for anyone with a good memory it was a breeze. I had continued to shine in history throughout the three years, both for Dr. Maine and Dr. Dorland. Shortly after Christmas I told Dr. Maine that I didn't intend to teach High School, which would have meant going to the Ontario College of Education in Toronto, and asked him about other possible jobs. He kindly volunteered to ask a friend of his in a hiring position at the London Life, in those days a very big employer of young women, and very soon I had an interview, followed by a job offer which I accepted eagerly. It paid at the rate of a yearly $600 for the first six months, going up then to $650. Upon graduation I was to go into the Actuarial Department. There was also talk of being in charge of French correspondence, but that came to nothing. I certainly wasn't thrilled by the prospect, and I had gone to see Dr. Tamblyn, the Chairman of the English Department, to ask him about the possibilities of Graduate School, for that was now my dearest wish. However, when he suggested Harvard, he might as well have been suggesting the moon, and I quickly retreated to reality.

Brandy left in January as planned, Morley entered into negotiation with Mutual Life in Waterloo and with the London Life as well. The rapidly expanding war-time Dominion Meteorological Service appeared on the horizon as an after-graduation choice for him, a fortunate development, for the compulsory C.O.T.C. had rapidly made the army totally uninviting and in fact was treated by many of the men as something of a joke. By this time he and I were an established couple among our families and fellow students. He had been at Grandma's for Christmas supper and to our place for meals, and I had been entertained at his place, and had attended several of the Christmas-week dinners that his family celebrated every year. We actually got tired of the winter procession of formals at Western and stayed away from several of them, but I was wearing his Delta Upsilon fraternity pin and in our minds we were engaged.

As spring and exam time approached we both worked very hard indeed. I was at home in Strathroy when the prize results came out in the Free Press, and my Uncle Evan was the one who called the house one morning and told me I'd won the Governor-General's Gold Medal for English. I ran all the way downtown to see the paper, and there I was, my graduation picture and the notification. I was more pleased about that than about any prize I've ever got, perhaps because there was a good deal of muttering at home about my London Life decision (teaching was considered more the proper thing, though no one was forthcoming about how I was supposed to afford Toronto for a year).

Graduation Day itself was a splendid time for me, if not for Morley. The men were in the Thames Valley army camp, suffering bad food and wretched conditions all round. They had to march in to graduation (a good three miles) on a hot day, wearing their heavy battle dress, and were not exactly happy about it. Brandy was there from Camp Borden, looking smart in his second lieutenant's uniform, my family was there in force, Mother and Father, Vi, Evan and Grandma, Annie, and, for Morley, his mother and grandmother. We attended all the ritual events for the graduating class, and I spent a couple of weeks at home before beginning my job at the London Life. Fortunately I was able to stay on at 805 Richmond, a great blessing. Joyce, who had taught for a year just north of London, was planning to work the next year at the London China Shop, and would, once again, room with me.

I graduated with two ambitions, both of them obsessive. At some point, though I did not know just when, I was determined to go back and do graduate work—and Morley and I were going to get married very shortly. I can remember talking about both of them to one of my classmates as we combed our hair that day before joining the graduation parade.

Chapter VII

Bright's Grove and The Three Poos

In the summer of 1938, Dorothy Cole (Stevenson), Ruth Sands(Longmire) and I founded the most exclusive Club in Canada. We were, forever after, 'The Three Poohs'. Ruth is gone now—Dot and I are still members, calling each other Pooh on all occasions and remembering with joy the summer when it all began. In the winter of 1998, holidaying in Florida with the Stevensons, we realized that we were marking the 60th anniversary of the Poohs. We celebrated all week!

It all began at Western when as a freshman I got to know Dot Cole at the Gamma Phi Sorority House where she was living. She was in her graduating year. We had much in common, especially Bright's Grove on Lake Huron about ten miles north of Sarnia, where Jack Kennedy's dance band had long since become the summer focus for both Petrolia and Strathroy teenagers. Our Strathroy 'gang' had danced regularly at Bright's since third form, and we had all become rabid fans of the resident orchestra, Jack Kennedy's. Sometimes on a starry August night I can almost capture again the sound of music on the breeze that was so familiar to us then, drifting over the grove from the open-air, terrazzo-floored dance hall next to Nicholsons' store. Jack Kennedy was a smiling young man, basically a piano player, but one of those naturally talented musicians who could pick up and play almost any instrument and who had a special talent for arranging. At the peak of the Big Band days, there were many orchestras, all striving for distinctive styles and sounds. Jack's major successes were in producing arrangements which imitated Sammy Kaye—he and his boys were really very good at that—and sometimes Glenn Miller, whose "Chatanooga Choo-Choo" and "Blue Orchid" remain among my happiest memories. His vocalist in our time was Cy Strange from Exeter, who had an easy, melodious 'crooner's' voice, and who later became well-known on C.B.C., especially for the early morning "Fresh Air" program.

In the winter at Western, mulling over our summer employment possibilities, Dot and I decided to try for Bright's. Lloyd and Del Nicholson, brothers, were owners of the store and the two dance halls, one open-air and beside the store, one closed-in and further over in the park. To our delight, we were hired at $5.00 a week each and our board. I arrived first, in mid-June. Our summer home was a former hot-dog stand in the Grove a short distance from the store. When the let-down side was put up it became a snug little cabin about 12x9 feet. I speedily made myself at home, working for a week or two with a French-Canadian girl who was about to leave. Certain hard and fast rules were established. I was happy to waitress on the restaurant side of the store, less happy to serve on the grocery side, and absolutely opposed to going outside to service the gas tank. That I did not do!

When Dot arrived we settled in happily, shortly finding out that the Nicholsons proposed to hire a third girl. Not only were we dismayed at the thought of an invader of our territory, we knew, as it happened, the perfect third girl—Ruth Sands, at loose ends in Strathroy until she went to train for nursing at Toronto's Wellesley Hospital in the Fall. I called Ruth and on the Saturday of the first of July weekend she arrived, her thick dark-red hair resplendent in the pageboy wildly popular at the time and with her several pieces of expensive luggage, for until her father lost his job and income she had been an only and a pampered child. She was an exotic sight in the midst of a weekday afternoon in the restaurant at Bright's; she continued to be an exotic sight all summer long! We settled in nicely and proceeded to rule the roost in our fashion, one of us usually off duty, the other two on. Two beds, a dresser and a washstand had been installed in our 'home,' the former hotdog stand. There we set ourselves up happily, thinking nothing of what we lacked—a bathroom, toilet and running water mainly. There were public toilets further over in the park, as well as many handy bushes—and as for bathing facilities, didn't we have all of Lake Huron in front of us, as well as an outside tap near us in the park, installed for the convenience of picnickers?

For our $5.00 a week we worked 13-hour days, until the last customer was served after the nightly dance ended at midnight. But we were far from grumbling, because we had certain hard-and-fast arrangements among us. For instance, when the man-of-choice for any one of us was around, it was understood that two would cover and one would dance. We went over the St. Clair River to Port Huron and smuggled back peasant aprons (smuggling was a popular pastime at Bright's and not for us alone)— green, yellow, red and black. These were our uniforms, we wore them interchangeably, and attractive they were. Because the Nicholsons approved of us, or because, in spite of our making our own rules we did work well, they let us go our own way. Also, usually, they let us get our own food, which was sketchy. There was a bad-tempered cook whose specialty was hot dogs, bacon and tomato sandwiches, and bacon and eggs. The menu didn't run to much else. We served the soda fountain, the counter and tables, and became proficient in making all manner of sundaes, sodas, banana splits and 'Bright's Grove

Specials.' The soda tanks were re-charged by way of a trap door and steps to the basement behind the counter.

One busy Saturday I stepped back into the open hole, a drop of 8 or 9 feet. No one had warned me that the trap door was open. I was not noticeably hurt, much to the Nicholson brothers' relief, though many years later a doctor discovered a swelling on one rib, probably the result of a rib cracked that day. I don't even remember taking the rest of the day off. The Nicholsons' roster of employees included Harvey, who barbered in a little room off the store, Stan, a groundsman and the one who ran the ticketing for the dances (5 cents a dance), Albert, the cook, and a boy, Bert Such, who absolutely infuriated Ruth and Dot, often to the point of yelling, and sometimes to the point of throwing things.

We had a totally wonderful time, both on and off duty. Soon, Dot's special way of looking at us when Ruth and I would get carried away by some discussion or other resulted in her being christened 'Pooh.' Ruth was a life-long fan of A.A. Milne's Christopher Robin, Winnie-the-Pooh books. Soon all three of us were calling each other Pooh, as we do to this day. There were certain store items we effectively reserved for ourselves—for me it was Cherry Blossom chocolate bars which we kept out of the sight of customers, under the counter. Each one of us had her eye on a special man: for Dot he was Bill Ewener, former Sarnia Imperials' foot-ball player, now a Western medical student and this year Bright's resident bootlegger; for Ruth, Cy Strange, the pleasant band singer, who, as far as we could tell, lived on fried eggs and toast which he ordered and ate in our lunch-room; for me, Ross Drummond, a U. of T. dentistry student, a friend of the Downhams and long since considered by the Strathroy gang to be the star dancer of Bright's. It was lovely nonsense and fun for all of us, and the special sound of Kennedy's orchestra lives on forever in my head.

For awhile Alice, who was brought in as the band's girl singer, in band lingo known as the 'thrush,' bunked with us, an unsuccessful experiment because Ruth took a violent dislike to her, mostly because she was a clothes-borrower. Alice did like our clothes, especially mine, which fit her well—this infuriated Ruth. Sometimes Agatha Cavers, my friend from Strathroy, came and stayed with us weekends. I don't know where we put her to sleep, but Aggie could always fit herself in anywhere. Sometimes we would be tired to the point of hysteria —but never tired enough to miss a dance. Sometimes two of us would be off together to make an expedition to Port Huron. I can remember wearing four garments one over the top of another back through customs. This was, of course, the day of the ferry when smuggling was easy or the officers were lax. Probably both. The bridge had not yet been built. In the ordinary course of a week we really spent nothing—food and dances were free—and so by summer's end we'd have $40.00 or so to spend on clothes for Fall, a handsome sum in those days. It would buy a great deal. I especially remember a green wool skirt with small buttons down the front from waist to hem—very smart. That was only one of my purchases for the Fall of '38.

I returned to Bright's for the summer of '39, but I was on my own. Dot was working in Petrolia and Ruth was in training. They both came for Civic Holiday weekend, though, and worked with me. And Aggie came for part of the summer too, as a willing though unpaid helper. I enjoyed the second year, but it was nothing like the constant fun and games of the first, when Ruth, Dot and I were forging the friendship that has always continued to mean so much to us. By the summer os '39 Morley and I had become seriously involved and the immanence of war certainly hastened our commitment. There was no more uncertainly about 'who.' The only uncertainly now was 'when,' and 'where,' for like all the young men, he know that his future would be bound up with the war effort in some major way.

Each one of us has a special summer preserved in golden memory—for me it is our first summer at Bright's, THE SUMMER OF '38.

Chapter VIII

1941-1945: Wartime

From June of 1941 until May of 1942, when Morley and I were married in Winnipeg, I worked at the London Life, unhappily, and experienced, happily, the first money I had ever earned which was mine alone to manage and spend. Summer money had not only been negligible, it had also been slated towards clothes for the next year and expenses, the sorority fee, for instance, which I believe was then $35.00. At the $5 a week from Bright's and $10 a week from Oakwood the 'expenses' were, of necessity, minor ones. For the first months after graduation until October, Morley was at the London Life as I was, and he was also in the Actuarial Department, though his prestige as a male and a Math and Physics graduate was infinitely higher than mine. I was placed in the Cash Surrender Values section, under the supervision of a young woman whose first name was Doris, and who seemed to find running an adding machine and calculating the poor little sums policy holders would realize from surrendering their policies a thoroughly satisfactory career.

Never have I suffered, at any work before or since, such sterile, boring and frustrating weeks and months. To begin with, the regimentation of the London Life workers, after my cherished freedom of activity and movement, was well nigh intolerable. At 9 in the morning a bell rang and all the girls trooped in to their desks. At twelve, another bell rang, and all the women rose and went next door to have a prepared lunch subsidized by the company. It was, I must admit, both tasty and nutritious. At 1.00 another bell summoned us back, and finally, at 5, came the final bell and release, after which the hundreds of London Life girls, the "pick of London's female youth," poured out the doors and dispersed. I could not imagine then, and I certainly cannot now, how young women could possibly put up with such authoritarianism, however benign. Now, surely, it must be radically different. Added to the daily boredom Doris, our supervisor, relished times when we stayed overtime—2 1/2 hours for an extra 50 cents—for she was getting married in the spring, and she had a purpose budgeted for every penny. However, I was still happier to be in London than to have gone, somehow, though there was no money, to the Ontario College of Education in Toronto, a move that would have doomed me to High School teaching for awhile. Truth to tell, I had become a scholar in my last two years at Western, and, always obsessive, wanted only two things—to marry Morley and to go to Graduate School at some as yet unknown time in the future.

    I began at the rate of $600 a year, and I think that was higher than the non-degree girls made; after six months I was raised to $650.00. We were paid, as I recall, once a month, and our cheques, with the various deductions even then compulsory, were for $49.00 and change. The men began at $1000.00. Still, it was all mine, and when I remember what I bought that year, it seems riches. It also seems that I managed money far better then than ever again! Joyce was living with me again, working at the China Shoppe of London amidst superb china, glassware and silver. Together we paid $5.00 a week for our room at 805 Richmond, and one of our first purchases was, for $12.00 second hand, a so-called continental bed, a couch that pulled out into a bed, which allowed us to get rid of the double bed and make our room into a real bed-sitter. For next to nothing I bought drapery material, green with a rosy sweet pea pattern, for window drapes and to cover a storage box that I'd brought from home. The Bertrands kindly supplied us with a couple of easy chairs, and we were all set, in our own minds very much the young career girls. This was the day of the 'young career girl' movies, Rosalind Russell, Katherine Hepburn and Jean Arthur, and like hordes of others we cherished the thought of being independently employed and living the 'bachelor girl' lives of the Hollywood role models.

In October Morley left for Toronto to be trained as a Met Officer after which he was to be stationed at one of the many proliferating R.C.A.F. stations as a Forecast Officer, a weatherman, so necessary to the training of airforce personnel. I missed him a whole lot, and hated going to work even more bitterly than I had before, but I did have a variety of compensations. We knew that we would be getting married in the spring. I had the pleasure of picking out my engagement ring at Birks in London in the late Fall, and the joy of feeling its security.

I had managed to begin marking essays for the English Department at Western, thereby making welcome extra money, and also for Drs. Maine and Dorland of the History Department. The pay was minimal, but I loved the work and the continuing contact with both Departments. I spent hours and hours pondering on a choice of dinnerware, and proceeded to buy it from Joyce in the China Shoppe, setting by setting. After much pleasurable dithering, I settled on the Aynsley Forget-Me-Not pattern, much enhanced in my mind then and now, by its descent from a famous French Limoges pattern and by the fruit and soup dishes that I was able to buy in the old original. At the same time I decided to collect International Sterling in the Pine Tree pattern, place setting by place setting. These were the years when International really strode forward in its advertising and price, to attract a market among brides- to-be that had formerly been the preserve of Wm. Rogers silverplate.

I don't know that I'd have thought of it on my own, but Dot Stevenson, who was already married to Charlie, though keeping it secret (she'd have lost her job driving a truck for Autolite had they known she was married), was buying sterling. She was always a very canny shopper and I followed her lead, thus causing a first-class family hassle. In the eyes of my aunts, especially Dot, I was acting as if I was better than the rest of them, and when I asked for a place-setting for Christmas, all of 5 pieces for $21 at that time, my mother was incensed, my father was sad and confused, and I was dumbfounded by the nagging fuss. I did not give in, though, I am happy to say, though I wasn't allowed to forget my misdemeanor for many years, if ever. Until 1983, when our house was broken into and papers strewn destructively everywhere, I treasured the receipted bill from the China Shoppe for six place settings of china and a lustre ware tea service for $47.50. Incredible now! I bought my china, silver, at least two dresses, my yellow wool wedding suit, had some lingerie made, and bought an 18 carat gold Western signet ring for Morley (35.00) out of my meagre salary, plus the few dollars I earned from marking. I also paid my share of our living expenses.

In January, his course finished, Morley was posted to Dauphin, Manitoba and our wedding planning began in earnest. In the first listing, he had been appointed to Gander, Newfoundland, to the very important Forecast Office there, the last stage before the transatlantic crossing for the all-important Ferry Command. When he found that there were as yet no quarters for wives, he traded postings with another meteorologist, and reported for duty at the Service Training Flying School in Dauphin, about 100 miles north of Winnipeg, in the first week of February, 1942. As events transpired, accommodation for wives at Gander was made available very soon. We would both have loved the Newfoundland adventure, and ever since, we have both regretted missing it. However, Morley settled in the Officers' quarters, began to look for a place for us to stay, and I began to plan in earnest to join him in May.

I had grown up with a customary and seemingly rock-solid small-town protocol for pre-wedding preparations. Any divergence, such as my high falutin' buying of sterling silver was unthinkable: the bride's family and the bride assembled a 'trousseau' of clothes, dishes and cutlery; the bride's friends gave 'showers,' a 'kitchen shower,' 'bathroom shower,' 'miscellaneous shower,' and the like. Friends and relatives also gave more substantial gifts of bedding, lamps, silver candlesticks and sometimes, though not often, money. Then the bride's mother and the bride asked everyone involved to a 'trousseau tea' where everything was on display, and a special 'dainty' lunch was served. Finally, usually exhausted and nerve-razzled, the bride was free to participate in her own wedding, usually held in her home. Church weddings were not yet an accepted feature of small town society.

I had announced soon after Morley's posting that I was going to Winnipeg to meet him and that we would be married in a United Church there. My father was seriously upset, though Mother made very few waves about that, being on the whole glad, I believe, to miss that part of the proceedings. The official reason for our decision, so we said, was a lack of money for both of us to make the trip and Morley still professes to believe that to this day. It was, of course, just an excuse. My father would have found the money to pay Morley's fare, if necessary; so would his mother. In fact, I was dead set on marrying in a church, which I couldn't do in Strathroy, and just as dead set on avoiding one of the parlour weddings, dripping with sentimentality, that were the Strathroy norm.

As it turned out, I was given some treasured showers, some of whose gifts we have used with pride ever since; the trousseau tea was a success with my aunts Marge and Annie on hand to help, and Mother in her element cooking for it; and two of my sorority friends from Western, Beth McKenzie and Marnie Van Horne, volunteering to go west with me by train. They both had railway passes, Beth because her father was an M.P., Marnie because her father was an employee of the C.N.R. With my father still sad and depressed, my mother and I relieved to be finished with the whole Strathroy bit, and my grandmother the happiest among us, and a goodly group of friends and well-wishers to see us off, we embarked from the London train station in the evening of May 21, 1942 We spent two nights and the next day, my twenty-third birthday, on the train, and arrived in Winnipeg on the morning of the 23rd, Morley having arranged for our marriage in Yonge Street United church later that same day.

Morley had two friends, also Forecast Officers, Ray Walkden from Winnipeg and Bill Jarmain from London, present for the occasion, so there were six of us, a genial minister who by chance had grown up close to Talbotville himself and the church setting we had chosen. Ray had his father's car for the occasion and after the ceremony took us for a tour of Winnipeg, including a rather depleted zoo, and then we went to the best-known restaurant in Winnipeg, Moore's, for a turkey dinner. We actually had a suite at the Fort Garry for the whole of our week's honeymoon, a splendid living room as well as bedroom and bath, for which, I believe we paid twenty-five dollars a day. Our week was full of the usual satisfactions and surprises that most young newlyweds experience, overlaid by a deep satisfaction in being again together. We took the night train to Dauphin enriched by several important possessions, a few books, including a copy of *Gone With The Wind* and The *Pocket Book Of Recipes*, a Kodak and several 78 rpm records for Morley, a dinner ring with an emerald green stone and an Underwood portable for me.

On first sight, the town of Dauphin was dominated by a fine, large, onion-domed Ukrainian Catholic church and our first home, a mile or so out of town, by its site, on the banks of the Vermilion River and surrounded by sizeable gardens, flowers, trees and berry bushes. Mr. and Mrs. Lys, our landlord and landlady, were an elderly English couple who had emigrated to Manitoba after W.W.I. and had founded a nursery outside of Dauphin. Mr. Lys was badly crippled with arthritis and confined to bed for most of the time; Mrs. Lys was a worker and an artist, looking after her husband, the house and grounds, and finding time for her avocation and delight, landscape, bird and flower painting. She also found time twice a day to put out food for the birds, and therefore had veritable flocks of them always around. The most beautiful to me were the goldfinches which I had never seen in profusion before. She had painted the walls in many of the rooms of the house with flights of imagination and enthusiasm greater than skill, the bathroom with bulrushes and birds, the dining-room with rank upon rank of trees, right up to the ceiling. Our two small rooms upstairs, bedroom and sitting room, had plain cream-coloured walls, and we were free to decorate them ourselves. In the kitchen was a large and intimidating coal and wood range which, under the tutelage of Mrs. Lys, I speedily became able to use, though never with the skill of a practiced hand. We were soon settled and when the barrel of dishes, silver, bedding and wedding gifts arrived from Strathroy we were speedily ready to begin married life.

Dauphin, and the many stations of the British Commonwealth Air Training Plan, then well underway all over Canada, were grand places for newlyweds in 1942. Morley had got used to station life in his months there and soon we were caught up in its rhythm, meeting other newly married couples, attending the weekly dances at the Mess and, for me, making friends with other brides, particularly Sylvia Gibson, Ruth Stoney and Norma Edgar, whose husbands were all officer instructors. All of these girls were Western by birth and very much 'western' in their friendliness and hospitality. Dauphin was, I believe, an especially favourable spot for young couples, because it was too far from the big city, Winnipeg, to provide an easy getaway on short leaves and weekends. Haliburton Wilson, the Commanding Officer of the station, was a former Royal Air Force type, though a Canadian himself; he upheld a good deal of Airforce protocol, but his sense of social and military hierarchy was not oppressive. Dr. John Patterson, Head of the Meteorological Service had fought and won the battle to have his men recognized as of officer rank, but to keep them out of uniform and subservience to the military.

The demands of training for all personnel were rigorous, very few people had cars, and in general, we stayed where we were, made friends and entertained ourselves and each other. It was fun to share and compare new recipes, and to meet at each other's rooms—no one had self-contained apartments, and as far as I remember there were no such buildings or 'suites' as they were called west of Ontario, in town. The townspeople, though, had been swift to open their homes and to rent rooms when it became obvious that such accommodation was sorely needed, and though some landlords grumbled a little, Mrs. Lys among them, and a few were difficult, most of them gave a hospitable welcome to the servicemen and their wives. We women really had a very good time, always visiting in one or another's homes, and always welcome at special occasions, including a wives' club, in the Mess. We had been there for a few months before any of the Women's Division were posted to the station, but then we were fortunate in the arrival of Corporal Barbara McLennan, former school teacher, present Met Assistant in the Forecast Office, destined to become a special, life-long friend.

In August we had leave and it was simply taken for granted that when on leave, one went home to visit. We made the long train trip again, were feted and feasted by our families and, when Morley had to return, I stayed on for an extra week or two and then returned to Dauphin early in September. On the way back, with a stopover of a day in Winnipeg, I paid one of the most important visits of my life: I went to see Dean Argue at the University of Manitoba, and asked him to allow me to take a course toward an M.A. in English. He immediately acquiesced and sent me to the office of Professor Broderson, who taught a senior course in World Fiction, and in no time at all, was enrolled as an extramural student. So I read, progressively more and more engrossed, *Madame Bovary, Anna Karenina, War And Peace, The Brothers Karamazov* and *Jude The Obscure*. There were other novels on the course, but those have stayed with me. Early in my stay in Dauphin I had discovered the Library, a room in the Town Hall, stacked with books on shelves and in piles on the floor. The quality was strikingly good: not only did I find the classics I needed there, I was also introduced to some famous Detective Story writers, Dorothy Sayers and Josephine Tey among them. The initiative for my U. of Manitoba course, like my marking and my job at the London Life, was largely due to the suggestion of Floyd Maine of Western's History Department whom I had gone to see while at home, and who had also suggested my teaching an Extension course for Western's English 20 survey course, in Dauphin when I returned. Dr. Maine himself would shortly join the Khaki College branch of the Army, go into uniform and take leave from Western, spending the rest of the war years overseas, engaged in courses for servicemen. He was a staunch and a loyal friend to me, and both then and ever since I have been in his debt.

I publicized the Western opportunity as best I could on the station at Dauphin, but certainly without notable success. However, three students became regulars, our friend Barbara, Pilot Officer Trickett, later killed overseas, and another young man whose name I simply don't remember. The Fall passed agreeably for me, with much to-ing and fro-ing with my friends and playing of knock-rummy, the station craze, with our husbands, and festivities, Christmas particularly, keenly anticipated. Real life entered in with a vengeance when one day, in the midst of a wives' meeting on the station, Wing Commander Ball opened the door and announced: "Two of you women have just lost your husbands." There had been a crash—one of the training Cessnas had 'pranged,' as the slang went, and two young men were gone. That stunned us and the entire station as well for a short time, but morale was too high and the personnel too young for gloom to prevail. It is safe to say, though, that no one there ever forgot the occasion.

We had a fine Christmas, my first experience of cooking a turkey and in a wood range at that. Mrs. Lys was patient in her instructions and the bird had, fortunately, lots of grease, for I had to dump two lots of porridgy gravy out into the snow before I achieved an edible version. We had a gathering—Barbara came, also a new Met man, Eric, who had recently been posted to the Station. By that time a posting for us had also come through. We were to leave for Dunnville, Ontario, shortly after the New Year. I was overjoyed at that, partly because of sheer old-fashioned homesickness, an emotion I had never known before, and partly because I anticipated setting up further ties with Western and the graduate course I so desired. There was a constant turnover of postings among all the station personnel and all our particular friends were either leaving or about to leave; once again we boarded train for the long trek home, stopping in Winnipeg en route to spend an entire $100.00 on my first fur coat. I had the money because I had just then become beneficiary of a $100 insurance policy which Father had paid into (5 cents a week) since my early childhood. It was a 'wallaby' coat, dark brown glossy fur, from Eaton's. Wallaby is, of course, a kind of kangaroo, but I have never known what animal had really worn my coat. It was quite handsome though, and for years I was both proud of it and warm in it.

Our stay in Dunnville was by no means as pleasant as Dauphin had been. Though we were within visiting distance of families, and that was a boon, we were also in a station where people normally left when on weekend leave. There was nothing like the community of young people making their own recreations that we had known in Dauphin. There was also not the same aura of western friendliness among station personnel, their wives or our various landlords. We lived with Mrs. Spencer—I never saw her husband that I remember, though I remember a small boy called Bobby. Hers was a handsome house and a relatively new one, but we had the attic floor, where we could walk upright only straight down the middle, and where we had to creep under the sloping roof to go to bed. We shared a bathroom on the second floor with the family and another couple of roomers as well. Even among makeshift station accommodations, it was substandard, and very shortly, oppressive. I tried a couple of part-time jobs, working for a Victory Bond Drive—quite stimulating—and being a nurse's aid at the cottage hospital—a disaster even before it got underway, for I was not cut out to be a nurse and simply walked into the hospital and out again early one morning.

I kept on with reading for the University of Manitoba course and in the spring made arrangements for the examination to be sent down to Western for me to write, which meant that I got two welcome spells of studying and staying for a few days at the Sorority House in London. The first time around, Manitoba's Registrar's Office sent down the wrong exam and I had to come again the next week for the right one. In the midst of all this, I went to see Dr. Tamblyn of the English Department about the possibility of doing M.A. work the next Fall, and to my delight, he not only accepted me on the spot, but also informed me that he thought Fred Landon, the Librarian, had a job open. Indeed Mr. Landon did, and when I hot-footed it over to see him he offered me $100 a month, the assurance that I could take time off for M.A. courses, his own on American History among them, and a ten month working year, so that I could spend the next summer with Morley. When I visited Vesta and found that I could board with her beginning in the Fall, my satisfaction was complete. Morley moved into the mess after Labour Day, and I moved to London. The Library experience gave me two of the best years of my life. I was so happy to be back in the university atmosphere, and moreover to be paid for it, that I almost danced up the hill and to work every morning. In fact I did dance, daily, from the tunnel in the Arts building over to the Library, practising twirling all the way over.

I was given a desk in the workroom. Miss Kate Gillespie, the senior Librarian who effectively ran the workaday schedule, was a pleasant and patient Head, and I thrived. I began to learn seriously to type and thoroughly enjoyed the cataloguing work always in process. The card-file cards were shipped to the Library from the Library of Congress in Washington; they had various categories of essential information already printed on them, but there were still Western's own information to be added, and thus there were always stacks of cards to be attended to. There were several professional librarians, Catherine Campbell, Miss Foster, Margaret Hughes, Lilian Benson, and Associate Head Librarian, James J. Tallman. But the most important of these, and the one who became a close friend, was Elsie Murray, a Canadiana Specialist, a History M.A. from Columbia, and a veteran of both the U. of T. and Toronto's Public Library system. She befriended me, encouraged me, and gave me a great deal of important information on Canadian books and their histories, especially when she realized that I was going to do my M.A. thesis on Canadian Novelists from 1920 to the present. I spent about half of the time in the downstairs workroom and the other half on either the main desk on the third floor, or the Reserve Desk on the second. In off times on the Main Desk I explored the stacks and so became especially familiar with the literature sections, particularly the Canadian and American shelves.

In short order I began to attend Mr. Landon's graduate course in American History, one of three students that year. Western's graduate faculty was never large at that time and the war had diverted many potential male students into the services. Dr. Tamblyn had volunteered to give me, all by myself, a course in Aesthetics, and so I plunged into reading Santayana and Croce, both of whom I found fascinating, if somewhat impenetrable. The history course was pure delight. Mr. Landon was at the peak of his career, having recently published his *Western Ontario And The American Frontier*, funded by the Carnegie Foundation under the Headship of James Shotwell of Columbia, the famous Strathroy old boy. In 1944, Mr. Landon would publish his *Lake Huron*, one of the prestigious Great Lakes' Series. His work had brought recognition to both Western's Library and History Department, he was full of enthusiasm for his subject and was a fine lecturer. I have always felt privileged to have experienced his class, especially in such a close and intimate group.

Through Elsie Murray I speedily became a part of another division of the Library, Wilfrid Jury's domain, the Indian artifacts Museum on the ground floor. Jury was a crotchety maverick who, with his father, Amos, had started long before to collect Indian artifacts and to reconstruct the early culture of Ontario's Indian tribes, not only at the Museum in Western's library but, more importantly, through archeological digs in several sites in Southern Ontario. When I began to be aware of all this, he was just beginning his work on the Jesuit Fathers and their sojourn among the Hurons and final martyrdom. He and Elsie were then in the process of a courtship that would lead them to marriage and a fruitful professional partnership as well. *Ste Marie Among The Hurons* was their definitive account of the long work of excavation and reconstruction. Wilfrid had very little formal education: always a rebel, he had run away to join the navy during W.W.I., had come home with damaged lungs, and had since given himself over to the archeological work that his father had begun as a hobby and avocation from farming and horse- trading. By professionals, and especially, in his mind, by Dr. James Tallman, Jury was considered a rank amateur, and between them there was a ever-active feud, of no danger to such an outsider as myself, but a source of much entertainment. For the chosen few, Jury held court in his Museum, where the major display was certainly impressive—a model Indian village built by himself and his father. He also kept a bottle of rye on hand, and his favourite practical joke was to spike the 'tea' of a novice with a goodly shot. Needless to say, I fell prey to this very early, as no doubt, did everyone who came in contact with him. In general, though, both Wilfrid and Elsie were very good to me, treating me as a young apprentice to their markedly original points of view. I was delighted to learn all that Elsie could teach me about the book business, and I benefited from her friendship, which continued for many years.

    I had returned to Western with some vague idea of doing a thesis on Thomas Wolfe, whose *Look Homeward Angel* was one of my discoveries in the Dauphin library, and whose combination of stunning prose and small-town insights, albeit Southern small-town, made an enormous impression on me. However, Dr. Tamblyn directed me to talk to Frank Stiling, their most recent addition to the

Department, about possible topics, and he wisely steered me away from Wolfe and toward a more manageable and, as it developed, useful topic, Canadian novelists. I had a fine time looking up names and dates, cheered on by my library colleagues, and especially enjoyed devising a questionnaire to send out to all those whom I could locate. It was, of course, a very amateurish questionnaire, but it brought forth many many answers, and not a few letters giving me more information than I had asked for. It also brought about a very few furious letters from authors who thought I was invading their privacy. By far the majority, though, were so unused to being sought out that they were obviously flattered by the attention, and gladly gave me all sorts of information about themselves.

I also wrote to William Arthur Deacon, Literary Editor of the *Globe And Mail* and author of the popular and newsy weekly column "The Flyleaf." That letter turned out to be my very best and most politically fortunate move: Deacon responded with enthusiasm and total encouragement, inviting me to come and see him in Toronto and promising help. As good as his word, he gave me a copy of the membership list of the thriving Canadian Authors' Society, sheets upon sheets of pink tissue paper on which were the names and addresses I needed.

In the spring Morley and I went down to Toronto for the 24th of May weekend, stayed with Dot and Dick at Port Credit, and I went to see Deacon at the *Globe And Mail*. He took me to the cafeteria for lunch where we had roast port, applesauce, potatoes and gravy, very good and very hearty, and Deacon's welcome was as warm as he had promised. I came home much inspired by his cordiality and enthusiasm—he talked and acted as if I were doing something rather important, and certainly something that hadn't been done before. At the end of May we moved to a spacious apartment that Morley had found for us in a big old run-down house at the beach in Port Maitland, within easy distance of the station for Morley, an ideal place to work for me. There I wrote my thesis, really an alphabetic catalogue of novelists giving all the data on each one that I had been able to collect. It was a straightforward piece of prose, no criticism attempted and none suggested by anyone at all with whom I worked. Therefore, the writing was not as much of a challenge as it might have been otherwise, but on the whole I was fortunate, because the information I had gathered was valuable and remained so, while my critical opinions, at that stage of my life, would hardly have been so.

On June 6, 1944, came D-Day, the long awaited invasion of the continent by the Allied forces for which we had been waiting so long. Ever since he went overseas in 1941, Brandy had been a faithful correspondent. After his father died in 1942, he had named me, along with his mother, next-of-kin. I had many many letters from him that summer, the most crucial of them telling of the wound he got on the beaches that day, of his hospitalization and his breaking free and hitching transportation back to France to the First Hussars, his regiment. He was very shortly brought up before General Crerar for that serious breach of discipline, but after the mandatory raking over the coals, the General had added an understanding congratulation for his determination to rejoin the fighting men. That was the last really good news we had for some time, although the letters kept coming: the Arnheim disaster and the Battle of the Bulge were unlooked for blocks to an early Allied victory, and the war dragged on through the Fall and another winter.

When summer ended, and with it our visitors—

Morley's mother, Vesta and Harry, Mother and Father, various friends—I went back to Vesta's and to Western with a finished thesis. As I recall it that Fall was very satisfying: not only did I get the thesis through with no trouble at all, and, in fact, no Oral, but I also got the degree at Fall Convocation. Best of all, to our minds, I became pregnant. I have always credited the combination of the academic goal realized and Vesta's benign presence for that, but whatever the case, I was due in July, and began to go the famous Dr. Evan Shute, who was at that time London's best known obstetrician and had been Annie's doctor as well for the birth of young Arthur in 1939. Edith Whicher (Morrow), who had roomed with me for our final term in '41, was back at Western that Fall, finishing up her Nursing degree, her training at the Hamilton General completed. She was anxious that the two of us should set up housekeeping again and we found quite a large apartment in the upstairs of a house on Hellmuth Avenue. We had much more room there than in our former Richmond Street bed-sitter, and we even had some of our own furniture. We each had a bedroom as I recall, and a living room, kitchen and bathroom besides. Ede was courting with John Morrow, the brother of my friend, Miriam, and a medical student, in uniform at that time, with another year to go on his course.

We had a good winter. I sailed through pregnancy with sleepiness my most troublesome manifestation. When I was staffing the desk at Western I used to fight to keep my eyes open, especially in the mornings. However, it was a small price to pay for the general delight—our own, and the family's, particularly Mother's, to whom it gave a new lease on life. My brother Vernon had just finished his training at Aylmer and had gone overseas to be a Flight Engineer in a bombing squadron, and this took mother's mind off the inevitable anxiety. I fear that it did nothing for my father, though, who simply added worry about me to his already huge anxiety about Vernon. Ede and John Morrow were around a lot, I was busy and happy, my academic ambitions for the time being satisfied, and the months passed pleasantly. In April, I stopped work at the Library and prepared to join Morley in Kingston where he had been posted. After weeks of searching, for Kingston was perhaps the most crowded spot in Canada, Morley had found us a one-room apartment with attached kitchen and bath, on the first floor of the same building where our friends, Ruth (Ruth Sands of Strathroy, Western and Bright's Grove comradeship)and Bert Longmire had the third floor.

On our way to set up housekeeping in Kingston we stayed again with Dot and Dick at Port Credit, and at Toronto's Eaton's made some of the most important purchases of our lives. We fell in love with the solid maple furniture, called 'Rock Maple,' at that time imported from Quebec and sold at a ridiculously low price. The breakfront still in our living room today was $45, the dining room table, our present table in Strathroy, $15, and four chairs and the coffee table still in our Toronto living room, were $52 altogether. To sleep on we bought a 3/4 continental bed, much to Dot's horror, who thought we should first of all have got ourselves a real bed. We, however, were happy as larks, thrilled in fact with our furnishings, and the maple pieces have stayed our favourite furniture ever since. The breakfront arrived water-damaged a week or two later in Kingston, and I, not about to put up with that, wrote a letter addressed to John David Eaton himself. With splendid result—another spotless breakfront arrived with speed! Such was Eaton's service in those days—"Goods Satisfactory or Your Money

Refunded" meant just that!

We settled down to wait for the baby in great good form, walking, seeing lots of the Longmires, and as we couldn't get into our apartment until the middle of May, spending the waiting weeks in a rooming house. We were quite happy there even though one night the bed on which I was reading and eating an orange partially fell through the floor, taking orange peels and me with it.

As the spring advanced, so did the allies in Europe and at last, on May 8, the Liberation of Europe was accomplished. We celebrated with the Longmires, very mildly, for by that time, I was quite a size and also quite uncomfortable. I had changed to a Kingston doctor as soon as I got there, though he, poor man, was so overworked at that time with enormous numbers of service couples' babies that he scarcely registered on me and to this day I can't even remember his name. The final month seemed to go on forever, but at last one night we walked across the park to the hospital and I was admitted.

Chapter IX

Family Matters

Stephen Morley Thomas was born in the Kingston General Hospital about 6 o'clock in the evening of July 25, 1945. He had been as impatient to be born as I was to have him, and had been giving me fake contractions, without pain, off and on for some days before Morley and I walked across the Park at two in the morning and I was admitted. Between VE Day and VJ Day was a good time to be born in 1945, the best since the start of the war. We all felt that new days, already beginning, were bound to be better days. Ruth Longmire had long since constituted herself my mentor. She got all dressed up in her nurse's uniform and came to the hospital early in the morning, but, to her disgust, she was discouraged from staying. I only remember a few moments of pain in the delivery room before the doctor gave me anaesthetic and then surprisingly, Steve arrived. I was in the hospital a good week, 8 days, I believe, at $5 a day, and by the time we came home the baby was being bottle-fed, absolutely standard procedure then, and made even more assembly-line by wartime's lack of hospital staff and crowded conditions. Ruth made 'Clara's first pregnancy' a better and better story as the years went by, and at least in her story I was the most laid-back expectant mother in the country.

Vernon was overseas and Mother had stopped work, ostensibly because she was not well, but really because she was in a nervous state about Vernon who was with a

Bomber Squadron. Her fears were absolutely justified, as we now know, but then we heard a great deal about the success of bomber missions, and little about their terrible casualty cost. She thoroughly enjoyed being a new Grandma, however, sleeping upstairs in the Longmire apartment while they were on summer leave back in Strathroy, and in the daytime—*cooking*. Morley had a bicycle in Kingston and she sent him speeding off to the store for supplies daily, so much so that our food bills for the couple of weeks she was with us cost more than Steve did! She was bound that I would gain back all the weight that I had lost and then some, being of the old school who believed that being 'stout' was a sign of health. Steve was the first baby in our family's or most of our friends' circles, and gifts poured in, which of course, we tried on, laughing at the baby's bemused appearance in all the finery as we wheeled him around in his strictly utility carriage.

Steve was not a happy baby, and the panacea of our pediatrician, Dr. Suddaby, was pablum, pablum and more pablum. By the time he was three months old, he was being fed seven tablespoons of it twice a day. It seemed gross and probably was, and especially horrified Grandma Thomas, who wrote to Aunt Floss that we were force-feeding our child (we never heard the last of that one). But Steve gobbled it up smiling and I now believe that he had the beginnings of the piloric stenosis that afflicted John when he was a month old, and that Suddaby's feeding methods stretched the baby's stomach muscles so that he could take food without discomfort. By the time we had been parents for five months, we were finished with that stage, and a relief it was. I believe that Morley and I and Steve too would have been better off if we had been on our own. We were over-supervised by both Mother and the Longmires and I was far too nervous a mother and amenable to both of them.

VJ Day and the first weeks of peace passed almost unnoticed, because Steve was very much centre stage. Then Morley closed the Kingston Station and was posted to Toronto, leaving me to move out of the apartment on November 1 as our lease required. We moved upstairs with the Longmires until just before Christmas, when in Mrs. Thomas's car, packed high with all our equipment and with our furniture to follow, we moved to Port Credit to stay with Dot and Dick until our flat on Humberside Ave. found by Morley after some weeks of pavement-pounding, was available. Meanwhile we had had lots of company: Vernon was demobilized and visited on his way home, Joyce and Harry Whicher came, as did the Stevensons and Aggie, newly demobilized from the C.W.A.C.

Our flat at 204 Humberside was the ground floor of a house owned by Frank and Ida Dean, sons John and David, and Grandma Dean. They moved upstairs where they had a partially finished third floor as well as the second floor. We had the living room, bedroom, kitchen, pantry, unheated and terribly cold, and joint use of quite a broad front hall. Upstairs we shared the bathroom and toilet, in separate rooms, with the Deans. In the basement there were laundry tubs and I had already bought a hand-turned wringer. Dot and Dick were heroic to take us in, in the interim, for they lived over the Bank of Commerce where Dick was Accountant and their apartment was already cramped, with Elizabeth about nine years old. They moved out of their bedroom for us, and there we were, charity cases, though people were doing all kinds of those things then, housing being wartime scarce still. Steve was a happy baby by four months and the month with them passed uneventfully. We went home to Strathroy by train at Christmas time where Mother had a lovely time fussing over Steve's vast appetite, though both she and Father, especially Father, were terribly worried about Vernon's difficulties in settling down.

New Year's Eve and New Year's Day we spent cleaning up the Deans' place for our move. It was a mess, for they were indifferent housekeepers at best, and we remember thousands of grapefruit pits all over the floors and cupboards of the pantry, even under the linoleum. They had sold us an old bed and mattress so beat up that later on, when we bought a bedroom suite, the Salvation Army wouldn't accept it. We also got a second-hand crib to replace the baby crib we had had in Kingston. Our furniture was delivered without disaster, and finally, joyfully, we were in our own place with our beloved maple furniture and our treasures around us. It took very little time to settle because there wasn't much to settle, and a good thing too, for we were immediately deluged with company. Our friends were then being demobilized in great numbers at the Exhibition grounds, so Toronto was a central rallying point. Brandy was the first, and his initial and many many later visits were high spots of joyful reunion. He speedily got a car and used to drive down to Toronto from London so often that when I was walking Steve in the afternoon I would always half-expect to see his car as I rounded the corner towards home. Then Jack Fowlie, army as well, then Joan, demobbed from the Air Force, came to Toronto to find herself a place to live and to begin working for the Dietetic Association. Miriam Morrow also came, intending to start work for the Bell in Toronto. Ede Whicher and John Morrow came, planning their marriage in the summer, Don McCormick and his wife Florrie came, then Hilda, Florrie's twin sister, and Willie Downham. The Longmires came in the early spring for several years in a row to write accounting exams. A happy horde! All of these people stayed at least one night and most of them were repeaters.

During the war we had all become accustomed to being on the move and in the burgeoning peace we certainly kept it up. Those first months of demobilization were especially happy, though certainly not without memories and talk of those who hadn't come back. Steve soaked up all the happiness as well, showing off to great advantage in the many snappy clothes that Mother loved to buy for him. We cannot now remember just exactly how we coped with sleeping arrangements but of course the three-quarter couch in the living room, our former Kingston bed, was always in use, and for $14.95 we bought a folding cot from Eaton's which we kept in the pantry for frequent spill-over. I don't remember being in the least upset at everyone having to go upstairs to the bathroom, or at having to go up there to bathe Steve when he grew too big for a tub on the kitchen table. But I do remember Dot calling that bathroom the muskrat den, and I will certainly never forget Brandy bringing Carol to stay on their honeymoon. Carol, daughter of the rich General Spencer, Commanding Officer of the First Hussars, in a gorgeous negligee heavy with ecru lace, had to trail away upstairs, like everyone else, undoubtedly meeting some of the Deans en route. Vernon and Pat also stayed with us on their honeymoon and countless other visitors including our parents—and all with unfailing good nature.

I loved all our company and having people to cook for and was especially happy when Mr. Dean partitioned the hall, making our part of it wide enough to take the maple table and chairs. Then we had what we could pretend was a real dining room. Among the courting couples we entertained were Mary Dampier and Ron

Mathieson, both working at Ontario Hydro and just beginning to get seriously interested in each other. Mary brought Ron for dinner, I cooked roast beef, gravy, the works, and Steve was delighted to show off his first pair of shiny brown boots, with which he tramped all over Ron who sat bravely on the couch all dressed up with coat, vest, tie and one of the stiff, high collars that he used to prefer. One weekend that winter, when Morley went to Talbotville to visit his mother, Joan and I, determined to have an outing, carried Steve to the Art Gallery via the Dundas street car, a tough load! We have marvelled ever since at our stamina, but, as I recall, we all enjoyed it.

In the spring Brandy was going to take us to Boston where he was enrolling at Harvard in the Ph.D. programme. To our horror Steve became very sick with diarrhea. That was when we first met Dr. Varty, who became our family mainstay. Our Toronto pediatrician was the famous Dr. Garnet Hamblin, one of the team who had been to Callander to look after the new-born Dionne quintuplets. He was totally of his time, a martinet, and I was as terrified of him as was Steve. A rigid schedule was the only thing he would tolerate—in those days, even Dr. Spock was all for letting babies cry and cry to keep them to their prescribed routine. However, at this crisis, Hamblin was on holiday and we 'lucked in' to Varty, just out of the army, absolutely no bedside manner, but friendly and gentle. He looked Steve over and said, "I've seen babies who had polio who weren't as sick as this." Some comfort! This, Steve's first experience of sulfa, which he grew to loathe because of all his ear problems later, had one good outcome—we got a fridge. No longer would we be vulnerable to spoiled milk, which may well have caused his sickness. Though all electric appliances had been long since discontinued, we found that Wright's in

Strathroy had a Westinghouse, and we found the money it took.

Steve, the first child, had very different early experiences from John, who was born in 1951. Every afternoon I took him walking up to Dundas and Keele to meet Morley, we began taking him to the movies very early, and he got used to going to restaurants and behaving himself at a very early age. His first movie was at Shea's downtown, the long-gone Toronto landmark with the big organ that rose out of the bowels of the theatre with the famous Ruby Ramsay Rouse at the console. The movie was *The Emperor Waltz* with Bing Crosby and Steve was two. From then on we were away—the Beaver was just to the north of us on Dundas Street, and the West End just south of Dundas on Mavety. Joan and I were movie buffs and also used to take Steve with us to the Runnymede on Bloor to the west of us. It was notable at that time for showing British films, one of which gave Steve memorable nightmares. It starred as I remember, Patricia Roc, a Hebridean tragedy with bleak rocks, gulls screaming and the adulterous woman set adrift in a boat with a fish tied to her head for the gulls to peck. I can't remember that we were particularly concerned about this, though it may well have toughened Steve up to attend a double feature of *Lives Of A Bengal Lancer* and *Four Feathers* for a treat on his fourth birthday.

Very soon after his return Brandy gave me the honour and the job of editing the wartime history of the First Hussars, written in a slapdash way by Foster Stark another officer whom we knew from Western and whom they had bribed with plenty of booze to do a rough draft. I speedily began to mark masses of history papers for Drs. Maine and Dorland, and Morley coached Meds football at the University. In the late spring of 1946, Longmans

Green, the publishers, suddenly erupted into activity and hired a man to edit my M.A. thesis which they planned to publish in June. I was, of course, delighted. I was also luckier than I deserved. Earlier Longmans had written to me about publication, but fixated in pregnancy I had refused to be bothered with editing. Both Deacon and, when he heard of it, Mr. Landon were shocked! This was all William Arthur Deacon's doing; furthermore, he had an intriguing master-plan in process: the Canadian Authors' Association was meeting in Toronto and he proposed to give specially bound copies of my book, *Canadian Novelists, 1920-45*, to the Governor General's Award winners and to the incoming executive. All this happened as he planned: Morley and I went to the gala banquet at the Royal York on a very hot night in June, at the price of joining the C.A.A. ($10 I remember), and watched with great pleasure as Hugh MacLennan and E.J. Pratt accepted copies of my book and Deacon beamed on the entire assemblage with pride at becoming its president. On Civic Holiday weekend that summer I went up to Wiarton to be Matron of Honour at Edith Whicher's and John Morrow's wedding, another excitement and honour. All in all, we were never bored in those early years at 204 Humberside.

We always went to Strathroy and Talbotville for holidays, sometimes getting away to London for a dinner out with Brandy, but more often staying home to enjoy the family company, Marge and Slim from Jackson, Michigan, Vernon and Pat, Annie and Art and in Talbotville, the welcome cherishing we received from Grandma and Aunt Nellie. We usually had Christmas Eve dinner in Talbotville and Christmas Day dinner, as of old, at Grandma McCandless's. Evan, Vi and Mary were always there, as were Roy, Elizabeth and Larrie, Evan the high point of attraction for Steve as, really for all of us, with his infectious laugh, good humour and general enjoyment of the occasions.

In the late summer of 1947 Dr. Maine called me to ask if I would like to teach Extension for Western that Fall in Welland. I was overjoyed at the chance, also at the prospect of the $400 dollars it paid. So began the happy extension saga which went on for many years all over Ontario, as well as on the Western campus in the summers, and climaxed with my returning to school in 1957 for a Ph.D. In the summer of 1949 I also got the chance to teach summer school at Western, the first of many times, and of course jumped at it. Steve and I stayed with Grandma and Aunt Nellie in Talbotville, Morley came weekends, I rode over to Western each day with a neighbor, Miss Futcher, who was taking a course, and we all had a thoroughly good time. Earlier that summer, before Summer School, we had gone on a trip to Ottawa and to Abbotsford, Quebec, to visit Willie Downham and Walter Bowley. Then we had an unforgettably gorgeous trip up the Saguenay to Arvida to visit Joyce and Harry Whicher, who by that time had two girls, Sandra and Celia.

The next year Morley had a chance to attend a Geography Summer School at Stanstead College in Stanstead, Quebec. With the Bowleys we took a cottage nearby on Lake Massawippi and had a grand summer. It included a visit to Bishop's University where Arthur Jewett, formerly Head of Western's English Department, had become President. After a splendid afternoon tea on the lawn, he wrote to me, offering me a job in the English Department combined with the Deanship of Women which, need I say, I sorely hated to turn down, but which was absolutely out of the question. Not only were commuting marriages still a thing of the future, but just then, after eagerly trying for some months, I had become pregnant, and was looking forward to our much-wanted second child.

A move from our flat on Humberside was now imperative. What I had been longing for for some years—I had even developed a recurring dream of finding more unknown rooms in our present quarters—now became absolutely urgent. I called Brown's, the first large Real Estate add in the telephone book, and asked whether or not they had any houses for sale under $10,000. "Just one, on Mountview Avenue," answered the dealer, and I asked to see it immediately. Fortunately, our salesman turned out to be the father of Margaret Hallman, the wife of Eugene Hallman, Morley's colleague and our friend. We saw the house that night, Mr. Torrens expedited our purchase, and with a loan from Grandma Thomas and a small second mortgage from the vendors, we were all set. We were to move in in mid-October. Meanwhile, excitement and anxiety together had somewhat upset the baby and to my horror I was threatened with a miscarriage. Dot put me to bed in Port Credit for a few days, Morley and Joan, our stalwart friend, nobly coped with the moving as well as Steve, who had just started to school, and all was well. We were in our own place, to our total joy and celebration. Mary Markham my co-teacher at Western in the summer of '49, moved in to board with us in the middle one of the three upstairs bedrooms and immediately became a treasured member of the family, a surrogate sister to me and a beloved 'aunt' to Steve. We didn't take a chance on travelling that Christmas, but revelled in our own home, and in putting together one of the many special 'sets' that were always a Christmas Catalogue feature of Eaton's. Cowboys and Indians, forts, plastic figures and tin constructions: for years the boys looked forward to the Alamo or whatever was the starring set for that year—John in fact developed into a toy soldier fanatic.

I have an indelible picture in my mind's eye of Steve and Mary curled up together in the big wine chair in our living room reading *Alice In Wonderland* as Morley and I left for the hospital in the late afternoon of March 30, 1951. I had read the famous Grantly Dick Read book, *Childbirth Without Fear*, and I really took it to heart, so much so that we barely got to the hospital on time. John David Thomas was born about 6 p.m. on March 30, 1951. Morley always says that he just had time to hand me over to a nurse, go to the kiosk, buy a newspaper and light a cigarette when Dr. Varty arrived to tell him that he had another son. It was as easy as birth could ever be, and I was one happy mother back in my room for a restful week, fending off suggestions that I go to mothers' meetings and, instead, marking essays from my extension class that had finished only the week before and that I had brought to the hospital with me. When I got home I had a short-lived time of absolute joy before I developed phlebitis and had to stay in bed for ten days. Grandma Thomas came down to look after the house and we managed, but that was the beginning of several years of milestones, both lucky and unlucky. John developed piloric stenosis at one month, a tight muscle around the stomach opening that has to be clipped so that food can pass through. He was operated on in the Sick Children's Hospital (just lately I came across the bill from the famous Dr. Farmer for $15. When I called, the nurse said it should have been $150, but settled for $75). Though Dr. Varty assured us that he would be fine and he was, it was a blow to doting new parents. We all recovered in due course and continued to be happy in our house. When

Mary left after two years to teach in Kitchener, Ginny, another Western Grad attending O.C.E., boarded with us for a year and, though never the close friend that Mary became and remained, she was fun to have with us and has always stayed in touch with us.

Meanwhile, my mother, working at the Artistic as always, loved buying the boys both toys and clothes. They had a red metal car, big enough to sit in, a trike, toboggan, everything up to and including a Lionel train. Vernon and Pat adopted Martha and when it became plain that Pat was seriously mentally ill, schizophrenic, Martha stayed with us for several months and went to school with the boys at Keele Street school across the street. Life speeded up considerably during the fifties; I was teaching Extension each Fall, sometimes every two weeks, sometimes every week. I had a nasty spell of exhaustion and depression from sheer over-tiredness and worry about Vernon and his family that spilled over on us from Mother's constant vocalizing of her own nagging concerns. But we made strides forward as well—when I felt better I began a Sunday School class of teenage girls that I loved. In 1954 I began to teach Summer School at Western regularly, an adventure we all loved, for North London was an ideal place for the boys in the summers. Finally, in 1957, I began the Ph.D. Programme at the U. of T.

Chapter X

The Apprenticeship Years

1. Teaching for Western
1947-1961
2. Toronto's Ph.D. programme
1957-1962

Sometime in the spring of 1947 my most important, life-shaking phone call happened when Professor Maine, who had always been particularly good to me, called to ask if I'd like to teach an Extension course in the Fall. Needless to say, I was absolutely thrilled. I had kept in touch with Floyd Maine ever since graduation, and beginning in '46 he had been sending huge packages of essays to Toronto for me to mark. His classes had always been large, and they were especially swollen with returning veterans in the post-war years. I began what speedily became a marking 'factory,' handling vast numbers of history essays for Drs. Maine and Dorland for many years. But the chance to teach was something new and very special. I was to teach two courses, English 20 and English 38, every other Saturday, going to Welland by train from the Sunnyside station in Toronto in the morning and coming back in the evening. Each class was for two hours, and with one beginning at 10 o'clock and one at 1.30, and a return train in the late afternoon, the timing was perfect.

I had absolutely no nervousness about the adventure, though I hadn't anticipated it at all and owed it to the potent combination of my friend, Brandy Conron, now a very active member of the English Department, and the willingness of Maine to give a rookie still another chance to prove herself. Once before when we were in Dauphin, Manitoba, in 1942, he had encouraged me to offer English 20 to men and women on the Service Flying Training School. I was certainly flying high with happiness as Morley took me to the train that first Saturday in September '47, and when I returned in the early evening, I was just as happy. The Extension classes were held in one of the Welland schools, and they were very well attended. I couldn't have had an easier group for my first real practice teaching. Teachers themselves, they made things easy for me, were easy to please, and certainly more appreciative of my efforts than ordinary undergraduates would have been.

In those early post-war days, Western's extension network was peaking. It had been built up since the thirties, basically to satisfy the needs of elementary school teachers who were working toward a B.A. and therefore a higher teaching status and more pay. There were many centres across the province as well as Welland—among them Orangeville, Collingwood, Woodstock, and Peterborough to all of which I went more than once. There was even one in Victoria College in Toronto in 1950/51. I taught in it when I was pregnant with our son John, wearing a borrowed academic gown to disguise, I fondly thought, my pregnancy (John was born a week after classes finished, and I went to the hospital with a suitcase full of essays. When I opened the essays I discovered many "good wishes" appended to them. I had not been as disguised as I thought!). Western was far ahead of the rest of Ontario universities in Extension work, partly because its first Director, Dr. Kingston, a mathematician, had imported the idea from the University of Chicago and had a real mission about its promotion. Western had set up a popular Summer School "Tent City" on its campus in the Depression years, and its reputation had steadily grown since. In the post-war years, with returning servicemen eager for instruction, centres proliferated.

The courses were exactly the same ones as were given intramurally, and the examinations were the same. Teaching Extension, except in London and St. Thomas, handy for faculty, was not particularly popular at that time. Intramural classes were crowded, teaching loads were heavy, and Extension pay was very low. In my first years, the fee for the two courses I gave every two weeks was something like $440 for the entire year, though by the time I gave it up in 1961, it was about $1000. Therefore, each year when Dr. Maine set out to staff the various centres my name was accepted with little or no opposition from the English Department. Furthermore, English 38, the American-Canadian course, was a popular one with teachers, and I was willing and eager to teach it as well as the survey, English 20 which, at that time and for many years thereafter, every first-year student at Western was required to take. The age of specializing in one's field was beginning to limit the offerings of scholars, but Clara Thomas was more than ready to pick up any one or two of a variety of courses, anything, in fact, that was suggested to me. During the next 14 years, for I taught Extension and Summer Schools until 1961 when I went full-time as a faculty member to York, I taught many courses, including first year French, and Renaissance and Reformation history, as well as almost all the pass courses offered by the English Department. Always the staple course was English 20, one I still believe to be the best survey ever designed, especially for the many years of the two-volume Baugh (Brooke, Chew, Malone) Anthology as text. Its introductions to the various periods were excellent, as was the range of its offerings. In those days, the canon was well agreed upon, and it stretched right from Beowulf to Virginia Woolf. I have always given my utter familiarity with it much of the credit for my later passing of the University of Toronto 'Generals,' that rigorous series of examinations that was a major hurdle in Toronto's Ph.D. programme.

After 1949 I didn't teach Summer School again until 1954, for John's birth intervened and he was three years old when we trekked down to London once more. Then it became a regular thing. We rented a house and Morley came weekends in the little beige Anglia we had bought after my first Summer School. At the end of the summer we took a cottage on Lake Huron or, one special summer, took the boys on a trip around the lakes. We had some splendid houses—three years in the 'Buck House' at Richmond and Regent, two years at the Klincks' on Grosvenor near Gibbons Park, and various other dwellings, all pleasant adventures for all of us. Beginning in 1955 we also travelled with our precious cat, Pooh, who always had a litter of kittens in the course of our stay and so we ended with considerably more than we began! I had picked up a very little kitten on a parking lot on campus, and she grew into a beloved household fixture and, finally, the mother of a total of sixty-five kittens.

North London was a splendid milieu for the boys, who learned to swim in the Gibbons Park pool and in general enjoyed themselves immensely. For me it was a priceless addition to my apprentice professionalism. By this time the Summer School had become so large that many of the Department taught summer courses and because I was temporary, certainly no threat to anyone, everyone talked to me, from Dean Stiling to all my English Department colleagues to many other colleagues from other departments. I learned a enormous amount about the inner workings of Western and of the English Department in particular, and I was privy to all the institutional and personal turf wars then in play. Brandy Conron was, of course, my old and close friend and confidant, and from him as for years past, I learned the most. In general, however, the Western Arts Faculty and the English Department in particular were remarkably homogeneous at that time. There had been unprecedented growth in the few years after the war and a group of young men, several of them veterans, had been recruited then. By the mid-fifties, they were busy founding families and bringing up young children, and they got along well, both professionally and socially.

In the spring of 1949, after two years of Extension teaching, I had first applied for admission to Toronto's PhD programme. This was a major step for me, and I did it fearfully, for I was only too familiar with all the horror stories about the programme, and I certainly knew that women were welcomed for M.A. work, but were looked upon as poor candidates for the higher degree. Very few women were hired full time by Ontario universities—in fact the only one I knew was Flora Roy of Waterloo Lutheran, (now Wilfrid Laurier) an affiliate of Western. But Flora had given me more encouragement than she knew when, at a meeting for Extension teachers, she had assured me that I could indeed do a Ph.D. if I really wanted to. My first application was speedily discouraged by a scathing letter from Brandy in which he accused me of competing with Morley, and threatened to pull out his support for my teaching if I dared to go any further. It was really a wicked letter, and the fact that I heeded it without question speaks for the position of women in the scholarly world at that date (also for the priority Brandy's opinions had for me!). But it seemed that Carl Klinck was hoping to get his student, Harry Weaver, accepted for Toronto's Ph.D. programme that year, and the warning signals were up: "no one else with a Western affiliation need apply."

I went down to the campus to withdraw, and to ask Professor Woodhouse if I might take one course, and to my mingled amazement and dismay, he insisted on calling the Graduate Dean to ask him for a Fellowship on my behalf. I was flattered and thrilled when he told me that my application had been one of the best, but I had to make it clear that I could not go on with it—and so my entrance was delayed by seven years. As I later realized, I had not the confidence to hold my head up and do the work just then, and it was just as well that my attempt was aborted. But I certainly never forgot Brandy's tirade, though he did, and later took credit for persuading me to enter the programme in the fifties.

As it was, I comforted myself by enrolling in Woodhouse's "Victorian Thought" course, met Earle Sanborn who, with Mary, his wife, became staunch life-long friends, and developed an enormous admiration and affection for Professor Woodhouse, his learning, his seminar management, and, not least, his wit. It was a splendid course, introducing all of us to the landmark thinkers of the 19th century, particularly the Mills and Carlyle, and leading me especially in the way I wanted to go. I already knew that I wanted to explore the work of Anna Jameson someday, and Woodhouse assigned me Wanda Neff's exhaustive survey, *Victorian Working Women*, as my major seminar topic.

Years later, a practiced teacher both during the year

and at Summer School, I finally made the firm decision to venture into the programme again. In 1957 John was in Grade I, Steve in Grade VII and my days were relatively free. All the same, I took care to take courses that were scheduled in the afternoons, for the boys came home for lunch. Now such fussiness seems absolutely unreal, but then, even with such careful planning, some supposedly dear friends looked askance at my activities, all of our friends found me strange, and I always was an easy prey to guilt. The years of the conservative fifties were still repressive ones for women, who were ideally like Beaver's mother, June Cleaver, housebound, busy whipping up tuna casseroles or attending Home and School meetings and, supposedly, happy. My ever-lurking guilty feelings circumscribed my choices and consequently I lived with a stiff measure of resentment against my restrictions—one of my later, lasting regrets being that I never experienced Northrop Frye as a lecturer because his classes were timed when I felt obliged to be home. The reluctance even to find a sitter stuns me now, but it was very much a part of our ethos then. But I did take Woodhouse's Milton, and I also sat in on his fourth-year Spenser course. At the same time I developed almost total recall for all his lectures.

I began my adventure by going to see Professor Wilson, at that time the English Department's Graduate Secretary. He was a gentle scholar and seemed agreeable when I outlined to him my plan of action: two courses in my first year, one course and the two language exams in my second year, the General examinations in the third, and then the thesis. Thanks to Murdo McKinnon at Western, I had been well briefed in my approach: he knew that I hoped to work on Anna Jameson for my dissertation and he was positive that it would be a great advantage to me to have a topic at the ready. He was right. From Professor Wilson I went to see Woodhouse, again on Murdo's advice, and when he wasn't in his office I proceeded to Victoria College, where I did find Frye on hand. He accepted me kindly, and advised me to go away and write a formal thesis proposal on Anna Jameson to be handed in to Woodhouse's office. This I did forthwith, with help from the *Dictionary of National Biography*. Very shortly Woodhouse, meeting me in the hall, told me that my proposal had been unusually good, and that Professor Frye had offered to be my supervisor —only many years later, a supervisor myself, did I realize what a giant step that had been, and how fortunate I was!

I have long since realized that my welcome was, in part, because of the mutterings that must have been already swelling about a forthcoming Ontario university expansion, a massive enlargement of the whole system. Brandy especially had begun to take my ambitions and my teaching devotion seriously. In fact, seven years after thoroughloy discouraging my ambition, he was now telling me that I absolutely "must" get a Ph.D. Whether or not my friends gave me some introductory publicity at Toronto I do not know, nor do I know whether or not the Toronto men knew of the publication of my *Canadian Novelists* (it didn't occur to me to tell them), but I do know that my welcoming by both Woodhouse and Frye was much more genial than I expected and totally contrary to the current mythology. My first hurdle was the passing of the qualifying examinations. I hadn't written an exam in thirteen years and my examination techniques were rusty, to put it mildly. To enter the programme, over 70% was required and it took me two tries to achieve that. Once again, I was encouraged by Woodhouse, who spoke to me as if I would certainly be successful on the second try—and I was.

I enrolled for his Milton course and for a course in Renaissance History given by Professor Powicke. The Victorian Thought course I had taken in '49 counted as one of my four required courses, and because I had taken Anglo-Saxon at Western many long years ago, I was excused from the Old English component of the Ph.D. requirements. Furthermore, and another case of special treatment, because I had worked for two years in the Western Library, I was excused from the compulsory bibliography requirement. Professor Endicott was in charge of that, and he excused me after a short interview in which he asked a few questions and then said, "Of course, having worked in a university library, you'd know that." I see now that I was indeed given some preferential treatment. I chose Renaissance history as my extra-departmental course because I had marked essays for Dr. Maine for so long and had also taught it in Extension twice. I couldn't have been luckier in my choice. I was one of only five students, the others doing Graduate History. I found the whole experience fascinating. I seemed to be covered with luck in finding pertinent books in the Library and I gradually got over my feelings of inadequacy among History specialists. The whole year was a liberating experience for me, including son Steve's emergence as a great spaghetti cooker on Tuesdays when I came home at dinner time to Chef Boyardee and some imaginative salads. I also enjoyed meeting other students. They treated me with great friendliness as a senior citizen and a kind of unofficial counsellor in their midst. Robin Matthews, then called Danny, became a good and life-long friend, a veteran of many impassioned discussions, academic and otherwise, in the Hart House coffee shop, the only place in those sacred male precincts where women were then allowed to venture.

In year two I had one course left to take, a compulsory course in Middle English, a Chaucer course given that year by Father Shook of St Michael's, and a very intimidating experience. As he gave it, the course was really centred on philosophy, and I found Boethius, an enthusiasm of Shook's, both almost incomprehensible and infinitely boring. The course was lightened somewhat by the presence of Jane Appelbe, who became a dear friend and study-mate, and a New Zealander, Roly Frean, a gentle and genial classmate. A feisty and funny Irishman, Eugene Benson, who has spent his academic career at the University of Guelph, was also one of us. During Lent, Father Shook went to sleep during each week's session, a considerable annoyance for the student whose seminar presentation was in progress. I, however, was quite happy while Shook dozed, for I felt completely out to sea throughout most of the classes. The language exams, French and German, which I also wrote off that year were no problem, and by the spring of '59 I was ready for the big hurdle, the General Examinations coming up in the spring of 1960. During this time I kept on teaching Extension, of course, and also moved with the boys to London for Summer School, welcome diversions from scholarship and, as always, great confidence builders. I was also a teaching assistant at the U. of T., as were all Graduate English students, instructing dental students in their compulsory English course, not the challenging Extension work I loved, but teaching, nonetheless. And I also was cook-housekeeper at home and in the day, the primary care-giver, for it was still unthinkable that a husband would miss his work for any reason except grave illness. As I learned and often said later, there was no margin for dealing with the domestic crises that are sure to happen from time to time. There is no margin in university teaching either, for we do not have the substitute teachers that are a part of the secondary system. Consequently, people like myself lived with a tension level that always made for considerable unease and often anger, though it was usually well-suppressed.

In the Fall of '59, Jane Appelbe and I began to study seriously for the Generals, Jane coming out to our house for a whole day a week. We had to write six papers—Anglo-Saxon, Old English, Chaucer, Renaissance, Shakespeare, Eighteenth Century; and, for me, a three-hour exam in Victorian, my major field. At that time there was no Canadian field as such. We must have had access to former exams, though I don't remember them specifically. But I do remember sharing the reading load with Jane, and organizing ourselves very strictly on that basis. I also remember going through the entire year with lists of Anglo-Saxon verbs pinned up over the sink, to be memorized while doing dishes. And I also remember making up trial exam questions and writing out the answers endlessly, for I still felt rusty in the techniques of examination writing. Several of us read through *The Faerie Queen* in all day sessions, as well as a great deal of Chaucer. After Christmas Jane and I were joined weekly at our house by a Polish Commonwealth Scholar, Yvonne Nowotny, who turned out to be a great thorn in our flesh. She had looked upon us to befriend her from the beginning of the year, and this we had done. Unfortunately, she had a very elevated view of her own knowledge and took a very dim view of ours. I think she was harder on Jane than on me, for Jane had won scholarships to no end on her path through school, and already had a B.Litt. from Oxford. She did not take kindly to the condescension that was Yvonne's forte. Fortunately, Jane and I share a sense of humour, and with much grumbling and, in private, laughing, we managed.

By examination time in the early spring, we considered ourselves as stuffed full of assorted bits and pieces of knowledge as we would ever get. Eight of us wrote the exams—four passed, and Jane and I were two of the four. We have always been extremely proud of that—and rightly so!! In those days, 50% was a normal failure rate, and it was most unusual for women to be as successful as male candidates. The process ended with a three-hour Oral for each one of us, taken before a panel of English Department members. Woodhouse, Priestley, McGillivray, Roper and Macpherson were my examiners, and the session was undoubtedly the most nerve-wracking I have ever experienced. At half time I was given a ten minute break and Miss Stevenson, the Department secretary and a formidable woman indeed, spoke words of encouragement that were so unlike her usual closed-up demeanour that I have treasured them ever since: "Don't let them get you down, Mrs. Thomas!" For years I could replay every question and every answer in my mind—even now, thiry-seven years later, I can remember a great deal of what went on. Our friend, Jim Nelson, was at that time in the programme and staying on campus with Ian Macdonald, then Dean of Students at University College. After the oral, Jim took me in hand and fed me sherry until Morley came to pick me up.

There were many stories told about those Orals, especially as they had affected women candidates. The best one, though surely apocryphal, was supposed to have happened when the first female Ph.D. candidate came up for an Oral in the days of the famous Professor Alexander. She, it was said, had fainted, whereupon Professor Alexander had looked around the table and said," Should one of you gentlemen not loosen her stays?" In the three days or so before we heard the results, Jane and I walked miles, both of us convinced that we had failed, and when Professor Priestley called me to tell me that I had passed, I was dazed with joy. Jane, of course, had passed too, but Yvonne had fallen by the wayside and was shortly persuaded to move to languages, where she did get a Ph.D. in Russian Literature, and eventually taught at York until her sadly early death.

After the successful Oral, the field was clear for my thesis writing and I began to do research on Anna Jameson. Though I had been fascinated by her life ever since Professor Spenceley's course in Canadian Literature at Western in 1939, I had had no idea of her prominence in so many areas of 19th century life and literature. The old library at the U. of T. was strong in the Victorian field and this helped me a great deal. I can still feel the thrill of opening one book after another and finding Anna there in some capacity—as an art critic, a friend of the Brownings or Lady Byron, as traveller in Canada or the States—she seemed ubiquitous as she must have seemed to many of her contemporaries.

I was also still teaching for the U. of T., an Honours Bibliography course this time, and as usual doing two courses in Extension for Western. The Fall of 1960 was abruptly shattered when Morley's mother had to have an exploratory abdominal operation that revealed inoperable cancer. From that time on until February 1, when she died in the Toronto General, she was with us a great deal. She didn't know how sick she was, and the strain of keeping everything as seemingly normal as possible was terrible. Furthermore, in late November Morley was scheduled to go to London for meetings which were to last for three weeks. I encouraged him to go, because it seemed to me that his mother, the boys and I could get along with perhaps less strain than when he too was at home, feeling broken up about her condition. Through my cousin Ethel Laugheed, I got a kind English girl, Nancy, to stay with Mrs. Thomas while I was at the university and we carried on. Just before Christmas Morley got back home, and on Christmas Eve itself, Dr. John Morrow, a true friend through all this, insisted that Mrs. Thomas must now go to the hospital. She was becoming dangerously dehydrated because she was eating very little. There followed a month of failing strength, and she died on February 1. Our friend Edith Whicher Morrow insisted on getting back into uniform and nursing her for the final few days.

All through these months, getting down to the university had been my lifeline, and in February shortly after the funeral, came another twist in my future. Jane Appelbe, my study-mate and staunch friend, had been a great source of strength to me through the Fall. She was in the process of having interviews for university positions. One day she came back to our office in the cloisters after having seen Hugh Maclean at Falconer Hall. Hugh was looking for someone for the brand new York University English Department, housed temporarily in Falconer Hall on the U. of T. campus, but destined to move to Glendon College at Lawrence and Bayview in the Fall. Jane urged me to go to see him: "He'll never take anyone without teaching experience," she said, "and you're just right for the job." So I went. Hugh and I clicked at once. He was a Toronto Ph.D., a Renaissance specialist and a Woodhouse devotee, and we were close to the same age. Before I could really realize my luck, I was interviewed by Murray Ross, the President of York, and hired. It never occurred to me to have any requests, let alone demands, of my own, and when Ross told me my pay would be

$5000, I was delighted. I didn't exactly appreciate his reminding me that it was a generous sum to pay a woman, especially one in English, where many candidates were available. But I was in no mood to demur by so much as a word.

I had honestly not expected to get a job, particularly a job that I could manage along with the family, the house, the multitudinous responsibilities. I had gone into the Ph.D. programme because it was the one thing in the world that I wanted to do, and because my friends at Western had begun to suggest that only the 'union ticket' would give me security in the future for the teaching I loved. My combination of astonishment and satisfaction at the York appointment was sealed when, shortly, I met Woodhouse, and he congratulated me, saying, "I sent your name to York. I thought you'd be alright with MacLean." He was still, as he had for many years, placing his people all over Canada and I was more than honoured to be one of them. Morley and the boys took the news more calmly than I felt—they had always thought I'd get a job, or so they said. I pressed onward with my thesis and went down to Western to teach that summer with my morale sky-high.

The story of my dissertation, "Anna Jameson: The Making of a Reputation," and its later rebirth as her biography, *Love And Work Enough*, has been for me a thrilling saga. In my interest in women of the past, I've been nothing if not tunnel-visioned—the public speech for which I won the Robinette medal when I was fifteen was called "The Pioneers," and in it I was more interested in the meagre information I'd collected on 'women's work' than in anything else. In our course at Western, Susanna Moodie, Catharine Parr Traill and Anna Jameson bulked large and I read avidly of their experiences. Later, as I worked in Western's Library in 1943/4 and 1944/45 I shared in the excitement of publication when our Canadian specialist, Elsie Murray, published an edited version of Jameson's *Winter Studies And Summer Rambles.* Later still, when I taught the American-Canadian course in Western's Extension and Summer School programmes, I became firmly fixated on Anna Jameson. I can remember standing in the cafeteria lineup beside Murdo McKinnon, the Department Chair, and telling him that I'd like to publish an article on Anna. I'd already had my M.A. thesis published by Longman, but no one, least of all myself, was impressed by that, and I was not surprised when he laughed unbelievingly. He did, however later give me the valuable piece of advice that certainly assisted my admission into Toronto's Ph.D. programme. In the course of submitting a formal thesis proposal, I had read the extensive write-up on Anna in the *Dictionary Of National Biography.* I ended that proposal with a flight of fancy, likening what we knew of Anna to the strong colours and pattern on one side of a tapestry and promising to unravel the myriad threads on the other side. Woodhouse liked that too, for he told me so, much to my delight, and now, decades later, to my chagrin, when I want my exact wording it is irrevocably gone. Parochially Canadian then, and believing the *Winter Studies and Summer Rambles* to be the heart of her work, I was completely dim about the importance of her art criticism to say nothing of her *Characteristics Of Women*, the study of Shakespeare's heroines that, in the 1830s, established her as a well known writer both in England and on the continent.

    I found her name and fame recorded everywhere in 19th century volumes, for she had been a participator in London's literary life from the 1820s to the '60s. While there were those who couldn't abide her, there were few, if any, who could ignore her presence. By the fall of 1961 I had the first draft of the thesis expertly typed, thanks to the interest and Dutch doggedness of Tina Vandermeer, the Department Secretary at Western. While teaching at Western that summer, every day Tina would type the pages I had polished the day and evening before. If I hadn't done ten pages, Tina would nag me, good-naturedly. It was the first summer I was largely alone in London, for Steve was at Cadet Camp at Ipperwash on Lake Huron and, for part of the time, John was at a Young Men's Christian Association camp on Beausoleil island. I was free to work, and work I did!

I had had only two consultations about the whole thing with Professor Frye, on the first of which he asked me how much of her life I was going to cover and I replied, "the whole thing." On the second meeting I told him that I thought I'd found a place to stop, and he said, "Good. I was hoping you'd say that." And so "Anna Jameson: The Making of a Reputation" became my thesis, tracing her rise from an unknown, ambitious young governess-writer to a 'Literary Lion' on the London scene after the outstanding reviews of *Winter Studies And Summer Rambles In Canada* in 1838. My friend, Jane's thesis research took her into the same 19th century period. We 'talked 19th century' together regularly, and felt as if we had a large gallery of mutual friends and acquaintances. After beginning to teach at Glendon in the Fall of 1961 I spent some months revising once again and then submitted my thesis to the committee. In April I was examined by a daunting committee chaired by Brough Macpherson of the Economics Department and at Convocation in June I became a newly-fledged Ph.D. The thesis oral was by no means the terrifying ordeal that the

Generals had been, partly because the key members of the committee had signified their approval beforehand, and partly because Professor Woodhouse kindly met me outside the room and told me not to worry: "It will be alright."

It didn't take me long to begin planning a full biography. If I had hesitated at all, I was pushed from all sides, from well-wishers at Glendon to friends at home. I was soon on the hunt for letters, instituting a two-continent search, with a large map on my office wall at Glendon and a series of letters to every library I had ever heard of, inviting information. The replies were, once again, astonishing. From New York's Berg to California's Huntingdon, including of course the major collecting libraries such as the Widener, Wellesley, Yale and the University of Texas, I was informed of letters to and from Anna Jameson and virtually every literary figure on the 19th-century scene. Both the libraries' generosity in making me copies and their hospitality in inviting me to come and see their holdings were astounding.

Early in 1963, the Humanities' Association granted me $1,200 for research and I treated myself to a thrilling trip to Harvard, Yale, Wellesley and New York's Berg. At Yale I talked to the director of the great German collection there. I had hoped to get a visa to go to Munich, where there is a collection of about 200 letters from Anna Jameson to Ottilie von Goethe, her dear friend and the daughter-in-law of the poet. The Yale professor discouraged that idea thoroughly—so I stopped trying. I didn't much want to go to East Germany by myself anyhow. When Professor Needler of the University of Toronto's German Department retired at age seventy, he and his wife had gone on a lengthy trip to Munich, where he had copied out all the Jameson-Goethe letters later published by the University of Toronto Press, and the last thing written about Anna before I arrived on the scene. The German connection was to remain unexplored—the Iron Curtain prevented that. That brief research trip was thrilling for me, however, even if I had to cram it all into four days, so much in fact that I have only the sketchiest memories of those great libraries. A pity, and one I never rectified later, though I became an habitue of the Bodleian, Lincoln and Manchester College Libraries in Oxford, and the British Museum Collection in London.

My main bonanza, however, came with the publication of Malcolm Elwin's *Lord Byron's Wife* in the spring of 1963. In order to do my research son John and I were slated to leave for England on a U. of T. charter at the end of May, a month before Morley and Steve were to join us on our long-planned family trip overseas. We were booked into the Commonwealth Services Club on South Parks Road in Oxford, guaranteed as an ideal place for us by my Glendon colleagues, Don Rickerd and Denis Smith. I wrote to Malcolm Elwin in care of his English publisher, John Murray, asking for correspondence information, because I had long since realized that Anna and Lady Byron were close friends for years. When we arrived in Oxford there was a letter from Elwin waiting for us, inviting me to his home on Putsborough Sands in North Devon, where he would have waiting for us a ledger-book full of letters, some two hundred in all. To call that a thrill is to put it mildly! From start to finish the English trip was a dream-come-true and a great adventure: I became a permanent acolyte, especially of Oxford, the centre of our English experiences for many years.

Devon and the hospitality of the Elwins was yet another high spot of this first expedition, perhaps the high spot of the whole research. I went on a reconnoitring trip myself, taking a taxi from the railway station at Braunton to Putsborough, absolutely entranced by the wonderfully rugged views of cliffs and sea and by the movement of the tides which I had never seen before. Malcolm Elwin, his niece, Ginny and her husband, Brian Fell, welcomed me for lunch, provided beer, shrimp salad and home-made bread—and 19th-century conversation. As a professional biographer Malcolm had written of so many famous figures that he was absolutely saturated in their lives, loves and ways of speaking. To listen to him recall them as if he had been talking to them only yesterday was to feel totally validated in everything I was trying to do. He presented me with the ledger book and invited me to come back and copy it, letter by letter if I wished. Malcolm had total access to the huge store of Lovelace papers assembled by Lady Byron throughout her life. They were stored at that time in Coutts Bank, and he would go up to London and bring home the ledger books into which they had been copied word for word, a lifetime's project for one of her descendants. Out of this treasure hoard he had a whole series of Byron-Lovelace works planned, three of which were published before his death. To me, an unknown scholar, his generosity was largesse and friendliness beyond my dreams.

A few days later, John and I retraced the Oxford-Devon journey and registered at the Putsborough Sands hotel, a short walk along the cliff from the Elwins, looking out over the sea to the island of Lundy, dimly showing in the distance. Every day for most of a week we walked along the shore, John with his beloved toy soldiers, and increasingly fascinated by the rock pools left by the tide. Leaving him to play on the beach, I climbed the cliff to the Elwins' eyrie, a semi-circular, many windowed house of great charm and distinction, built right at the cliff's edge. I copied letters all day, breaking to take John back to the hotel for lunch. I met Malcolm's wife, Eve, only once on that trip and found her presence as imposing as one of the great stage Dames, Edith Evans, for instance. But later, and even that same summer when we all returned to the Putsborough and Morley and I were entertained to tea, she began to be the warm friend that she was thereafter.

When I had finished making my dissertation into a biography I found a willing typist in Marja Moens, the wife of a young colleague in biology, Peter Moens. That began one of the lengthiest and most satisfying friendships that York brought to me. Marja and I still meet several times a year. She has developed another identity as Maria Jacobs, accomplished poet, writer of a compelling memoir of the war years in Holland, *Precautions Against Death*, and, with a partner, proprietor of a successful poetry-publishing company, Wolsak and Wynne. Early in the revising process I had contacted Macmillan's, who rather snippily turned down my manuscript. Then Northrop Frye, who assured me that a biography would be eminently publishable, suggested the University of Toronto Press, of whose Board he was a member. I handed in the manuscript, finished in the last months of '63 and early '64, and settled in for a long wait. When, finally I got the news, it was good: Francess Halpenny brought me the message as I sat in the reception area of the old U. of T. Press quarters above the U. of T. Bookstore. She had forgotten my appointment and was apologetic, but she assured me that it would be "alright."

It WAS alright, but it was not speedy, finally coming out in the Centennial spring of 1967. By the summer of 1965 it had passed the Humanities' Association inspection and was promised a publication grant, Diane Nelles had been assigned as copy editor and the book was well underway. I did hope that it would be published in 1966, thinking that it would drown unnoticed in the midst of

The Apprenticeship Years 147

Centennial hoopla, but all was well. Mary and Ron Mathieson gave me a splendid publication party at the Engineers' Club, the reviews in Toronto papers were good, especially Carl Klinck's in the *Globe and Mail*, and I basked in the pleasure of a really fine design and production. Meanwhile in England, Malcolm Elwin, who was a reader and advisor for Macdonald's, had recommended it for publication there; greatly to the delight of both myself and the Press, they bought pages for an edition of 1,000 for publication in England. When Morley and I were in England later that summer we were lavishly lunched by one of their editors, and I took the keenest pleasure in picking up a copy in Blackwell's and having Morley take my picture setting it in their front window. There was one miserable review in the annual "Letters in Canada" section of the *U. of Toronto Quarterly* by a young (very young) historian, Michael Cross, who wondered why the Press would publish a book about a "whining, self-pitying woman," but otherwise the whole thing was a splendid experience. I often wonder how Cross fared during the yeasty years of the Women's Movement, just then on the brink of plowing down such sexists as he. Some years later it was also gratifying to have it republished by the Press in a quality paperback edition. Only a few short years had passed, but no male reviewer would have dared then to question the publication of one of the 19th century's 'New Women.' Feminism had arrived!

But the best part of it all was that first major adventure in research, with material which turned out to be so lavishly supplied in 19th-century publications, and after that, in preparation for the biography, with the treasure hunt which brought, as a bonus to it all, dear and lasting friends, the Elwins, and from the Commonwealth Services club, Anne Innes, the manageress, and Jim and Trudi Rowe, the Club's Director and his wife.

Chapter XI

Glendon in the Early Years

On a Monday morning in early September, 1961, I made my lengthy trek from 88 Mountview, just west of Keele and Bloor, to Glendon College, at Bayview and Lawrence. It took me about an hour, on bus and subway, and my main anxiety then, far more than my faculty appointment in a brand new university, was how to work in the travelling problem with being at home with home-and-mother responsibilities. Steve was fifteen and in Grade twelve; John ten and in Grade six; my appointment was the delight of my life, but for all of that, there was no way to alleviate the not-so-vague guilt I felt in beginning to be a full-time working woman. I'd already been teaching part-time for Western for fourteen years, but that was all relatively easy, for summer classes were in the mornings only and winter Extension was always on Saturdays. Even then, I had been plagued by guilt, enhanced by the overpoweringly mother-in-the-home context of the time, the 'Leave it to Beaver' world. No amount of guilt could completely dim the triumph of the new job, however, or the knowledge that my Ph.D. thesis was in its final stages.

Glendon had been the impressive old Wood estate, and its beauty and spaciousness were well in evidence that September day, with the newly constructed York Hall in the final stages of readiness for the influx of students the next week—110 freshmen and women plus the original 70, who had spent their first year at Falconer Hall

Glendon in the Early Years 149

on the University of Toronto campus. For those first years, York gave Toronto's three-year Ordinary Degree course and students were awarded a Toronto B.A. The new university's site had been leased from the University of Toronto for a token sum. The control centre of Glendon that day was the present dining room. There the various secretaries were set up, and there I met Florence Knight, the English Department's secretary, and Hugh Maclean, the 'Acting Head' of the Department who had recommended my hiring (there were only the two of us). I was dazzled by the spaciousness of the office I was given, on the north side of the ground floor, overlooking the ravine, just then on the verge of turning to a glorious Fall gold. I was quickly introduced to Hugh's favourite people among the Faculty members, Douglas Lochead, Librarian, Lorna Fraser, his assistant, Norman Endler of Psychology, Donald Rickerd and Vicky Draper, the Registrar and his assistant.

I was also quickly indoctrinated into the official workings of the university, for there was a Faculty Council that very day. York's minimal Faculty at that time included: Donald Rickerd, Bursar, Mr. Langille of Physical Education; Bill Small, the Comptroller; John Armour, the on-site Engineer and Superintendent of Building; Art Johnson, Physics; David Fowle, Biology; John Seeley, Sociology; Lionel Rubinoff and John MacFarlane, Philosophy, Lester Pronger and Donald Jackson, French; Alice Turner, Mathematics; Norman Endler, Psychology; John Bruckmann, History; Denis Smith, Political Science; and two members just arrived from overseas, Douglas Verney, Political Science; and George Doxey, Economics. The senior statesmen were Irwin Pounder, retired Head of the Mathematics Department, U. of T.; and Edgar McInnis, also retired, a former U. of T. History Department Head.

George Tatham, Geographer, was already well into his life's vocation as Dean of Students, totally committed and tirelessly enthusiastic. Alice Turner was the only other woman, and she took me under her wing from the start. The star turn was Murray Ross's arrival at the Council in his gorgeously embroidered presidential robes; the air around Maclean and some of the others frosted over whenever Ross or Seeley spoke, and there was no delay between my arrival at York and my awareness of the factional nature of the faculty, even at this early stage.

Before this first day was over, Dr. Pounder had asked me if I would like to drive back and forth with him, thereby alleviating my greatest source of anxiety, for he lived within two blocks of Mountview, and he drove me every day for that first year, becoming my friend and wise mentor in university ways as well. Before the week was over, I was completely at home with the prevailing political climate; for certain members of the Faculty, who for me speedily became my party of choice, Seeley and Ross could do no right. In fact there was a daily underground of memos amongst the 'men of goodwill' who were constantly torn between frustration, disbelief, rage and amusement at many of the wilder ideas that were landmarks of York's beginning. Seeley was the instigator of many of these, and the most outstanding occasion of pained embarrassment on the part of my friends was his writing and delivering of an "Ode to York" at one of many public occasions in those first years. There were many doomed endeavours to make York into an elite small four-year Arts College—no one who had been living in Toronto for the previous decade, reading the *Globe And Mail*'s excellent educational commentator, Bascom St. John, could fail to know that the province was on the brink of a major university boom, and that the Metro

Toronto area, of all others, was the least likely to be funded provincially for an elitist luxury.

The students arrived and teaching began—no great strain on any of us in those early days. My load was only five hours a week, and unlike all the men, I was not involved in planning committees—a definite compensation in being female and too lowly to qualify as a partner in any of the major decisions that were made daily, and almost as often, unmade. It never occurred to anyone in authority that, with fourteen years of teaching behind me, and a great deal of knowledge of the inner workings of Western in general and their Extension Department in particular, I might have had a few good ideas about the immanent beginning of Atkinson College, designed to be York's adult education and night school wing. Instead, absolute newcomers were hired and in some cases imported, who had absolutely no experience or knowledge of the Canadian university scene. Some, like Harry Girling who came to us from South Africa, were quick and willing learners; others, like Neil Morrison, formerly of the C.B.C., were charming and affable people, but scarcely born educators. Others simply had no notion of what the Canadian educational system was all about, or what its customs and traditions were; a few, alas, were too arrogant to care. The amazing thing is not that York had many an anguished growing pain, but that it successfully grew at all. Only the unrelenting provincial and public pressure for its success was stronger than the often wild and disaster-prone planning and factional feuds that went on day in day out.

York had successfully courted publicity as it began to function, a good deal of it being announcements of one kind and another about its enlightened attitude to students. "Tea and Talks" was one such innovation, a series of informal gatherings of students and professors or well-known figures such as Morley Callaghan. Seeley loved to function with a group of students literally sitting at his feet, drinking in the master's words of wisdom. To me, used to the more impersonal student-faculty relations of Western and the University of Toronto, such occasions were artificial and nonsensical and I don't remember that they continued beyond that year. The faculty-student advisory system was undoubtedly a good idea, though it was carried too far into a Big Sister-Big Brother, hand-holding pattern in those early days. Fortunately, that too dwindled and died quickly. A certain pressure was put on faculty members to take part in coaching or otherwise involving themselves in various sports—that, too was completely out of the question as far as I was concerned though some colleagues did honestly enjoy their involvement and were good at coaching their sport of choice.

Dining-room etiquette included a dictum from Murray Ross that all students should wear jackets and ties, and that there should be no brown bag lunches, another mercifully brief attempt at elitism. Silliest of all, in the opinion of many of us, was the tradition of the 'High Table' at which faculty were supposed to eat in splendid isolation from the students. Much was made of the first Senate, and its members' names were engraved on a brass plate at the Senate Chambers' entrance, and on public occasions, much was made of the distinguished academic antecedents of certain of the Faculty, Hugh Maclean among them, who was enraged to hear himself being introduced as a "graduate of Andover and Princeton." Notice might even have been taken of me, had I remembered to tell either Maclean or Ross that I had had a book published in 1946, but I quite honestly did not think of that in the course of my interviews with either of them, and Hugh only found out to his great surprise when I showed him the programme for my Ph.D. Oral examination in the spring of 1962. 'Publish or Perish' had yet to become a term of universal academic awareness.

The first 70 students had been treated as such a special breed and with so much press publicity that they were notably inclined to prima donna behaviour and the influx of the second group that Fall came as a distinct blessing. Furthermore, the numbers were such that student activities could really begin to flourish, everything from the first *Protem*, the student newspaper, to the councils and committees that are so much a part of campus life. The campus was lively with activity, some for students and faculty together, some for faculty alone, for no week passed without some visiting expert arriving and being feted at reception or dinner, and the whole place was awash with sherry, the preferred drink of college conviviality. On very special occasions, Murray Ross entertained faculty and guests at the York Club—black tie occasions were a commonplace. Every secretary dutifully made and served tea, coffee or the ubiquitous sherry as part of her job. Those secretaries deserve a special chapter in any story of the young York: many of them, Florence Knight, Florence Allen, Vivienne James, Gladys Neilson, for instance, were highly experienced women trained in the old-time tradition of secretarial service that speedily made them the backbone of Glendon's structure. Their secretarial skills were impressive, and so were their social skills, for they became the discreet confidantes of faculty and student body alike. My good friend, Florence Knight, had no great opinion of my interest in tea-brewing—on one rare occasion when she was unavoidably away, she called me to say, "Mrs. Thomas, Please try to make Professor Maclean a good cup of tea."

As each building on the campus was completed, its

official opening was the occasion for yet another grand event. John Bruckman, of the History department, had written a Latin song for which the brand new choir's director, Mr. McAuley, composed the music, various notables were assembled—on various occasions Leslie Frost, John Robarts and Maryon and Lester Pearson added lustre to the occasions—the Faculty, suitably gowned, the students sometimes obligingly adding a touch of pressworthy highjinks to the scene, the Board of Governors, staff, and assorted parents all assembled to play their parts in yet another ritual celebrating yet another early York milestone.

'Traditions' were formulated and established with the greatest of ease: a much publicized competition for a suitable motto was won by a High School student from Scarborough with his entry, *Tentanda Via* (The Way Must Be Tried).The colours red and white and 'the white rose of York' speedily became part of the scene, and the blessing of England's York University was conferred by a visit from its Chancellor, Lord James.That occasion remains particularly vivid in memory for the spur-of-the-moment largesse of Mrs. John David Eaton, one of our Board of Governors. A number of Canadian paintings from her private collection were on loan around the campus at the time, one particularly handsome Riopelle gracing the dining room wall behind the High Table dais. After the visitor had spoken in due praise of the entire York undertaking, making special mention of the painting behind him, Mrs. Eaton was seen to whisper to George Tatham who rose, removed the painting from the wall, and presented it to Lord James on the spot, a stunning example of a generosity for which the Eaton family has never been particularly noted. Members of the Board were very involved in the early days, particularly Mr. John Proctor of the Bank of Nova Scotia, who was the Board's supervisor of building, and Peter Scott of Wood Gundy, the Board's Chairman. Anything was possible in those early days; visiting V.I.P.s were a dime a dozen, so much so that having lunch at High Table was almost never a quiet and private affair; whether for or against the rapidly growing establishment, one's days were never dull!

From the beginning, the designing of a curriculum was the faculty's chief concern. Emissaries were sent far and wide, all over the States and on various junkets abroad to observe and report on the various curricula of small, four-year Arts Colleges. Endless meetings were held, from which I, I now know, was fortunate to be excluded, for feelings ran high, factions formed, broke and re-formed, often bitterly, and the cost in human carnage was high. There was a great deal of pressure on a very few people who often behaved like the famed Polish Parliament who regularly met on horseback and rode off in all directions. The separation of Departments and Divisions, the matter of compulsory courses, the establishment of "Modes of Reasoning," a brand of up-market mathematics, these and every other item of the curriculum to be, when the day came that York should separate from the U. of Toronto and be off and running on its own, were matters of high concern and impassioned rhetoric. For the few of us who were almost entirely spectators of all this, there was also a daily calling to mind of the fabled ant-covered log going down the rapids, with every ant thinking he was steering. The experience of Professors Pounder and McInnis in matters academic and procedural was crucial, and essential steps towards orderly progress were achieved when Ronald Earle, retired Dean of Queen's, arrived early in 1962. The appointment of Jack Saywell as his second-in-command, and then within the next two years as Dean, heralded an achievement of balance that was precarious indeed, but was recognizably and in time solidly, academic.

It was not long before the fate of the much touted, exclusively four-year curriculum was seen to be on quicksand and it became necessary to plan as well for a three-year 'Ordinary Degree.' It was also not long before the spectre of forced growth began to haunt the die-hard devotees of the small college concept that had been so attractive to a number of the first Faculty recruits. The day that Premier John Robarts, speaking at one of our 'Great Occasions,' announced that we, as well as all Ontario universities, must prepare to admit students with Grade 13 percentages of between 55 and 60, lives in my memory in a kind of "told-you-so" way. My many friends and former colleagues at Western had known what the future held for some time, and talked of nothing else than the swiftly approaching unprecedented growth. The rumours and mutterings about a large campus grew speedily to a roar, the interposing of Valleyanna Drive made it impossible for York to grow towards Sunnybrook, and the 400-odd acre tract in the city's far northwest became the scene of hectic building activity. A great deal of moving and shifting among early Faculty took place in the midst of all this, often with deep disappointment at the rapid disintegration of the early dream that had brought some of them to York, and sometimes with lasting bitterness.

I finished my thesis, "Anna Jameson: The Making of a Reputation," in the spring of 1962 as I had undertaken to do when hired. Northrop Frye, my supervisor, gave it his approval, and in late April I was examined and passed. In fact, in terms of the long, often anxious process, begun five years before, the final Oral was an antilimax. Still, it made me a valid academic, consolidating my position at York and giving me a certain glow of satisfaction in the approval of family and friends, especially the friends at Western who had given me so many teaching opportunities for so long.

Hugh Maclean was angry on my behalf because my salary wasn't immediately adjusted, and because of the three of us who had been hired at the same time, all Ph.D's unfinished, I was the only one who finished on schedule. I wasn't particularly disturbed, however—the satisfaction of the degree achieved was for me of paramount importance.

* * *

On May 27, 1963, son John, 12, and I flew on a U. of Toronto chartered Britannia aircraft to London, the beginning of our family's long-planned trek to England and the continent. On Coronation morning ten years before, the four of us in bed together listening to the Abbey ceremony and dazzled by it, we had promised to take the boys to England ten years hence. Then Morley would have a long leave after twenty years in the Meteorological Service, and then we would have saved money, mostly summer-school money, for the great adventure. Very shortly our friends the Stevensons of Petrolia joined in the plan, their two girls, Jane and Judy, just in between our Steve and John in age, and their mother, like me, employed, though she became a full-time teacher of Commercial in the Petrolia High School some years before my York adventure began. John and I were going ahead of the rest on that May flight, however, because I had received a Humanities' Association award of $1,200 to assist me in extending my Jameson thesis into a full biography of Anna. Glendon colleagues Donald Rickerd and Denis Smith had enthusiastically directed me to the Commonwealth Services Club in

Oxford, and Anne Innes, its Manageress, had welcomed us by letter, even offering to keep her eye on John while I explored the Bodleian, the mecca of all libraries for scholars travelling to England.

We arrived in England one early morning after a thirteen-hour flight in a Britannia turbo-prop, settled at the Rubens Hotel on Buckingham Palace Road, and embarked on a few days of sight-seeing all the landmarks that Morley had seen two years earlier when he spent some three weeks at meetings there. On an idyllic June 1, after watching the Trooping of the Colours, we arrived in Oxford at the Club that was to be my favorite place in all the overseas world until its closing in 1969. Two old ivy-covered Victorian houses joined by a glass-covered walk-way, it had been the Parks Hotel before the war, the Coal Board Headquarters during the war, and shortly thereafter had been taken over by the Colonial Office to provide a residence for men training to be colonial administrators. In its first years, the men had been British, destined for the many imperial holdings abroad, especially in Africa. As time passed, and the weakening of imperial ties accelerated, the residents came more and more from abroad to be trained in administration and then to go back home to their own countries to be a part of their various administrations. The whole place was warm and welcoming, verging on threadbare in its furnishings, but always, under Anne Innes, with the help of two full-time au pair girls, Franco, the temperamental cook, and various part-time helpers, extremely clean and well run. All the bedrooms were large, high-ceilinged, provided with single couch-beds, wash-hand basins, gas heaters, old-fashioned wardrobes, and full bathrooms down the hall. John and I were given a kind of suite, a small room, which pleased him no end, and opened out of a large one for me.

We overlooked the garden, a large, treed, green expanse, with beds of riotously blooming roses along its borders and a vegetable garden at its back, up next to the impressive tower of Manchester College. The strange, low, windowless structure in its midst turned out to be a former air-raid shelter. Croquet was played with ruthless enthusiasm by the inhabitants of the Club; in the long early summer evenings, the "thunk" of mallets and balls punctuated our evenings. The very first night, as the players left the lawn and darkness finally fell, I heard my first nightingale, a fountain of song, and a culminating enchantment in what was for me a fairy-tale situation. My Jameson adventures, especially with the Elwins in Devon, have already been recounted. The entire summer was magic for me, and our tour with the Stevensons was a six-week part of it. We travelled England in a Volkswagen van with Morley driving, and covered a good part of Europe on a Global Tour bus with a fine courier called Franco who kept us all, especially the children, both informed and suitably under his thumb—and we ended up as firm friends as we had begun. An achievement that has been unceasingly and deservedly a source of pride ever since!

Chapter XII

The Golden Years
1968-1980

I moved from Glendon and began to teach on the York campus at Keele and Steeles in the Fall of 1968. From that time, and through the first half of the seventies, we enjoyed what we now call "the golden years." They were wonderful growth years, not only for Ontario's new universities, of which York was the oldest by a few months, but for Canadian Literature in particular and the rise of Canadian Studies in general. The public's intense enthusiasm for Pierre Trudeau combined with an equal enthusiasm for Canada's centenary celebrations in 1967, produced a fertile soil for all things Canadian, including literary studies. 1968 was the year that Douglas Fetherling arrived in Toronto and met Dave Godfrey who, with Dennis Lee was then in the process of founding the House of Anansi Press, one of the many entrepreneurial projects then simmering among young Toronto activists. Godfrey and Lee were two of the busiest movers and shakers of cultural nationalism, Dave having recently returned from teaching for C.U.S.O. in Ghana—hence the adoption of the name Anansi, the ubiquitous spider and trickster god. Fetherling's *Travels By Night*, the first volume of his autobiography, contains a warmly reminiscent account of those days, when anything seemed possible and many remarkable things were.

To a generation accustomed to the variety and, often, the elegance of design and production of contemporary Canadian books, the sheer surprise and visual satisfaction

The Golden Years

of Anansi's innovations must be stressed. For decades of students the Department of Education's prescribed High School text, *Short Stories And Essays*, and the University of Toronto's undergraduate Text, *Representative Poetry*, had inflicted on the young the absolute nadir of book design and publishing. We teachers were accustomed to visits from salesmen from the publishers, most of whom seemed to take a perverse delight in discouraging suggestions for new publications: "you couldn't guarantee us any sale on that," or, "we'd never make any money on that—or that—or that" was the common response. Now, suddenly, to see Margaret Atwood's *The Circle Game*, or Godfrey's *Death Goes Better With Coca-cola* was to have the door open on another world. Both of them were among the first half-dozen of Anansi's publications and wonderful to behold!

But even more important for the spread of Canadian literature throughout our school system were the splendidly innovative works that Anansi published. Where before the few of us who taught the literature were always its most hopeful proselytisers, suddenly people were reviewing Margaret Atwood's *Survival*, Northrop Frye's *The Bush Garden*. Our field was given a powerful and continuous momentum from the outside. Anansi's publication of Roch Carrier's *La Guerre, Yes Sir!*, translated by Sheila Fischman, as Jim Polk wrote in *A Canadian Forum* article of 1982, "almost overnight became the book a student read to learn about The Other Solitude." Those of us who were part of that time, whether in the midst of the yeasty brew or on the margins, as I was, remember those days and their prime movers with affection and gratitude. Our literary landscape changed then, immeasurably for the better. Courses sprang up in every university because students began to demand them, and the 'poor relation' among departmental course offerings quite suddenly became the darling of students and administration alike. I had offered the first York Graduate course in Canadian Literature in 1968/9. I had three students including Frank Birbalsingh, a recent arrival from Guyana who was studying for a Ph.D. at the University of London. The next year I had 22 in my Graduate seminar, really not a seminar, but a class, all of them eager for some training in the Canadian field, and several of them determined to go on to Ph.D.s. Nothing shows more clearly the sudden rise in interest than that class enrollment, a number that continued at that level until early in the seventies when our department imposed a capping number on individual classes.

From 1967 on Canadian nationalism was at its height, a period of a few years which saw Canadian content appear on secondary school courses as well as university ones. I undertook to write the guidebook to Canadian Literature, *Our Nature-our Voices*, because former students who were training for the teaching profession at O.C.E. kept telling me that they had no resources in the Canadian field and that they intended to see that Canadian fiction and poetry were on their agenda. Two Carleton University academics, Robin Matthews and James Steele, kept up a constant barrage of publicity for Canadian content in all courses and for Canadian teachers to teach on every level of the educational system. Tom Symons, the President of the recently established Trent University in Peterborough, was named Head of a Royal Commission to look into Canadian content in curricula all across Canada, and, in general, Canadianism was flowering as, a few short years ago, we could never have hoped that it would.

Ryerson Of Upper Canada, the book that was written

in my sabbatical of 1967/8, was published in June of 1969. In May, Mother had died after some months in hospital with her chronic kidney condition; almost immediately after I had gone to England for a three-week trip, a combination working and relaxing trip. When I left, I was still more than a little rocky emotionally, and I simply caught the plane, a students' charter, almost literally without money. I had changed $25 into English money, and landed at Gatwick airport at two in the morning to find that the Rubens Hotel, to which I had written for a room, did not have a room, and I had only the Commonwealth Services Club in Oxford as a refuge. Miraculously, one of the cab-drivers who showed up to serve numbers of travellers, found several fares for Heathrow, and good-naturedly assured me that he'd go on to Oxford with me. He did—and for something under 10 pounds he took me to the door, barrelling through the countryside in the middle of the night with me feeling as if I was in the midst of an English mystery story, by Ngaio Marsh, perhaps, or Margery Allingham. We arrived in Oxford about 6 o'clock, he dropped me off, accepting without a murmur a pitiably small sum, to which I'd added a bit of change that Morley had saved from an earlier trip. The Club was never locked, I sank into one of its shabby arm chairs and felt blessedly at home. Sigrid, Anne Innes's Swedish helper, came downstairs about 7.30 and by nine o'clock I was having a wonderful mid-morning nap!

That was the June of the closing of the Commonwealth Services Club, the place that had been such a haven for me since 1963. It was a particularly poignant time, with the last class of Commonwealth, mostly African, students in residence, Anne feeling very badly, but indefatigably planning outings for everyone, and a final great party in the last week of the month. I went with the club on a bus-tour to Longleat, the occasion when

Anne and I, in the queue of sight-seeing visitors, came upon a Holbein portrait swinging on the wall—someone had just crayoned a moustache on it. The line passed quickly on, no one wanting to be implicated, I suppose. This was also, as I have recorded elsewhere, in a chapter on our friendship, my first meeting with Margaret Laurence, when I went by bus to Penn to have lunch with her at Elm Cottage. It was also the time when my usual trip to visit the Elwins was considerably dampened by Malcolm's illness. He had had a heart-attack and was still in bed, but he and Eve and Sally greeted me with all of their usual warmth and I was made to feel that my coming had lifted his spirits.

Almost immediately after the publication of *Ryerson Of Upper Canada* in 1969, and very shortly after Campbell Hughes, of Ryerson Press, my publisher, had granted me $1,000 to do research on my guidebook, the Press was sold to McGraw-Hill, an American firm. There was a huge outcry against the sale, for the atmosphere of vociferous nationalism still prevailed; for me the result was, of course, the take-over press's complete lack of interest in the book in preparation, to say nothing of their complete burying of *Ryerson Of Upper Canada*. The last thing they wanted was further public reminder of the former Ryerson Press. Dave Godfrey, with whom a warm friendship had developed after my first, small *Margaret Laurence*, in a series of which he was the General Editor, was now involved in another publishing venture, New Press. With no hesitation he took over *Our Nature-our Voices* and shortly published my guidebook, a handsome production lavishly illustrated with photographs from the National Archives that I had gathered on an overnight trip to Ottawa in the summer of 1970. Since the mid-sixties Dave had been a friend and supporter of Margaret

Laurence. He had first of all admired her Ghanian stories, a bond forged by his own Ghanaian experience. His *The New Ancestors*, a novel that won the Governor General's award, was set in the newly-liberated Ghana. Dave was influential in Margaret's appointment as Writer-in-Residence at the University of Toronto in 1969/70. I remember with affection and gratitude our association and the times when he and Ellen, his wife, and their children, John, Rebecca and Sam, came to our place to visit Margaret and us. In the mid-seventies he also spent a year teaching in the Humanities Division at York, a very special year for his students and myself. When he lost faith in Toronto as the hub of good things for Canadian culture, he moved to Victoria, taking a position at the university there, and devoting much of his time to the burgeoning world of computers. He was, and is, a 'Renaissance Man,' vastly talented in many areas.

The seventies were my times of maximum variety and professional satisfactions. In the summer of '70 I taught Summer School at Trent in Peterborough, renting my former colleague, Denis Smith's large and historic old house and enjoying various visitors, Morley on weekends, of course, Carl and Margaret Klinck, Mary and Earle Sanborn and Mary Brown at other times. Steve and Linda, his wife, had gone overseas to travel before settling down to teach at Eerde, a private school at Ommen in Holland, for a year, John was busy being a counsellor at Camp Kandalore, and for recreation I was writing my guidebook as well as sewing madly, a hobby that I had taken up during mother's final illness and one that gave me much relaxation and satisfaction. My menopausal syndrome, I always called it, and I believe it was that!

After Summer School, Morley and I went to England, visiting Margaret at Elm Cottage and then going on to see

Anne Innes in Oxford and the Elwins in Devon. On this trip we took a very large, sun-ripened August tomato over to Margaret, a treat she never forgot. I came back to York having become a brass-rubbing enthusiast, thanks to Nancy Whitla, my colleague Bill's wife, who took me in hand and oversaw my rubbing of a splendid brass at Waterperry near Oxford, one which has hung in our upstairs study ever since. I did a great many brass rubbings after that, specializing in brasses of women, and delighting in having friends at home who asked me to bring a rubbing back for them. I was fortunate to be an enthusiast in the very last decade of easy access to brasses. Now it is necessary to go to rubbing centres and work on mock-ups, for eager hobbyists such as I were ruining the brasses all over England by over- rubbing.

That was the Fall that I instituted a new third year course at York, English 334, English and French-Canadian literature, the French Canadian in translation. Even though I, like most others, was enthusiastic about the Trudeau government's policy of bilingualism, I was also soberly convinced that most students had better know about Quebec literature in translation, because they were unlikely ever to read it in French. Consequently I had a grand time devising a course that included some of the classic Quebec novels, Ringuet's *Thirty Acres*, and Carrier's *La Guerre, Yes Sir!* for instance, as well the many novels available in English Canada, from Laurence's *The Stone Angel* to Margaret Atwood's *Surfacing*. Only in a new university could we have instituted such a course so easily, and even so, there were some murmurs from the French Department at this eroding of their legitimate field. However, none of these were in any way serious, and the course remains a popular and constant offering in our department. For some time we had had a large Canadian survey course for second year. Now, with a new third-year course, as well as specialized courses planned for 4th year, our Canadian offerings were much enhanced. From that time on I taught a Graduate course in Canadian Fiction, the third-year course, and a fourth year course in African and Caribbean Literature. Late in the seventies, I instituted a fourth year course in Canadian first person narrative fiction and autobiography which was a new and major interest.

In the summer of 1971 I taught at the University of British Columbia. Donald Stephens and Bill New had both asked me, but it was Donald's Graduate course that I was to be in charge of. We rented a house from one of the men in the English Department, Morley came with me for a month, and then for a final two weeks I lived on campus in U.B.C.'s luxurious Faculty Club, given to the university by a wealthy lumber magnate. We had a good summer, travelling up to Whitehorse to visit Morley's colleague Herb Wahl and Dorreene, his wife, over a long weekend, and thoroughly enjoying our experience of the north. We came away equally impressed by the Wahls' hospitality and by the vast distances which residents take so for granted—also tired, very tired, for we weren't used to the almost constant daylight of the northern summertime or the general busyness of life there. In Vancouver various colleagues at U.B.C. and Simon Fraser were most hospitable, and my class was small and easy.

It was a good experience, but U.B.C. seemed overly regimented after the experimental nature of so many initiatives at York, and I was glad to get back on familiar academic ground. Petty rules and regulations were something new to me: I was astonished when Donald asked me to hold my classes in his office, explaining that it would be too difficult bureaucratically to be assigned a classroom. I had gone to Vancouver with a prescription for vitamin B12 shots from my doctor. I was used to having it administered by the nurse in our Health Centre at York—not so at U.B.C.: in fact they absolutely refused to honour the prescription, seeming horrified that I would even ask. The final evidence of U.B.C.'s rigidity was the difficulty in collecting my pay cheque: all faculty had to stand in line and present identification. The man just ahead of me was Kenneth Hare, formerly President of U.B.C. When he failed to have the proper identification, the clerk refused to serve him. He told her that he was a former President—it made no difference. All in all, I flew home with relief.

In the spring of 1971 I had attended the Learneds at Memorial University in Newfoundland and had become President of A.C.U.T.E. (the Association of University Teachers of English) for the year '71/72. This had been arranged previously by Michael Collie, a colleague who had taken on the Presidency for a two-year term the previous spring, but who had been appointed York's Dean of Graduate Studies and so felt forced to give up the Association position. I was delighted—years back, Marion Smith of U.B.C., later Brock, had been one of the founders of A.C.U.T.E., but there had never been a woman President, and I was happy to serve. As in many situations at that time, I was fortunate in being in the right place at the right time! I was not in the least surprised when, at the meetings at Memorial, Collie told me that he would announce my name at the final banquet and not before, in case of possible objections. I was, however, obstreperous in demanding and getting a place at the Head Table on that occasion, in order to make my own little speech of acceptance. Such were still the politics of academic feminism, and Eliza's Chorus, "Just you wait, 'Enry 'Iggins, just you wait" played often, if silently, in our heads.

A.C.U.T.E. was some fifteen years old then, and had a membership of between three and four hundred academics across the country but it was still a gangling adolescent, relatively unorganized, with no constitution, no bulletin or news letter, and no Journal. Membership lists and other records were haphazardly kept, there was no policy of preliminary vetting of paper-proposals for the annual meetings, no financial support from the Canada Council, and no standardized agreement of support from the executive's home university. Every two years the executive moved, establishing the records in yet another university (a good way to insure maximum chaos). There was, however, a fairly well-established tradition of support for the aggregate of 'Learned Societies' on the part of the various universities, one of whom agreed every year to host the Learneds as an entire group. Thanks to the busy and knowledgeable activism of various other member societies, notably the historians, political scientists, psychologists and sociologists, the Learneds had flourished.

Janet Lewis, a friend and colleague in our department, agreed to be secretary-treasurer, and quite soon we began to have a very good time indeed. Jack Saywell, York's Dean of Arts, agreed to give us part-time secretarial support. Along with our normal teaching loads, we managed to organize the books and the membership list, as well as instituting a cross-country survey of women English Department Faculty. It was certainly the first one, and perhaps the only one ever done, and one which also went to Ottawa, for the Status of Women Survey under the leadership of Florence Bird was just then getting underway. Our survey gave us all kinds of useful information about our colleagues, and some that then seemed esoterically charming, such as "Fencing" listed as the favourite hobby of Juliet McMaster, a well-known Alberta professor. I had a weekend planning meeting at McGill, the future site of the 1972 meetings, with Peter Buitenhuis, who had agreed to be McGill's representative. Most important, I went to Ottawa to ask Marcia McClung, at that time a Canada Council official, for support money. Credit for that move must be shared with Douglas Verney, a friendly York Political Scientist, whose society had been collecting such a bounty for some years already. Once we knew about the precedent, we were swift to follow up, and once we made personal application, the Canada Council came through nobly at so much per membership, though I have long since forgotten the exact figures.

At the end of my presidency, the Annual Meeting of 1972, A.C.U.T.E. ratified a constitution that was the result of a one day's committee meeting early in the winter, attended by our Vice-President, George Baldwin of Alberta, Paul Fleck and Ron Bates of Western, who had agreed to be President and Secretary-Treasurer-Elect, Peter Buitenhuis of McGill, Janet and myself. At the same meeting we set up an official journal planning committee. Their proposals were ratified the next year, and *English Studies In Canada*, its first editor Lauriat Lane Jr. of U.N.B., was on its way. Peer vetting of paper proposals was an acknowledged early necessity, as was a proper newsletter and a membership list containing information about our colleagues' various fields of teaching and research.

With no rules or strictures in place, Janet and I had the intense pleasure of devising the entire three-day programme for McGill, the task much expedited by our fashioning of a large chart that hung for the entire year on my office wall. We marked it off in squares for days and hours and began with our wish-lists for plenary sessions —panels of distinguished scholars and writers who would, we knew, draw the entire membership into their orbits. For the other sessions we sent out a call for papers, and much of our time was spent in balancing the contents of those squares on my office wall among the proposals from colleagues in the various literary fields and the various sections of the country. It gave us a wonderful illusion of power, never to be so fully realized again by an executive, as it happened, for by the next year a system of vetting was in place.

As for the hopeful plenaries—no one turned us down: Malcolm Ross of Dalhousie chaired a panel, Roy Daniells of U.B.C. another. Edith Fowke and Northrop Frye, old friends and for many years co-workers on *The Canadian Forum*, and Carl Klinck, editor-in-chief of *The Literary History Of Canada* were star panelists; Balachandra Rajan of Western and Eddie Baugh of the University of the West Indies were enormously effective speakers in other special sessions. It was on the plenary panel of writers—Hugh MacLennan, Margaret Laurence and Dave Godfrey—that Hugh MacLennan told us that he would have to retire from McGill the following year with a pension of a miserable $2,200.00, a joltingly memorable statement. Working on the thesis that banquets were boring, especially in Montreal, the city of enticing restaurants, I negotiated instead with Jack McClelland to give the membership a wine and cheese party. Just then, in the heyday of the New Canadian Library's stunning success and the pinnacle of optimistic Canadianism, he was happy to oblige, instituting an A.C.U.T.E. tradition that was to continue for a number of years and then was taken over by Jack David and Robert Lecker of ECW Press.

The very small book exhibit, usually the University of Toronto Press's virtual monopoly, was much enhanced that year by a large trailer of Canadian publications master-minded by Dave Godfrey and James Lorimer, yet another successful manifestation of their boundless cultural entrepreneurship and, in those days, its success. Janet and I and our helpers, Mary Louise Craven, John Lennox and David Silver, former students, good friends and colleagues from York, swam around happily, stimulated by the obvious approval of our membership. Strangely, but understandably, we were not invited to the party given by Donald Theall, Chairman of the McGill Department: against his protestations, I had insisted on a report at the General Meeting from a committee headed by Theall and so earned his lasting enmity. For me, the meetings were a warm vindication of more than two decades of involvement in the career that I loved. As well, and throughout the year I thoroughly enjoyed various meetings of other committees and societies to which I was bidden as President of A.C.U.T.E. Most particularly I enjoyed attending various conferences at various universities throughout the year, especially a George Eliot conference at Western, a Bibliographic one at U.B.C., and a Writers' Conference at U.N.B. I firmly believed in "consciousness raising" across the country on behalf of A.C.U.T.E. Personally, my feeling of having moved from margin to centre was sweet indeed. Janet and I loved to congratulate each other on our success—and we were justified. I really didn't know until it happened how eager I had been to prove myself in a cross-country organization.

The Learneds, so called half in fun, half in affection from the French version, 'Sociétés Savantes,' had come to life in the latter half of the fifties, one of the beneficent aftermaths of the Massey Report, envisioned as a yearly gathering of scholars from all disciplines and from every university from coast to coast in a convention that would help to collapse vast Canadian distances and forge a true "community of scholars." I believe that 1957 was the inaugural year of A.C.U.T.E., but it had been preceded by the foundation of the Humanities Association in the late forties, a project that A.S.P. Woodhouse, all-powerful Head of the University of Toronto's English Department, so enthusiastically supported that he made his one and only cross-Canada trip in aid of its foundation. The Humanities' Association was designed, ideally, to link town and gown, with meetings at which academics in the Humanities' disciplines would cross-fertilize fruitfully with interested citizens in their own areas. The success of its branches was always in direct ratio to the organizational energy and enthusiasm of its local supporters and it remains one of the Learneds' member associations.

In contrast, A.C.U.T.E. was seen from the start as a professional association, strictly limited to university teachers of English and for too long too exclusionary to admit even Graduate Students either into its membership or its programmes. Its primary aim, however, was swiftly achieved—it was indeed a jamboree where once a year old friends, colleagues, and rivals met to exchange ideas, sometimes, and academic gossip, always. When I first attended in 1960 the meetings were dominated by a handful of "senior statesmen" who tended to be Heads of their home departments and were accustomed to running their bailiwicks with firm hands: Roy Daniells of U.B.C., Claude Bissell of Toronto, Malcolm Ross, Dalhousie, Carl Klinck, Western, Reg Waters, R.M.C. I recall one of them leaving a session with a decisive slam of the door because the paper presenter had gone over his allotted time. In recent years, as habitual ignoring of time-limits becomes more and more scandalous, I have longed to do the same thing. Alas, civility—or chicken-heartedness—

prevails, but I do wonder why we put up with such gross egotism.

Anecdotally, the Learneds are rich in my memory. The first meeting I attended in the early fifties, pre-dating the formation of A.C.U.T.E., was a Humanities Association gathering at Western at which E.J. Pratt was the distinguished speaker. A Pratt speech was always a grand occasion, his warmth and high spirits reaching out to the audience and carrying them with him, usually back to Newfoundland about which he loved to talk. The speech on this occasion was memorable, certainly, but what sticks most vividly in my memory was the descent of the entire group on the London Hunt Club then adjacent to the campus, where we were being entertained by the Board of Governors. Open Bar—Free Booze—frenzy! The first, but not the last time that I realized just how thirsty a group are the academics of this country. Small wonder that such largesse was speedily replaced by the comparatively pallid vin d'honneur!

In the mid-sixties, at U.B.C., a group of us dining in the Faculty Club were holding an informal wake for A.S.P. Woodhouse, who had died suddenly the previous Fall. He had been the controlling agent in the careers of most Canadian academics and we were warmly and noisily remembering his witty as well as his autocratic dicta. This one for instance: "I have sent your name to Alberta, Kreisel. And I shall give them only one name!" Henry Kreisel and Murdo MacKinnon, the two best Woodhousiana raconteurs in the country, were of the group that night, as were a half-dozen others, among them John Graham, Anne Bolgan and Ross Woodman of Western. We had absolutely no consciousness of the broadcasting we were doing to the entire room, until another diner came over to thank us and urge us not to stop—Earle Birney. No mean raconteur himself, his arrival was a grand intervention. There was also the forever memorable time in Winnipeg when Murdo MacKinnon and I, on an evening A.C.U.T.E. junket by paddle-wheeler on the Red River, rounded up twenty-five or so of our colleagues and ruthlessly forced then to play "Caribou and Mongoose," to our intense enjoyment, if not theirs (a stamped, self-addressed envelope to me at York will get you the directions for the game, but beware, it is both silly and addictive!).

The most useful gambit I perfected at the Learneds was what Margaret Laurence and I called 'The Slink.' This was the technique of going to a gathering, assiduously but briefly 'working the room' and then vanishing, so that people who might conceivably be looking for one would say, "Well, she was right here a minute ago—Oh, well." This is an extremely effective defence against unwanted confrontation, boredom, and, most important in the days of few women, being included out of politeness in a dining group off to some far-flung restaurant where the evening becomes later and later, and male colleagues, well-trained in yesteryear's gentlemanly etiquette, become more and more adamant about paying. I devised this remarkably successful technique after a colleague insisted on buying me a meal and then told me that his wife would be very angry if she knew. Those were the days and such were the joys!

Were the goals that brought A.C.U.T.E. into being realized? Did the Learneds collapse our distances and make us a community of scholars? Insofar as such an ideal is ever realizable for large and disparate groups of individuals I firmly believe that our annual tribal pow-wow is enormously successful and the envy of our colleagues around the globe. A.C.U.T.E., now A.C.C.U.T.E.,

Colleges having been added to the acronym, is at once an arena for fruitful networking and a forum for assessing the changing parameters of our discipline and its fields. It has long since dropped the hierarchical elitism of it earlier years, and today a graduate student's paper is as likely or likelier to be a hotly discussed item on the programme as any other. Though all our associations are riven from time to time by inevitable controversies, as a group the Learneds have managed to escape the most tiresome of the politicizing elements that characterize our American counterparts. I was once asked to give a paper at a huge College Art Association convention in New Orleans only to find out a year or so later that my cordial invitation had been sent because I had been considered a 'safe' Canadian, unpoliticized by the controversy about the Equal Rights Amendment then splitting off the feminist membership. Had I known at the time, I, too, would have been a part of the split-off! In some four decades of the Learneds we have not yet been hammered apart by hard-core national political issues. And if I sometimes recall fondly the early days when everyone knew everyone else, I certainly wouldn't have them back in contrast to today's energy, diversity and, especially, acceptance of gender equity, surely the greatest advance of my long, long membership. That took a while, mind you. A few years after my presidency, at Western, Murdo McKinnon undertook to honour the past Presidents of A.C.U.T.E. who were present and omitted my name, though at the time he spoke I was standing beside him. I was too fond of Murdo to correct him publicly, but the omission has always rankled.

In personal terms the year 1971/2 was a hard one. John had just begun Queen's in the Fall, and early in November was rushed to Toronto to be operated on for a torn retina, the result of an old football injury. Needless to say, we were cruelly anxious. He was home until after Christmas, the operation a success, but the plastic bonding replacement gives him a wavy vision in that eye and is there permanently. Father's emphysema had been getting steadily worse, and in the summer of '71 the doctor had told him that his heart was bad. Typically, he made no fuss about it, and though he was progressively more disabled and depressed, he kept on until March 19, when he just had the time to call Vernon's number before a massive heart attack killed him. I had returned from Fredericton the previous evening, and, of course, had to resume teaching immediately after the funeral. It was fortunate , I know, that there was so little time to grieve. None of us could have wished for him to go on, disabled and terribly lonely as he was.

In 1974/5 I had a sabbatical, during which I did a good deal of travelling on behalf of Canadian literature. I had received a travel grant for that purpose from the Canada Council, and I had a fine time, in Winnipeg, Newfoundland, and at Dalhousie and Acadia. Of them all, the Memorial experience was the most memorable. I had been impressed and intrigued by St. John's on my earlier trip, and now I had a little more time to savour its uniqueness, to talk to students and faculty, and to spend a memorable evening, with the accompaniment of 'screech' at David Pitt's home. Finally I flew from Halifax to London to meet Morley, who was flying in from Geneva. We stopped briefly at Gander. This was my only visit to Gander, notorious during the war as the final North American post on the North Atlantic staging route. We stayed at a small hotel on Half Moon street, and from there I called Devon to tell the Elwins we would be driving down to see them. It was then I heard that

Malcolm had just died, of the lung cancer that had afflicted him for three years. It was a sad pilgrimage, but one that we very much wanted to make, and we had a comforting visit with Eve and Sally, her daughter. Then we went back, as always, to Oxford and the Old Parsonage Hotel, our home-away-from-home since the closing of the Commonwealth Services club. The Rowes and Anne Innes were, as always, warmly welcoming, and Anne joined us on a tour of England's East Coast, not as extensive as our Scottish tour which we had done the previous year in the final weeks of summer, but pleasant all the same. Before flying home we visited Sandy and Ian Cameron at Margaret's Elm Cottage. They, Sandy a York colleague and Ian, a former student, had gone over in 1969 to stay with Jocelyn and David Laurence when Margaret accepted the Creative Writer's post at the U. of T. They stayed on in England and, in fact, were to make it their permanent home.

II

In the Fall of 1976 Michèle Lacombe first arrived at York and immediately became my research assistant and my M.A. supervisee. Michèle was to become a major source of pleasure for me and for Morley from that time onwards. At the start, however, I just knew of her as a McGill graduate with long black hair, tight white jeans and a quiet shadowy boyfriend, Lee, who spoke little and appeared rarely. Michèle wanted to do her M.A. thesis on science fiction, about which I knew nothing, but our graduate director, Bob Cluett, had rightly suspected that Michèle and I would get along famously. When I found out that she was a Francophone, a French speaker by birth and a fluent English speaker by training, I proposed a bargain to her: I would supervise her M.A. thesis if, in her turn, she would do her Ph.D. thesis on something in the French-Canadian literary field. She agreed eagerly and immediately was appointed my research assistant.

From the start we had a wonderful time together, with much easy laughter as well as many research results, for Michèle was insatiably curious, quick and resourceful in combing through records and otherwise satisfying the assignments I gave her. My graduate course was also a delight to us both. That year I had begun for the first time, a course on Canadian women writers, a good many of them forgotten and neglected, but all of them fascinating subjects for research. We had fourteen women and one man in the class, a man who soon became a thorn in our flesh and who, luckily, didn't stay with us long. On one historic occasion, when he was fudging a seminar report and condescending to all of us, he became furious when we laughed and stalked out of the room slamming the door—at which we laughed harder. He came back in to warn us of his bad temper and then, enraged at being taken lightly, stalked out of the room and visited the Director telling him that he had 'personality clash' with all of us. Needless to say we wept no tears! It was good to be rid of him, not least because he smoked cigarettes made from vile, home-grown tobacco. Oddly enough they didn't affect the class's non-smokers, but made the smokers nauseous. In those days, no one banned smoking in seminars—I smoked and so did most of the students.

Once rid of the "ghost at the feast," we had a wonderful time, restoring to view numbers of our early writers. We didn't find breathtaking novels, but we did find a considerable body of important work, for some of these women, the Sadlier mother and daughter for instance, had been important and prolific writers in their day. Some of them, the Sadliers and later Agnes Laut, for instance, had written many school texts, some had written melodramatic romances, the 'bodice rippers' of their day; some, like Lily Dougall, were devoted to 'message writing,' and some, Sara Jeannette Duncan, Madge Macbeth and Evelyn Eaton among them, had been full-time writers and journalists. Eaton had achieved signal success with the historical romance, *Quietly My Captain Waits*, published during the W.W.II. The class became a weekly festival, enthusiasm was high, and together the students assembled an impressive array of information, opinion, and primary sources on these women. They all left their material with me. It is stored among my papers in the York Archives and it makes an impressive file. In my memory all graduate classes are special—this one was perhaps more so than most, for we were doing something new in Canadian graduate research, as many colleagues across the country were quick to tell me, and besides it fitted in wonderfully with the current preoccupation with feminism and women's concerns in general. This group also harboured good cooks! Twice they brought pot-luck dinners to our home, and twice they outdid themselves in providing tasty casseroles and desserts.

The previous year, 1975-6, had been a banner year for my graduate class as well, for one of our students was one of Canada' grandest old feminists, True Davidson. True had graduated from Victoria College in 1919, taken her M.A. at the U. of T. in the twenties and worked for a number of years as a cross-Canada sales representative for the Dent publishing company. She had gradually worked herself into municipal politics, until by the post-war period she was the much admired, respected, and sometimes feared, Mayor of East York, and a force to be reckoned with in Ontario politics in general. A tall, handsome woman with a hawk-like profile, True was noted especially for her plain-speaking on all occasions —and for her hats. As she explained to the class when they got to know her: "I was so often the only woman in a meeting of men, and I realized that if they were looking at my hat and complimenting me on it, they weren't so apt to notice what I was working towards. So I began to collect hats, and then people started to know me for my hats and to present me with hats, and now I have more than 200." That prompted another student to ask her about her public speaking, and her reply gave me the most unforgettable images of True that she treated us to: "I practise in front of a mirror," she said. "I've practised all over, sometimes in hotel rooms, in front of a mirror, wearing the hat I'm going to speak in and my slip." Smashing hats they were too, of all shapes and sizes, most of them in the very height of fashion, and a few of them, like a white mink number that I inherited, works of art.

Once the class got over their initial shyness, she

became walking history to them. Before she came to our class she had had two cataract operations: a friend, Emily Smith, who became her executrix, drove and escorted her everywhere, but once there the students were wonderfully attentive and eager to learn from her. As for True, she stood no nonsense: for her first seminar, she elected to deal with the picaresque novel. She came armed with various books in Spanish, French and English, asked the students piercingly how many read Spanish and went on to say that they must know that the picaresque began with Spanish and that they could certainly read it if they tried: "Just get a dictionary, and get to work." Before long they were taking her sterner pronouncements in good part, and even asking her about points that were pure history to them, and everyday past experience to her. The day we were discussing Sara Jeannette Duncan was especially memorable: one of the men, speaking of *The Imperialist*, refused to believe that young people could ever have spoken in what , he considered, was such an affected and stilted manner. "Indeed we did," said True. "When I was at Victoria in the teens, we didn't have dances. They weren't considered decent. We had 'Conversats' when men and women promenaded around Convocation Hall, arm in arm, to the accompaniment of music, making polite conversation. Then the boys went away to war, and when they came back, they would promenade us right out of the hall and upstairs to the dark classrooms. And THAT was when the powers-that-be decided that we'd be better off dancing. So we had dances."

True had been legendary, and something of a role model to me long before she joined my class. She was often in the political limelight and she knew the value of, and got lots of, press exposure. My first encounter with her, still from afar, was on a flight back from Ottawa to

The Golden Years

Toronto, sometime in the early seventies. She was in the old departure lounge where the whole of Canada seemed to turn up at one time or another. She was impossible to miss—it was the winter of the maxi-coat, and she was wearing a high-style long grey one, and, of course, a grand grey hat to set it off. When we boarded, a young woman, who obviously felt about her as I did, but who was alone and had plenty of nerve, moved to sit beside her and began to talk to her. Fortunately we were close, and I could hear. That was when I first heard her famous credo which I used many years later in writing her citation for an Honorary Degree from York: "Twenty years a warrior, twenty years a chief, twenty years an elder of the tribe." I loved it then and I love it now, a clarion call of inspiration for all women.

In the mid-sixties she had called our department Chairman, volunteering to teach a course in Canadian Literature. Needless to say, I was hoping to do the same, though Canadian Literature was still a chancy proposition, especially with a Chairman who was British born and educated, thought he was a dictator of the old school, and had no intention of featuring a Canadian course. It was early in the seventies when my friend and colleague, Edith Fowke, began to mention True to me regularly. When Edith was growing up in Lumsden, Saskatchewan, True's father had for a time been a minister there. Edith was an avid reader and the Davidsons had books—she was given access to their books and so she got to know True, who was about ten years older than she. Much later, living in Toronto, she and True often were play-goers together, their cordial relationship sustained by a deep respect for each other's work and achievement. One May day in 1975 Margaret Laurence and I went from our house to a Canada Day celebration in Hamilton. When I returned home that evening, son John handed me a sheaf of messages. "These are mostly from True Davidson," he said. "I don't know whether she wants to take your class or give it, but you'd better call her—right now." That was the beginning of my, and my class's experience, of True, a memorable year for all of us!

Handling True wasn't always easy, for she had very very strong opinions and she did carry on about them, sometimes at great length. However, the atmosphere she created was so dynamic and positive that we all thrived on it. One day, when she was being especially obstreperous, I pounded the table and said, "True, why are you being so bitchy?" And she replied. "Because today you are all being so dull!" That smartened us all up—also gave us all a good laugh. Susan O'Heir, who had taken a year off from being Associate Dean of Nursing at the University of Toronto, was in our class, and she also had a strong presence. Once, when I was going to be unavoidably late, I asked Susan if she would begin the seminar. I entered the classroom to an unforgettable moment: "Now True," Susan was saying, "I will let you speak in a moment. Just now Robert is speaking. Please let him finish." Before the class ended, I had them all to dinner at our house, a usual finish for my classes. I love hats too, and I was sorely tempted to wear one to greet them. But I didn't. That day, I remember, True treated us to a marvellous brown mink hat, and she was, as always, the centre of conversation. One of the girls asked her why she had never married: "Because in my twenties I realized that I talked too much for any man, and I certainly wasn't going to give up talking."

After my class and Eli Mandel's, which she also loved, she took several history classes. These didn't work as well as our English classes, because she did sound off about her version of history—and of course she had lived through a great deal of it. She also couldn't accept the way graduate history is now taught, a far cry from her own days of schooling when the assembling of data was the main thing, not the critical perspective that our historians cultivate. At any rate, her plans for a Ph.D. finally crashed and for a time, she told me, she was devastated. Being True, however, she picked herself up, moved off the York campus where she had taken a bachelor apartment in the Atkinson residence to be close to her work (when I saw it, the apartment was crowded with hats!), and made plans for travel to Australia and New Zealand. It was on this trip that she fell, and in the course of x-rays a cancerous growth was discovered.

She spent a long time in hospital, and she was there when her Honorary Degree Convocation was held at York. I wrote the citation, using as its touchstone the famous phrase I had first heard on the aircraft, and presented the hood and parchment to Edith Fowke who stood in for True. John Robarts was then our Chancellor, and as we stood in front of him, he said in his famous growl, "True used to come and see me by a secret door at Queen's Park and give me good advice." After the ceremony at York Edith and I went to the hospital to give her honours to True and found a small group of friends, let by Emily Smith, with a celebration in progress. York had sent a handsome bouquet of red roses to the hospital. "I think there must still be something for me to do, even at my age," she said to me. "There must be a reason, otherwise I wouldn't still be alive." I read the citation aloud and she liked that, although something about it was not quite right, she said. I can't remember just what. Not long after that, and still in hospital, True died. I went to her funeral as York's representative, and again the university had sent flowers.

She left York all her books, her papers, and $5,000. I decided that we should raise funds to augment that legacy and Edith joined me in a drive for "The True Davidson Collection of Canadian Literature." I had a marvellous time doing that—hectically busy, in the midst of term-time, but great fun, the two extra-special events being readings for the students, one week by Margaret Laurence and the next week by Margaret Atwood. On both occasions June Callwood, who was President of the Writers' Union that year, came along as Chairperson. We took the largest amphitheatre at York, one which officially holds between 600 and 700 students. We charged them only $1.00 admission, and both weeks they were sitting in the aisles. It was a lot of money easily and enjoyably made. We had persuaded Ian Macdonald, York's President, and our librarians, that one of the Reading Rooms in the Archives should be called the True Davidson Room. When our fund-raising drive had reached about $35,000 and York as a whole was about to embark on a massive fund-raising project, we were asked to call a halt to our effort. We then had a grand opening of the True Davidson Room, with Pauline McKibbon, the Lieutenant Governor, unveiling a fine framed photograph of True, wearing one of her famous hats, and with various friends and interested university colleagues attending. I had assembled a very special group of patrons—Isabel Bassett, Edith Morrow, Doris Anderson, Bill Kilbourn and Mavor Moore among them, and most of them were present. Also present was a visiting professor from the U.S.S.R., a pleasant lady whom we hoped would return home thinking that such occasions were an everyday affair in Canada.

In the latter half of the seventies I began an enjoyable

and busy adjunct to my York career—membership on various Ottawa Boards and Committees. As I had loved the A.C.U.T.E. experience, so I thoroughly enjoyed this later work—three years on the Board of the Killam Foundation, judging their yearly competitions for Fellowships and prizes, another three years on the Academic Panel of S.S.H.R.C.C., judging its competitions, and still more years on the Aid to Scholarly Publishing committee, representing the fields of English and Commonwealth Literatures. I became, as Morley already was, a frequent visitor to Ottawa for meetings, and it was commonplace, and a family joke, that we were apt to meet in the old Ottawa airport, where the departure lounge was often like the crossroads of Canada.

The life was stressful, and as is always the case with a university teaching career, there was no margin—there are no supplemental teachers in the system, ready to take over a class in case of illness or emergency. But there was Strathroy to escape for we had taken over the family house after father's death. Not only in the summertime, when I rested, relaxed and wrote there, but also throughout the year, I would escape by train for a few days, especially when Morley was on one of his frequent trips to Geneva or elsewhere. We had a swimming pool installed there in 1975, and it became a holiday focus for the entire family as well as being my delight and certainly my safety valve.

In 1977 John Lennox and I received a major research grant from S.S.H.R.C.C., enabling us to begin the three-part project that became a biography, *William Arthur Deacon: A Literary Life*, a letter collection, *Dear Bill: The Correspondence of William Arthur Deacon*, and the *Deakdex*, a computerized index to the very large Deacon Collection, the property of the Thomas Fisher Rare Book

Library at the University of Toronto. My association with Deacon, as I have written earlier, goes away back to the days of my M.A. thesis, when I wrote to him as Literary Editor of the *Globe And Mail* and the man whom, I knew, was keenly involved with Canadian Writers. He was unceasingly helpful, and it is to him I owe the publication of *Canadian Novelists* in 1946. Through the years I had heard very little about him, though I was a faithful reader of "The Flyleaf," his weekly column of literary news and gossip. He had retired in the 60s—and it was Claire Pratt who told me one day that his papers had been sold by the family to the Thomas Fisher Rare Book Library. She had known for years that I was grateful to him and she suggested that I should think about a biography. For some years I backed away from any thought of such a mammoth task, but in the late seventies, John Lennox and I began to talk of a possible major joint project. The Deacon papers were there, ready and waiting, and after some months' delay while the librarian looking after them got them arranged to her satisfaction, we were given the go-ahead.

Both of us were somewhat leery of such a vast collection to be dealt with—some 18,000 pieces, much of it correspondence with writers since the teens of this century, when Deacon was an aspiring young writer, shortly to find his real metier in journalism. S.S.H.R.C.C. granted us a large sum with which we were able to hire Michèle Lacombe, now a Ph.D. student, full-time for two years. Richard Landon of the Thomas Fisher secured spacious quarters for us in the Robarts Library and we were off and away! Each of us had a sabbatical while working on the project, and besides, we were able to arrange our teaching schedules to allow for time at the Robarts. For several years I spent both Thursday and

Friday at the Robarts, and our large second-floor room became a meeting place for our colleagues from near and far. We had the whole Deacon collection at our fingertips, there in the room with us, and we worked superbly well as a threesome. *William Arthur Deacon: A Literary Biography*, was published in 1982 and a letter collection, edited by John and Michèle, called *Dear Bill*, a couple of years later. It was a totally successful enterprise, and the three of us came out of it with friendship and respect for one another undimmed.

Suddenly, it seemed, my retirement date was just around the corner. Twenty-three years since I made my first trek to Glendon from Mountview Ave. in West Toronto? I was not to be cut off completely, however, since it was accepted then that a retiree would still teach one course, and this I did until 1988. The greatest boon of all was the invitation in 1983 to become a Canadian Studies Research Fellow for the Library and to be given a roomy office in the Scott Library Archives. I learned too that there is absolutely no expiry date for fanatically devoted faculty members such as myself. For the past ten years I have happily joined John Lennox as a partner in his Graduate classes—not a silent partner, Heaven knows, but one who has all the fun without any of the final responsibility that being on the payroll exacts.

III
May, 1984

The culminating event of my entire teaching career was the retirement party which John Lennox, Michèle Lacombe and Mary Louise Craven arranged for me in late May, 1984. John has been my student, my teaching colleague and my staunch and dear friend since he graduated from Glendon, the first class to be awarded a York degree, in 1967. He and Jane, his wife, began in 1963. Jane Rooke was one of my special advisees in her first year, and they both took my American-Canadian class in third year. In their fourth year, I taught Commonwealth Literature to the two of them and a third, Heather Pantry, of whom I haven't heard in many years. Jane always lived in residence and so, of course, was close to 15 Lewes Crescent. We quickly developed a special relationship—Jane, completely competent and unflappable, would come over to help me the odd time, when I was having special dinner parties. Of course she became good friends with Sandy Bracken, chief Don in residence, and a friend of mine since our first year together at Glendon. By their fourth year John and Jane were firmly paired together in my mind, and their marriage, in 1971, after Jane had spent two years with CUSO in Ghana and John had got his M.A. at the University of Sherbrooke, was, and has remained, totally right and fitting. By that time John was back at York in our Department, but shortly thereafter, he and Jane went to Fredericton where he got his Ph.D. He came back to York to become a stalwart Department colleague and always, a dear and loyal friend. Now a family of five, with their daughters, Mia and Anna and son, Jeff, the Lennoxes have a very special place in our galaxy of friends and colleagues.

Since Glendon days John had been especially interested in Canadian Literature and his dissertation was a comparative study of certain Francophone novels with fiction of the southern United States. On his return I was happy to have his collaboration in the various courses we were offering in the Canadian field, and our relationship, personal and professional, has continued fruitfully to this day. Since my retirement, for many years, he has welcomed me as an enthusiastic volunteer for his senior and Graduate classes, on Canadian fiction, or, more recently Life-Writing, a field that is relatively new to our discipline, but is particularly rich in the Canadian field. In the chapter, Biography, I have written of my early experience and our later joint efforts.

Michèle Lacombe along with Mary Louise Craven, another former student and present colleague, teamed with John some months ahead of my May retirement date in 1984, to plan a gala evening. I was not entirely unaware of the goings-on, but I certainly did not know the extent of their plans, nor did I have any idea of their success until the night itself. It was unique, certainly one of the very greatest events of my life. They were joined in their planning by Michael Darling who, with John. planned a Festschrift, and by Jack David and Robert Lecker, founders of ECW Press, also former students, who undertook to publish the Festschrift as number 29 of their Journal *Essays In Canadian Writing*.

John had asked me where I would like to have the party and I requested the dining room at Glendon, scene of so many first impressions and first experiences of York. They planned the menu and the entertainment. I was stunned and delighted by the turnout—about 125 people, a full house for the dining room, and by the speakers, from Janet Lewis to Margaret Laurence, to President Ian

MacDonald. Friends and colleagues came from all over: the Klincks and the Conrons from Western. the MacKinnons, Waterstons and Killams from Guelph, the Fryes from Victoria, Francess Halpenny from the U. of T., Lorraine McMullen from the U. of Ottawa, Jane and Craig Campbell from Wilfred Laurier. There was also a wonderful cross-country turn-out of former students: Gwen Davies from Acadia, Robert Lecker from McGill, Les Monkman, from Queens, Ken McLean, from Bishop's, Jim Nelson, from the U. of Alberta. Edith Fowke and many other York colleagues also attended: Ramsay Cook, Maurice Elliot, Bob Cluett, and Don Rickerd, the original Registrar of the early Glendon years, and my entire graduate course of '83-84. Besides Margaret Laurence, writers Chinua Achebe and Adele Wiseman had come, as had Beth Appeldoorn and Susan Sandler of the Longhouse Bookstore and all my dear friends of the group we fondly called "The Drama Guild of Canada" were there in force. Of course, all my family were there, John, Steve and Sherry and Morley. At two years, grandson Tyler was left at home. I had a hard time believing that such a festival in my honour was really happening. When I look at all the excellent pictures that Paul Craven took that night I can hardly believe in it yet. To cap it all, they presented me with $500 for the True Davidson fund for Canadian Literature.

The rewards of a teaching career are never-ending. My dearest pleasures now lie in the many former students who have become friends and who visit me, E-mail me, and generally, keep me in touch with other generations and their vital concerns and interests. Prime among them, and the very next in my affection to my close family, is always John Lennox, whose friendship and close collaboration have meant such an enormous amount to me, since our first meeting thirty-five years ago.

Chapter XIII

Canadian Literature Abroad

The great surge of nationalism that accompanied Centennial celebrations in 1967 also meant a surge in enthusiasm for Canadian Literature abroad as well as at home. Beginning in the late 60s it was part of the Trudeau government's policy to encourage (that is, subsidize) conferences, speaking trips, books, and all other aids to Canadian Studies. These fundings by the Minister of State reacted, of course, to Canada's advantage. I once asked a colleague from Rouen why they had begun a Canadian Literature Centre at the university there. "Simple," he said, "Three-quarters of France's trade with Canada goes through Rouen." But even before European Canadian Studies became a part of my picture I was involved in teaching Commonwealth Literature, as it was then called, in my case West African and Caribbean. With Morley and son John, I attended the International Commonwealth Association Conference in Jamaica just after Christmas in 1970. We arrived on the Mona campus, a beautiful site, built on the ruins of an old sugar plantation, some miles out of Kingston, late in the afternoon, three novices, me wearing a brown wool pant-suit and all of us already panting from the heat, which we should have anticipated but didn't. With some delay, we were housed in one of the university residences, unprivate, by our standards, for the partitions didn't go up to the ceiling and the washrooms seemed a long walk away.

I had had a message from Sandra Djwa of Simon

Fraser before we left home, asking me to get in touch with her as soon as we arrived so that our two boys could keep each other company. I went in search of Sandra in the residence, found her—and found her son, who was a two-year-old. John at that time was in Grade 13, determined to go to Queen's in the Fall. They were hardly compatible. We left the Djwas and set out to explore the campus. Nothing can be darker than a Jamaican night. We eventually found ourselves in the hospital complex, where we certainly should not have been. Much of it was open, crowded with patients, relatives and friends, and very noisy. We were not used to the gregariousness of Jamaicans, nor the largely open-air buildings we were encountering. We did realize, however, that we were, if not actually on forbidden ground, right next door to it, and we made our way back to the residence with some stumbling around in the dark, and a lucky discovery en route of a wayside shop selling chocolate bars, for we were very hungry,

Our Western friends, Brandy and Carol Conron, were staying at a hotel close to the campus, and there we went to find them the next day, our first excursion after Morley had walked into the city and rented a car in the morning. That morning we also met Eddie Baugh and so began one of the most fruitful friendships of our lives. I was standing in line for some information at a central conference registry when Eddie introduced himself and asked us if he could help us in any way. Earlier, in Canada, we had registered for a campus flat, said to be available, so that the three of us could be together. Eddie went to considerable trouble to see to that, taking us in his car to get the bedding and the household gear that we needed, and then moving us in. John still lived in the residence, but he was able to come every morning for breakfast, and we were able to get our own meals in private when there were no official functions. It was a nice little place, all grown over with poinsettia and, to our wondering eyes, totally exotic, and, now that we were in lighter clothes, just what we thought Jamaica should be.

The conference was to open in the Arts Centre, a fine modernistic structure recently built on the campus. We were not yet used to Jamaica time and were surprised on the morning of the opening, which was to be attended by the Prime Minister, the Vice-Chancellor of the University and other dignitaries, to find ourselves, with the Conrons, all alone in the auditorium. Shortly a technician or two appeared on the stage and set up speakers, microphones and all the paraphernalia, and then slowly, slowly, the international delegations assembled. The very dignified and welcoming opening speeches were delivered and the conference proceeded to its first session. That was my first sight and hearing of Prime Minister Manley, not, I am happy to say, my last. It was also my first sight of Dr. Figueroa, the Vice Chancellor, and a revered elder statesman of the University of the West Indies.

There was a considerable delegation from Canada: John Matthews had brought several students from Queen's, Bill and Peggy New of U.B.C were there with their young baby, as well as Sandra from Simon Fraser, ourselves and the Conrons. Dorothy Livesay was much in evidence, as well as senior writers from the Caribbean, including Sam Selvon, George Lamming and V.S. Naipaul, the latter easily the most famous of all those assembled. Jamaica was in a period of high nationalism, like Canada, but her people are much more voluble and feisty than Canadians. Edward Kamau Braithwaite, the historian and poet, was a campus leader, an impressive figure, already known for his poetry of exile, and a wonderful reader of that poetry. I will always remember his impassioned shout: "If our laws make 75% of our children illegitimate, they are bad laws. We are not bad people!" Derek Walcott, not yet widely known, but obviously a poet and playwright of remarkable power, was present. There were various performances of their work, and they gave their own writing credos from the stage of the Arts Centre. For a North American, unused to the emotional vocal dexterity of Caribbeans, the reception of Naipaul was an unforgettable experience. He was challenged, in shouts, as he spoke of his writing, domiciled in England as he was then and is now. His compatriots told him in no uncertain terms that he should be ashamed of himself not to come home and work for his people. "You should be shot," someone shouted at him from the audience. "One is a writer, and one writes," he answered in a voice so soft as to be barely audible, "and when one is finished writing of one subject (meaning Trinidad, his native island), one writes of something else."

Sessions always began later than the appointed time, but once going, the participants, especially West Indians and Africans, would go on and on and on. And no matter how loud and passionate the discussions had been in the question periods after the papers, participants would laugh, joke and fraternize outside on the steps afterwards. The whole thing was a wonderful, concentrated learning experience such as I had never had before, and for Morley and John as well. Although John had come down with a wretched case of the flu, he managed to attend everything and so learned, as I did, about a culture so adjacent to ours, but so different.

There were various entertainments arranged, official receptions and the like, the most enthralling of which was a performance in the Arts Centre by Olive Lewin and her Jamaican Folk-singers. Miss Olive, as she was known, had just got nicely underway in her lifelong project of finding and perpetuating the wonderful music of her people. I heard her group perform twice more on successive years, and in 1995 was thrilled to receive as a gift from the Baughs a 90-minute video of her group combining their music with enactments of traditional settings of the music in magnificent Jamaican scenery. All through our stay Eddie Baugh continued to befriend the Thomases, on one occasion taking us along with Mollie Mahood, an Africanist from the University of Kent in Canterbury, England, on a tour to Port Antonio, his birthplace, where his father had been a talley-man, a buyer on the plantations for the thriving banana industry. Back in Kingston we visited his home where Sheila, his wife, proudly displayed the newborn baby, Sarah, just a month old at that time. We also had our first trip to the famous Pantomime, the variety show held every Christmastime in the big old theatre downtown on Kingston's 'Parade.' That was a spendid occasion, for it was our first experience of Jamaican 'creole,' the folk-dialect of the island, and its most famous poet and performer, Miss Louise Bennet. We were fortunate indeed, for the creole is fast disappearing, Miss Louise is aging and lives in Canada now, and we saw the Pantomime twice more, on successive years.

Morley and John left just after New Year's Day, and a trip by car to Port Royal after a rainstorm that deprived Kingston of electricity for several hours. I stayed for the conference's second week and so became a lifelong fan of the Senior Common Room Hotel, to which I was able to move for the last few days, again thanks to Eddie Baugh. It is a roomy, airy structure, with an outside bar and swimming pool, and large, second-storey guest rooms with balconies and baths attached. It was presented to the university by the Aluminum Company of Canada and is used as a combined Faculty Club and stop-over for itinerant faculty and travelling scholars, for the Mona campus is one of three campuses of the University of the West Indies, another in Trinidad and one at Cave Hill in Barbados. There is a considerable itinerant population among faculty, and also a considerable guest population —hence the usefulness of a campus hotel. The manageress at that time was Mrs. Bourdillon, an Englishwoman, and of course the whole place reminded me of my beloved Commonwealth Services Club in Oxford where I had spent so many happy weeks since 1963. The S.C.R. Hotel, however, is new and well-maintained, in contrast to the aged and creaky Oxford residence. The dining room was well occupied by the Faculty every lunchtime when a hot meal was served, but in the evening only the residents were usually dining, in an idyllically cool and leisurely setting with food both delicious and intriguingly different from our home fare. By the time I had spent one night there I had resolved to come back and back and back, which we have done successfully for twenty-five years now, our latest visit being in December of 1994.

I returned to Toronto on the same plane as Brandy and Carol about January 8, and the first of our many trips to the University of the West Indies was over. I had made many connections that were to open up the teaching of West Indian and West African literature for me: most important, we had begun a friendship with the Baughs that was to grow over the years. In 1995 Sarah was married and though we were not able to attend, we were honoured to be asked, and to receive the mementoes of a beautifully decorated chapel wedding and a garden reception. Many winter holidays followed that first trip, when we had the leisure to explore the campus more thoroughly with no conference sessions to interfere. In subsequent years it became part of our routine to swim every morning in the Olympic sized pool down the hill a good hike from the Senior Common Room. We attended chapel in the old sugar factory which, restored, is one of the precious historic buildings on campus. The combination of its handsome dark wood interior, the brilliant red gowns of the choir and their enthusiastic and melodious singing is unforgettable. The flowers are always unforgettable too, bright, papery blossoms of bougainvillaea rioting everywhere, hibiscus blooming madly, flame trees, lignum-vitae, the wonderfully purple trumpets of the 'garlic vine,' and everywhere among the ruins of old plantation walls, the poinsettias in scarlet clumps. As an ever-present backdrop of beauty the mountains rise back of the campus, covered with a dozen shades of green and set off by the brilliant blue winter sky and white towering clouds. We have had rain in Jamaica, heavy rain, but not often, and in my memory the days are always sunny and hot until about five o'clock when darkness "falls"—and we never really knew what that phrase meant until we experienced it in Jamaica.

With the darkness comes the barking of many dogs in the hills surrounding the campus, the strange cry of the "creaky pump bird," so named by us for its hoarse call, the forgiving evening breezes of the Trade Winds and the long, leisurely dinner with, often, stimulating conversation among the lucky denizens of the Senior Common Room. My love-affair with Jamaica has been one of the most rewarding and never-ending treats of my life. It became habitual for us to go there just after Christmas, by ourselves except for once when Ruth and Bert Longmire came with us. That time we heard Olive Lewin and her singers again and also saw at the Arts Centre an early Tom Stoppard play, *Inspector Hound*, a mystery and great fun, if only to listen to the voices, including the fake Canadian accent of one of the characters. That year we also took Ruth and Bert and the Baughs to dinner at the adjacent old Mona Plantation hotel up the road towards Kingston. I always bought Jamaican cotton, then a thriving island enterprise, and made many of the robes that Margaret Laurence and I wore with such pleasure. I still have a few of them, as I have of the tablecloths I made from the brightly coloured and beautifully designed cotton.

After five years of such holidays on campus we tried the Shaw Park Beach hotel on the north shore. I did this unwillingly, but Kingston at that time was in a cycle of violence and Morley wasn't happy about the relatively open and unguarded campus. The hotel was fine, the service and food excellent, but for Jamaica both air and water were chilly, and it lacked entirely the exotic, other-culture ambience of the campus. Wherever we looked we seemed to be surrounded by guests from Toronto and the touristy patterns set up for their and our supposed delight. Everything changed again the next year when we tried St. Lucia, staying at the Holiday Inn there, now long since the St. Lucian Hotel. I was doubly motivated towards St. Lucia: it is Derek Walcott's home island and the site of his long poem, *Another Life*. Also, Sheila Baugh had tantalized me with tales of St. Lucian cottons from 'The Bagshaws.' In neither was I disappointed. The cottons are unique to St. Lucia and available only in the factory-cum-store close beside the Le Toq hotel outside of Castries, the capital city. The island rivals Jamaica in its beauty, an admission I never thought to make. Altogether we went to St. Lucia five times, twice to the Cariblue Hotel, once to Le Toq and twice to the St. Lucian. We met our academic friend from Sudbury, Claire Beauchemin, there, or rather, she picked us up there, for she was looking for company. So began a friendship that has brought much comradeship and pleasure.

The best fruit of our island ventures has been twofold: a continuing interest in Caribbean literature and our friendship with the Baughs. Besides his permanent appointment in the English Department, Eddie has served as its Chairman and as Dean of Arts, and he has also continued writing the poetry for which he is increasingly well known at home and throughout the Commonwealth. Recently he was fittingly honoured by his university for his various achievements. On every trip he has opened doors for us, introducing us to fellow academics, taking us on exotic tours—to Harmony Hall, another old plantation house made into a gallery and gift shop, or to their home for dinner, or on a marvellous drive right over the island to a luxurious villa loaned them by a friend. The very change from a Canadian winter is a blessing, as is the gorgeous bloom, the soft, warm air and blue sky with the hills an ever-changing and always beautiful backdrop. The special lilt and musicality of a Jamaican accent is a constant joy to me.

Bordeaux and the French Fact

In March of 1978 Morley and I went to a conference at the University of Bordeaux at which I was to give a paper called "Seeing Niagara and After," a bibliographic description of the proliferating works on Canadian Literature in the late sixties and seventies. We flew first to England, as was our custom, drove immediately to Oxford, had dinner with Anne Innes and lunch with Jim and Trudi Rowe, and then flew on to Bordeaux, arriving somewhat tired to find a friend and former student, Mary Louise Craven, then Pigott, waiting for us. She was at the university as an assistant that year, working with Pierre

Spriet, who had been responsible for my invitation and who was well known at York. She had a shabby, spacious apartment in one of the many elegantly designed 18th-century houses in downtown Bordeaux. Almost immediately we were due at a dinner party at the home of Pierre and Claire Spriet. I was really not up to much of the rabbit stew, delicious, but not to my taste, and I was more than relieved when the evening ended.

The next day official functions began with a bang, for Bordeaux and York were becoming 'twinned' with a good deal of publicity. The university, under M. le President, Dr. Escarpit, was determined that the Canadian Studies Centre would be well publicized, and grand, not to say grandiose, functions had been laid on right and left. In the all-too-common Canadian manner, I felt tongue-tied among French speakers, and certainly got off to a bad start at the initial reception, for Mme Escarpit, *Tres* chic and *Tres* cool, made me feel anything but at home practicing my halting French. Later, at a select dinner, in the famous words of Susanna Moodie, "Bad as things were, they steadily got worse." The guests included Naim Kattan, already a cordial acquaintance of many years, my York colleague and friend, Jack Warwick, our then-ambassador, Gerard Pelletier and Cecile, his wife, the President of the University of Moncton, a good sort, but the butt of the Escarpits' unconcealed scorn for his Shediac accent, and ourselves. We joined the Moncton colleague in a taxi to the Escarpits, and his greeting to Morley was, "President or Dean?" He took the information that I was the delegate quite calmly however. It was one of those interminable dinners with everything passed by the maid, and passed several times. The conversation was stilted at best. At one point I heard Mme Escarpit say, in French, of course, of me: "She can speak French but she won't." Whereupon Mme. Pelletier leaned toward me and said, condescendingly, "You are very fortunate to be here among the Bordelais." To which I replied, in like tones, "In what way?" I don't remember what came next. I think my reply was a show-stopper. Mme Pelletier seemed the only human one of the group, especially since M. le President himself was called away from the table to deal with erupting student unrest on campus. When at length, he returned, Pelletier congratulated him on his bravery. Escarpit answered, with a fake humility I found nauseating, "Après la résistance, il n'y a pas de peur."

When the papers began the next day, I realized that many, maybe all, of our External Affairs men from all over Europe were present in the amphitheatre. I thought it hilarious to be all of a sudden the focus of such attention when I gave my piece. It mattered to them, it really did, what was said about Canada and Canadian Literature in France. Having always been a nationalistic pan-Canadian I had nothing to worry about, but a year later, when John Moss, a good friend of mine, gave a paper in which he seemed to applaud the idea of the separating of our two literatures, I speedily found out that he was unlikely to be funded for European conferences from that time forward. Our External Affairs Department was not about to exercise its largesse or even its tolerance on a potential separatist sympathizer.

After a huge reception at Bordeaux City Hall, the major memory being of huge arrangements of roses, six dozen or more in an urn, I had had enough. I pleaded feeling unwell, and Mary and I had a grand dinner by ourselves, while Morley kept himself company. The next day one of the consular women told me she had made my excuses, adding wisely, "I knew you had diplomatic flu." On the final day, thanks to Mary and her beat-up little car, we had a wonderful drive to the coast, through countryside blooming with mimosa, hanging from the trees like great swatches of yellow mist. We had an omelette at a little roadside restaurant, and on the way back to the city I bought my beautiful yellow blazer, my only article of clothing tagged "Paris" and my showpiece for fifteen years. I wore two jackets back home and was rather warm in the plane, but happy in my purchase—happier than in my first, and last, experience of the French on their own ground.

It was not a happy experience, thanks both to the self-consciousness that afflicts most Canadians of my generation in the presence of French speakers, and the condescension, or, to put it plainly, downright rudeness, of the Bordelais hosts. That conference was by far the least pleasurable of all our overseas travels in aid of the Canadian Literature enterprise. Aside from Pierre Spriet and Simone Vauthier, academics who became deservedly and affectionately well-known in Canada, it might also be said that of all the visiting professors we have had, and have, at York, those from France are usually the most difficult to satisfy. They tend to come in the early Fall, just when our classes are settling down, and it is most difficult to entertain them. Robert Mane and Jacques LeClair were eager Laurence scholars, and though Margaret absolutely dreaded French involvement and did everything in her power to avoid it, being resolutely unilingual, they were always persistent. One year, arriving at her home in Lakefield unheralded, and finding the doorbell unanswered, they had the colossal nerve to tie a bottle of wine to her doorknob with a message saying, "We will return." Fortunately we could laugh at most of these antics, including Mane's impassioned eagerness to entertain us in France, which he expressed in the most overblown prose. Another learning experience indeed!

The Sicilian Connection

In March of 1983 Morley and I flew to Rome, then Catania, Sicily, to take part in the Italian Association of Canadian Studies' conference at Piazza Armerina in the hills above Catania. The gathering of Canadianists from all over Italy, as well as guests such as ourselves, was hosted by Giovanni Bonanno, already a friendly visitor to York and an enthusiastic and powerful Canadianist at the University of Messina, his academic home. There was a goodly group of us from Canada, both academics and writers. Adele Wiseman was there, Eli Mandel and Anne were there, Jack Granatstein, a colleague from York's History Department, was there, as was a favourite friendly colleague from the University of Ottawa, Pierre Savard. The conference was to be a three-pronged affair —literature, history and political science. Of course, there were also a number of our External Affairs people, including a young Mr. Seaborn who, with his colleague from Rome, turned out to be something less than tactfully diplomatic. We were housed in style in a posh hotel and, very shortly, reassembled in order to attend the opening ceremonies in a historic 12th-century Templars' church in the little town. That occasion was the coldest ordeal I have ever suffered. The chill in the ancient building had been gathering since the 12th century, there was absolutely no heat, and we were all, in a word, frozen. I had on a wool dress and my all-weather coat, fortunately quite warm, and even more fortunately, I was equipped with the woolly cap I always carried. Morley wore his trenchcoat. We were, it would seem, adequately dressed, but many of the men wore only jackets, and no one was adequately protected from that chill. There was considerable delay as lights were set up and television cameras placed themselves, for this was a first-time occasion for Sicily and, when speeches from notables began, it was to be broadcast. The official opening ceremonies seemed to go on forever, certainly a good hour and a half, while we all grew steadily colder. Finally, blessed relief, we were bused again, this time to the Town Hall, past a square inhabited by men, middle-aged to elderly, well wrapped in long overcoats, scarfs and gloves. On arrival we were offered Scotch! Never were there more thankful, or speedier drinkers. The noise level in the Hall rose to deafening heights as the fiery liquor warmed us, and we left for the buses again, an hour later, restored to the living. There were lasting bad effects, though: Eli, for one, caught a cold that turned into a dangerous chest infection. He had to be hospitalized a few days later.

Except for that initial gruelling ordeal, our treatment was princely. We ate all together in a bright hotel dining-room, with large, colourful pitchers of wine on every table to start us off, pitchers which were often refilled. The meals were gorgeous, dangerously lavish until we all realized that the huge platters of pasta were just starters, and that we would be served with entrees also. Most of us made the mistake I did the first time, loading up with the pasta, thinking it was the main course. Very quickly everyone became everyone's friend. The Italian scholars, of whom there were many in a number of disciplines, made a point of sitting among us, and we found out then, if we hadn't known before, that Italian hospitality and bonhommie is definitely the best and the most memorable among all our off-shore experiences.

The papers began the next morning, and were given in separate sections, with Italian academics as well as Canadians performing. I read my paper on Frye and Laurence, "Towards Freedom," early in the proceedings and so was able to enjoy the remainder of the programme without stress. I found myself reacting so eagerly to the expressiveness and enthusiasm of the Italians that I rushed up after one paper on W.O. Mitchell and congratulated its author, only as I spoke realizing that he had read in Italian and I had really no notion of what he had said. Much too tactful to ask me what part I had enjoyed most, our friendship was cemented there and then. That was Professor Rizzardi of Bologna. One of our External Affairs men congratulated me in a truly back-handed way: "You have certainly done a lot for Margaret Laurence," said he. "I hope that applies to Northrop Frye, as well," I said, to which he replied: "Oh, Frye, of course, doesn't need it."

There were various special treats laid on for the whole group, the most memorable a conducted tour of Greek ruins at Argentine, in process of excavation. It was truly eerie to see the well-defined amphitheatre, and just as strange to a Canadian to see wild hyacinths already in bloom. Prickly pears, the huge cactuses with bulbous leaves, are everywhere in Sicily, another new sighting for us. This was the trip on which we saw and heard, to our dismay, our two External Affairs Officers trying to persuade a uniformed member of the carabinieri to wear on his uniform a plastic Canadian flag pin. A stunning mistake in diplomatic tact, confirming our already poor opinion of the two young men.

On the final night of the conference, the Italian Association for Canadian Studies was having its Annual Meeting. I went down from our room to the auditorium to take a message to someone and found the assemblage in the process of roll-call. Surprising to us, who conduct meetings far less formally. Even more surprising was the noise level of passionate argument that arose for a couple of hours, as they elected their hotly contested President for the coming year. Most surprising of all was the aftermath of what sounded like a real donnybrook: someone began to play the piano beautifully and the whole group sang and danced for a long time. We didn't get to sleep until very late that night, but we did learn a good deal about the political side of the association.

In 1992 we had our next Sicilian adventure, this time invited by Gianni Bonanno to his yearly seminar for students at Naxos, on the eastern coast of Sicily, with Mt. Etna brooding above. This time, Etna was in the process of eruption, and put on a fabulous show for us, with streams of molten lava running down the mountainside and puffs of gas and smoke rising in the air by day and night. Before Sicily we had gone to a conference in Milan, where we were housed in a beautifully restored monastery and, again, among the kindly and hospitable Italian professors who made us just as welcome as they had years before. John Lennox travelled with us, greatly adding to our enjoyment, and once we had landed at Catania, after a slightly scary trip, when we were all instructed by the pilot to move to the front of the plane as it was having trouble getting off the ground, the stay was idyllic.

This time we were housed in individual chalets in the midst of a large lemon grove, in which about a third of the trees were in blossom, scenting the air deliciously, another third were in bud, and in the final third the fruit was being picked. The whole scene was magically exotic. A three-minute stroll led to the sea, the very spot where Aphrodite rose from the waves. There were about a dozen academics, Anglophone and Francophone, and about seventy students from Sicilian universities, Messina and Catania. Giovanni Bonanno was in charge of the whole thing, ably seconded by an assistant, and, in the meals department, by a good-looking, talkative maestro called

Carlo. We all ate together and were superlatively fed, really two dinners a day, with a pasta starter and then a meat or chicken entree and a fruit dessert. Lots of wine, as always.

The students, second and third year, were very good, their English already easy and their understanding certainly on a level with our own students'. They seemed exceedingly well-dressed and bejewelled to us—gold bracelets and chains were prominent. There were usually two groups, one housing English, one French, with separate seminars on Canadian Literature, Political Science and Geography. Part of each day was given over to excursions, a bus-trip up the mountain to Taormina, a tea at a very fashionable hotel, a dinner given by the head of the English Department, University of Messina—in fact more than I could handle. Gianni treated me like a queen. Far up in the hills on the bus tour, he came to ask if I were tired. When I said "Yes," he called a taxi and had us taken home—some dozen miles. He also told me privately that he had told the students that I was "the bigga cheese!"

Gemma Persico, one of the friendly Catania faculty, took John, Morley and me on a tour of the city, ending up for lunch at a trattoria in the midst of the most crowded and ancient part of Catania and one in which the hazards of driving her little car were immense, but didn't ruffle a hair on her head. Time after time she rammed us through streets where there wasn't room for us, and once got out to have a shouting match with a storekeeper who had objected to her careening over his sidewalk. We lived through the experience, to my amazement. We also had a final dinner at the beautiful old taverna on the grounds of the hotel. At the last session, when the students themselves were going to report on what they had heard and learned, our consul and various other dignitaries were present. In honour of Canada, our hosts began, they thought, with our national anthem. But what came out of the speakers, blaring, was not "O Canada," but "Rule Britannia." A funny, funny mistake, especially if, as I did, you happened to catch the eye of the consul and barely suppressed a terrible fit of the giggles. Yet somehow, that such a thing would happen fit the whole experience—an out-of-this-world kind of fairy tale conference, presided over by magnificent Aetna, spewing streams of fiery lava every night—for our benefit.

We left Naxos for Catania airport at five in the morning, flew to Rome and then home, a long long flight, but livened by an interesting elderly stone sculptor called Cox, who sat beside me and talked all the way. His first wife ran off with Earle Birney, he said, but lives in Toronto again just now, and they do the *Globe and Mail* crossword by telephone every Saturday! A gossipy end to a perfect, perfect overseas adventure, the greatest among all the far-flung conferences of our past.

In the Fall of 1989 we flew to Brussels for a conference at the Free University there, the academic home of Jeanne Delbaere, who, over the years, has become a valued friend and one of the most enthusiastic promoters of Canadian Literature in Europe. The spring before, at the Learneds in Quebec City, I had been presented with the Northern Telecom Canadian Studies Prize, an enormous gold medal, and a cheque for $10,000. The honour was entirely a surprise, unlike most things in the academic world, in Canada at least. I was dumbfounded, and in the first instance it was my former student, Gwen Davies of Acadia, who was responsible for my nomination. The prize had been awarded for some seven years, but never to a woman, and Gwen obviously decided that it was time for such an honour to come to me. So, at a splendid dinner at the Chateau Frontenac, I was duly presented, and duly gave an acceptance speech which was a great pleasure and satisfaction to write.

Travelling to Brussels that fall was a grand follow-up and the conference was a well-attended and congenial affair. I gave a paper on Carol Shields' *Swan*, there were various fine receptions and dinners, as well as papers by old friends, Philip Stratford and Bob Kroetsch among them, and we returned home after a stay of a few days in London. We were both stricken by a nasty bug, which somewhat dimmed the enjoyment of the latter part of the trip, but for us, and also for Michèle Lacombe of Trent, our dear friend and former student, the conference was a satisfying one.

In 1991, we also agreed to attend an early spring gathering of Canadianists at the University of Edinburgh. Neither of us had been to Edinburgh before, and staying at a very comfortable hotel in Charlotte Square, adjacent to Princes Street, we found the whole thing a splendid initial exploration of a most beautiful spring cityscape. As we are accustomed to do, we began our stay with a tour of the city, sitting in stiff breezes on the top of a double-decker bus. We saw the sights, but I caught what turned out to be a vile bug, which somewhat, but not entirely, dampened our travellers' enthusiasm. This conference's theme was the influence of Scotland on Canadian Literature hosted by Ged Martin of the U. of Edinburgh. It had been preceded by a biography conference which was attended by a number of Canadians, our friend Francess Halpenny among them. Again, Michèle was with us, as was John Lennox, and so we had a congenial home-from-home family. The hospitality was excellent, the bus-trip to Abbotsford, Sir Walter Scott's magnificent home, was memorable, and all went well.

We left to drive south to St. Deniel's in Wales, a research centre I had been told of by my York colleague, Douglas Verney. This is a well-funded foundation situated in Hawarden, William Ewart Gladstone's home turf, and the site of the magnificent library which he left to the nation. It is run by the Church of England, and the residences are capable of housing about 50 visitors very comfortably and very reasonably. Here I had about ten days to recuperate from my Edinburgh cold, to enjoy the rural spring around the village, and to savour once again the delights of living institutionally, an experience that, ever since the Commonwealth Services Club, has been dear to me. We were fortunate to find ourselves sharing the premises with a group of about forty men and women from Winston Salem, North Carolina. They were having a combined episcopal and holiday tour, and perhaps because they were residents with us, the meals, three a day plus coffee and biscuits in the morning and tea in the afternoon, were particularly good. The rooms were not spacious but very cleverly designed to give a maximum of closet space and up-to-the-minute built-in detail to residents. Baths were plentiful, and all the natives, from the Warden himself, an Anglican clergyman, to the waitresses, were cordially friendly. It was a splendid experience, enhanced by spring flowers and woodsy paths through the large woods where Gladstone had relieved stress by felling trees. I loved reading in his oak-panelled library, an imposing 19th-century Gothic building containing a memorable theological collection and a smaller, though still considerable, general 19th-century collection. In spite of the misery afflicting me, St. Deniel's is a cherished memory.

Chapter XIV

Biography

In the Fall of 1977 I first began to teach a course on First Person Narrative. Under that rubric I meant to include autobiography and autobiographical fiction, a shining example of the latter being Margaret Laurence's *Bird In The House* and of the former Anna Jameson's *Winter Studies and Summer Rambles in Canada*. At that time the formal study of autobiography and biography was almost unknown, though fiction written in the first person had been for some time a growing field for critics, in large part the result of *The Rhetoric of Fiction*, the influential work by Wayne Booth, which had enlarged our critical vocabularies by the introduction of "unreliable narrator" as a profoundly useful concept. In my teaching experience, Sinclair Ross's *As For Me And My House* had been the first Canadian beneficiary of the term, Mrs. Bentley, the narrator of the entire work, a tantalizingly apt candidate for unreliability. The inherent possibilities of the term broadened and deepened the impact of that work and many others immeasurably.

By the time I introduced my course, my own interests had become focused on texts that were in considerable part autobiographical or were presented as such. My required reading list began with the three outstanding 19th-century stalwarts, Susanna Moodie, Catharine Parr Traill and Anna Jameson and went on to our three everfascinating con-artists, Frederick Philip Grove, Grey Owl and John Glassco, before climaxing with the work of

Margaret Laurence, Gabrielle Roy, Charles Ritchie and, the most recently published, Percy Janes's Newfoundland-set *House of Hate*. At that time Douglas Spettigue was busily stirring up the Grove stew, convinced that little or nothing about his subject's early life was as Grove had portrayed it in *In Search of Myself* and *A Search For America*. Grove had told and written the story of a rich young man, brought up in a castle in Sweden, who, when his father died and the family fortune was lost, had to emigrate to America and there travel, penniless, from coast to coast, a casual labourer and an incipient writer. Finally, he had come to rest in Manitoba, and this finale was verifiable, for there he taught school and married Catherine Wiens, one of the Mennonite community in which, at long last, he settled. Together they suffered the early death of their daughter.

Spettigue, who had been set off in his search years earlier by a chance remark of Northrop Frye's about Grove's "lying," was vociferously and often nastily opposed by an old guard headed by Desmond Pacey who had, as he thought, marked out the Grove territory years before as exclusively his. He would have none of the "upstart Pettigrew" or his theories. It was, however, the time for young iconoclasts, and with a highly commendable mix of stubbornness and research, Spettigue persevered in the face of stone-walling, even at the hands of the notably fair-minded George Woodcock, until he was finally able to publish *FPG: The European Years* (1973). In it he demonstrated, with the complete cooperation of Grove's son, Leonard, that far from growing up princely rich, Grove was in fact Felix Paul Greve, a German from a very ordinary background who had indeed had a propensity for writing and who had dwelt on the fringes of a literary group that included Andre Gide, making his living from translating and living well beyond his means. In fact, he "sowed his wild oats" so effectively that he spent some time in prison for fraud and upon release, faked suicide and sailed for America, leaving a wife and his considerable literary production, including two novels, behind. Spettigue's assiduous detective work effectively scotched the old and ushered in a new and far more interesting Grove, giving the study of the field just beginning to be called "Life-Writing" an enormous boost in this country. It did not, however, and no one has yet, solved the mystery completely—there are missing years between Grove's documented flight from Europe and the documented teaching post in Manitoba. There has been a broadening of knowledge about his companions both in Europe and America, notably because of the efforts of Paul Hjartarson of the University of Alberta who effectively unearthed one of Grove's lovers, the wild and wonderful Baroness Elsa, the friend of the well-known American writer, Djuna Barnes, whose novel, *Nightwood*, features the goings on of the fast set in New York's Greenwich Village of the teens and twenties.

At that time, we knew nothing of John Glassco's comparable fabrications and every word of *Memoirs of Montparnasse* was considered a true and moving portrait of the youngsters, Buffy and Graham, sowing their wild oats in the Paris of the twenties, Graham paying for his dissipation with a long drawn-out, life-threatening illness climaxed by radical chest surgery. Such a reading was enhanced by the handsome production of the published book, its introduction by Leon Edel, unquestionably the senior biographical scholar on the continent at that time, and its clever alternation of Glassco's present and much younger voices, beautifully differentiated in the text by the use of an elegant italic print. One of that first year's students whose friendship I still enjoy wrote me an outstanding essay about *Memoirs*, considering the entire text as a series of boxes within boxes, a very fitting way of dealing with the book as it was produced for us and as we accepted it then. Edel provided that outer box, then Glassco in the present, then Glassco at the supposed time of writing and finally, the earlier, extremely youthful Glassco. It was years later that Fraser Sutherland and later, Philip Kokatailo, were able to consult the manuscript and establish its hoax factor, one of the crucial pieces of evidence the simple but incontrovertible recognition that the ball-point pen, with which the manuscript was written, did not exist at the time Glassco claimed to be writing out his adventures in Paris. Undoubtedly he was an adventurer in Paris: his name crops up, along with his friend, Graham's, in the memoirs of Gertrude Stein, Hemingway, and Morley Callaghan, and there is also the evidence of Callaghan's waspish short story based on Buffy (Glassco) and Graham, "Now That April's Here." Nor did the unmasking of the Glassco of the *Memoirs* have any negative impact on the reputation of the real Glassco, writer, translator and horseman, for decades a feature of the Eastern Townships clique which also included Hugh MacLennan, A.J.M. Smith and Frank Scott. Canada's literary community appreciated yet another well-done hoax and continued to admire its vehicle, the *Memoirs of Montparnasse*.

    The same masking of reality still applied to Grey Owl when my course began and for some years later. When, about 1980, I became friendly with Viola Pratt, the poet's widow, and talked to her about Grove, her explanation of the staying power of the fable he made of his early life was utterly simple and correspondingly convincing: "The men wanted to believe him, you know," she said, "and so they did." The desire for European glamour in Canada's small, colonial, literary culture outranked all probability or suspicion of fraud. As in the case of Grove, publishers, poets and readers were so happy to believe in Grey Owl as a self-taught child of nature, our very own noble savage, that they preferred to ignore his blazing blue eyes and all the rest of the evidence that suggested that his blood was not the Indian mix he professed. His publisher, Macmillan, was hugely successful with his works and the book tours they arranged for him. Their chief editor, Rache Lovat Dickson, toured him around England, even to an audience with King George VI and the princesses, in costume and playing his Indian role to the hilt. "Greetings, cousin," he saluted the King, in what must have been a climactic moment for Archie Belaney, who had grown up an orphan in the care of maiden aunts in Hastings, England. Well into the eighties, holidaying in St. Lucia in the Caribbean, I met an Englishwoman of about my own age who had read his 'beaver book' as a child at school and could still recite paragraphs of it from memory. That he was a fake made not the slightest difference to her—he was an early hero-author, and such he remained! Small wonder that he died young, of alcoholism: the pressures of acting that total life-style were wickedly draining. Of all his many readers the British were and remained the most devoted: it is especially fitting that Sir Richard Attenborough is at this moment in Canada(1998), making a movie of his life.

While the three G's—Grove, Glassco and Grey Owl —were our most spectacular frauds, they were by no means alone. Emily Carr is a case in point. When in her middle age, she began to write, she adopted the persona "Small" and portrayed herself as the child she felt herself to be, often badly used by her sisters, and, in fact, abused, often "whipped" she claimed, by one of them. In the late seventies, shortly before Maria Tippett's major biography of 1979, Francess Halpenny, at that time Dean of the School of Library Science at the University of Toronto and an accomplished actress as well, wrote and presented Carr in a one-woman show, accepting totally her version of her early life in a very affecting performance. It was the Emily that we all wanted to know and honour, and even now it is with pleasure that I remember her portrayal and regret that it was superceded so quickly by Tippett's biography and then by the works of Paula Blanchard and Doris Shadbolt. Our forced acknowledging of Emily's incorrigible fictionalizing of portions of her past was not accepted easily or with good nature.

Meanwhile, in 1977, concurrent with the introduction of my course, both the study of Life-Writing and the women's movement surged forward. When Leon Edel retired from Columbia and settled in Hawaii, the university there established the quarterly journal *Biography* in his honour. This was in 1978; it was certainly in that journal that I first encountered the term "Life-Writing." Before that Roy Pascal's study, *Design And Truth In Autobiography*, was effectively our only critical enquiry into the genre. His thesis, that the genesis of autobiography was the urge to confession, harking back to Augustine's *Confessions*, while obviously arguable from the start, was also at that time, convincing, though not for long. The critical articles began immediately, and before long we had assembled a considerable roster of them, in those early years much concerned with 'truth,' honesty and the implicit contract established between writer and reader. It took a long time for students to accept without stern moral judgments the tricksterism of Grove, Glassco and Grey Owl, in whose works its machinations are particularly blatant. Even now there is a certain unwillingness to do so.

More and more though, as time has passed and the 'realism' that was such a large factor in modernism has given over to 'post-modernism,' blurring the lines between genres that were once so firmly delineated, we, our students and all readers have been forced to accept the distortion and selection of detail, both planned and inevitable, that occur the moment a writer, or any one of us, begins to write.

My colleague, John Lennox, asks me to join him in his Graduate course in Life Writing every year, and it attracts exceptional students, for it has been one of the most popular fields of the last decade. Not only do critical works proliferate, autobiographical works proliferate as well, many of them inspired, or at least affected by Carolyn Heilbrun's *Writing A Woman's Life*, a short monograph of a particularly timely topic. Heilbrun was a Columbia professor for many years, and an outspoken feminist. Her earlier *Reinventing Womanhood* has been and remains particularly important to the entire feminist project, though the situation in the United States for women, both students and academics, is significantly different from ours in Canada. Under the pseudonym Amanda Cross she also writes ingenious murder mysteries with a decidedly feminist slant.

The three nineteenth-century stalwarts, Jameson, Traill and Moodie, hewed much more closely to the facts of their lives than did our major tricksters. Yet Jameson herself had begun her writing career with a ruse so successful that she became famous in London's literary society overnight. She had gone as a governess to the continent with a wealthy family, touring through Europe, down through Italy and back through France. She wrote up her trip as *The Diary Of An Ennuyee*, the story of a young girl who, heart sick and sad from a broken love-affair, listlessly travels around Europe nursing her broken heart and finally dies and is buried in France, lovelorn, pitiable, and forever far from home. Although Jameson had already been writing for some years, this, a Childe Harold for young women, was her first success, and it set her up in a career that was to make her one of the most successful literary women of her time. By the time she came to Canada, ostensibly to join her estranged husband, Robert Jameson, who was about to become Vice-Chancellor of the Canadas, the colony's highest legal position, she had behind her several travel books and one best-seller, a consideration of Shakespeare's women called *Characteristics of Women*, an early example of 'feminist' literary criticism. She was, in fact, a consummate book-maker, no stranger to any number of literary techniques designed to enhance the reader-appeal of her works.

She came to Canada unwillingly and with no intention of staying, for she and Jameson had lived separately for some years, but she couldn't refuse to be present to act as his hostess when he took over his important legal appointment, especially if she hoped to persuade him to give her an annual allowance. But she left her dearest friend, Ottilie von Goethe, the poet's daughter-in-law, and their mutual male friend, Robert Noel, most unwillingly. It was to Noel that she addressed the journal that was the basis of her *Winter Studies* and once again, as she had earlier, she portrayed herself as a melancholy exile, this time without the saving interest of the famous sites of Europe, but rather as one besieged in the harsh climate of wintertime Toronto, in the midst of a society that was a cultural wasteland. By this time in her early forties, Anna had already been for years a confirmed traveller, and she knew very well when she set sail for Canada that she would produce a book from her experiences. She arrived in Canada in the months immediately before the abortive rebellion of 1837 and this circumstance gave interest to her work by the time it was published in England by Bentley in 1838. More important than that, though, were her travels; for from her arrival she had planned to make and exploit an extended trip from Toronto to the west and up Lake Huron, a 'summer ramble' which would show her off as an intrepid traveller and a keen observer of largely unknown territory, hitherto unreported by lady travellers. In this goal she was, of course, considerably aided by her status as "Chancellor's Lady," a position which brought her special treatment. No matter what the state of her marital relations, she was the wife of a high official and as such she could command aid and respect wherever she went. Furthermore, by this time she had many connections to well-known people in England—her visit to Colonel Thomas Talbot, "the old eagle," as she called him, in his lonely estate on Lake Erie, was undoubtedly one of these, for Talbot was notably inhospitable, and a lone female guest who not only visited him, but stayed for several days, was an amazing and almost certainly unwelcome phenomenon in his solitary isolation.

However aggressive Anna may have been, she was through and through a professional writer. When her planned trek got underway, her very best traveller's side surfaced, and the woman who made light of all the hardships on her way and the most of every mile of her journey, is a far cry from the bitterly lonely and heartsick exile whom she portrayed in her "Winter Studies." She was keenly aware of her female readership and made a special point of observing women, in this case especially native women, for she had become friendly with two sisters, Mrs. MacMurray, the wife of the Anglican clergyman at Niagara-on-the-Lake and her sister, Mrs. Schoolcraft, the wife of the Indian agent and early anthropologist at Michilimakinac. Their mother, Mrs. Johnson, was a Chippewa Chief, according to that tribe's matriarchal custom, in the area surrounding Sault Ste. Marie. Anna was quick to exploit the possibilities in discussing the position of Indian women from the vantage point of her nascent feminism, finding them in some ways more favourably situated than their white counterparts. "I have never met a contented woman in Canada," she said, and as was usual with her, she blamed a miserably inadequate "education" for their discontent.

When in 1960/61 I wrote my Ph.D. thesis, "Anna Jameson: The Making of a Reputation," I made as much as I dared of Jameson's early feminism and of her various crusades in her works to raise the standards and quality of women's education. I had always to keep in mind, however, that I was doing my research for the University of Toronto, until recently loath to have women in its Ph.D. programme at all, let alone a woman who argued too vociferously for the "New Woman" aspects of Jameson. The Second Wave of the Women's Movement, as it is now called, was in its infancy and Ellen Moers' ground-breaking work, *Literary Women*, was not to appear until 1965. I was inhibited and cautious, for I was already doubly fortunate in my work with Northrop Frye as my thesis supervisor and the easy acceptance by the department of my own part-time schedule for my work. In 1977, ten years after its original publication date, the University of Toronto Press issued a paperback of the work and I was able to add an introduction that gave Anna at least her partial due as a 19th-century feminist. It was not until the mid-eighties that she was 'discovered' and celebrated by various young women scholars and featured in such publications as *Amazing Space* as the committed champion of women that she had always been.

She herself had been as prudent and circumspect

about her convictions as I had been, and with more reason, for she had depended on her writings, not only for her own livelihood, but for the support of various members of her family. Jameson had never paid her the allowance he agreed to, and, when he died, had left his estate, including considerable land holdings, to a Canadian woman friend. Now, thirty years after its publication, when I look at *Love And Work Enough: The Life Of Anna Jameson*, I am on the whole pleased with the way it has weathered the years. I think I could write it all now with more grace, but my reading of Anna would not essentially change. I was deeply engaged then: as I wrote in my first introduction, omitted at the insistance of readers who said I had a "strange relationship" with my subject, I wrote with the feeling of Anna herself looking over my shoulder. I am still deeply engaged with that gifted, hardworking, often tiresome, many-faceted woman.

In contrast, the Strickland sisters, the others of the famous threesome, have undergone sea-changes, both of them, since I began to write of them in the sixties. When Professor Spenceley gave us our first Canadian Literature course in 1939 they were the two prototypically contrasting Upper Canadian settlers: Susanna, the unhappy, unwilling emigrant whose early experiences recorded in *Roughing It In The Bush*, she called a life "in the prison house," and Catharine, the gentle, godly earth-mother, whose *Life In The Backwoods* was intended to encourage and instruct prospective women settlers. Shortly after I completed my Ph.D., Malcolm Ross, General Editor of the McClelland and Stewart's burgeoning New Canadian Library, asked me to write the introduction To *The Backwoods Of Canada*. The request, to a still novice academic, was like a Royal Command, and it was given with firm instructions as to length, both of the introduction and of the text, which I was to cut to requirements—absolutely no possibility of a fully reprinted version, though I tried to argue for one. The work had first been published in 'Knight's Library of Entertaining Knowledge,' one of the first paperback series, selling for sixpence, and designed to instruct the rapidly growing working-class reading public. The Stricklands were a family of writers, though Catharine had been the first to be published, well before her marriage, but one of her sisters, Agnes, was the author of *Lives Of The Queens Of England*, and was a well-known and successful author by the time Catharine settled in Canada. She and Elizabeth, another stay-at-home sister and writer, together edited Catharine's letters home for publication and shepherded them to publication. Even then it seemed obvious to me that the letters had been written in two parts, one for publication and another for family perusal only. It was to be thirty years, though, before the publication of Traill's letters, *I Bless You In My Heart* would reveal just how very different her reality in Canada was from her first published version.

Traill's work cannot be considered in the same league of deliberate hoaxes as can the works of the three G's. Rather, both she and her sister were writing for specific audiences; both were writing for money that they badly needed, and it is unsurprising that they chose to stress and enhance the aspects of their Canadian experiences that were the most fitting for their purposes. *The Backwoods* is bland: Catharine chooses to spend pages on the flora and fauna around her and to radically downplay the dreaded cholera epidemic that was raging when she and her husband landed and that she fell prey to in Montreal. She resolutely dwells on the beauties and opportunities of the new land, as she does in her follow-up work, *The Female Emigrant's Guide*, which a student once rightly termed our "Whole Earth Catalogue." What is astonishing to me now, three decades later, is how very far those texts portray the realities that Catharine and her family faced, not just on their arrival in Canada, but for most of her long life here. First and formost it must be said—Thomas Traill was not the material of which successful settler-pioneers are made. A gentle and delicate man with artistic leanings, he was already a widower and was forced to leave two sons by his first marriage with his family in the Orkneys. Like many another, as a British officer, now redundant, he was powerfully attracted by the free land he could claim, and he was led to emigration by the will-o'-the-wisp dream of becoming a landed gentleman. That dream was still affecting the English as late as the large emigrations of the 1940s and fifties—to an island nation and one in the grip of a rigorous class system, the vastness of Canada looked like the land of golden opportunity and dreams come true. Unfortunately, for Traill as for so many others, the dream, without capital or the ability to endure years of slogging hard work, was all too readily transformed into a nightmare.

When I wrote the introduction to the N.C.L.'s *The Backwoods Of Canada* I was still very close to my first experience of England and particularly to the magnificent paintings of the National Gallery. Gainsborough's "Mr. and Mrs. Robert Andrews" was my special favourite and the one I associated with the Traills. The painting shows two attractive young people, garbed in 18th-century fashion, the lady in a blue silk dress seated on a garden seat with her husband standing beside her and their dog relaxed at their feet, both of them looking out toward lush, cultivated fields and a softly curving landscape. It is an idealized picture of the prosperous gentleman-landowner and his wife, and it seemed to me at the time the very embodiment of the benignly civilized couple that the Traills personified. About the essential personalities of Thomas and Catharine Traill I was right; about their fortunes in Canada I could scarcely have been more wrong. In the 1970s three scholars, Beth Hopkins, Michael Peterman and Carl Ballstadt began a serious search for letters and documents relating to the Traills and Moodies and before long they had unearthed a very great deal of material. With many many descendants dispersed throughout Canada and the States, their efforts eventually uncovered hundreds of letters, whose first fruits concerning the Traills, the collection *I Bless You In My Heart*, was published in 1995.

It is a wonderfully well-chosen collection and still only the tip of the iceberg, for hundreds had to be set aside in the interest of producing a manageable book. Michael Peterman is now in the final stages of writing Catharine's biography, a work which will throw still more light on their fortunes in Canada. Far from being in any way like the idealized Gainsborough sitters, the Traills all too soon became impoverished and remained so, their misfortunes exacerbated by Thomas Traill's ill health, depression, and, before their large family was grown, death. Everything unfortunate that could happen to settlers happened to them: isolated land, inability to clear and farm it, sickness of one or other of their nine children, and, the last straw for Thomas Traill, a disastrous fire. Sometimes the children could not attend school because they did not have shoes; sometimes they did not have enough warm clothing; sometimes they were dependent on neighbors for food, and neighbors were often some miles away. Always Catharine tried to make a little money by her writing and always, too, she was in demand as a midwife, a training and aptitude she had brought with her to Canada. In reasonable circumstances she would have been every inch the ideal settler: she never lost her quiet faith and optimism, and she hung on to the standards of a gentlewoman. As she wrote, believed, and lived by, the wife of a British officer had a secure standing and no need of fashionable externals. As it was, her goodness shone throughout a long life illuminating every word of her letters.

The case of her sister, Susanna Moodie, is comparable, though in *Roughing It In The Bush* she herself presented the dark side of her experience so vividly that scholars, myself among them, had no need to feel they had been absolutely wrong in their assessment of the Moodie's siuation as more and more letters were gathered and more and more facts were expanded and made plain. *Letters of a Lifetime*, again collected and edited by Ballstadt, Peterman and Hopkins, did not radically reorient what we knew and thought about the couple. In particular, we have found our initial opinion of Dunbar Moodie improved, rather than weakened, by late-accumulated evidence. Like the Traills, the Moodies were unfitted for settlers' lives, and like the Traills they were led into some rash decisions and expenditures of precious capital by the chimaera of a landed gentleman's estate. But Moodie was more rugged, both physically and mentally, than Traill. He was also quick to take a chance to better himself, out of both loyalty and expediency hastening off to join Her Majesty's forces at the first news of the Rebellion of '37. Likewise Susanna, left alone with the children and sadly in need, did not hesitate to write to Governor Arthur asking for some preference for her husband; nor did she hesitate to set herself up squarely in centre stage in her *Roughing it*, as the beleaguered heroine who battles her way through poverty, loneliness and every misfortune that the wilderness could bring and finally is rewarded with a sheriff's appointment for her husband and a home in the comparatively congenial town of Belleville.

Like Catharine, Susanna was a practiced writer before she came to Canada, but she was very different in her writing style. Catharine was of a factual, scientific turn of mind; she was a patient amateur botanist before coming to Canada, and she became an authority, writing two works, *Canadian Wildflowers* and *Studies Of Plant Life In Canada* about Canada's native plants. Susanna's temperament was romantic and sentimental; she was a fictionalist who, before Canada, had practised a gothic and melodramatic style and had published a good many stories in that mode. Life in the backwoods gave her the setting which outdid in its menace anything she had encountered or imagined, and she made the most of it. She was also blest with, she sometimes considered cursed with, a lively sense of humour: she didn't mind making herself the butt of her stories, and her various housewifely disasters make consistently compelling and entertaining reading. As Carl Klinck was the first to point out long ago, she set herself up as her own romance heroine: no matter what the ordeal, she survives, sometimes laughs, and always learns. *Roughing it* will always be the book we read by choice, as Catharine will always be the sister whose goodness we admire. Some twenty years ago Margaret Atwood found herself haunted by Susanna: her *Journals Of Susanna Moodie* will remain a major memorial to a gifted, vital woman. Catharine, became "Saint Catharine" to Margaret Laurence in *The Diviners*, and the lovingly ironic relationship between Morag Gunn and Catharine Traill is another permanent memorial.

Since its publication in 1908, millions of girls have read *Anne Of Green Gables* and then gone on to be enchanted by Anne's further life and the stories of her successors, particularly Emily whose three sagas, *Emily Of New Moon*, *Emily's Quest*, and *Emily Climbs* are given particular credit by many writing women, Alice Munro among them, for early encouragement and inspiration. Page of Boston, who published *Anne Of Green Gables* and whose salespeople called it "a Home and Jesus novel" in the popular tradition of *Rebecca of Sunnybrook Farm* and stemming of course from *Little Women*, its great foremother, certainly had a success with it at the time, but no one could possibly have prophesied that ninety years later it would still be read world-wide, that it would have been a code book of the Resistance movement in Poland in W.W.II, or that in Japan it would have been for some generations, a runaway success. Like most of the girl readers of my generation, I found it at about age 8. It had several profound effects on me, perhaps just the enhancing or underlining of attitudes already present to me, but certainly important to my life, then and now. The first of these was friendship—the idea of "best friends," of a "kindred spirit" as Anne called Diana Barry, was taken over and practised by everyone I knew; in fact I remember saying to a new girl at school, with self-conscious, total seriousness," I would like to be your friend." I meant "best friend" and I meant "kindred spirit", and I can still remember the keen pangs of jealousy I felt a year or so later, when a third girl joined our twosome. To jealously guard the territory was certainly not a good thing, but to be initiated into the special and lasting good that close friendship brings certainly was a good thing, one that many women have treasured throughout their lives. L.M. Montgomery's Anne showed that to my generation and to every generation since.

 I also credit Anne with instilling in her readers a militant sense of individualism and fair play. The idea that a child had rights, was as entitled as any adult to her own possessions and her own privacy, was not a widely accepted tenet of child-rearing in the early years of this century. Again, I can remember vividly my impassioned partisanship when Anne was falsely accused by a grown-up, or was put in a humiliating position. More than that, I can remember taking my own first steps toward the defying of unfair treatment by adults and, most important, I can remember my first small victories. Finally, and also of prime importance, I believe that Anne and all of Montgomery's works imparted and encouraged a healthy appreciation of the natural beauty around us. Sentimental indeed were Anne's naming of "the lake of shining waters" and Anne's high-flown fanciful language, but beautiful indeed were the plentiful woods around us and the flowers at our feet in the borderline rural Canada I grew up in: our appreciation of these was surely enhanced by Montgomery's work. At just about the same time, Gene Stratton Porter's *Girl of the Limberlost* celebrated the teenage years of her heroine, Eleanora, unloved and poor, who roamed the vast swamp of northern Michigan and loved it as did Anne her Prince Edward Island habitat. However, Stratton Porter's work demonstrates one crucial difference from Montgomery's that now seems to me to illustrate perfectly American hustling entrepreneurship, for Eleanora made herself money from her swamp: she collected and sold specimens of rare moths and finally was able to finance herself at the University of Michigan. The natural beauties that Anne loved were not a source of income; her love for Green Gables and its setting was absolutely untouched by consumerism.

Small wonder that when Elizabeth Waterston and Mary Rubio, both of the University of Guelph, first began to edit and publish Montgomery's Journals, hitherto kept private by her family, the shock of finding a Lucy Maud who was radically different from her sunny Anne, was considerable. In the sixties, as Centennial approached, the University Women's Club sponsored a book of articles about outstanding Canadian women, *The Clear Spirit.* Elizabeth Waterston wrote the chapter on L.M. Montgomery; I wrote the one on the Strickland sisters. I have a vivid memory of first hearing from Elizabeth at that time, of the recurring religious melancholia of Ewan MacDonald, Montgomery's husband. I believe that her article was the first bringing to light of the very dark side of the MacDonald's marriage. The *Journals*, four volumes up until 1939 now published and still another to come, are a revelation, not only of the actual progress of Montgomery's life, but especially of her ever-present writerly compulsion. She possessed a self and market awareness that led to her copying her original journals, editing them herself with an eye to future publication.

For a picture of village life in Prince Edward Island, in volume I, in the Ontario village of Leaskdale, volume II, and Leaskdale and Norval in volumes III and IV, the journals are unparalleled in our literature. For a picture of housewifery and the duties of women in the closing years of the 19th centurry and the first two decades of the 20th, as well as the challenges faced by a minister's wife who was also a successful and prolific writer, they are unmatched. Always Montgomery was a high-strung and difficult woman; during the years of WWI, she was overwrought and nervously unstable. But throughout, her Journals gave her the release she sadly needed, and her editing and calculation of their eventual publication is a matter of the utmost gratitude for her readers. For me she has provided a climactic early figure in a Canadian Life Writing field that has steadily become richer, more varied and more popular with students and teachers alike.

Chapter XV

Grandma's Story of her Life, written at age 90

Martha Elizabeth Martin McCandless, 1863-1957

Strathroy, January 25, 1953

My father's name was Samuel Martin, my mother's Beulah Miner Martin and my name is Mrs. Martha Elizabeth Martin McCandless. I was born in the township of Adelaide, in the year 1863, on the 20th of May.

We lived in a white frame house next to Down's for three years; then my father sold out and bought a farm in Caradoc on the 9th concession about a mile from the Saxton schoolhouse where I attended school until we left the farm for town life in Strathroy.

I don't remember how old I was when I started to school, likely 6 or 7. My first teacher's name was Miss McIntyre. She boarded at Mr. John Saxton's. She went home for dinner and when we saw her coming back from dinner a lot of us little girls would run to meet her and all try to get hold of her hands, 3 or 4 for each hand. We must have liked her a lot, I think.

The next teacher, I think, was Miss Lizzie Stuart: she left for some reason and her brother took her place. Then a Miss Pilgrim came; she used to make the pupils cross as she would take a bite of their pencils when doing their questions and eat chalk also. She was very pale and needed some kind of medicine, I imagine.

Then Miss Kidd, red-headed and Dr. Charles Reynolds, a dentist of Strathroy, used to come out to see her. I remember a concert we had and he was there and I suppose she had to see that everything was alright before leaving the school house. He got a little impatient and said, for he lisped a lot, "are you tummin, Miss Tidd? Tum on, tum on!" The young people older than I was had a lot of fun out of that. He was still in Strathroy after I was married. He married and moved to London, passed away some years ago.

Another one was Miss Edwards, next Miss Carrie Oakes, aunt of Mrs. John Burdon on Colborne St. She married Mr. Cady. Miss White was the last teacher I had. She married Truman Crealy.

The older boys had to stay home in the summers and work on their fathers' farms and go to school in the winters and some were pretty dumb, never got out of the first book, I guess. The boys played ball, marbles and shinny: the girls played house, waded in the creek in summer and anything else they could think of. We had to make our own amusements. In the spring my girl-friends would always invite me to their sugar-bushes the day their fathers would sugar-off and I would stay all night. It was always after four o'clock. I just loved the hot sugar in the woods. We always made taffy in some snow or ice.

In winter we would sleigh-ride down hill and going home at four, we would catch on sleighs if any were going our way. We always had a concert in the winter which was the big event. The boys decorated the school with cedar and the older girls made tissue-paper roses to trim with. I can remember the smell of the school as I like cedar.

We had singing for old and young. A Mr. Robert Curtis of Mt. Carmel was the teacher. It was held in the

Saxton school house. He would have the staff and scales all printed on the blackboard and started the singing with the tuning-fork. He was a good teacher and how we did sing Do Re Mi, we almost raised the roof! But it was fun and did so much good to all the young people around that 9th concession and other parts.

The Baptists held their meetings Sunday afternoon in Saxton's school house and Rev. Thomas Collins was the minister all the years we lived there. There was no Sunday School, so my sister Electa and I walked through the fields to town to the Methodist Sunday School on North Street. Our parents were Wesleyan Methodist, but could not get to church, so went to the Baptist church.

In 1875, they built the Caradoc Zion church and we all went there, had Sunday School and Mother led the choir, without an organ for awhile, with Mr. Collins still our preacher, no salary. The choir was made up of the ones who had gone to singing school and they tell me I was in the choir also. The choir used to practise for the opening of the church at our home. They rented an organ from town and a Mr. Rose to play it at the opening and Tea-Meeting Monday night. Oh, what a pleasure they all had practising: I can still hear some laughing at the mistakes I suppose. I remember the tune and a few words of the chorus of one piece they sang at the Tea-Meeting— "It's six o'clock, it's six o'clock, it's six o'clock P.M. Ring out, ye bells, glad whistles blow, "tis six o'clock P.M." I must have been thrilled with it, to remember it all these years.

Bees were all the rage—paring bees, husking, barn raisings and threshings. We liked the paring bees. Three or four would bring the little apple-paring machine, just small things fastened on the table like food-choppers. A little fork stuck out on one side, the apple was stuck on that and a little crank turned. The apples were thrown in a big pan and some would quarter and core them, then others would have cord cut in long lengths, a knot tied in one end, then the quarters were strung on those strings with a big darning needle. When the string was full, the ends of the cord were tied together and hung on poles above the cook stove to dry. Then they had to be put in bags to be tied up to keep them from flies. They always had a big lunch and games and music after the paring was over. They did enjoy themselves.

May 12, 1953.

As I think of spring on the farm, it was a very interesting and busy time. So many cows to milk and butter to make, soft soap to make by putting a barrel on a slanting little platform and filling the barrel with ashes and pouring water on the ashes until they got wet enough to begin to drip the lye down through the grooves on the platform into an iron kettle. Then we put scraps of rinds and grease in the lye, perhaps something else and boiled it down after the scraps were taken out. Men used to come around to buy ashes and gave tin-ware or yellow bar soap for pay. That was fun for us, to go out to the enclosed wagon with a high spring seat in front and look at all the tin-ware. Perhaps we would get a dipper or wash-dish, pie-plate or a tin cup, or part of a bar of brown soap. Then Mother made tallow candles in moulds that would be interesting to children of today. We had coal-oil lamps also in my day, but used candles for lantern and cellars and carrying around.

What lovely apples and cherries we had—no worms! We would dry them for winter use as we didn't have glass sealers, just stone jars that had to be sealed up. Potatoes had no bugs. I remember the first bugs on our potatoes and I remember the first celery I tasted. I thought it was horrid. Another thing was ham-smoking time. We had a smoke-house and the hams were hung on poles across and a fire of corn cobs on the ground, as they didn't burn up like wood, just smouldered to get the smoke and not blaze. The hams had to be put in bags and sewed up tight—to keep flies and bugs out.

We cleaned our knives and forks by taking them out doors and pushing them up and down in the ground, but we made them shine. Then a scouring brick came along. We put one on a little board and shaved some brick off and rubbed with a dampened cloth. That was an improvement.

I could ride horse-back and drive horses and do everything but plough. We hoed and weeded the garden, carried sheaves to be stooked up, raked after the loads when harvest time was on. I couldn't take time to tell all the work we used to do, but we had our play times also. The big event of the year was the big picnic held on Queen Victoria's birthday, the 24th of May, in the pine grove across from the cemetery. They had horse-races and Bell's Family Band, the only Band Strathroy had at that time. I was always thrilled to hear them play, for I loved Band music. There was one little girl about my age, Christie Bell. How I wished I could play like she did. She passed away a few years ago, three or four, on Metcalfe Street. Her sister, Mrs. Bateman, still lives there.

August 10, 1953.
    This is the big day (liquor vote). I have just been down to vote at the school house. There will be lots of excitement tonight likely.

September 30, 53.
    Well, my man got in alright, but I don't think there was much excitement down town. I was more excited over the liquor store vote, however we won and I was very thankful. The Lord said "Him that honoureth me, I will honour" and he always keeps his word.
    Father sold our farm and we moved into town. I went

to school till something happened and the man couldn't pay for the farm and father took it back, so he and mother had to go out to the farm every morning and I stayed home to look after Till and May. They went to school, so a new kind of life opened up for all of us.

I started to take piano and guitar lessons from Miss Carrie Cutten, a music teacher. She was the organist and member of the little old brick Baptist church. She got me in the choir, I sat at her right hand and sang alto. They moved away to Woodstock. She was hired as music teacher in the college and married a student, a Mr. Farmer who later on was Rev. Dr. Farmer of McMaster University.

Miss Ella Frank took the organ and when she married Mr. Dick Robinson and moved away, I took the organ and played for seven years, until I married in 1887. After Miss Cutten left, my guitar lessons stopped, but I started piano lessons with a Miss Napper who was a good teacher, also my last teacher. I was on my own then. Music seemed to be my hobby all through my life from a little girl of six or seven years old singing with Hattie Saxton in that same little brick church. When we lived on the farm, our big sisters took Hattie and me to town to sing a song, something about "Tiny little snowflakes". Our sisters sang in the choir at the time.

I took lessons in sketching and painting in black and white. There were no oil-painting teachers in town at that time or I would have chosen that. Miss Lloyd was my teacher: she had a large class which all met at her home for our lessons. They belonged to our church. Old Mr. Lloyd was run over by a train and Mrs. Loyd and daughter moved away. I was working in a dressmaker's shop with a room-full of girls till that family moved away. My teachers all seemed to be on the move, but not until we all got a good start.

In the Fall of 1887, I started to get ready for my wedding on the 16th of November. My Bridesmaid-to-be offered to come and make my dresses as she was a very fine dressmaker in Sarnia. She made three, a wedding dress, cream cashmere with a little train and all the trimmings you could imagine, all lined and finished to perfection, with a veil. Another was part garnet silk and part cloth, the skirt of silk with gold stripes going round and with it I had a hat of garnet plush with ostrich tips. A travelling dress of grey nubby cloth and little hat or bonnet shape, made of the dress goods and trimmed with grey corded ribbon with a nubby edge. A dark brown Sealette coat brought over from Port Huron looked something like fur—some thought it was.

I resigned as organist of our church with Mr. Dayfoot as minister and my sister May took the organ for about two years until they could get an organist for the new church. I had about fifty or more at my wedding, all the choir and brother or sister, wife or husband who weren't in the choir, some friends and relatives. We had a turkey dinner. I guess it was good, as Mother invited a cousin of ours, an extra good cook to come and help her. I only remember one thing we had—that was grapes. The west side of our house was covered with grape-vines and two kinds of grapes. I had read how to keep grapes for some time by melting beeswax and resin together and picking the nicest bunches and dipping the end of the stem in the mixture, wrapping each bunch in brown paper and packing loosely in a big box. They were fine for my wedding day.

Mr. Dayfoot came down the day before and brought a lovely raw fruit, hand-painted china dish, set in a silver basket, from the church. I think we must have been married about six o'clock and left on a train at nine o'clock, going East. There were no cars at that time; there was a man in town, we all called him the Old-for-hire. He had a two-seated carriage, I have forgotten its name. He came and took us to the old station at that time.

When we came back, we went to our new house, upstairs over our meat-shop. That winter Sam made me a present of a new organ which added a lot of pleasure to the home and we had lots of company, living on Front Street. The next year the corner-stone of the new Baptist church was laid, and the church finished the next year, I think. Then Victor came along. We had moved to English street as it was so hot upstairs and Victor was born there. We moved back over the store in the Fall and the next summer we went to Roach's Hotel and boarded for the hot months. Mr. Roach was a good customer and we had a nice time there. They were building the new Post Office. Mrs. Roach and I would sit in the sitting-room and watch the men lay brick. We used to say we knew every brick that went into that building. It was very interesting to watch everything going on. We went back in the Fall, when Victor was about two years old.

Jim Smiley and Polly lived south of St. Thomas, on a rented farm and were at our place visiting. He told Sam about a farm about a mile from their home and got him in the notion to farm, so we sold out and moved four miles south of St. Thomas for two years or more. Roy was born there. Then we moved back to Strathroy, on a farm in Adelaide for a couple of years. Evan was born there. Then we moved to another farm nearer town and Sam bought another meat-shop. Basil was born on the last farm.

We moved to Metcalfe Street, next door to my old home. While there, Grandpa McCandless passed away in his home on English street. After a few months we moved to the Murby house, east of the station. It was a nice large brick house with a verandah on both sides. The children had a tricycle and would race around at great speed. The room over the kitchen was their play-room and warm. The trains passed quite close to the house and I always went out to the verandah when passenger trains went through, for sometimes someone would wave at me. Of course I couldn't tell who they were, but it got to be a habit to go out.

While there, Grandpa's farm in Caradoc was to be sold and shares paid off, so Sam thought it might be a good move for us to take the farm, pay off the shares and live out there. We could have a slaughter-house and pasture for some cattle, pigs, chickens, cows, horses and raise all our own living almost but wheat. We had lovely apples and some berries and garden stuff galore and lots of all kinds of meat and maple syrup was only 75 cents a gallon at that time. We bought 22 gallons that year. There were generally eight people to eat: we boarded the hired man and I kept a girl nearly all the time we lived there, for $2.50 a week. The men drove home to dinner always —no cars, no phones. The children went to the same school I did when I started to school. The building was frame but brick now. Basil started the last year we lived there. We were on this farm for six years.

We went to town to church and Sunday School and Victor started to go to the High School on Caradoc Street. We got all the shares paid and started saving money to buy a home in town. Wes Prangley owned this place on Colborne Street: it looked like an ideal home for us, with horses, waggons and chickens. There was a mortgage on the Nichol house and lot. We paid it off and had the big square lot. We moved to town in the Fall and the children all started school there.

Later on, we made some changes to the house, put doors on the arches to make it warmer, put red shingles on the house, tore down the old verandah, built a new one, planted the hedge and took away the fences. We sold the Nichol house and lot and two other ones, one to Gladys and Jack Brown and one to Mrs. Butler. She changed the barn into a house. Three or four years ago the boys sold the farm.

Some time after moving here I had a surprise. Two ladies were visiting me from Inwood when a man came to the door and said they had a piano from Ernie Wright's store or factory. I said, "Oh, I think you have made a mistake," and he grinned and said, "It's yours all right," and started taking the organ out and bringing in the piano. You can't imagine how pleased I was, as well as the whole family. The boys all took some lessons on piano, but Basil was the only one to stick to the lessons and now he plays well and enjoys it.

I stayed with the choir until three or four years ago, when I wasn't well, so never went back. the choir always used me well, from the time I was a young girl and joined it. While I was playing the organ in the old church, the members of the church made me a present of a purse of money on the Christmas tree. The didn't pay organists in our church at that time. All worked to help the church get along.

I belonged to the Ladies' Aid and Mission Circle, had Life membership in both Home and Foreign Missions. On one of my birthdays, the Ladies' Aid gave me a Card Shower, then went down in the basement to a banquet. Another time the choir and some friends gave a lovely banquet in the basement with place-cards, flowers, candles and Birthday Cake covered with candles for me to blow out, and last, a lovely present from the choir—a box with comb, brush, mirror, powder and jewel glass jars. The whole party was wonderful—the Rev. Smith gave three or four chicken dinners which we all enjoyed so much too. Years ago, the Aid gave me a present of a beautiful floor lamp and fernery at a social in the basement which was a big surprise to me.

I intended to write down a few things we used to do when we were children which might be interesting to the children later on. We would go to the woods and dig up crinkly root to eat—it grew underground. Also ground nuts grew underground, about the size of a hazel-nut. And a vine called squaw-berries grew on top of the ground. It had little red berries which we ate. They were about the size of a currant. We ate May apples too. We were taught what was good to eat. We gathered wild plums—they made lovely flavoured preserves and were good to eat.

We also gathered yellow sand-cherries for preserves. They grew on very sandy land. We gathered grain-bags full of hazel-nuts and dried them in the sun and shelled them later in the winter. We kept lots of bees and honey all the time. When it was time to pick the geese, they tied their legs and wings and put a stocking-leg over the head of the goose and picked the down and small feathers from the breast and under the wings and kept them for pillows and feather-beds. We had to fill ticks full of oat-straw and later with corn-husks instead of mattresses. They also braided out straw by putting the straw in warm water to make it soft—almost like rag mats and then we sewed the braids into hats for the men in summer and for all of us.

In sheep-shearing time we had to help drive the big flock of sheep to a creek or pond to be washed. The one we went to was on the Mt. Brydges road opposite the farm that Fred and Bill Fisher live on now. The creek had been dammed up and made quite a large lake with a big saw-mill and dwelling house. A pen was there to put the sheep in. One sheep was washed at a time in a little pen on the edge of the water, then let loose. As soon as the wool was dry on the sheep, the men sheared it off and it was sent to the woollen mills to get carded and made into rolls or whatever you wanted—cloth, blankets, yarn. Mother spun our rolls into yarn and we all knit mitts and stockings and made clothing.

All animals roamed the woods, so one cow would have a cow-bell on it and one sheep would have a sheep-bell. At night, at milking time we had to go to hunt the cows. Sometimes they would be turned around and eating along towards home. We would hear the bells. At last the law said : "Keep all animals on the farm, build all fences high so nothing can jump over them." That made the men so much work splitting rails and building fences—I often wonder how people could live so long and work so hard.

Father set a trap in our woods one time and caught a black fox—the first one trapped in that part of the country and everybody so surprised.

Chapter XVI

Telling Dot's Life Like a Story

In memory of my aunt who died in 1991

One of Dot's great gifts was story-telling. We've all listened spell-bound as she told about her past. I've had more chances than most to hear her— seventy-two years of loving kindness in fact, and hours upon hours of listening. Besides, Dot and I were the two redheads of the family, and that gave us a special bond from the beginning. I'll tell it as she has told it to me, my memory selecting the details, of course, as her memory in her turn also selected the elements of her story. What she told me was true in spirit, not complete (what story of a life can be?),and what I tell you will be true in spirit as well.

Dorothy Eileen Sullivan was two and a half when Rachel, her mother, died in 1906. The family always said that Dr. Jones from Watford was drunk when he came that time to deliver Rachel's baby, but it is just as likely that Rachel was worn out. She had had six children in close stairsteps, Vernon, Frieda, Mabel, Harold, and Marge, two years older than Dot. Rachel and Will were working hard on their farm on the Second Line of Adelaide, about ten miles northwest of Strathroy, but they certainly didn't own it outright, and Will was always at least as interested in local, county, provincial and federal politics as he was in farming. He had become Reeve, to his great pride and pleasure, and his political ambitions were boundless. Of all the Sullivans he was the one who was the most adventurous and who loved learning more than any of the others. He had gone to High School in Strathroy for awhile, boarding at the Shotwells, where Jim, the clever son of the house, was already showing the aptitude for study that would eventually lead him to a very great reputation as a Columbia historian and Woodrow Wilson's advisor at the birth of the League of Nations. The climax of Will's young life was his most adventurous feat of all—he ran away and shipped as a cattle hand on a voyage to England, taking the family savings in a sock with him. When he got to Liverpool he looked around for a few days, and then shipped right back —if he remembered much of anything about his trip neither Dot nor I heard of it, though he was proud to relate how glad his father was to see him again—so glad that the lifting of the sock was forgiven and forgotten.

Will was shattered by Rachel's death, not only by the loss of his beloved wife, but by the loss of the companion who was as interested in community and political affairs as he was, and whose encouragement he could always count on. Like many country girls of her day, she had been a teacher and a good one. She had as good a brain as her husband, and she liked to use it. Will was also stunned by suddenly being left with the children, but like many another widower of his time, he was rescued by his own family, to the best of their ability. Mabel went to live with his younger brother, Ed, and his wife, Clara; Harold to his older brother John; Marge to friends, William and Stella Langford, and later to cousins, the Woontons in London; Frieda, old enough to be lost and desperately unhappy without her mother, wouldn't be budged from her father's side; and Vernon was old enough to stay with him and help with the farm.

Of all of them, Dot was the most fortunate. She was too young to realize what had happened. She had never known anything but a comfortable and sheltered babyhood, and Rachel's mother and father, the Clark grandparents, took her home with them to carry on the loving care that had surrounded her. Elizabeth and James Clark had very little to live on. Grandpa Clark had been a notorious wild one in the family, and though he had sobered with age and had become thoroughly respectable, he had never made a success of farming, and by the time their daughter died, he and Grandma lived frugally in a little house in Kerwood, about six miles away from the Sullivan farm and Grandpa earned bits of money doing odd jobs here and there. Grandma was the strong one in that family. Elizabeth Brown by birth, always called Lib, or Tib, she was one of a large and flourishing connection. She lived by a combination of godliness, loving kindness, common sense, and a strength of will that made her rise above the various ups and downs of her married life, remaining steadfastly loyal to the husband who had often let her down. Above all, she retained a great capacity for warmth and love that she poured out on the granddaughter whose presence she took as a gift from God, not as a heavy responsibility in her late middle age.

In her house Dot flourished, and, understandably, lost all feelings of connection to her own father and her brothers and sisters. Late in her life she told with regret of one of her earliest memories of her father when he came to visit her at Grandma Clark's and she was so frightened of the dark stranger with a moustache that she ran away and hid—to his disappointment and dismay, of course. When she was about seven her grandmother took her on a long visit to her mother's sister, the Clarks' other daughter, Aunt Em Sifton, who lived on a large farm in southern Manitoba with True, her husband. She began school there and absorbed such vivid memories that to the end of her long life she could tell—and draw—stories about prairie dogs(gophers), about belting across the prairie on a wagon with her brother Vern, who by this time was teaching school in the west, and about all kinds of details of life with her good, but repressively strict Methodist aunt and uncle. It was here that she had an early indoctrination to religion that was evangelical, fundamentalist, partly uplifting and partly terrifying to her for many years after.

Meanwhile, after three years of being alone and seeing both Vernon and Frieda well into High School, Will Sullivan remarried, sold the farm and settled in Strathroy. His wife was Margaret McColl, only daughter of Hugh McColl, a very clever man of Highland Scotch descent who at one time had been editor of the local weekly newspaper, *The Age* and who, when his daughter married, held the important town position of Postmaster. Widowed and with a comfortable salary he lived with his daughter in Rose Villa, one of the big yellow brick houses on Victoria Street in the "Quality Hill," as it was called, part of town. He welcomed Will Sullivan as a man in whom he recognized true affection for his daughter, honesty, and an intellectual curiosity and competence equal to his own. For his part, Will set about building an addition to the house that would hold all his scattered family, and he and Margaret also set about having a family of their own, first Annie, then twins, Hugh and Lloyd. Like Dot, Margaret McColl had been brought up a treasured only child, and very much a town girl, used to an active life according to the considerable cultural opportunities of books, music, church and social affairs that a thriving Ontario small town, fortunately on the main line of the Grand Trunk railroad, afforded in the late nineteenth century. Sadly, she was handicapped physically. From birth she had been hard of hearing; she had had cataract operations on her eyes at the shockingly early age of eleven and her sight was never good; and in fact she had met Will Sullivan when she was in hospital with a broken leg, the result of a street accident, one that left her permanently lame. He had suffered a broken arm in an accident on the farm, and their joint hospital stay had instigated and consolidated their romance.

After Will and Margaret, Maggie as she was always called, were married Dot was left with the Clarks in the quiet and warmly loving atmosphere that she had always known. Mabel, Marge and Harold joined their father in Strathroy. Dot was not sickly, but she was never rugged and it was undoubtedly a wise decision for everyone concerned to leave her where she was so cherished—"the little golden-haired granddaughter," as they loved to call her. The change in her life came like a thunderclap: she was ten in 1914 when Grandpa died, the Kerwood house had to be sold, and Grandma Clark, with no resources of her own, had to go west to live with Aunt Em and Uncle True. Dot was suddenly uprooted to the family home in Strathroy. From being the treasured only one, she was flung into the midst of a wild and noisy zoo, for not only were Will's children obstreperous teenagers, resentful of their stepmother and, with true Irish contrariness, bound to make things as hard for her as possible, there were also Margaret's own children, Annie and the twins, though Lloyd was not to survive babyhood. From being the precious one, around whom the household circled, Dot suddenly became one of a crowd—and a crowd that were as alien to her as beings from another planet, and just as frightening. To her Annie and Hugh were bound to seem like usurpers, demanding much of everyone's time and attention. Certainly nobody had much time for Dot, and when her own brother and sisters bothered with her at all, it was usually to make fun of her for her timid ways, "old fashioned" to them, or her red hair which she had been taught to be proud of, but which to them was always good for a teasing put-down.

Not to be with Grandpa and Grandma Clark was bad enough, but to be absolutely cut off from them was shattering, and of course, Grandma in Manitoba might as well have been at the end of the earth. Dot found the affection and understanding she craved in Will, certainly, for he loved all his children dearly, tried to do well by them always, and was not afraid of showing his feelings toward them. Mabel, Marge and Harold too were fond of her really, but far too involved in rebelling against their own situations to be of any real help to her, and Margaret, who really tried to do her best by all the brood, was really not up to the job physically. Just to keep things running from day to day was almost more than she could do, let alone cope with six children, including a rowdy threesome of teenagers who were bound to make her life a misery in as many ways as they could think of. Being a stepmother has always been horrendously difficult—in those days, tragically common though the situation was, it was almost a foregone conclusion that a constant guerrilla warfare was waged between the step-children and their father's new wife. Certainly it was so in the Sullivan family, and though Dot was too much of a newcomer and too gentle by nature and training to be a part of it, she was sadly affected by it. To add to Dot's insecurity, a local woman took a fancy to her and wanted to adopt her—that too was in that day a frequent answer to the problems of a widower with a brood of children. Will, however, would not hear of such a thing, for he was intensely proud of all his children and, by hook or by crook, was determined to keep them all together.

When she was twelve, in Mr. Cuddy's High School Entrance Class, Dot's health broke down completely, and, a deep sadness to her for the rest of her life, her schooling ended. She was in bed for weeks, dosed with the tonics that were standard medicine then for the breakdowns that were all too common, especially among girls, and that were usually thought to be an unfortunate aspect of their development into adolescence. In Dot's case though, as she knew very well, and as she often talked of throughout her life, the whole thing was the result of the change in her situation that for her was truly traumatic. Her memories of life at Rose Villa were anything but happy: once, for instance, she was left at home to look after Hugh and Lloyd, while the rest of the family was visiting at Aunt Hettie's (Dad's younger sister, Hettie, was married to Peter Anderson, who had recently retired from his farm near Watford to a house on the hill at the corner of Kittredge and Caradoc). At some time in the evening, she never said just when or how, Dot became aware of a fire in the attic. In a panic, she left the twins and ran all the way down to Aunt Hettie's to get Dad, a good quarter mile. It must have been a chimney fire, a common occurrence then, for the twins were safe and the house didn't burn down—though Dot never forgot her terror and the family didn't allow her to forget her leaving of the twins. Another time, when the family had gathered at Aunt Hettie's for Christmas dinner, Heaman Armstrong, the clergyman husband of Ethel, Hettie's older daughter, lay ill in one of the bedrooms. Dot was sent up to see him. "I'm going to die, Dorothy," he said to her, and then, "Are you saved?" Whatever she reported downstairs was taken too lightly by the assembled Sullivans—Heaman did die that night, of a burst appendix and peritonitis. When her health broke down, a fearful religious sensibility went along with her weakness and depression, a terrifying consciousness of sin that was a direct legacy from the hysterical brand of fundamental Methodism that she had witnessed out west with Aunt Em. She never ceased to marvel at her father's loving care at this time. When she was in bed, he stimulated her to read books that he would talk to her about for hours—a translation of *Les Misérables* was always the one that she most remembered. When she was well enough to be up, he would walk with her, patiently comforting her and talking her out of her overpowering sense of sin and fear of hell's flames.

In time, she did get well, but never to go back to school again. Instead, she began quite soon to make a little money, working as a "hired girl" for Howard and Williston Downham, who were just starting their family and Howard's nursery. That didn't last long, though. Howard got a little fresh with her, she reported to Dad, he tore a few strips off Howard as only a Sullivan in a righteous wrath could do, and Dot retired permanently as a household help. In many ways she was a naturally domesticated young girl, however. When I was born in 1919 she lived at our house looking after me for a good while. When I was six months old, Mother and I both got mumps. Mabel was really sick, and, as was the invariable McCandless custom, we moved into Grandma and Grandpa's house, Mother, Dot and I. She loved to tell me about that early time, when she'd rock me for hours at a time, and Grandma would praise her nursing. My experience of Dot's mothering instincts began very early, and continued all my life. Unlike Mabel, my mother, she was openly affectionate always, finding it easy to cherish others as she herself had been cherished. Her nurturing by Grandma and Grandpa Clark had made her quite unselfconsciously demonstrative, something that neither Mabel nor Marge ever found possible. When I was still very young, in the early twenties, she began working in Prangley's restaurant as a waitress, then in MacPhail's bakery as a salesgirl, then, a step up in the social scale, at Arden Sutherland's Coal Yard as an office girl, and finally in the office of Downham's Nursery, where she was to remain quite happily until her marriage in 1933.

II

All the Sullivans had a sticky pride, but Dot, I think, had the strongest combination of pride and a strong will of any of them. During this period of her life, from Grandpa Clark's death in 1914 to about 1921, she proved herself as a survivor, and more than that, as a determinedly independent and happy young woman. Snapshots of her in her early teens show a frail, bedraggled, unhappy young girl; snapshots in the early twenties show her transformed into a self-confident young woman. Those years were a time of testing for the whole family. When he and Margaret married, Will Sullivan thought, with good reason no doubt, that he would be chosen to follow Hugh McColl as Postmaster, a traditional political perk that, as a good Liberal and a good son-in-law, he seemed destined to be given. He was mistaken, sadly disappointed, and without a job. Hugh McColl died shortly after the marriage, and fortunately, Margaret was left with a little money and, just as important, with the good will and concern of her relatives, the Evans family, who had ample means and were amongst the Strathroy's 'gentry' as owners and printers of *The Age Dispatch*. For some years Will took any job he could get, usually doing rough carpentry, until, early in the twenties, he was made caretaker of the Strathroy Cemetery, a position he was proud to hold until he died. Some of my early memories of him concern riding out to the cemetery with Dad, as all the family called him, pulled at quite a clip by his blind but fast horse, Bob. The cemetery was a beautiful and peaceful place, and there my brother, Vernon, and I used to have picnics on the gravestones. Dad liked to joke that, as the caretaker, he had hundreds of people "under him."

At the beginning of World War I, in 1914, the same year that Grandpa Clark died and Dot's happy life collapsed, two of Will's children, Vern, age 20 and Frieda, 18, were already started on a teaching career, Vern in the Peace River district of Alberta and Frieda in Mattawa, in Northern Ontario. Mabel was 16 and hard to handle, Harold 14 and notorious in town for his mischief-making abilities, Marge, 13, gentler, but always an ally of the older ones in their many escapades, Annie only 3, and Hugh a baby. The prime mystery of the Sullivan family is the question of how on earth Will managed to see Vern, Frieda, and later Marge and Annie through Normal School, and Mabel through Westervelt Business College in London. But, though seemingly without resources, he did so, and a great credit it is to him, and to Margaret as well. Even with all possible suppositions about family assistance, it seems a triumph of determination over circumstance. Dot, of course, could not qualify for the teaching training that was his ambition for all his daughters, and that was her ambition too, something she never ceased regretting—and a fine teacher she would have been. Annie went through a stage of wanting to train for a nurse, and a fine one she'd have been, but Dad was intensely old fashioned about nursing, and was violently opposed to any of his daughters being exposed to hospital conditions, nudity, of course, being the great taboo.

A year after war was declared in 1914, Harold, then only 15, lied about his age and joined the Middlesex Regiment, then being recruited to the tune of much excitement and patriotic propaganda. Dad was distraught, but also proud of the harum scarum whom everyone in town knew as incorrigible. In the west, near Fairview in the Peace River District where he had homesteaded, Vern promptly resigned his school and came home to sign up and, according to the family myth, look after Harold. According to the rules of the time, the brothers were to be allowed to remain together in the same unit, but certainly, in Vern's many letters home, there is no mention of Harold's presence, and if Harold wrote home, none of his letters survive. Because of the deep-rooted loyalty to England of the day, Will was proud of his two sons, but he was also exceedingly anxious. The arrival of Vern's letters, copies of most of which survive today, were family occasions of great joy, and often of publication in *The Age Dispatch*. In certain ways, small towns of that time were a kind of extended family for their people, and certainly 'letters from the Front' were sought after and valued far beyond the family circle. As it happened, Vern's letters were outstanding, revealing a thoughtful, philosophical young man, exceedingly well-educated and well-spoken for his age and experience, and with a talent for writing that might have developed into something outstanding. That was all lost in the mud and blood of Flanders. In 1918 Vern was reported "missing," the cruellest of all the War Office telegrams, for it left the bereaved families with agonizing hopes and disappointments, often for years after. When my memories begin, in

1922 or 23, Dad Sullivan was still following up news of amnesiac veterans, hoping against forlorn hope that one of them might be his lost son. Meanwhile, Harold came home, but with a badly damaged back and a rheumatic condition that could never be cured and that meant the wearing of a hip-to-neck cast for the rest of his life.

Vern's death was a sorrow that Dad carried with him always and, of course, it affected the rest of the family massively also. Mabel, always in revolt against her situation, and one who remembered Vern well as a hero-worshipped older brother, was just beginning to work in Ross and Bixel and was enjoying courtship with Basil McCandless, a Royal Bank Teller, but more important than that to the young people, one of the town's best ball-players. They used to go off to London to celebrate winning games at Wong's Cafe, where Base could enjoy a few beers free of the restraints of his Baptist family. After one such excursion in the late summer of 1918, Mabel found herself pregnant. She and Base were married in March of 1919, Clara was born in May, and somehow or other the Sullivans weathered yet another major crisis —for in those days, and in the puritanical Baptist bosom of Strathroy (for Will and Margaret were Baptists as well as the McCandless family) a pregnancy before marriage was counted a deadly sin. Each side of the family rallied around, however, and in fact Marge and Dot came closer to Mabel than they had ever been, though from that day to their deaths, Mabel and Margaret Sullivan hardly spoke and Basil and Will kept each other at arm's length. For myself, for some years I didn't know I had grandparents on my mother's side, and not until I was 6 or so was I ever in their house, and then I was taken there by Annie, now a teenager.

Meanwhile, Dot had missed the worst of the shattering events in the Sullivan house by the simple expedient of moving out as soon as she was making a little money of her own. She had only two personal memories of Vern, one of them during her trip to the west, and though she dearly loved Harold, he and she had known each other very slightly before he went away. On leaving home she went first up to the north end of Victoria street to board with Mary Thomas, a friend of Will and Margaret and a happy-go-lucky landlady who kept a number of young boarders in her rambling house just across the corner from Downham's Nursery. For a bit of board money and a bit of household help, Dot had a grand time being a kind of favourite 'little sister' to all the young men there, among them Art and Frank Fidler and Bill Patterson, all Downham employees. Dot blossomed under their good-natured teasing and their obvious admiration, for she had gained weight and colour, learned about attractive dressing and, above all, her bright golden-red hair made her outstanding, then and always. She simply couldn't thrive in what she always called the "terrible confusion" of Rose Villa, but once out of it, she was free to love and admire all the Sullivans in her own way.

Then, quite soon, and I have no idea what put the idea into her head, she moved again, this time to live down on Front Street West, almost across from the United Church, with Aunt Rate Ward, a childless sister of Grandma Clark who had been widowed in 1921. Dot always said that she simply went down to see Aunt Rate and said "I want to live with you"; with no fuss or bother Aunt Rate agreed and she moved in. Certainly the move was of great benefit to both of them. Aunt Rate found a companion who added her small but necessary board money to the upkeep of the house, and she also found a great-niece who was temperamentally totally congenial to her. Dot, for her part, found a companion who was calm, firm and loving, just as she remembered Grandma Clark. Each one of them found bonuses in the other—a lively sense of humour, a down to earth common sense, and a valuing of things of the mind and spirit. As long as she lived Dot liked to quote Aunt Rate for such wise sayings as, "Remember, Dorothy, you're just as good as anyone else; but also remember, you're no better."

Aunt Rate had a remarkable personality. Deformed from childhood by severe curvature of the spine, she had still married her childhood sweetheart, Richard Ward, and borne him several children, all of them, sadly, born dead. He had moved from the farm to Strathroy as the Clerk of Metcalfe Township, and though there was little money, there was enough for quiet good living. I began to go to Aunt Rate's with Dot when I was very young; a meal there was one of my greatest treats. You walked into the house from Front Street along a verandah and directly into the kitchen which always smelled deliciously of apple wood being burnt in the range on which all the cooking was done (those who have never smelled apple wood burning have missed something! It is even worth snitching a branch or too and putting them in a fireplace over a light bulb to enjoy the distinctive aroma). Aunt Rate was a wonderful cook, and under her influence Dot speedily became one too. The house was a rambling white frame, with a fairly large back garden of flowers, vegetables, berry bushes and a couple of old fruit trees. It was a little dilapidated on the ouside, but cosy on the inside, with a good piano in the parlour, a horse-hair suite —settee and two chairs—and, another vivid childhood memory, two glass bells full of dried flowers and butter- flies, those popular Victorian ornaments. When I was a little older, my favourite time for calling was Sunday afternoon after Sunday School, for Aunt Rate loved young people and welcomed any and all of them, and I often found myself part of a group including Hugh and his friends, Doug Parker and George Thompson. They had a habit of regularly bringing Aunt Rate their Sunday School papers. Often we'd sing, and I'd play accompaniments to hymns and, especially, to "Danny Boy," the one piece above all others I loved to hear Dot sing.

As she grew up she developed a wonderful clear soprano, and once at Aunt Rate's she began to sing in the United Church choir and also to take lessons from the town singing teacher, Professor Gordon. That poor man was subsequently the subject of a scandal and had to leave town, and I remember a good deal of family muttering—also laughing—and Harold going to him in righteous wrath about Dot's safety. As it happened, she had been perfectly safe with him, for much later I gathered that his preference was for boys. What he taught her about singing and breathing properly she always valued. She also began to teach the youngest children in Sunday School, and I have some friends now who remember her warmly. She was good with little children, a natural story-teller, and until her marriage she presided over the Primary Department. Two other nieces of Aunt Rate's, Eva Pooke, a High School teacher whose career Dot always envied just a little, and Effie Brown, housekeeper to a London family, visited when they could, sleeping on the feather ticks and under the goose-down comforters that I so loved when I got to stay there overnight. Both Dot and Aunt Rate had the lifelong gift of contentment, and they were for years as happy and peaceful a household as one could imagine.

III

There was a great deal of talk and laughter, always, among the Sullivans, about who was courting whom, and they all felt perfectly capable of being either loud in praise or equally loud in damnation of current boyfriends. After Mabel and Base were married, their house became the centre for family gatherings that always included big meals, for my mother loved to cook (with the McCandless grocery and butcher shop, there was a never-ending supply of good food, huge succulent roasts and lots of eggs and butter for the baking Mabel loved). At our house, by now on Hull Road, 'up on the hill,' there was much talk, laughter, piano playing by my father and singing by everyone. For some years they specialized in New Years' Eve parties, but any excuse was good enough for a party, for the Sullivans had grown up to be a very clannish bunch, often fighting with one or other of their members, but always preferring their own family's company to almost any other. Marge was away teaching, first in Rainy River and then in Windsor. Once there she found it easy to get to Strathroy for weekends and holidays. Harold had married Beatrice Burdon and started a trucking business in Strathroy. Frieda was far away and very homesick—finally she had a complete breakdown and, in the early thirties, took her own life, another traumatic tragedy for the family to face. Annie, as she got older, loved the company of the older family and was with them every minute she could be. They all had a tremendous sense of humour and certainly Mabel and Harold also had the true Irish 'gift of the gab,' though neither could Marge, Dot, or Annie be called exactly tongue-tied.

Dick Davis came to Strathroy as a Teller in the Bank of Commerce in about 1923. He and Dot were both 19 that year, and they met when he began to go to the Methodist Church, soon, in 1925, to become the United. He and Dot began to go out together very soon—when I say "out," I mean the small-town things of the day, walking home after Young Peoples' meetings or having a soda in Prangleys ice-cream parlour. They became serious about each other almost immediately, and I remember absolutely no nonsense teasing from the family, either. Not only did they approve of Dick and his obviously serious intentions, but also in his favour, by the end of the twenties the family had come through the shock of Marge having married Slim Durocher, a French-Canadian Roman Catholic. By the time I was eight or so, "Dot and Dick" were as much of a family item as "Mabe and Base," or "Harold and Bea." They always knew it would be years before they could be married, because the Bank didn't allow marriage before their young men had become Accountants and, in fact, Basil had had to leave the bank when he married Mabel in 1919, a crushing blow to him. But when Dick was moved away from town there was always room for him at Aunt Rate's over long weekends or on his holidays, and they were a settled, contented couple very early in their courtship. Harold and Bea loved driving people around, and I remember all of us going to Exeter to see Dick's mother. I also remember many picnics, especially at Rock Glen near Arkona, and one historic outing to Boblo island in the Detroit River. Dick must have given Dot her very beautiful diamond solitaire about 1930, and in 1933, when he became an Accountant in a Toronto-Davenport branch, they were married.

I was 14 then, old enough to be involved in various showers, at which Dot was deluged with good wishes and gifts, many of them pieces of silver, and all of them cherished for all of her life. Late in her life, she pointed out all the loaded shelves of her china cabinet and I heard once again her stories of each piece of silver and reminisced over the wedding book which she kept complete with all the cards and verses of good wishes. Like the scrap-book which she kept before her marriage, that collection is a precious heirloom, though now Annie and I are the only ones left who remember the events. But Dot was an active church worker, choir member and Sunday School teacher, besides being a popular resident, and her wedding created quite a stir. To marry a banker was to marry well!

I was disappointed that Dot and Dick weren't going to have a romantic church wedding, with white veil and all, because I was in the throes of the romantic teen years, and very much under the spell of Hollywood on the one hand, and the wedding of Princess Marina and the Duke of Kent on the other. I mourned their choice of a totally private ceremony in the church, with only Harold and Bea present, though when it came to be my turn to marry I chose exactly the same thing, though a thousand miles or so away, in Winnipeg. However much my nose was out of joint, I loved all the preparations, admired Dot's beautiful grey crepe dress with fur-trimmed grey coat to match, and especially appreciated her long-accumulated trousseau of silver, dishes, linens and treasured underwear. If I showed my disappointment at not being present, it was dispelled the very next Easter, when Dot asked me to come to Toronto to see them for the holidays, the major outing of my young life and my first trip to Toronto. I went, of course, by train, wearing a new navy blue spring coat with a cape, and carrying, not a suitcase, for no one in the family had one, but a discarded Downham's sample case, the kind the salesmen carried, about as long and wide as a good sized suitcase, but only about six inches thick. Some sight I must have been, and some crushed my clothes! Dot and Dick had an apartment in a new building somewhere very near Bathurst and St. Clair. I often wonder which one as I pass. It was magic to me. I had never stayed in an apartment building before, much less been taken to the Royal Ontario Museum, the very new Eaton's College Street, Timothy Eaton Church filled with lilies for Easter, or Shea's theatre, where there was still vaudeville and "The Largest Pipe-Organ in the British Empire."

So good to me they were, both Dot and Dick, both then and always. So fortunate I have been. So rare they have always been in their unfailing strength and affection and in the willingness to broaden and develop, as their daughter, Elizabeth, grew up—the most outstanding, astonishing and admirable characteristic of their later years.

Chapter XVII

Vi and Evan
1925-1993

Written shortly after Vi's death in 1993

One chilly November night in 1925, when I was six years old, all the family were assembled for supper at Grandma's. This wasn't unusual, goodness knows, because we seemed to be there at least as much as at home, but it was a party occasion with Grandma's best dishes, company food, and of course a great roast of beef at the head of the table. Along the verandah and in the side door came Evan with Vi, his bride, just back from their honeymoon. I thought Vi was the most beautiful sight I had ever seen, and I remember vividly her yellow crepe dress, her cloud of very fair hair, and her coat which was called Hudson Seal and was just about the poshest fur that Strathroy ever saw. I don't remember regretting the loss of my laughing uncle, who had let me jump all over him ever since I was a baby, and who invariably treated me as a very special person, because from that moment on there were two of them in my life, both with unfailing kindness and acceptance. The words "unconditional love" weren't used in those far-off days, but that is what I remember about both Vi and Evan, from that day to this.

When they were first married they lived down on Front Street East in a double house, just across the street and down from the house where we lived until 1928. On one great and early occasion, they asked me over for dinner with Evan's great friend, Bill Sutherland, who was in the furniture business. To my delight I had my first taste of home-made spaghetti and meatballs, a dish so exotic that it was unheard of in Strathroy, in our house at least. Early in their married life, Vi's mother lived with them for a time. She was very old, as old as Vi was when she died, I think, but in that day there was no place where she could be well cared for as in the present Strathmere Lodge, and so there she was, in the same condition as Vi's in these last nine years, but a daily responsibility and care.

From those first years, Vi used to make me dresses for Christmas—I remember a black sateen one trimmed with green piping that I loved, also a black and white print one, and in my early teens a wonderful mauve flowered organdy in which I felt like a princess, and no doubt preened as if I were one! She was a gifted sewer, designer, and refurbisher ("making over" we called it then), and in a day when every penny counted, there was a lot of it done. Because I had several aunts on the Sullivan side of the family, I fell heir to a fair number of their castoffs, and "take it over to Vi" became the watchword. I think now of how much I took all this for granted, and how much Vi did for me with great good nature. She was a wonderfully precise seamstress, and I remember very serious conversations about, for instance, the attractiveness of a green belt as opposed to a black one, for I always loved clothes, and had a grand time during these weighty operations.

By the time their daughter, Mary, was born, Mrs. Fisher had died I believe, and as we had moved up to the hill in 1928, the neighborly running across the road stopped, though the family was still together a lot. Grandma used to have a lunch ready for the men after the store closed on Saturday nights, not until 12 o'clock in my early youth, and sometimes I was thrilled to be allowed to stay up for that. Then I always came home from church with Grandma and Grandpa, went to Sunday School from their house in the afternoon, and then the whole family were there for Sunday supper. Both Vi and Mabel, my mother, were very fond of their in-laws, and the affection was certainly reciprocated. Once, years later, I told Grandma that she was very good to her daughters-in-law. She looked at me with total surprise and said, "I've always thought I was so lucky to have such nice girls marry the boys." In those days, though, neither of 'the girls' was allowed to do more for those many meals than to help with the dishes, for family entertaining was Grandma's big pleasure. As long as she lived, until her mid-nineties, she baked every Friday as she had every week since her marriage in 1887. Apple pie, hot-water cake (a kind of gingerbread), sugar cookies, biscuits with currants in them, and a plain and tasty drop cake called "rocks", were her regulars.

Just about the time we moved up to Hull Rd., on the hill, I remember a lot of talk about Mrs. Farthing's house, just across and down Colborne Street from Grandma's, which Vi and Evan bought and moved into when Mary was little. And then, of course, I was in on a lot more of double family things. I remember, for instance, going into "the shop" as the store was called, with Evan and Grandpa one Sunday after church and finding that thieves had been there in the night. Some three hundred dollars had been taken, I believe, besides cigarettes, and some other produce, but there was not an awful lot of confusion, and certainly the thieves had not trashed the place. I don't know whether or not they were caught, but I have a feeling they were. I also remember well another great crisis for the store, when the Geddes Block next door to it on Front Street burned down in 1929. That was a real disaster, and the adjacent wall of the store was threatened, but the fire stopped spreading in time. The Geddes dry-goods store had been Strathroy's finest, and its building contained, besides two floors of women's wear, a Concert Hall, called Albert Hall, which along with the Lyceum Theatre on Frank Street had been host to important entertainments, both local and imported.

A great many important things happened in that period just around 1930. The store was doing well, obviously a part of the boom that preceded the big crash of 1929. I remember Grandma and Grampa acquiring the big green Essex car, the store was completely refurbished with the big walk-in refrigerator and new counter arrangements, new furniture at Grandma's house—and then the big blow struck—Grandpa got sick. I don't know how long it was before his illness was diagnosed as stomach cancer, but he was in bed in the upstairs centre room at Grandma's all one Fall and Winter, because I remember that we were all there on Christmas day as usual, and I went up to see Grandpa in bed. He was 76 when he died in May and Grandma was 69. For the first time since long before my birth, Vic, the oldest son, a railwayman in Vancouver, came home in the early spring to see his father and briefly, the four brothers were together again. His death marked the beginning of a decade of anxiety for Evan and Base, because the Depression hurt their business as it hurt everyone else's. In all the lean years, however, they never faltered in their support of Grandma in her own home, and for that they deserve enormous credit, something that all of us just took for granted at the time.

Vi and Evan

I was thirteen when Grandpa died and for a long time afterwards I would go down to Grandma's on Friday night to keep her company and stay the weekend. I loved that—Grandma was a night-hawk, as the family always teased her. We would listen to the radio, and often listen to the Metropolitan Opera broadcasts on Saturday afternoons, for music was a necessary part of Grandma's life. I got into the habit of going over to Evan and Vi's to have a visit when we came home from church on Sunday, while Grandma was getting our dinner—usually my favourite food, plain macaroni cooked with onion and butter, meat-loaf and custard pie. No one has even been able to touch Grandma's custard pie, or her meat loaf and macaroni for that matter. I would sit and gab away to Evan, Vi and Mary with the greatest enjoyment, always feeling that I was the most welcome guest in the world, and always loving the atmosphere of Evan's great laughing good nature and Vi's affection. There was a long spell which must have been very hard for them all, for Mary had a bout of rheumatic fever and was in bed for a long time in the bedroom adjoining the old-fashioned kitchen. I was too young and thoughtless to know how anxious they must have been.

The dressmaking went on, and all the other handwork that Vi did so superbly, and I was always an eager watcher and listener, because though not in the least gifted as she was, I loved hearing about it and seeing it, and I was especially intrigued by her passion for antique furniture, her collecting of it and her refinishing skill. For instance, I remember when she was drafting plans for making an old organ into a wonderful cupboard for the living room. She spent ages at that. She was spectacular at using the old, ornamental bits in the most telling way, and the finished piece was a work of art. She had all kinds of patience in this as in all the handwork she undertook, and her results were fabulous. If as the saying goes, "Genius is the infinite capacity for taking pains," Vi certainly had genius. Much later, when we took over our Strathroy house after father's death, I went to Vi for lessons on furniture refinishing and had some wonderful times doing it myself, but never attempted the intricacies of her work! Not by a long shot! The first piece I did was Grandma's old pine bake-board which Vi gave me, and when I showed her the finished (as I thought) product with great pride, she immediately turned it over and looked at the unfinished underside, teasing me about having stopped halfway through the job.

All through the thirties, Vi was working part time at Butler's Dry Goods store, and saving for the major renovation of the house that she was planning. That was another thing that fascinated me and I loved to hear her describe what was going to happen. When it all did happen, some time during the war years I believe, it was a major transformation of the space, the adjoining living rooms with the arch between, the gracious dining room, kitchen and bathroom where the old kitchen and bedroom had been, and of course the lovely display of furniture pieces that Vi had been collecting and working on all those years. I have never before or since known anyone with her artistic gifts—today they would have developed into an extremely well-paid career.

From the beginning too, the musical skill of Vi and her brothers, and the violin-making of their father were parts of the family lore. It was very glamorous to me to think of Vi filling in when the Lombardos needed a pianist in their early days. And of course, everyone remembered the Fisher Brothers' Orchestra, with Vi the pianist, Bill the violinist, Fred on the banjo and Martin

Pincombe the drums. At the funeral home, Bernice Freele, a double first cousin on both Vi's and Evan's sides of the family, remembered the orchestra coming to Teeswater in 1919 and staying for a week to play for the Old Boys' Reunion. Vi carried on her love of music in the church, singing alto in the choir with Grandma McCandless and Mabel also in the choir. Great was the excitement in the thirties when they did selections from the Messiah one Easter. My mother couldn't read music, but Vi and Grandma could, and the whole choir was stretched to its furthest limits that spring! It's too bad that Evan didn't sing in the choir as well, because he had a lovely tenor voice. I used to love the singsongs both at Grandma's and at our house, father playing everything from jazz to hymns. Evan was especially good on "Jeannie with the light-brown hair" though once he and I hit a flat instead of a high note, had the giggles, and disgusted Grandma to whom it was almost a sin to hit a bum note. That was the Christmas of 1955, when Grandma was 92 and Evan had come in to find her with one foot on top of the piano and one on top of the stepladder, putting up her Christmas streamers as if she were a 40-year-old.

When I was at Western Vi began to give me beautiful crystal plates and goblets for Christmas, and when I was getting ready to go to Winnipeg to be married, she made me some beautiful nightgowns. There was no one who could do delicate work with lacy trim like Vi. All through High School I had loved getting the Christmas nightgowns she'd make me and like most other girls of my time, I kept them all done up with a bit of perfumed soap in a bottom drawer—a kind of hope chest! Grandma and Vi had a wonderful tea for me before I left for Winnipeg, asking dozens of Strathroy people and many friends of mine from London. It was both an afternoon and an evening affair. The house had been all redone then, and it looked grand—a great occasion, if exhausting, but neither of the hostesses ever complained of that. It was a beautiful party, and as I've got older I've appreciated more and more just how much care and work went into it.

After father died in 1972 and we took over the house, I was able to see both Evan and Vi for more than just the brief visits we had had for years. I was down a lot during Evan's illness, and after his death Vi and I visited many times. She was always glad to see me when I'd walk down, she often had me for supper, and quite often she'd also come up to our place for lunch or a cup of tea. As always I was fascinated by all her projects, especially the one she embarked on shortly after Evan's death, when she made a beautiful tailored suit out of one of his grey suits. The hours and hours of precision work she spent on that produced a truly spectacular piece of work. One evening we spent a long time looking through her old patterns, for she had kept every single one from her wedding clothes on, and at that time, late seventies, I was in a sewing fit myself. Not in Vi's class, I hasten to add! But I was struck by the sheer complications in the patterns she chose. She liked best to work on difficult things, inserted pleats and such, the like of which I'd never dare touch. Plain sewing wasn't much of a challenge to her—she was all for the intricacies and demanding know-how of the involved Vogue or earlier, Butterick patterns. Sometimes Mary's cat, Panther, would be with her, sometimes not, depending on where Mary was at the moment.

Vi was a care-giver, to Evan and Mary, to Mary's twins, Jane and Emily, to her mother, her brothers, to many others, my aunt Dot, for instance, whose friendship had begun when they were both in their teens and, in the ways I needed her, to me. We had good times together always, and I remember her over a lifetime of kindness, favours done, and many laughing moments. She was an unusually gifted woman, in Evan she had an unusually devoted partner, and all those of us who knew them were blessed.

Chapter XVIII

My Friend, Agatha

The most glamorous thing that happened on our street about 1930 was the arrival of the Cavers family. They had come to Strathroy from Detroit, and that in itself gave them and all their doings an aura of romance to me. Besides that, they were like no other family I had ever known. They had a bad-tempered parrot called Cora, who actually talked, and whose chief diversion was to escape from her cage and fly to the topmost branches of the Whiting's old maple tree beside them. And when Mr. Cavers had to climb the tree after her, Cora would look down tantalizingly at him and croak," Silly bugger, silly bugger." They had several cats, probably only one or two, but I remember them in numbers, and certainly I do remember one litter of cuddly kittens. They had a radio, always turned on, as I recall, and a lot of bright colour, especially a red-beaded lampshade—again, I am almost certainly remembering more than there were, but beside our decent, muted colours, the inside of their house seemed to me like a gypsy fortune-teller's tent. Certainly the house that they rented was brick and painted a dark and rather ugly red.

There were the parents, Cavers, Robert and Christian —everybody called her Chris and believed that her name was Christine. She had just a slight and musical Scottish accent (her father, Adam, the caretaker of the High School, had a thick, rolling brogue, and his wife had brought so much of Glasgow with her across the Atlantic that almost no one in town could understand her). Chris's specialty was playing the violin, another exotic note, and she was soon in demand at church teas and concerts. Her favourite piece was Fritz Kreisler's "The Old Refrain," a melody I thought then and think now is achingly beautiful. There were two sons, Ronnie and George, and in between the boys, about eight years old, Agatha.

Agatha speedily became the wonder-girl of the neighborhood. She was little, fine-boned and quick, and she had taken tap-dancing and acrobatics in Detroit. She could turn handsprings, do the splits, and, to our eyes, dance to rival any of the child-wonders just coming into their own as Dr. Bowes' Amateur Hour beamed weekly over the continent's air-waves. More than that, she was friendly, eager to make and keep friends and, even at that young age, had a receptive adaptability and loyalty that made her outstanding among us. I loved to go to her house, partly for its general aura of difference, and partly because at 5.15 every week-day we could listen to a programme called "Chandu the Magician" that my mother called "trash"and wouldn't have on. Chandu, like the Cavers household, seemed thrillingly exotic compared to Amos 'n Andy, Myrt and Marge, Lum and Abner, and all the other, tried and true, certified wholesome, family entertainments.

Furthermore, and most important of all, Aggie was a reader—and that meant a born reader of anything and everything, from all the library books we could lay hands on, to the weekly American papers with their whole sections of funny-papers and hair-raising tabloids to the movie magazines, then in their hey-day and always, seemingly, in bountiful supply in their house. Aggie was the one who shared the Anne books with me, and after that the Emily books, as well as lesser series, Ruth

Fielding, for instance, and The Campfire Girls. Aggie was the one who spent Saturday afternoons with me, roaming in the gully that ran from Hull Road back along Victoria Street, a heavenly place for transposing ourselves into versions of Anne Shirley's, or, later, Tarzan's world. We didn't have a Lake of Shining Waters, but we did have a stream, a swimming-hole, wild-flowers in abundance, a deserted house with thickets of lilac bushes gone wild, carpets of wild violets in springtime—and solitude to wander and explore, with nobody to worry about our whereabouts or infesting our make-believe kingdom.

In the enthusiasm for Tarzan of the Apes, which struck when I was in Entrance Class, 1931-2, and which was a by-product of the movie with Johnny Weismuller and Maureen O'Hara, we even practised swinging on the abundant wild grape-vines, though we swung neither far nor high. In the high summer the swimming-hole end of our magic kingdom was the scene of almost crowded activity, for then all the neighborhood gathered daily and the bigger boys were given to making caves and tunnels in the sand hills of the gully. But in the Spring and Fall it was ours alone, and we loved it. In the summer of 1932, when my uncle Roy, a druggist in Sarnia, married Elizabeth, they had a large cottage on the lake a few miles west of Sarnia and asked me out for a holiday—with Aggie. We had a wonderful time, and probably our most vivid memory is of Elizabeth insisting on roping us together when the waves were high. For two summers after that, eight or nine of us were at a ten-day C.G.I.T. camp at Hillsborough, also on Lake Huron, sleeping in tents, Dorrie Fowlie and I in a pup-tent the second year, and having a thoroughly good, early teens, still boyless time.

Aggie was behind me in school, three years, I think,

as befit our ages, but when I began to High School our friendship continued as always. Sometime in the mid-thirties her father was made caretaker of the school, replacing her grandfather, Adam, and her family moved to a house on the High School grounds. At about the same time my mother began to work at the Artistic full-time, and it became a part of our pattern for Aggie to walk home with me after school and help me with my job, the dinner dishes, and, especially, to spend Saturday afternoon at our house, washing our hair, listening to the radio, making peanut butter or chocolate fudge, and, as we got into the mid-teen dancing days, planning our strategies for the Saturday Night dance in the Town Hall.

In the thirties that dance was the high-spot of the week and certainly it was a marvellous feature of young life in the town. The girls learned to dance as soon as they entered High School, because we danced in the auditorium every day at noon-hour with one of our number, usually Dorrie Fowlie, playing the piano. But the boys didn't learn until they started, at about fifteen, to go to the Saturday Night dances, with music by our own town orchestra, the Casa Royals, with Dony Marshall, one of the Walker boys, one of the Snelgrove boys, Donald Oakes and others unremembered, in the orchestra. We were just coming into the Big Band era, and dancing became our passion—we *and* the boys speedily became first-class dancers, as we always bragged, then and now, with complete conviction. Only Petrolia dancers, and a few from Sarnia, could rival the Strathroy crowd. Aggie was the best. I can still see her jitter bugging with Donny Leitch—no Judy Garland-Mickey Rooney combination ever looked better.

When I was seventeen, Bright's Grove, on Lake Huron, ten miles north of Sarnia, became our Mecca, and

Jack Kennedy's orchestra, with its Sammy Kaye arrangements, our own 'Big Band.' In the summer holidays Willie Downham asked several of us to spend two weeks at her family's cottage, about a mile from the Grove and the dance-hall. Libby Lambert, Jean Swift, Dorrie Fowlie, Joyce Houston, Grace Crawforth, Aggie, Willie and myself were all driven out by various parents, laden with food, and set up for a grand holiday. The boys in our lives, George Downham, Walter Bowley, Cecil Wright and Jack Fowlie, pitched a tent next door, and most of the time ate with us—and all of the time danced with us. Such freedom we had—and I doubt that any of our parents spent a moment worrying. Certainly they had no need to. We swam, ate, and ate some more, lazed on the beach, walked back and forth to the store at the Grove, and above all, made preparations in terms of hair-washing and nail-polishing, for the big event of the day, the nightly dance.

The summer of '36 and the summer of '37 we had our two weeks of dancing, beaching, bliss, all of us developing crushes on one or other of the boys 'from away,' meaning Sarnia or Petrolia, whose teenagers were Bright's regulars too. Both before and after our solid two weeks, Aggie and I spent most of our Saturday afternoons at my house, hoping that one of our faithful locals, Cecil Wright or Jack Fowlie, would get gas in the car and take a load of us to Bright's. Strange to look back on, they usually did. We all went in a group—no pairing off, though from time to time the boys would make moves in that direction. But we were a "crowd," a happy crowd of teenagers, and we just wanted to get there and dance all night, preferably with as many different boys as possible. There was indeed quite a rivalry in that direction. But a good-natured rivalry. The Bright's fever didn't wear off, either. When I got to Western in the Fall of '37 and met Dot Cole from Petrolia, it wasn't long before the two of us had the brilliant idea of working as waitresses at Bright's the next summer. That turned out to be the summer of the Poohs, a landmark time in all our lives, and one which Aggie shared often, for she would turn up to stay weekends at our shack in the Grove, and we had no problems in packing her in. After my two summers as a waitress at Bright's, she followed in my steps, and was there for at least one summer, maybe more.

Even before the Cavers family came to town, I was a dyed-in-the-wool movie fan, sent off to Saturday afternoon matinees with my young brother in tow, I found a mate in Aggie. She loved films, had been weaned on them, knew all about the "world of Hollywood," and eagerly joined me. All through High School we used to go to the movies twice a week at the King Theater, and we saw a great many of the old classics that histories of movies analyze today. Those were the days of movie glory, and even small towns had first runs. The odd ones, *Tarzan Of The Apes* or *King Kong*, for instance, that did not come to Strathroy, were a matter of wangling a trip to London—Mr. Fowlie took us to *Tarzan*, my Uncle Harold to *King Kong*. We talked endlessly about the movies and the well-publicized and publicity-laundered "romances" of the stars, and we definitely had our own roster of Greats—Garbo headed the list. I began to make a scrapbook of Garbo pictures in my mid-teens, and Aggie was an avid collector with me, even tearing out a photo from a magazine she found in Vic Summerhayes' office where she had been sent for some crime, lateness probably. To take a picture from under the nose of the lion himself was devotion indeed!

When I went off to Western, it was always an understood thing that Mother would let Aggie know when I was coming home for the weekend, and then we'd pick up just where we'd left off, movies, dancing, and not least, all the goodies that Mother baked for my homecoming—butter tarts and spare-ribs especially. Just before Morley and I got married, Aggie joined the Canadian Women's Army Corps. She arrived at our house a week or so before I left for Winnipeg looking absolutely smashing in her uniform (it *was* the most attractive uniform of the three women's services, and it suited her to a T). When we came back from the west to Ontario, and I began to work at Western's library and board with Vesta and Harry Stocks on Epworth Ave., she became a regular visitor. She would come around to my bedroom window and scratch on the glass, and I'd let her in for the night. Whether or not Morley was there made not the slightest bit of difference. We've joked ever since about the number of times the three of us shared a bed. Vesta was our dear friend, and both she and Harry found Aggie as endearing as we did.

We've kept together all our lives, loyalty being an outstanding quality of Aggie's, together with a letter-writing flair that makes me wish I had all of the last 50 years' crop. They'd be a better read, and a funnier one, than most books. She was the person I wrote to the day after our wedding in Winnipeg in 1941. She was the first person who came to see us after Steve's birth in Kingston in 1945, and her visits to Strathroy and Toronto in the last twenty years have been landmark occasions, filled with laughter, nostalgia, and the unbreakable bonds of long, long friendship.

Chapter XIX

Jim and Trudi Rowe

In early June of 1963 when John and I arrived at the Commonwealth Services Club in Oxford, we first of all were made welcome by Anne Innes, the Manageress, and then, a couple of days later, by Jim Rowe, the Secretary. Anne was in charge of all the housekeeping arrangements for the Club, as well as having a great deal to do with the well-being of all its inhabitants, their food, the upkeep of the rooms, and their entertainments. She was a housekeeper, but a glorified housekeeper, because her experience and abilities at management were more than adequate for her job.

Jim was the titular Head, the appointee of the Commonwealth Ministry to whom he answered, his "Masters" as he called them, and the man in charge of the various students from all over the Commonwealth and their direction into the courses they had come to Oxford to take. The Club had been set up to train British candidates for administrative posts throughout the Empire, and then, gradually, and more and more speedily, its clientele had changed to Africans and Asians who were being trained to administer their own, soon-to-be-self-governing countries. When John and I ate our first meal, the Saturday of our arrival, we were the only two whites in the dining-room. I was somewhat daunted, and through nerves, didn't hear half of the kindly questions that came our way, but John, nerveless at 12, was without inhibition and had a fine time. He speedily found himself befriended and treated to numbers of games of bar-billiards by good-natured Africans and East Indians to whom a child around the halls was a welcome novelty.

At first I was much in awe of Jim Rowe. When, about mid-June and before Morley and Steve joined us, there was a 'Club Night' with dancing to records and Jim asked me first to dance and then to go for a drive to see the various College Towers illuminated, I was almost tongue-tied. However, I behaved myself well, obviously, for later, when the four of us were all staying at the Club, we were asked out to tea at East Hanney, where Jim and Trudi had bought a Manor Farmhouse as their retirement home. And then we began to know something about Britain's overseas administrators, made famous by so many writers, notably Joyce Cary, and soon to vanish forever.

Jim had been educated at St. Edmund's Hall, the "poor boys" College, as he always said, and had gone into the Foreign Service in the twenties. His mother had been widowed when he was very young and when we knew him first, he had one living sister, an Anglican nun, a very very large woman who, when I saw her, wore a worn and rusty black habit, and came to Jim and Trudi for holidays. They always referred to her more dutifully than lovingly, as "the holy woman." Trudi was one of two daughters of an artist. Where she and Jim had met I don't know, but in 1963 they had already been married for 30-odd years, and Trudi had been a staunch partner in his African career. He had risen to be a District Commissioner in Tanganyika under Governor Twining (of the Twining Tea family) and he and Trudi were still dear friends of Lady Twining, who had retired after her husband's death to Kenya, and who was once on one of her periodic visits to the Rowes when we, too, were guests.

It was a marvellous and on-going experience to be made part of Jim and Trudi's close circle of friends and we savoured and treasured the experience for more than twenty years, until they both died and their beloved Manor Farmhouse had long since been sold. They had no children and Trudi had developed acute arthritis rather early in life, so that, when they retired in the mid-50s, she had spent months in a famous Oxford Orthopaedic Hospital and had finally emerged walking, but with one leg considerably shorter than another. A cane and special shoes permitted her movement, though I don't think she was ever completely without pain. She was indefatigably active, however, and one of her most important skills and hobbies was cooking. A mistress of delicious meals, she told me once or twice about her favourite African cook, and how she had often vowed to publish a cookbook incorporating many of his recipes. She never did, but she did become proficient in Swahili, and for many years she was an examiner for Oxford-based examinations in Swahili.

Perhaps because we were class-clean Canadians, an advantage we often felt in England, perhaps also because we were at first about the age their children might have been, had they had any, Trudi and Jim were loving friends and correspondents from the start. Many, many times we slept in their large bedroom, some of the beams brought overland from ships that had fought at Trafalgar, as they often told us. Their house was the realization of the dream they had had throughout their African service. Instead of taking the pension owing to them, they were "lumpers" as those who preferred a lump sum on retirement were called. They had spent many months looking for just the right place, while living temporarily at the Club on South Parks Road in Oxford. When they finally found their house, they were happy to spend their retirement years on its improvement.

It was a picturesque, long stone structure, one end of which they had given over to make a sizable dwelling for Olive and Percy who, with their son, were regular helpers with the grounds and the housework in return for their comfortable living quarters. In 1963, when we first knew them, the expectation of servants was still a living tradition among Trudi and Jim's 'class' and in Africa, of course, they had been used to a plethora of servants, often more notable for their kindliness than their efficiency, but some of them responding effectively to Trudi's training. She was a careful and enthusiastic housekeeper—once in Tanganyika, challenged by friends, she attached a pedometer to her ankle and found that one day she had walked 33 miles in the course of her household duties. Many were the delicious meals we ate at their splendid mahogany table, where Trudi, in spite of her lameness, served the meal from a trolley that she pushed around to each one of us. She had beautiful china, silver and crystal. The meal was pleasantly formal, but not too formal, and the table was always decorated by a large bowl of flowers in season, for Trudi had been thoroughly trained in the flower culture so much a part of post-war housewifery in England. No room was without its flowers, but the bouquets were especially works of art on the dining room table and in front of the sitting room fireplace when there was no need for a fire.

The downstairs of Manor Farmhouse had a wide entrance hall, opening from a small portico, a relatively small sitting room and larger dining room, a study and TV room and a warm and spacious kitchen, where Trudi's large, beloved Aga cooker held pride of place. An Aga, we soon learned, was the unfailing sign of a really well-equipped kitchen. It burned both coal and gas, and had spacious top-of-the-stove burners, oven racks and warming oven. The Aga was equipped to take care of all cooking eventualities and was, and is still, a luxury item.

Upstairs a long hall led to separate bathroom and lavatory and three large bedrooms. There was 'central heating,' not by our standards but by theirs, governed by the popular Dimplex electric heaters which only came on at low-service times of day and never at all from April to November. I have been colder in August in the Rowe's fine bedroom than anywhere else in England, and that in spite of the electric blanket on the bed, strangely, by our customs, under not over the bottom sheet. In the sitting room there was often a glorious fire in the fireplace—and always. even if the rest of the house was cold, the welcome was warm, and the food and drink lavish and delicious.

Their favourite time to start entertaining was, of course, tea, for which Trudi would wheel in a laden tea-wagon, with sandwiches, scones, hot cheese goodies, cake, cookies (biscuits), and many, many cups of hot, hot tea. Usually by the time tea was over, Jim was ready to begin 'drinks time,' at which sherry, whisky, or gin was favoured and which went on and on until Trudi was ready to announce dinner. Then there was a general removal to the dining-room, where the splendid mahogany table was set with fine china and silver and where, once again, Trudi's tea-wagon was wheeled around to serve us while Jim poured the wine with a generous hand. Coffee, of course, was taken in the sitting room and after that, to no one's surprise, the evening was as good as over. Trudi was an early-to-bed person, and guests followed her rule, in fact a general English hospitality rule, we found—to be given encouragement to withdraw to one's room and be alone. A wonderful way to give guests time and independence!

As befitted a veteran of decades of colonial service, especially of his years as District Commissioner in Tanganyika, Jim was an impeccable planner. Each time we visited he had planned a 'safari,' to take us to some point of interest, a neighborhood stately home, or a famous garden. We had many many treats of this kind, Wilton, for instance, a magnificent stately where Eisenhower's headquarters had been during the war. Sometimes Trudi would be with us, sometimes not. But always we were magnificently supplied with sandwiches and tea, and always we were back at Manor Farmhouse for the ceremonial tea-time. Sometimes he would take us up on the Berkshire Downs to see the prehistoric horse scratched in chalk on the hillside, and when I was in my brass-rubbing phase, he took us to the East Hanney church for some grand rubbing of down-to-earth Dutch-like housewives, the only examples of that type I'd seen. Sometimes we'd go to one of the Rowes' favourite pubs for lunch, and in those days there were many pubs retaining their old-time charm, with darkened oak furniture and authentic brasses —and again, always grand bouquets of flowers on the bar-counter.

Jim and Trudi were the last of their breed, men and women who had served the Empire and believed implicitly in it. Jim could and did move with the times, but Trudi couldn't get over her resentment at the speed of independence and what she thought of as ingratitude on the part of the former colonies, especially the African colonies. She predicted dire woes for the future, and alas, too many of those predictions are all too real now. When the Commonwealth Services Club closed for good in 1969, a bitter blow to Jim and to our dear friend, Anne

Innes, as well, Jim took on several part-time positions, particularly one with Worcester College, as bursar for their American Summer School, just then a very new idea, and one that has grown enormously in the part 20 years. We were asked to a couple of fine occasions at Worcester because of Jim, and at a pre-dinner sherry-party at one of them, the Head of Oxford's Extension Department, a Dr. Jessup, who looked like a benevolent shark, said, with a gloating smile beaming at the students in the room : "And just think, each one of them brings us two thousand dollars—and they don't take one penny home!"

In the years between 1975 and 80, Morley stopped off in England on his way to or from Geneva and had several visits by himself with the Rowes. Always he and Jim would go on a 'safari,' sometimes miles of healthy walk, for late in life Jim had joined one of the many popular hiking clubs, and with them, or by himself, he walked many miles at a time. The last time we saw him, in 1983, when he was already over 80, he had walked 24 miles with his club the previous day. For twenty years we were firm friends, the hospitality all being on the Rowes' side, unfortunately, for Jim and Trudi were not keen travellers in their retirement, savouring all the delights of the beauties close-by instead. One of my most memorable visits was in June of 1969 when, just after my mother died, I went to England on a three-week combined Toronto-York student excursion. Jim took me out to their place for the weekend and laid on several wonderful excursions to famous houses and one to a particularly well-known garden. With us that day was Allison, their dear friend and across-the-road neighbour, whom, years later, after Trudi's death, Jim married as Trudi had wished him to do. He and Allison were happy for a few years before Jim's decline and death in 1987.

There are wonderful memories from the Rowe visits, one of the funniest to me, the occasion, again on my lone trip in 1969, when Jim and Trudi entertained all the residents of the Club at tea, and they arranged themselves as in an old-time picture of the Raj, with Jim, Trudi, a very large African and his very large wife in their native costumes in the front row with the Rowes' two little dogs stretched out in front of them, and the rest of us in rows behind. I felt truly back in the 19th century. That June trip saw the closing of the Club and a splendidly noisy final party, with the Williams family all present. The Williams were also old Africa hands, with whom we had become friendly on our first, 1963, visit to the club.

We were wondrously fortunate in knowing the Rowes and the Commonwealth Services Club, as well as Anne Innes, Manageress of the Club and her husband, Albert. They became our friends at the very end of Empire. One night, at Worcester College with the Rowes, we heard a British academic speak approvingly of the separating of the African nations from Britain, then in full spate. Trudi was especially upset and disgusted by the speech, for she was convinced that separations were being engineered too speedily and carelessly. Such a residence as the Club and such Empire servants would not be possible to find today. It was our lucky timing to find them and to have them share with us a long and unfailingly warm friendship.

Chapter XX

Malcolm and Eve Elwin

Once upon a time, in England between the wars, it was possible to say "I am going to be a writer," and to be somewhat confident of living by the pen. This was before the writer-as-academic days, before the spate of new universities providing appointments for men and women of letters, and long before such a thing as a Creative Writing class had been dreamed of, let alone countenanced. From 1963 until his death ten years later, I treasured and enjoyed the friendship and patronage of such a writer, the biographer Malcolm Elwin who, with his wife, Eve, lived on a clifftop in North Devon, looking out over the Atlantic to the island of Lundy, in a house called "Sedgebanks" near the town of Braunton.

The bonuses of scholarship have been many for me, none more so than my chance connection with the Elwins beginning in the late spring of 1963 when I was avidly collecting letters for my biography of Anna Jameson. I had a small Humanities Association grant of $1,200 to go to England a month before the four Thomases were joining the four Stevensons for a long anticipated tour of England and Europe. Shortly before John, 12 years old, and most unwilling to leave his baseball team, and I were to set forth on a University of Toronto Charter (on an old Britannia aircraft, a 13-hour trip to Heathrow), I had read a review of Malcolm Elwin's just-published *Lord Byron's Wife*, and excited by that book's account of Anna Jameson's and Lady Byron's friendship, had written to

Elwin, in care of John Murray, his publisher. When on June 1 John and I arrived in Oxford at the Commonwealth Services Club where we were booked to stay, a letter awaited me with the stunning news that Malcolm Elwin had some 280 letters between Anna Jameson and Lady Byron which I would be welcome to see if I came down to Devon.

John and I had gone over armed with British Rail passes, and it took me no time at all to make arrangements to travel to Devon the very next week. What stunned me, as a Canadian newcomer to the miniature quality of Britain, was finding out that I could be at the Elwins in North Devon for lunch and back to Oxford by dinner time in the evening! The trip was one of the great adventures of my life: I left John with Anne Innes at the Commonwealth Services Club, changed trains at Exeter, and was met in Braunton by a taxi, ridiculously cheap by our standards, arranged for by the Elwins, the driver a burly character whom they called "the pirate," and who always drove them because they did not have a car. Then we drove through the winding, impossibly narrow, and high-banked Devon roads, along a wonderfully scenic cliffside to, finally, easily the most gorgeously-situated house I had ever seen.

Malcolm Elwin, bearded, blue-eyed, genial and sixty-ish, gave me sherry in a living room whose windows looked out over the Atlantic; as I shortly realized, the entire house was built to provide a sea vista from most of its rooms. Its front was a half circle, all glass, and my first impression, never subsequently modified, was that every wall that wasn't glass was completely covered in books. In the living room there were a couple of huge old oil portraits, one of an Elizabethan gent who looked like (but wasn't) Elwin's ancestor, elegant, shabby, pale yellow slip-covered sofas and chairs, and a large glass bell filled with butterflies, the product of some Victorian collector's mania. Malcolm had ready for me a ledger-sized book, completely filled with the Jameson-Byron letters, copied decades before by an employee of the Lovelace family, Lady Byron's descendants, and housed for safe-keeping at Coutts' Bank in London. Malcolm loved to "talk 19th century," as I came to call it, and he was a superb talker, never sitting down, but walking back and forth in front of the windows, lighting one cigarette from the butt of another, delighting in a myriad of anecdotes that made the men and women he spoke of as real as himself, and delighting in my obvious enthrallment to some of the same characters he knew so well.

By the time we had lunch, in a glassed-in porch at the back of the house with his niece and nephew Ginny and Brian Fell, a lunch of shrimp salad, home made bread and butter and beer, I knew that I would have to come back to copy letters from this gold-hoard, and by the time I left, again with the pirate, I felt as if I had been accepted into a new and entirely wonderful literary world. On the way back to the railway station, we passed the Putsborough Sands hotel, like Sedgebanks perched on top of the cliff overlooking the sea. I rushed in and reserved a room for John and myself for the next week, and then, such being the miniature size of England, the train took me back through Exeter to Oxford again, to the Club in time for dinner.

By this time, John was acclimatized to the quick changes and new vistas of England and he, like myself, was enchanted by the sea. Neither one of us had ever seen tides before, and when we got to the Putsborough, greeted kindly by Mr. and Mrs. Palmer, the proprietors, we made for the sands immediately and then, for the three days following, we made our way down the beach immediately after our breakfast and, while John amused himself with castles in the sand and his ever-present toy soldiers, I climbed the cliff path to the Elwins and copied Jameson-Byron letters. Morning and afternoon I was brought tea where I worked, this time by Eve Elwin, a woman whose handsome presence and offhand kindly manner seemed to me much in the line of one of the great theatrical Dames, Edith Evans perhaps. She also took treats down to John on the beach and, since we both had been supplied with lunchtime sandwiches from the hotel, we were well looked after. So well, in fact, and so furiously did I write, that I developed a bad case of spotty fingers, small warts, they turned out to be, but well worth the experience and cured a week or two later at the suggestion of an Oxford doctor who advised me to lick them whenever I thought of it. It worked! By the time we left the Putsborough Sands to go back to the Commonwealth Services Club on the weekend, I was resolved to bring our party back during our forthcoming tour of England with the Stevensons, and the Elwins assured me of a warm welcome for Morley and myself. I had mined the ledger-book for all the letters that seemed useful to me, and I was glowing from this unexpected windfall and, especially, from this totally lucky, generous and unexpected compatibility.

We did go back, all 8 of us, and the Stevenson girls enjoyed that wonderful beach as much as John and Steve. Steve even had the nerve to swim in the sea there, although it was much too cold for the rest of us to contemplate. When we said goodbye to the Elwins, it was to an invitation to come again and a vow on my part to do so. It was also with Malcolm's offer to read my thesis and advise on the biography that I was embarking on. Not only was he the veteran of many biographies, he was also a reader and editorial advisor to Macdonald's, the publishers, and best of all, he was endlessly interested in and supportive of would-be biographers, especially if the work-in-progress was set in his beloved and familiar 19th century.

Between that first halcyon visit and my next one, two years later, my thesis, the basis of the biography-to-be, accompanied Malcolm Elwin on the strangest episode in his long, individualistic and often eccentric career. After a year, when he hadn't been in touch with me, our English friend, Ken Jones, wrote to him offering to pick up the thesis and get it back to me. This sparked Malcolm into a letter, explaining that the long delay was caused by a move he had made away from Sedgebanks up to Woolacombe, some twenty miles up the coast, a move that necessitated the removal and resettling of his 2,000 books. It was not until I got over and again visited Sedgebanks in the summer of 1965 that I heard from Eve the whole strange story. Just after the summer of 1963 when we met, Malcolm and Eve's marriage underwent a serious crisis during which she encouraged Malcolm to advertise for the woman who had been his youthful sweetheart long ago and who had subsequently been married to a butcher for some thirty years. His long-lost love answered his ad and, stranger than fiction, agreed to leave her husband and join Malcolm who, with his books and chattels, moved himself to a rented place on the Woolacombe cliff, leaving Eve at Sedgebanks alone. An emotionally conservative Canadian then and now, the story stunned me. It still does. Neither Eve nor Malcolm was at all happy with the chaotic situation they had created and, on the surface, so calmly accepted, and in due course, after almost a year of heart searchings, confessions and inevitable damage on both sides, they came together again. "I had suddenly fallen out of love with Malcolm," said Eve, as if that explained everything, or anything. As for Malcolm, he was given to calling himself a fool for the entire episode, and blamed the heavy book-moving efforts forever after for weakening his heart and making him susceptible to the heart attack that felled him in 1969.

When I returned to see them at Sedgebanks in the summer of 1965, much seemed as it had been two years earlier, with the pleasant addition of Sally, Eve's younger daughter by her first marriage, an artist who loved the Devon cliffside even more than she loved her vocation as a painter. From then on, Sally was 'home' whenever I visited, and for some ten years I became almost a commuter across the Atlantic. Sometimes Morley was with me at the Elwins' sometimes not. Every time, though, we sat in that livingroom overlooking the sea, Eve and I in the yellow chairs, Malcolm on his feet, a cigarette hanging out of his mouth, pacing up and down, up and down, and 'talking 19th century.' He was a great Byron man, despising Lady Byron and various of his hostile female biographers, "those women," as he called them. He was absolutely full of anecdotes about all the Romantics, "old Wordsworth" and the rest, all of whom had been subjects for one or other of his books. He had had considerable success for many years, book club selections, good sales, enviable relationships with publishers and agents, "old Pollinger" the most famous agent of all. Finally he was persuaded to undertake the mammoth Byron project, persuaded and blessed by Lord Lovelace, the holder of an immense treasure trove of papers collected by Lady Byron (in the course of my Jameson work, Lord Lovelace gave me permission to quote from the collection on House of Lords paper, which I ostentatiously showed to my colleagues). Out of the collection Malcolm published three volumes, *Lord Byron's Wife, The Noels And The Millbankes,* and *Lord Byron's Daughter,* none of which were exactly compatible to him, labours of necessity rather than of pleasure. In his very last years he turned with relief to the Powys brothers, and particularly to the letters of John Cowper, always an enthusiasm of his.

Malcolm was a wonderful and non-stop raconteur, and he was also an eager listener. The literary past was present for him and for any enthusiast who shared his delight in his subjects—his old friends, really, for he knew them more intimately and more amusingly than, in the stage of life when I knew him, he bothered to know many of his contemporaries. He had been, until his mid-fifties, an eager cricketer, a well-known county player, and though that was one area where I could not follow his stories, I could catch his enthusiasm for vanished victories and celebratory feasts which Eve had shared with enthusiasm. When they met in the thirties, he was a rising young biographer and a restless young married man, mated with an incompatible wife and already far beyond her reach in literary interests and ambitions. He was a graduate of University College, Oxford, "Univac," as he always called it, and in youthful married days he had lived on Boars' Hill, outside of Oxford.

Eve, with two young daughters, was married to an American academic, later diplomat, named Conelly, an ambitious writer herself, and bowled over by Malcolm's energy, erudition, literary reputation, flamboyance, sensitivity, and virile sexuality. She had grown up on a vast ranch in Colorado, in a notable family who took servants and private schools as a matter of course and who were proud of their most famous relative, Buckminster Fuller, but who were also quite comfortable and confident in their own identities. Eve was used to having what she wanted, and she wanted Malcolm, both for the glamour of his writing life which she longed for herself and the reality of his virility. They broke with their partners and lived together for some years before divorces freed them both, and Malcolm once confided to me that he thought their extra-legal status had been extremely hard on Eve. I'm not so sure of that, though I am sure that learning to cook and clean, to take responsibility for the upkeep of a house and the getting of its meals, was hard for her to adapt to. She had been used to servants, always, in America and in England, but she undertook housekeeping doggedly, and shortly, efficiently, and her willingness was certainly both test and proof of her love for Malcolm. During the war he was a conscientious objector, as were so many writers in England, and worked as an agricultural labourer, while also eking out time for his writing. He encouraged Eve to write as well, and as Mary Evelyn Turner (her maiden name), she published several romances, very much of their time, very much the Boots Lending Library kind of book, though far less melodramatic than the story, as she told it, of hers and Malcolm's romance.

To my lasting good fortune, the Elwins, and Sally Conelly, Eve's daughter, took me in as if I were a friend of longest-standing, instead of a newcomer. Malcolm was also a splendid friend in a literary way, advising Macdonald's to buy pages of *Love And Work Enough*, my biography of Anna Jameson, from the University of Toronto Press, and to publish it in England, in the summer of 1967, shortly after its Canadian publication. And so I had the great thrill of seeing my book in the window of Blackwell's on Broad Street in Oxford, the centre of the world of books for me at that time, as for most Canadian academics. In 1965 I went to England, stayed for a time at the Commonwealth Services Club and then went to Devon to visit the Elwins, staying for three days at the

Saunton Sands Hotel because the Putsborough was booked. In 1967 we were both over, staying with the Elwins for the first night, and then moving to the Putsborough, where we always felt at home. We had lots of time that visit because Morley had a six-week leave and we didn't go home until Thanksgiving. Seeing Somerset and Devon in their golden Fall colours was a new and special treat, as was my successful brass-rubbing all over as we tripped, including far out on the cliff at Tintagel, King Arthur's storied castle. Sally came to Oxford to join us for a further few days of touring colleges and countryside, and we hoped that she might visit us in Canada, but that never transpired. In all these years and visits, we in Canada were far more fortunate financially than our English friends, though they were so good at living well on little, a skill that they had developed to an art form during the war and its aftermath, that we were only very dimly conscious of their circumstances. In 1969 shortly after my mother died, I went over on another university charter, and again, on a side trip from the Commonwealth Services Club, I was in Devon while Malcolm was still in bed from his heart attack. But he had his spirit back, his warm kindliness, and his literary drive, and it was obvious that he was soon going to be on his feet and working again though Eve was very aware that the Byron project was a killing one for him. From then until 1972 when he died, I was there three times, once with both Morley and Shirley Doughty, soon to be Halevy, our acquisitions librarian at York who was interested in the possibility of acquiring Malcom's library.

All this time both Eve and Malcolm treated me as a cherished sister, with a generosity and an openness foreign to our comparatively standoffish Canadian temperament, wonderful to experience and forever remaining as a miraculous blessing, utterly unlooked for, undeserved. In 1972, after Father's death, we were over in August, and it was then that we had our last visits with Malcolm. He had been diagnosed as having terminal lung cancer just a short time before, and he was weakening, but his spirit was as of old, and he loved to sit outside in the sun and talk to us until he tired—talking 19th century in the same old way. A young academic couple from the University of Manchester, with their little boy, had camped in the field across the road from the Elwins that summer and had worked on cataloguing the library, a great boon and pleasure to both Malcolm and Eve. The gift of compatible enthusiasts meant a great deal to that final year's quiet of mind and sense of work well done.

In the Fall of 1973, on sabbatical, I met Morley in the famous small hotel on Half Moon Street in London. We were going on a trip with Anne Innes, around the east coast, through the fenlands and we intended to make some time to visit the Elwins in Devon, as usual. I called and Sally answered the phone to tell me that Malcolm had died that morning, and that they would love to see us the next day. We hastened to arrange our plans, drove down to Sedgebanks and spent several quiet, sad, but satisfying hours with Eve and Sally. The end had come peacefully, as Malcolm had weakened and loosed his grip on life, but without pain, and without regrets. Eve had been with him constantly, and they had talked constantly about the satisfactions their lives and their love had given them, until Malcolm was too weak to talk, and they lay side by side hands touching in final affirmation of their rightness for one another. To us from Canada, used as we were to the funeral parlour panoply of death, the experience was both very sad and very beautiful. Malcolm was to be cremated immediately, and then the ashes were to be scattered on the wild hillside above them, where he had loved to sit and write in his Wendy hut, or on good days to tramp through the golden sedge. Eve asked us to stay over, to be there for the little memorial ceremony of the ashes, but we couldn't, and besides, she and Sally were content to be by themselves, and at peace.

Our visits to Sedgebanks did not stop with his death, though, for we were always in touch with Eve and Sally, and ten years later, in March, we drove once again from Oxford out to Devon to have lunch at Sedgebanks. They had long since forged their own comradeship, and over the intervening years Eve had been very busy writing, particularly a novel that incorporated in lightly clothed fiction, hers and Malcolm's lives. Called "Celebration," it is as their love was, an old-fashioned romance, perhaps not saleable or even publishable today, but readable and gently reassuring for all that. I treasure the manuscript copy Eve gave me. She also gave me, but asked me to return, some 150 pages of typescript containing the story of Malcolm's life as far as he had wanted, or been able to, write it. The most utterly startling, not to say shocking, passage in it concerned him as a young child of three, sent away from his home to board with strangers because his mother had a baby and was not up to managing both young children. He told of watching longingly as his father walked down the street every day at noon, going home from his legal office for lunch, and how he was allowed one visit for tea a week. This went on for a long time, about three years. We are used to thinking the English strange in sending their children off to boarding school at a tender age, usually seven, but this custom, if custom it was, was right off the scale of family affection and caring, particularly since, to Malcolm's knowledge and memory, there was no more crucial reason for his exile than his mother's convenience.

We still correspond with Sally, though we haven't seen her since Eve died. She had to sell the house on the cliff (for a very large sum, seafront property being both scarce and precious), and, with great trouble and trauma, move all the books and belongings to a much smaller house in the village of Croyde, where she lives a lonely life but, I think, a contented one.

We enjoyed such acceptance, friendship and trust from Malcolm and Eve. We were blessed.

Chapter XXI

Friends and Sisters

Margaret Laurence

Reading *The Stone Angel* for the first time in 1965 was a milestone in my life. Never before had I been so deeply moved by a book, so aware of its speaking directly to me, in an idiom completely familiar, my mother's, my grandmother's, my own. From the start I thought it a turning point for Canadian Literature too, so much so that I had my students buy the hard-cover edition that Fall—a radical and expensive addition to their normal paperback book list. It was years before I could read the great "pride was my wilderness" passage without weeping. Even now I'm not sure that I can. What I do know, however, is that students were always long-suffering about that, and that many of them confessed to having a similar reaction. After the publication of *A Jest of God*, I began to say that I had to write something about all of Margaret's work, at that time consisting of *The Tomorrow-Tamer* stories, *This Side Jordan* and *The Prophet's Camel-Bell*. Two of the Manawaka novels had been published and some of the Vanessa Macleod stories, as well as the Somali translations, *A Tree For Poverty*. It seems only a little while before Dave Godfrey, at that time the editor for the McClelland and Stewart's Canadian Writers' series, asked me to write the first little book, *Margaret Laurence*, which I did in the Christmas holidays of 1968, my mother in the hospital in her last illness, myself at our kitchen table where I could easily watch various pots boil. From time to time one or other of my family would find me in tears, for the juxtaposition of Hagar's situation and my mother's was unbearably moving.

Margaret and I had corresponded a bit over that book. She told me some things about her writing methods—first draft in scribblers in pencil or ballpoint, for instance, a habit which she never relinquished; typed second draft, with a lot of revision going on at that time. Then usually a typed third draft before submission, and that one would ordinarily be the publisher's copy. Then, after submission, the anguish of waiting—and never did that anguish grow any less, even when Margaret was the best-known writer in Canada and her publisher would have been glad to publish her most random jottings. During the writing of every book, her characters became as real to her as her family or friends. Their fate agonized her. She always wrote for publication—no closet writer Margaret. She believed that to have her work published was the only way to justify it and to keep faith with her characters. When Jack McClelland—whom she always called "Boss," to whom she was fiercely loyal as were most of his writers, but also with whom she fought enthusiastically for her beliefs—wrote his tribute to her in the *Quill and Quire* of February, 1987, he said:

> One thing we may not yet understand is the deep courage of Margaret Laurence. She had to begin with the instinct and faith of all great writers. I refer here to the courage it requires for the simple act of submitting a manuscript to our publishing system. I learned something important from Margaret about writers: the anguish, the anxiety, that an author experiences while waiting for a judg-

ment from a publisher—the kind of uncertainty that remained with Margaret long after she had become an established star.

I began to know this, and much else besides, about the agonies and also the ecstasies of the truly born writer when I first visited her in Elm Cottage in England, just at the time of the publication of my *Margaret Laurence* book in June of 1969. I was staying at the Commonwealth Services Club in Oxford and went by bus to have lunch with her. "Elmcot," as she called it, was an old, old house in Penn, near High Wycombe in Buckinghamshire; she had first rented it through Alan Maclean, one of the senior editors of Macmillan, her English publishers. Shortly after her death Barry Callaghan wrote an article about interviewing her there. About the only thing that his article illuminates is the North American eyes and attitudes of Callaghan. He hadn't seen many English houses, or he would never, I hope, have described it as negatively as he did. In fact it was a lovely old house with many rooms, a tangled rose-garden and a large lawn at the side and back. The feature that I and many others noticed about it first was a very beautiful oil portrait of Lady Maclean, Alan's mother, as a child, hanging in the hall and acting as a kind of presiding 'angel in the house.' Margaret loved that house, as did the many Canadians who visited her there over the years; it still has happy memories for her children who, by the time I saw it, in June of 1969, had been living there for a number of years. Recently she had been able to buy the house from the proceeds of the film *Rachel, Rachel* (7,000 pounds as I recall, a minimal price when you think of what is now being paid for movie rights). Then, however, Margaret was overjoyed. She owned it at last, and had embarked on a great program of re-decorating and weather-proofing it, for it had become afflicted over the years with what the English call "the rising damp." This is one house hazard with which we don't seem to be afflicted in Canada. It means, simply, that the dampness of the climate slowly eats away and destroys the walls of the dwelling.

But that June, everything was in hand. She took me out into the garden and we sat down with pre-lunch drinks, mine a can of beer that Al and Eurithe Purdy had left in her fridge after they had recently visited her. She told me all about the genesis of *Jason's Quest*, recently published. The family had got up one morning to find the entire stretch of lawn we were sitting on all humped and bumped by mole-hills, not an uncommon occurrence in England. The lawn was ruined and in dire need of the local mole-man, an expert in controlling the little creatures who had suddenly caused all the damage. It took a season—but in the meantime, Margaret's imagination had got busy on the mole-civilization obviously thriving underneath her—and as she said, "the whole of *Jason's Quest* was given to me—just like that—a great and joyous gift." She had just finished *The Fire-dwellers* at that time, and the relief and joy she found in suddenly being given this mole-adventure to write of was, and remained, one of the crowning delights of her career. Calico and Topaz, the two cats who accompanied Jason on his quest to save Molanium, were the family's much-loved pets, and they, too, were very much in evidence that day. Jason himself was not. Do you remember the mole motto, inscribed in the Great Hall of the Moles? *Festina Lente* (make haste slowly). For Christmas, 1984, Margaret designed and had Birks make stirling silver pins for herself and her children and their spouses. These pins were the Laurences' own special family crest and they bore the motto *Festina Lente*.

That June day was the beginning of one of the most important and firmest friendships of my life—and our family's. When we did have lunch—steak and salad—Margaret spent a great deal of time thanking me for my little book—I was the one who needed to thank her, especially since that book was wretchedly edited and I've always been somewhat embarrassed by it. But when we parted in the afternoon, it was as friends, and our friendship grew and strengthened over the years. Margaret and I both knew very well that in middle age one is not usually lucky enough to find a dear friend, a "kindred spirit" to know and cherish. We were blessed; we quickly came to call each other "dear sister." When we met, we were both especially needy: Margaret was temperamentally a needy person—longing for warmth, acceptance, understanding; I was especially vulnerable at that time, mourning my mother's death, our temperamental mismatches and the long-drawn-out sadnesses of her last, ailing years.

Margaret was coming over that August to take up her first post as writer-in-residence at the U. of T., and we arranged that she would stay with us while she was getting herself settled and until she could move into the house she had already arranged to rent for the year. It was the first of scores of visits with us and the initiation of the room in our house that we will always think of as "Margaret's Room." We met her at the airport on a hot August night, dragging what must have been the heaviest suitcase in the world. Relaxing on our patio later, it was as if she, Morley, and I had known one another for a lifetime—in fact we talked so hard and laughed so much that our next-door neighbour leaned out of his bedroom window and told us in no uncertain terms to go to bed.

Morley took her to see the house she was renting and

to get instructions from its academic owners before they left on sabbatical. Both of them came back hysterically giggling and rather stunned—the venture remained one we reminisced about forever. The owners had such an array of instructions about lights, furniture, their 'priceless antiques' and all such, that Margaret was reduced to a nervous wreck and Morley to a total turn-off rare for him. It took several scotches and a lot of laughing to ease the anxiety about daring to move into such a homestead (for which she was to pay a hefty rent), and in the entire Fall and Winter of her stay there, Margaret was so nervous that she used only the study, the kitchen and the bedroom. The stories that evolved out of that first visit were legion!

Margaret had many friends. She made friends easily, and at that stage in her life, when she was already a successful and sought-after writer, many many people admired her and sincerely wished to befriend her—and, of course, to be befriended by her. It was not long before we realized how deeply she needed loyalty, people close to her whom she could trust and to whom she could confide freely her worries and doubts. Most of all, in those days of burgeoning and demanding fame, she needed a 'safe house' where she could be sure of welcome, understanding, affection and the opportunity, when she needed it, to unload her burdens. In her dear friend, Adele Wiseman (Stone) she had all that, but at that time, Adele lived in Kleinburg. We were, and are, honoured and grateful that from the start she knew, somehow, that she had found all that she needed with us too. We didn't know her children, had never met Jack or any other member of her family, and so we didn't have preconceived opinions and loyalties. We were exclusively *her* friends and increasingly *her* confidantes. She carried a great residue of regret and guilt about the breakup of her marriage and at that time she was also extremely sensitive about Neepawa and her roots there. It was some time, in fact not until the success of the film, *First Lady of Manawaka*, and its enthusiastic reception back home in Manitoba, that she felt the reconciliation that enabled her to return to her roots with joy.

That Fall and Winter we would talk endlessly, about writing, about her "kids," as she always called Jocelyn and David, who were then in their early teens and in the care of Ian and Sandy Cameron, Glendon friends of mine, about our kids, our families, worries, happinesses—everything. From the start we knew about Margaret's deep-rooted fears—of cars, where she was white-knuckled from start to finish of a drive, of traffic, subways (she would not go underground), and especially, of any hint of quarrel or confrontation. What we did not know, and never knew then or later, was the cause or causes of her extreme timidity. We speculated, of course: had she had a car accident in England or Africa? Was all this the traumatic result of the deaths in her family of mother and father when she was very young, of grandfather and her aunt, her beloved "Mum," later? We were not alone in our speculations: friends such as Dave and Ellen Godfrey didn't know either. Very soon we simply accepted Margaret with love and without such speculations, for these were the gifts of friendship she most wanted and needed from us and from others.

Morley loved all the talk and laughing too, and son John spent hours with his feet comfortably parked on the coffee table, just listening to us, both then and later. When he went to Queen's in the Fall of '71, we had a great family joke about how Margaret and he used to coincide coming home for weekends. It was a rich relationship for all of us, for our older son, Steve as well, though he was already married and wasn't around as much as John.

Sandy and Ian Cameron, who had gone to England to look after Jocelyn and David, had been Glendon College friends of mine, Ian, an early student, and Sandy, a biology lab assistant and residence Don. They were the beginning of what became a large trans-Atlantic network, for Elmcot became a drop-in centre for numbers of travelling young Canadians, some of whom stayed on, many of whom returned again and again, and all of whom loved and respected Margaret and her hospitality. She has given her own account of this period in her life in *Heart of a Stranger*. Sandy and Ian themselves remained in England where they are still, converts to a culture that has been congenial to them and their talents. Margaret and Sandy remained close until Margaret died and, of course, Sandy and Ian are in part responsible for *The Diviners'* songs and pen-portraits. Morley and I too were at Elmcot several times, once taking over a huge August tomato with us, that Margaret never stopped reminiscing about as the treat of her life. Elmcot had a glow for us because of Margaret's love for it, but that glow was stronger when we were across the Atlantic from it. We were, and are, spoiled by central heating. Elmcot was just a touch cold, even in August!

The year 1969-70 was a particularly hard one for Margaret. She and Jack had finally decided to divorce after six years of separation with rare visits. Margaret had to go back to England at Christmas time for the final hearing, a terrible ordeal for her, because she could never let herself believe that everything would go smoothly. She and Jack Laurence had loved each other very much and they had had a good marriage for many years. She often said that she would never have divorced him of her own volition, and she also said that she would always look after him if he were disabled, but long since she had found to her grief that she could not reconcile the demands of her work with her marriage. In truth, Margaret had grown out of her dependency on Jack, who, ten years older than she, had been a husband and lover, but had also been a father-figure to her. Now she had long since proved that she could make it on her own, in her writing and in the practical decisions of everyday living. Few people, I'm sure, have gone through with a divorce at such a cost in heart-searching regret or such a continuing sense of guilt.

She was now completely on her own financially. She had decided to buy property in Canada and she knew that she had to have a place within easy distance of Toronto, because she anticipated working as a publisher's reader, doing book reviews, and engaging in all the money-making asides that a free-lance writer must be prepared to undertake. One day that first Fall, sitting on the couch in our living room, she took a map of southwestern Ontario and drew a circle with Toronto its centre. Within that circle, she told us, she was going to buy a cottage, to which she would come summers, and to which she might well eventually return when her kids had finished their schooling in England. It didn't take her long, watching the ads in the *Globe*, to find what she wanted. So happened the buying of "The Shack" on the Otonabee, about six miles from Peterborough, which she enjoyed for ten years and in which a good part of *The Diviners* was written. Once she had found the place, she had a grand time furnishing it with some good old pine pieces from around that part of the country—and Eaton's catalogue. As for all of our generation, the catalogue had been a big part of her childhood. She said that she had always dreamed of having the means and the excuse to outfit a whole house from it. This she did—dishes, pots and pans, sheets, towels, etc. etc. When she moved in, in the spring of '70, it was to a complete, newly fitted-out place, and she loved it.

As soon as she moved up there and immediately had a phone installed, we began to get play-by-play accounts of the settling process. One of the first I remember, and the most important from everyone's point of view, was the day her well was divined. It was absolute magic to her. Her excitement made the wires crackle! And thus a good part of *The Diviners* was born, for the character of Royland is a composite of Jack Villerup, the old fisherman who had the next cottage, and the well-diviner of that always-to-be-remembered occasion. Through all the time of writing *The Diviners*, we were in constant communication. Since Margaret did not drive, she considered the telephone her car-substitute and thought nothing of using it. Her bills were horrendous—several hundred dollars a month was not unusual. But, as she was always quick to say, owning and running a car would have cost her much more. She kept close to her family and friends by means of the phone. Sometimes after a good day's writing she'd call and say: "It's wonderful—all I have to do is to listen to their words and put down what they day." Other times were "dry spells," worry—about "my kids", about the book, about everything.

For the rest of my life, I know that I'll always jump to the phone when it rings about five in the afternoon, her favourite time. She had a particular, breathless way of saying hello that I can hear now. When she was back in England we heartened each other with absolutely crazy correspondence, sometimes using silly names, and playing with all kinds of transatlantic tomfoolery. Sometimes

Margaret's letters would be all decorated with all kinds of little coloured flowers, fish and cats that were sure signs of a good day. They were Margaret's arty signatures and she took a really childish delight in drawing and colouring them. In fact, Margaret, like most, probably all gifted people, retained a large measure of childlike awe and wonder. Small good things were celebrated and magnified in her imagination, the good side of the coin, as opposed to her agonizing vulnerability to anxieties of all kinds.

The shape of *The Diviners* had been in her head for a long time. On that very first hot August night when she came to us, I asked her if she would like a book to go to sleep by, and offered her Willa Cather's *Song Of The Lark*, one of my eternal favourites. I'll always remember her look as she took it out of my hand and her saying: "That's so strange. I hope I'm going to write something like that. I've been trying to think about it as having to do with the growth of an artist, but I don't think I can do that. I don't know enough about it. I think the character will have to be a writer." *The Song Of The Lark* is about the growth of Thea Kronberg, from a little girl in a Nebraska prairie town, to an internationally-known opera singer. It wasn't strange that that was the book I offered Margaret. I had connected her to Willa Cather long since and had written an article about them both called "Proud Heritage". It was strange though, to find out what was already in her mind and her planning.

She worried a great deal about the future for herself and her children. Fortunately, the New Canadian Library had already published *The Stone Angel* and more and more her name was occurring among the lists of texts for courses, first in university Canadian Literature courses, then just beginning to boom, and a little later in high school courses as well. More and more she was invited to make public appearances—these she felt were part of her duty although they were agony for her—but she always did them, and as anyone will know who saw her on any platform occasion, she did them superbly. But she never lost her acute nervousness, and she never lost her nervous shaking. In fact, the main reason for her going over to the long gowns that became her trademark was to mask the shaking of her knees.

It was early in 1970, during that first stint as Writer-in-Residence that I made the first of many long gowns, all of them from the same pattern. I had gone into the "sewing fit" that I called my menopausal syndrome. I began making very simple things and Margaret fell in love with one of them,"The Robe" as she came to call it. The first one I made for her was of bright orange material, heavy, brilliant in colour and very becoming to her darkness. The fashion for robes and long skirts in general was just peaking then. I cannot remember on what occasion Margaret first tried out her robe, but it was a great success, and from this time forward she always wore these in public, when she read, spoke, or was awarded honorary degrees, something that began to happen very quickly. "The Robe" reminded her of African dress, for which she retained great admiration and, most important, it successfully hid her shaking—and she was always thankful that it was her knees and not her voice that shook!

Margaret chose the material for the first one, and from then on, I made her at least nine of them. We stopped counting at nine. Sometimes she would pick the material and send it to me when she was back in England. This was the situation in the spring of 1972 just after my father died, when I sent over two, one rusty coloured paisley silk, one green and blue in an overall silk print. I remember them especially because I had sent them with lacy black hemming tape on their bottoms. I left these to be hemmed by Margaret because of uncertainty as to length, but she wrote to thank me for the elegant lace decoration on their bottoms—we were neither of us what you would call fashion consultants. Sometimes Morley and I would go away and I would bring her back material for a robe. We began to go on yearly excursions to the University of the West Indies in 1970. I loved the brightness of Jamaican cottons and would always bring back a length for a robe for Margaret. One of those in a bright coral pattern she is wearing in one or two scenes of *The First Lady of Manawaka*. One of her robes is Finnish material, bright blues and greens on a white background. That came from a Finnish shop in Toronto and was in honour of our treasured house-helper, Hulda, whom Margaret knew well. They were together in our house a lot while I was away at York, and they became fond of each other. I can't remember all the robes, but I do remember the last one. It was made for her installation as Chancellor of Trent University and she picked out the blue-green, silky material and sent it to me. Edith Fowke and I went to the installation and I was proud to see her wearing it. Those were great years and great fun for both of us—Margaret used to love to say that she was the only woman in Canada whose dress-maker had a Ph.D. I loved that line too!

Once her commuting pattern between England and Canada had become established, she was very active in the burgeoning writers' movement in this country. The formation of The Writers' Union of Canada thrilled her, and she was one of its chief organizers, though she refused to be its first president once it had been organized. That honour she felt should go to Marion Engel. She was a faithful attender and played the part of a wise elder statesman at its Annual General Meetings for many years—until the early '80s when she resigned because she believed that the Union should not accept as much financial support from the government as it did. She was much missed. She always referred to all other writers as her "tribe," in her mind a great compliment, because her African experience had left her with enormous respect for tribal loyalties. She spoke fondly and idealistically of her "tribe" over all the years that I knew her, so much so that her belief, her naming, went into the vocabulary by which our writers speak of one another. After her death, the Union instituted a fund to provide for a Margaret Laurence Lecture on the first evening of every annual meeting.

Margaret was in Toronto and at our house when Beth Appeldoorn and Susan Sandler opened the Longhouse Bookshop in 1972, the first bookshop to stock Canadian books exclusively, and so another landmark for Canadian writing. Isabel Bassett, who at that time was in my Graduate Seminar, had volunteered to arrange and fund a gala opening party in honour of the first all-Canadian bookshop. That was a great occasion, much enhanced by Margaret's presence. Beth and Susan's Longhouse Bookshop became a drop-in centre for Canadian Literature enthusiasts here and abroad, and the partners were absolutely tireless in their enthusiasm and support. The walls of the Longhouse were garlanded with signed pictures of writers, the shelves were well-stocked with their works, and the owners were always ready with anything from bookish help to the latest gossip in the book world. And Beth and Susan, believe me, were the first to have all the gossip at their fingertips! When they retired, after years of hard work and stalwart support, they moved to Salt Spring Island, B.C., but not before they had been awarded Honorary Degrees by Trent University. They sold the Longhouse, and for a few years it survived under genial management, but now, sadly, it is defunct. Crucial in its time, it has left behind its memorable legacy of a total investment of time and money on the part of the two founders. When our cultural historians write of the yeasty 70s, Appeldoorn and Sandler must be among our prime literary benefactors.

After my father died in 1972 I decided to keep the house in Strathroy in which my brother and I had grown up. Margaret made her first visit to see it that same summer. She loved it, every old inch of it, but what I remember most was her first exploration of the house, when she opened a door in the kitchen and nearly pitched down the cellar stairs. How was she to know that those stairs were all that was behind that intriguing old door? It was on that visit to Strathroy, on a balmy summer night that she first told me in detail, play by play, the story of *The Diviners*. As always, she hadn't liked to talk about what she was working on, and though I knew a lot about good writing times and bad ones from letters and phone calls, I had no idea of the book's plot. But when she told me the story the book was finally in the press, the final manuscript typed by Jocelyn, a labour of love that pleased Margaret mightily. Some months before publication she gave me the final typescript to read, because I was about to work on *The Manawaka World of Margaret Laurence* and she wanted me to be able to include her new book in my study. She made me promise, though, not to try to see what had been blacked out in the mss with heavy black felt pencil, sometimes words, or lines, sometimes whole passages. I kept my word, except for the last two words on the last page of the manuscript.

It looked like this: "Morag returned to the house, to write the remaining private and fictional words, and to set down her title.

The Diviners

Margaret did a part of the final editing of the manuscript by telephone with Judith Jones, her much-respected Knopf editor, from our house in Toronto at Christmas time. They would argue over points, they would agree and disagree, and sometimes Margaret would consult us on various points of Canadian word usage. Sometimes one would give way, sometimes another, very much as Morag writes of her experience of being edited. Always they retained the highest respect for each other's opinions and Margaret always considered Judith the ideal editor—in fact, so much the only editor that when *Heart Of A Stranger* was published by McClelland and Stewart but not Knopf, she and the young Canadian editor assigned to the book gave each other some very hard times.

I had a sabbatical in 1973-4. Besides writing the chapter on biography for *The Literary History of Canada*'s second edition, I also wrote *The Manawaka World*, enlarging and adding a great deal to the earlier little *Margaret Laurence*. I also busied myself having a great many things done to the family home in Strathroy. It was the time for painting, re-roofing, wiring, decorating. At the same time Margaret was buying 8 Regent St., in Lakefield and doing all kinds of the same things to it. And then happened one of our greatest of many examples of mutual serendipity, E.S.P. as we liked to call it. Each of us, unbeknownst to the other, picked identical wall-paper for our hall and living-room areas. We were both working with old houses that we loved, ours built in 1871, Margaret's about the turn of the century. And of all the hundreds of wall-paper patterns available we picked the exact same one. Such a happy coincidence! I can't remember which one of us it was who first got to see the other's handiwork—but never will I forget our joint surprise and delight at what we found.

Margaret had happy years in that house, from 1974 until her death in 1987, and even in the months of her last illness she was able to be at home. David and Sonia, his wife, came back from San Francisco to be with her and had a partition between her part of the house and the attached flat removed so that she had access to a bathroom on the main floor. They installed a hospital bed, and, until November, when she had the terrible misfortune of breaking her leg, the day after she returned from Toronto and Jocelyn's wedding, she was comfortable there, where she could see and talk to her friends. The wedding, dear to her heart, was the last event she attended, and it cost her a great and gallant effort. She also had agonizing times in that house. The two attempts to ban her books from the schools were particularly hurtful because they occurred in her beloved home territory, one in Peterborough, one in Lakefield. It is impossible to overestimate the damage that these attacks caused to her personally and to her writing of fiction. I think it is safe to say that had they not occurred we would now have the novel at which she worked so hard, before finally giving up.

When she finished *The Diviners* she said that she would never write another novel. Many didn't believe her. I did, because she had said the same thing to me many times during the long haul of that book, and I had seen just how much psychic energy it had drained out of her. Besides, with it the Manawaka cycle was finished. It had come full circle. She used to say that she had had a kind of mission to write the Manawaka cycle, that all the novels had been there in her mind and imagination and that she had had to bring them to birth as it were. But she did start again, and she spent months and months planning—and writing. The book was not to be centred in Manawaka this time, but it was about three generations of a Ukrainian family in Manitoba. She had some hundreds of pages of first draft written, but she could never get the voices to come out to her satisfaction. That is all lost to us now. Had she not been so emotionally dashed by the banners, I think that we would have had that other novel. I am sure that it is also safe to say that the book-banners' activities shortened her life. She tried each time, but she simply could not rise above the attacks. She used to telephone me from the depths of despair, and even the tremendous support she got from literally hundreds of correspondents did not appreciably lighten the burden for her. I don't pretend to understand why these mean-spirited campaigns were so hard on her, but I do know that they undermined her health. For a very long time I underestimated the damage that the banners were doing to her. I was wrong.

For us the activities of the book-banners meant great loss, but she compensated in some measure by her devotion to good causes—the Peace Movement, Energy Probe, CARAL, Amnesty International, Project Ploughshares, all these and many more had her support in writing, speaking and giving, both energy and money. All her belief in the Social Gospel, so important a part of her western heritage—and Tommy Douglas, J.S. Woodsworth and Stanley Knowles were great heroes to her—came to the fore in those last years. She treasured a plastic pen Stanley Knowles had given her as if it were pure platinum.

She had become a loved and venerated figure countrywide very quickly after she began coming back to Canada, and especially after the publication of *The*

Diviners. Her honorary degrees began in the early seventies and accelerated quickly after that, so that sometimes universities seemed to be standing in line to give them to her, always, in return, expecting a convocation speech from her. These cost her enormous amounts of thought, research and effort in the writing. They never became easy for her, nor did she ever give the same speech on two occasions, though Heaven knows she was often tempted. But she considered them a part of her public duty and in spite of the horrible cases of pre-event nerves that she invariably suffered, she did them—and did them superbly.

Along with the gowns that hid her shaking knees, she downed massive doses of Kao-Pectate before such occasions, to quiet her stomach. In spite of complicated preparations and precautions, some near-disasters did happen —as the time in High Prairie, Alberta, when she found herself on a raked stage, in front of a lectern with wheels! Or the time at Simon Fraser University when, up on the top of that mountain she was in grave danger of freezing at an outdoor Convocation until a male friend loaned her a black wool turtleneck sweater to wear under her gown. In early June of 1986 the University of Manitoba gave her her last Honorary Degree, a very special one to her, though of course she had no idea that she would be mortally ill within two months. Manitoba meant a homeland and a specially-treasured vindication of her life's work.

In June of 1986 she was with me when York honoured me with a D.Litt., an occasion I was delighted to share with her and my family. In July, her Lakefield friend, Joan Johnston, had a 60th birthday celebration for her, another memorable occasion for a sizeable group of friends. On that day I presented her with some pieces of the "Manawaka Limoges" we had joked about so often, ever since the writer, Joan Hind-Smith, mistakenly mixed fiction and fact and reported that Margaret's mother had sold the family Limoges to send her to United College. I had spent a good deal of time looking for odd pieces, and when Margaret recognized the pattern I had brought her as indeed her grandmother's own "Bridal wreath" we were equally astonished and delighted. Within a month of that beautiful summer day, she found that she was terminally ill.

She had been honoured and pleased to become Chancellor of Trent university in 1979, and she took her duties very seriously. She had good friends at Trent, particularly Jean and Alf Cole, Michael Peterman, John Wadland, and Tom Symons, Trent's first President. Edith Fowke and I went to see her installed at Trent's usual out-of-doors Convocation on a day when it constantly threatened rain but didn't quite get us all wet, nor did the weather dampen our enjoyment or Margaret's obvious pleasure in the ceremony. She anticipated a livelier role in the doings of the university than the position of Chancellor allows for, however, and she took issue with some of Donald Theall's policies shortly after he became President. Unfortunately their disagreement was exacerbated by Margaret's relegation to a secondary place when Trent was visited by the administrative officer of the Royal Society as a possible site for a future meeting. Margaret and Tom Symons were the only two Royal Society Fellows at Trent; she was informed that she would be having lunch with the visitor's wife, while Theall and Symons would lunch with the Society's representative. One did not with impunity damage Margaret's pride; she was deeply and justifiably offended. She refused a second term as Chancellor, largely because of the oil-and-water quality of her relations with Theall. She was, in any case, far too much of a social activist to be satisfied with a purely honorary position, and she gave it up with a good deal of relief.

When she sold her papers to York in 1981, she asked me to read through all of them, in order to be able to advise the various scholars who would henceforth be able to use them. The decision to sell was an agonizing one for her: for many years she had been outspokenly against such a move, so that I simply never mentioned the topic to her and was astounded one day to receive a sudden phone call asking me if York would be interested. Naturally I lost no time in calling our chief librarian, and though Margaret suffered many tremors and it was a good many phone calls later that she firmly made up her mind, the sale went through. Before finally signing, she had gone through all her papers and she and Adele Wiseman had gone through all of their lengthy correspondence. She had removed only a handful of letters deemed too personal for dispersal and, in fact, when she was with Adele, engaged in this review, she called me in hopes that I would make a book of their correspondence. I was not interested then, but I am happy that John Lennox and Ruth Panofsky have now done just that and that their collection was published in the Fall of 1997. All through the years that I knew her, Margaret had times of gruelling anxiety about the financial future for herself, Jocelyn and David. It was only this recurrent worry that finally persuaded her to sell, and only the fact of our friendship that turned her thoughts to York, for any other university in the country would have been happy to purchase.

It was when I read through her papers that I realized just how much a part of her life Margaret's correspondence had become, how much of a joy, how much of a burden. Of course, she had talked about it for years, and many times, when she was finding it particularly difficult to keep up with her letter-writing I had urged her to use form letters, or to get some part-time help. When she was Chancellor of Trent, I had begged her to ask the university to give her some secretarial help but she would never do that. She did have some form letters made up, but she used them only a time or two, and then only to refuse to read or edit someone's manuscript. Until the months of her last illness, she answered every letter, often at considerable length—and she got hundreds of them. Quite often the initial exchange would develop into a continuing correspondence, and in a good few cases, into a treasured friendship. Always, finally, there were more positives than negatives in such a constant and voluminous mail, for Margaret spent many lonely hours of self-doubt, and the constant evidence of affection and respect pouring in upon her life was consistently heartening.

The age-span of her correspondents ran from eight to well over eighty. Whole classes of kindergarten children drew her pictures, inspired by *Six Darn Cows*, *Jason's Quest*, or *The Olden Days Coat*. Slightly older children printed tributes that were sent en masse by teachers. Teen-agers poured out their feelings about Pique, Skinner, Vanessa, Hagar and all the rest. One thirteen-year-old boy wrote her seven pages of appreciation of *The Diviners*. A man in his eighties, in a nursing home, wrote to tell her how much he had appreciated *A Bird In The House*. His wife, he said, had lent him her copy and then had thought him crazy when he said he was going to write to the author. A woman wrote: "Well!! Here I am. I've just finished *The Stone Angel*. I've cried so hard I'm a mess. Now I have to get dressed and go bowling. What am I going to do about that?"

All ages, men and women, boys and girls—hundreds

of people felt the need to communicate to Margaret what her work had meant to them. One special day began with this letter:

> Dear Mrs. Laurence: Some time ago you were one of several celebrities asked by *Chatelaine* magazine to name their favourite sports figure. You said that you did not know very much about sport, but that you had heard very good things about a young man named Wayne Gretzky. Wayne was grateful for your mention, and in return he would like you to have the enclosed autographed picture. And who am I? Just a friend of his, a nun, who helps him out with his correspondence when it gets too much for him. Yours sincerely, Sister Antonio of the Holy Cross, Edmonton, Alberta.

Margaret was especially amused and touched by that letter—the phone lines were busy that day as she told her friends. Her answer was a very warm wish for the continued success of Wayne who, she was sure, she said, lived as honourably as he played hockey. She sent warm wishes for Sister Antonio too.

These letters are quite apart from another major section of her correspondence, her letters from writers. Between 1965 and her death in 1987, virtually every writer in Canada corresponded with her at one time or another. The older, more established ones shared news and views of their craft. The younger ones wanted encouragement, often of a tangible kind, in the form of letters of recommendation to the Canada Council or other granting establishments. Mostly, however, writers wanted what the public wanted—to be in touch with her warmth and generosity, to communicate with a woman who had had spectacular success without losing one iota of her firm faith in humanity and hope for its future.

One of Margaret's passages that I think of most often occurs in the introduction to *Long Drums And Cannons*, published long ago, in 1968. That is her book about, really her tribute to, the astonishing group of Nigerian writers who blossomed just after their country's independence, the group that includes Chinua Achebe, Margaret's dear friend, and Wole Soyinka, a writer she admired enormously, and the one who was awarded the Nobel prize in the Fall of 1986. The day in October when that news hit the press, we had gone to Lakefield to visit Margaret. It was a sad visit—not only did we know of her mortal illness, but only the day before her beloved brother, Bob, had died of cancer and she had just had the word. Ken Adachi of the *Toronto Star*, also a close friend, called while we were there to tell her about the Soyinka prize. The news infused her with life and joy. For a few moments, we witnessed the Margaret we knew so well, the writer who rejoiced in the successes of other writers so wholeheartedly, and who inspired so many of our writers to their successes. But to go back to the passage I speak of—it is this:

> Achebe's writing also conveys the feeling that we must attempt to communicate, however imperfectly, if we are not to succumb to despair or madness. The words which are spoken are rarely the words which are heard, but we must go on speaking.... In Ibo villages, the men working on their farm plots in the midst of the rain forest often shout to one another—a reassurance, to make certain the other is still there, on the next cultivated patch, on the other side of the thick undergrowth. The writing of Chinua Achebe is like this. It seeks to send human voices through the thickets of our separateness.

Margaret's voice reached out to all of us and continues to do so. For Christmas of 1985, the last Christmas she enjoyed in health, she designed and had Birks make a sterling-silver medallion for her family and friends. It is an oval, inscribed with a Cross and a Star of David. With it goes her "Prayer for Passover and Easter," a final statement of her deep personal spirituality.

Prayer for
Passover and Easter

May our eyes and hearts be opened
To all faiths that praise
And protect life
May our lives be committed
To honouring and saving life
May we struggle all our lives
For lives of us all
For all the children
And may we strive with all our lives
Against destroyers   against wars
Against those whose distortions
Have taken and would take again
Beloved children to untimely death
May we oppose those hatreds
With every strength and word
In all our lives as long as life
Shall last, and may at last
Our fears be brave and may we praise
Life given   life lived   with hope
May our symbols of faith
Of caring and respect and love
Become one symbol
As our children are

Our mutual children
As the Holy Spirit
Breathes in us all
And may we learn
Not to hurt
May we lean
One upon another
Give and receive loving strength
And may we learn

We are one
People   in our only home
Earth.
        AMEN.

                1985

Index

Adelaide 232
Albright, Mrs. 71
Allen, Florence 153
Allen, Dr. 77
Allison, Helen 67
Anderson, Doris 186
Anderson, Hettie 250
Anderson, Peter 250
Appelbe, Jane 135, 136, 139
Appeldoorn, Beth 312
Argue, Dean 102
Armour, John 149
Armstrong, Ethel 250
Armstrong, Heaman 250
Armstrong, Mr. 44
Attenborough, Sir Richard 217
Atwood, Margaret 161, 186, 228
Augustine 218

Baldwin, George 170
Ballstadt, Carl 226, 227
Barnes, Djuna 215
Bassett, Isabel 186, 312
Bassett, Mr. 71
Bateman, Mrs. 236
Bates, Ron 170
Battle, Helen 71
Baugh, Eddie 171, 194
Beauchemin, Claire 200
Belaney, Archie 217
Bell, Christie 236
Bennet, Louise 197
Benson, Eugene 135
Bertrand, Ivy 74
Bertrand, Mrs. 74, 79, 83
Birbalsingh, Frank 162
Birney, Earle 175

Bissell, Claude 171
Bixel, W. 255
Blanchard, Paula 218
Bolgan, Anne 174
Bonanno, Giovanni 205
Bonanno, Gianni 208
Booth, Wayne 213
Bowie, Billy 32
Bowley, Jean 42, 73
Bowley, Walter 276
Bracken, Sandy 190
Bradford, Douglas 58
Braithwaite, Edward Kamau 195
Broderson, Prof. 102
Brown, Effie 258
Brown, Elizabeth 246
Brown, Evelyn 42, 73
Brown, Gladys 241
Brown, Jack 241
Brown, Joan 85
Brown, Mary 165
Bruckmann, John 149
Buitenhuis, Peter 170
Burdon, Beatrice 9, 259
Burdon, Mrs. John 233
Butler, Mrs. 241

Cady, Mr. 233
Callaghan, Barry 301
Callaghan, Morley 152, 216
Callwood, June 186
Cameron, Alison 36, 38, 63
Cameron, Ian 178, 306
Cameron, Sandy 178, 306
Campbell, Catherine 72
Campbell, Jean 67
Caradoc 322

Carr, Emily 217
Carrier, Roch 161
Carson, James 2
Cavers, Agatha 28, 40, 61, 92, 272, 273
Cavers, Christian 272, 273
Cavers, George 273
Cavers, Robert 272, 273
Cavers, Ronnie 273
Clark, James 246
Clark, Elizabeth 246
Cluett, Bob 179
Cole, Jean and Alf 318
Cole, Dorothy 88, 277
Collie, Michael 168
Collins, Thomas 234
Conelly, Sally 294
Conron, Brandy 74, 75, 84, 86, 110, 117, 120, 127, 130, 194
Conron, Carol 118
Cox (sculptor) 210
Craven, Mary Louise 172, 190, 191, 194, 201
Craven, Paul 192
Crawforth, Grace 28, 69, 276
Crealy, Truman 233
Cuddy, Laftus 34, 41, 43, 250
Curtis, Robert 233
Cutten, Carrie 237

Dampier, Edward 35
Dampier, Mary 32, 36, 37, 41, 53, 68, 118
Daniells, Roy 171, 173
Darling, Michael 191
David, Jack 171, 191
Davidson, True 181
Davies, Gwendolyn 210
Davies, Robertson 1
Davis, Rick 259
Dayfoot, Mr. 238

Deacon, William Arthur 109, 121
Dean, Ida 68, 116
Dean, Frank 116
Delbaere, Jeanne 210
Denning, Evelyn 36
Dickson, Norman 32
Dickson, Rache Lovat 217
Djwa, Sandra 193
Dorland, Dr. 77
Downham, George 276
Downham, Howard 251
Downham, Williston 28, 251
Downham, Willie 117, 276
Doxey, George 149
Draper, Vicky 149
Drummond, Ross 72, 76, 91
Duncan, Sara Jeannette 1
Durocher, Slim 260

Earle, Ronald 155
Eaton, John David 154
Edel, Leon 215, 216, 218
Edgar, Norma 101
Edwards, Miss 233
Elliott, J.C. 43
Elsa, Baroness 215
Elwin, Eve 145, 166, 287
Elwin, Malcolm 144, 147, 166, 287
Endler, Norman 149
Engel, Marian 312
Escarpit, Dr. 202
Evans Family 252
Ewener, Bill 78, 91

Farmer, Rev. Dr. 237
Farthing, Mrs. 265
Fetherling, Douglas 160
Fidler, Annie 72, 256
Fidler, Art 256
Fisher, Mary 264

Index

Fisher, Mrs. 264
Fisher Brothers' Orchestra 268
Fleck, Paul 170
Fowke, Edith 171, 183, 311, 318
Fowle, David 149
Fowlie, Dorrie 28, 40, 73, 274, 275, 276
Fowlie, Jack 27, 63, 117, 276
Fox, Miss 69
Frank, Ella 237
Fraser, Lorna 149
Frean, Roly 135
Freele, Bernice 269
French, Mr. 44, 48
Frye, Northrop 55, 132, 142, 146, 161, 207, 214, 222

Gast, Vesta 51, 80
Gibney, Sarah 20
Gibson, Sylvia 101
Gide, Andre 214
Gillespie, Kate 106
Girling, Harry 151
Glassco, John 213, 215, 218
Godfrey, Dave 164, 171, 299, 305
Godfrey, David 160, 163, 172
Godfrey, Ellen 305
Gordon, Prof. 258
Goulding, Hanah 24, 44
Graham, John 174
Granatstein, Jack 205
Gretzky, Wayne 301
Greve, Felix Paul 214
Grey Owl 213, 216, 218
Grove, Frederick Philip 213
Grove, Leonard 214, 218

Haight, Myrtle 36
Hall, Mrs. 44
Hallman, Eugene 123
Hallman, Margaret 123

Halpenny, Francess 146, 211, 218
Hare, Kenneth 168
Heilbrun, Carolyn 219
Hemingway, Ernest 216
Hind-smith, Joan 318
Hjartarson, Paul 215
Hopkins, Beth 226, 227
Houston, Joyce 28, 74, 76, 80, 81, 95, 276
Hulda (housekeeper) 311

Innes, Anne 147, 158, 163, 166, 178, 201, 279, 288

Jackson, Donald 149
James, Lord 154
James, Mr. 74, 79
James, Vivienne 153
Jameson, Anna 213, 219, 220, 223
Jameson, Robert 220
Jarmain, Bill 99
Jensen, Chris 71
Johnson, Art 149
Johnson, Edward 18
Johnston, Joan 317
Jolson, Al 23
Jones, Dr. 244
Jones, Ken 291
Jury, Wilfrid 107

Kalbfleisch, Dr. 77
Kattan, Naim 202
Kennedy, Jack 27, 88, 276
Kidd, Miss 233
Kilbourn, Bill 186
King George VI 217
Kingston, Dr. 217
Klinck, Carl 131, 147, 165, 171, 173, 228
Klinck, Margaret 165
Knight, Florence 149, 153

Kokatailo, Philip 216
Kreisel, Henry 174
Kroetsch, Bob 211

Lacombe, Michèle 179, 190, 191
Lambert, Libby 28, 276
Lamming, George 195
Landon, Fred 105
Landon, Mr. 107
Landon, Richard 188
Lane, Lauriat Jr. 170
Lang, Betty 66, 70
Langford, Stella 245
Langford, William 245
Langille, Mr. 149
Laurence, Jack 306
Laurence, Margaret 1, 164, 165, 171, 175, 183, 186, 191, 207, 214, 228, 299
Leacock, Stephen 1
Lecker, Robert 171, 191
LeClair, Jacques 204
Lee, Dennis 160
Leitch, Donny 275
Lennox, John 172, 187, 189, 190, 192, 208, 211, 219, 319
Lewin, Olive 196
Lewis, Janet 169, 191
Liddy, Kay 71
Lidicott, Doris 72
Livesay, Dorothy 195
Lloyd, Miss 237
Lochead, Douglas 149
Lombardos 268
Longmire, Bert 117, 199
Longmire, Ruth 117, 199
Lorimer, James 172
Lys, Mr. and Mrs. 100

MacDonald, Ewan 231
MacDonald, Ian 192

MacFarlane, John 149
MacKinnon, Murdo 174
Maclean, Alan 301
Maclean, Hugh 139, 149, 157
MacLennan, Hugh 171, 216
MacMillan, Sir Ernest 18
MacMurray, Mrs. 221
MacVicar, William 39
Mahood, Mollie 197
Maine, Floyd 77, 85, 103, 122
Mandel, Eli 184, 205
Mane, Robert 204
Manning, Mr. 44
Marcy, Earl 44, 48, 66
Markham, Mary (Brown) 123
Marshall, Dony 275
Martin, Basil 239
Martin, Beulah Miner 15, 232
Martin, Electa 234
Martin, Evan 239
Martin, Ged 211
Martin, May 237, 238
Martin, Roy 239
Martin, Samuel 11, 15, 179, 176, 232
Martin, Till 237
Martin, Victor 239
Mathieson, Ron 119
Matthews, John 195
Matthews, Robin 134, 162
McAuley, Mr. 154
McCabe, Dr. 45
McCandless, Elizabeth Slack 274
McCandless, Evan 7
McCandless, Martha, grandmother 6, 15, 18, 121, 232, 263
McCandless, Roy 7, 274
McCandless, Samuel 3, 30, 43, 239
McCandless, Vila Fisher 263
McClelland, Jack 171, 300

Index

McClung, Nellie 35
McColl, Hugh 247
McColl, Margaret 8, 247
McCormick, Anne 24, 44
McCormick, Don 117
McCormick, Florrie 117
McInnis, Edgar 149
McIntyre, Margaret 64
McIntyre, Miss 232
McKeen, Colin 72
McKenzie, Beth 99
McKibbon, Pauline 186
McKinnon, Murdo 132, 141, 176
McLennan, Barbara 102
Miller, Alice Duer 24, 61
Moens, Marja 146
Moers, Ellen 222
Montgomery, L.M. 60, 229, 231
Moodie, Dunbar 227
Moodie, Susanna 213, 223, 227, 228
Moore, Mavor 186
Morrison, Neil 151
Morrow, Edith Whicher 139, 186
Morrow, John 111, 117, 139
Morrow, Miriam 117
Moss, John 203
Murray, Elsie 106, 141
Murray, John 70

Naipaul, V.S. 195
Napper, Miss 237
Neilson, Gladys 153
Nelson, Jim 137
Neville, Dean 67
New, Bill 167, 195
New, Peggy 195
Newton, Florence 33, 34
Nichol House 240
Nicholson, Del 89

Nicholson, Lloyd 89
Noel, Robert 220
Nowotny, Yvonne 136

O'Heir, Susan 184
Oakes, Carrie 233
Oakes, Donald 275
Oakes, Frieda 51

Pacey, Desmond 214
Panofsky, Ruth 319
Pantry, Heather 190
Parker, Doug 258
Parker, Ralph 72
Pascal, Roy 218
Patterson, Bill 256
Patterson, John 101
Pelletier, Gerard 202
Persico, Gemma 209
Peterman, Michael 226, 227, 318
Pilgrim, Miss 232
Pitt, David 177
Pooke, Eva 258
Powicke, Prof. 134
Prangley, Wes 240
Pratt, Claire 188
Pratt, E.J. 174
Pratt, Viola 216
Proctor, John 154
Pronger, Lester 149
Pugsley, Mrs. 41, 68

Rajan, Balachandra 171
Ready, Norma 80
Reynolds, Charles 233
Rickerd, Donald 149, 157
Ritchie, Charles 214
Rizzardi, Professor 207
Robarts, John 185
Robinson, Dick 237
Rose, Mr. 234
Ross, George 1

Ross, Malcolm 171, 173, 223
Ross, Murray 139, 150, 152, 153
Ross, Sinclair 213
Rowe, Jim 147, 178, 201, 279
Rowe, Trudi 147, 178, 201, 279
Roy, Flora 130
Roy, Gabrielle 214
Rubinoff, Lionel 149
Rubio, Mary 230
Sadleir, Marjorie 31
Sanborn, Earle 131, 165
Sanborn, Mary 131, 165
Sandler, Susan 312
Sands, Ruth 71, 73, 88
Sarnia 238
Savard, Pierre 205
Saxton, John 232
Saxton, Hattie 237
Saywell, Jack 155, 169
Schoolcraft, Mrs. 221
Scott, Frank 216
Scott, Peter 155
Seeley, John 149, 150, 152
Selvon, Sam 195
Shadbolt, Doris 218
Shook, Father 135
Shotwell, James 2, 245
Sifton, Em 246
Sifton, True 246
Silver, David 172
Sinclair, Mary 71
Small, Bill 149
Smiley, Jim 239
Smith, A.J.M. 216
Smith, Denis 149, 157, 165
Smith, Marion 168
Spenceley, James 77, 85, 138, 223
Spettigue, Douglas 214
Spriet, Pierre 202, 204
St. John, Bascom 150
Steele, James 162

Stein, Gertrude 216
Stephens, Donald 167
Stevenson, Dorothy 74, 76, 78, 97, 157
Stiling, Frank 77, 108
Stock, Harry 278
Stocks, Vesta 80, 278
Stoney, Ruth 101
Strange, Cy 89, 91
Stratford, Philip 211
Strathroy 1, 12, 232
Stratton, Gene 230
Stuart, Lizzie 232
Sullivan, Annie 8, 53, 67, 99
Sullivan, Art 72
Sullivan, Clara Carruthers 12, 70, 245
Sullivan, Dorothy Eileen 244, 246
Sullivan, Dorothy 3, 8, 53
Sullivan, Ed 12, 62, 245
Sullivan, Frieda 8, 244, 245, 247
Sullivan, Harold 8, 244, 245, 254, 256
Sullivan, Helen Clarkson 12, 70
Sullivan, Hugh 8, 53, 247
Sullivan, John 14, 245
Sullivan, Lloyd 8, 247
Sullivan, Mabel 8, 244, 245
Sullivan, Mandana 14
Sullivan, Margery 8, 47, 99, 244, 245
Sullivan, Pat 125
Sullivan, Rachel 8, 244
Sullivan, Stewart 12, 16, 61
Sullivan, Vernon 3, 8, 10, 66, 111, 114, 116, 118, 125, 244, 245, 247, 256
Sullivan, Will 8, 244, 276
Summerhayes, Mr. 44
Summerhayes, Principal 66
Summerhayes, Vic 277
Sutherland, Bill 264

Index

Sutherland, Fraser 216
Swift, Jean 40, 276
Symons, Tom 162, 318

Talbot, Thomas 221
Tallman, James 108
Tamblyn, W.F. 77, 86, 105, 107, 108
Tatham, George 150
Theall, Donald 172, 318
Thomas, Hartley 71
Thomas, John David 124, 157, 291, 305
Thomas, Morley 58, 70, 78, 79, 83, 86, 96, 97, 115
Thomas, Stephen Morley 114
Thompson, George 258
Thompson, Jean 21
Thompson, Mrs. 44
Tippett, Maria 218
Torrey, Mr. 53
Traill, Catharine Parr 213, 219, 233, 224, 227, 228
Traill, Thomas 225, 226
Turney, Alice 149, 150
Turville, Dorothy 77

Van Horne, Marnie 99
Vandermeer, Tina 142
Varty, Dr. 119, 124
Vauthier, Simone 204
Verney, Douglas 149, 170, 212
von Goethe, Ottilie 220

Wadland, John 318
Wahl, Bert 167
Wahl, Dorreene 167
Walcott, Derek 196
Walkden, Ray 99
Walker, Jean 72, 275
Ward, Richard 257
Ward, Rate 256
Warwick, Jack 202
Waters, Marge 68
Waters, Reg 173
Waterston, Elizabeth 230, 231
Waugh, Marian 24, 44, 48
Wetherell, James 2
Whicher, Ede 117
Whicher, Edith 111
Whicher, Harry 82, 85
White, Miss 233
Whitla, Nancy 166
Wiens, Catherine 214
Wilson, Haliburton 101
Wilson, Mrs. 46
Wilson, Woodrow 3, 245
Wiseman, Adele 205, 304, 319
Woodcock, George 214
Woodhouse, A.S.P. 131, 132, 141, 173, 174
Woodman, Ross 174
Woontons 245
Wright, Cecil 27, 32, 63, 73, 276
Wright, Clarke 21
Wright, Ernie 241
Wright, Mary 61

Illustrations

1. 1924 — Grandma McCandless and Clara at Grand Bend

2. 1926 — Samuel McCandless

3. Morley Thomas

4. 1943 — Martha McCandless

5. 1944 — **Agatha Cavers**

6. 1944 — **Basil McCandless, Flight Sergeant Vernon McCandless**

7. 1944 — Mabel McCandless and Flight Sergeant Vernon McCandless

8. 1949 — Caroline and Brandon Conron, wedding photograph

9. 1951 — Alice Thomas and John

10. 1952 — **Clara, Steve and John**

11. 1952 — **Steve**

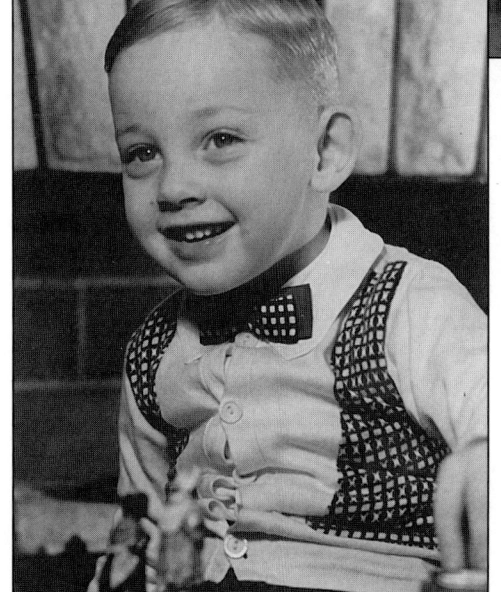

12. 1952 — **John**

13. 1952 — **Morley**

Illustrations 341

14. 1956 — The Sullivan Sisters, from left: Annie Fidler, Mabel McCandless, Dorothy Davis, Margery Durocher

15. 1960 — A.S.P. Woodhouse in his office. University College, Toronto.

16. 1961— Clara – first year at Glendon College, York University

Illustrations

17. 1967— Oxford, England, Blackwell's Book Store, – English publication of *Love and Work Enough*

18. 1977— Margaret Laurence's Honorary Degree from York University, Clara Thomas, Margaret Laurence, President Ian MacDonald, Chancellor John Robarts

19. 1982— **John Lennox, Clara, publication of** *William Arthur Deacon: A Canadian Literary Life.*

20. 1984— Retirement party at Glendon College, York University, Clara presiding over birthday cake.

21. Chinua Achebe, Eugene Hallman, Margaret Laurence

22. Northrop Frye, Carl Klinck

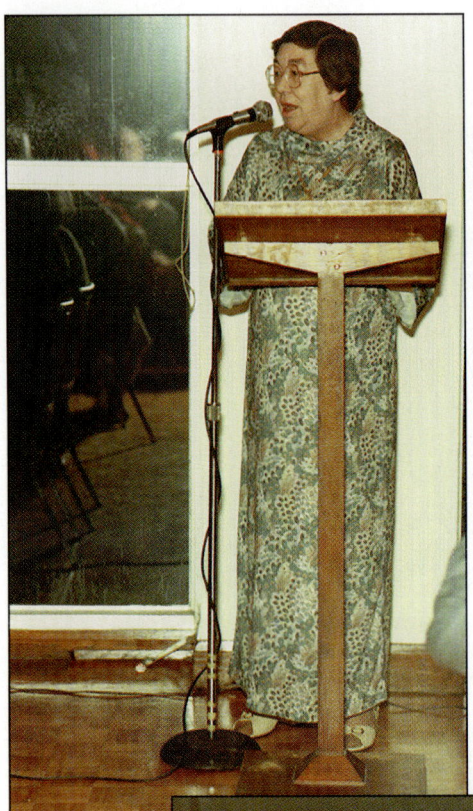

23. Margaret Laurence

24. Clara Thomas, Northrop Frye

25. From left, Adele Wiseman, Murdo McKinnon, Chinua Achebe, Ian MacDonald, Margaret Laurence, Jim Nelson, Elizabeth McKinnon

26. Clara Thomas, John Lennox

27. Michèle Lacombe

28. Morley Thomas

29. Edith Fowke

30. Margaret Laurence with Jane Lemieux, Mary Mathieson

31. Left Jack David, right Robert Leckert of ECW Press – publishers of Clara's Festschrift #29 of *Essays in Canadian Writing*.

32. Mary Louise Craven, who with John Lennox and Michele Lacombe, organized the retirement party, Northrop Frye in Foreground.

33. 1985— Rideau Hall, Ottawa, Morley Thomas awarded the Massey medal by Gov. Gen. Jeanne Sauve. From left, John Thomas, Morley Thomas, Steve Thomas.

34. 1983— Our grandson Tyler's Christening. Margarey Laurence, his godmother.